LONDON REVENANT

Previous Books by Conrad Williams include:

*Use Once, Then Destroy*
*Game*
*Nearly People*
*Head Injuries*

A NOVEL BY

CONRAD WILLIAMS

NIGHT SHADE BOOKS
SAN FRANCISCO & PORTLAND

Cover illustration © 2005 by Caniglia
Jacket layout and design by Claudia Noble
Interior layout and design by Jeremy Lassen

The lyrics on page 67 are from "Sugar Town" (1966), written by Lee Hazlewood

The exchange on page 217 is taken from the film *Taxi Driver* (1973), written by Paul Schrader

First Edition

ISBN
1-59780-010-4 (Hardcover)
1-59780-011-2 (Limited Edition)

Night Shade Books
http://www.nightshadebooks.com

For Ethan
I love you, little bear

Thanks to Rhonda Carrier for tough and tender encouragement, love and support.

Thanks also to Karl Sinfield at em foundation for looking after my website for the last few years, and to Shelley Eichholz for taking it over and giving it a great new look, Matthew Robinson and Caroline Johnson for their proofreading skills, The Chisellers, Anna Scott for a brand name, Louise Till-Hosier because I forgot last time, the rest of the Bristol mob, Ariel, Rick Cadger, Richard Coady, Jim Driver, Mike Harrison, Joel Lane, Robert Morrish, Fiona Neilson, Chris Reed, Hayden Williams, Charon Wood, Mum and Dad, Nicky and Tony and beautiful boy Ripley.

For this special edition, I'd like to thank Jason Williams and Jeremy Lassen of Night Shade Books, and Caniglia for his cover art.

My debauchery I undertook solitarily, by night, covertly, fear-fully, filthily, with a shame that would not abandon me… I was then already bearing the underground in my soul.

Fyodor Dostoevsky
*Notes from the Underground*

# PART ONE

## OUTSKIRTS

I was discovering here a paradoxical consequence of blindness: a blind person can no longer do anything secretly! Those poor people who can't see constantly fear being seen. In order to escape this unpleasant feeling, in a rather illogical reflex, I closed my eyes behind my black glasses.

Alain Robbe-Grillet, *Djinn*

I wandered through each chartered street,
Near where the chartered Thames does flow,
A mark in every face I meet,
Marks of weakness, marks of woe.

William Blake, "London"

Freedom is permitted.
Graffito, O'Neill's public house, London WC2

# CHAPTER ONE

## TERRORISM

It's so late, it's early.

It feels the tunnels radiating out like veins teased from Its body. Further along this platform stands an athletic man in trainers, jeans and a T-shirt upon which the words *Foo Fighters* are neatly stenciled. There's a woman reading the *Evening Standard*, the toe of her left foot tapping against the painted curb at the platform edge. She wears glossy black clothes; her legs are thin, her trousers tight around her buttocks. A courier bag filled with box files hangs heavily on her shoulder, as if it were some kind of penance. She looks like a tired raven. The last train to Upminster is a minute away. On the opposite platform, a couple are clinched, kissing each other greedily. There are no other people around.

It strolls down the platform and buys a Crunchie bar from the vending machine although It won't eat it. It can't abide the sickly sweet taste of Topside food, everything sugared and salted to hide how unpalatable it all is. How mass market. Its guts churn at the thought of the greasy junk that passed Its lips in the past. Those memories will help It now, the rage at the way It was forced to eat that rubbish, that shit. E numbers and monosodium glutamate and xanthum gum and riboflavinoids and disodium guanylate—whatever *that* is—and fuck it, and *fuck it all.*

The woman has turned to glance at It before returning to her newspaper, and It feels happy that it was just a glance. Because doesn't that mean It's still got some normal in It? It still blends in. Maybe It looks like a guy wending his weary way home from a building site, pock-marked with plaster dust and paint, the grime from a day's solid graft. But It really ought to be invisible for this. It can't afford to make these errors. It can't afford to be caught. Next time the world must be blind to It. Not even a glance. As if It were a ghost.

It assesses the way she is standing, the spread of weight, the lie of her fulcrum, her natural balance and poise. She weighs maybe a hundred and twenty pounds. She's on the back foot. That big bag of homework will need to be compensated for. Further… you can see, without trying too hard, how she would look naked. A bit of a belly on her; slim in the hip and thigh; breasts high, but slowly going to seed. Rounded shoulders. Too much time making eyes at the VDU. Emails and spreadsheets. It can imagine her in the morning, after the shower, sizing herself up in the mirror. After tonight, well, she won't ever wish for her youth back again.

From here, you can smell the woman's perfume despite the charred persistence of diesel fumes. *Foo Fighters* is rubbing his eyes and trying to focus on a paperback. Across the track, the kiss continues: he's holding on to the shivering meat of her thigh as though she were about to come apart in his hand. Her fingers flutter at his groin for a second. It wonders if he can taste any of the rubbish she will have eaten for dinner.

The breeze quickens.

In the moment before the grime-streaked snout of the train powers into the station, the lick of preceding blue light across the tunnel walls becomes almost liquid as time thickens and masses at Its shoulders. It becomes incandescent. Like the silent flight of black holes around It, Its focus diminishes until only she remains fixed within. The deliberate fold of her newspaper, the movement of her hand as she flicks an errant strand of hair from her eye, the shift of weight from one foot to another. The drop and tilt of her hips—all scorched onto Its retina as surely as if It were staring at messages written in the sun. In two steps, It is upon her. The way she stiffens tells It she's aware of something, even though It's moved silently… but anyway, she's too soft, too slow, too late now. One hand at the small of her back to counter her instinct to retreat; one at the dip between her shoulder blades: Its movement is fluid and inexorable. Her head flies back, her hair whipping Its hand as she disappears over the edge. The scream could have come from her, the witnesses, the train as it tried to abort its charge. No, the scream is coming from It as It flees through the tunnel marked NO EXIT. *Foo Fighters*, if he's pursuing, is not as lithe as he looks; more likely he's staring down at the rails in shock or trying to help. Its hand plucks a blade from the pocket of Its jacket and It slows down. Its heartbeat is steady. It went well.

It makes Its way quickly to the interlocking service tunnels, donning Its bicycle mask to protect It against the grime. Home is a long walk from here but It's done it before on dry runs for this very day. Next time, there'll be more choice.

It plunges into the infernal Circle Line, praying to God that she'll be all right.

# CHAPTER TWO

## TUNNEL VISION

Three a.m. moonlight, like radioactive milk. Like a soluble headache pill at the moment it hits water. Like a marble of wet electricity about to explode into a fireball.

*Adam is fine too, reading lots this summer, he looks*

The softness of the dream receded, replaced by the gradual return of solid shapes sucked back from the dark: a chair, a table, a bookcase. A suitcase vomiting clothes from its deep, slack mouth. The book on the floor that I was reading: *Dead Babies.*

The dream was almost too soft to hold on to but before it left me, I knew it had something to do with being in a place darker than shadows, where electricity crackled along the walls. There was something there with me, something with less substance than water, and it was either tracking me, or me it. Direction meant nothing and neither did purpose. In the dream, all that was certain was the weak flirt of blue light and the suffocating dark, smothering it as soon as it was born. I remembered getting on a train, arriving, getting off the train and falling into a blackness that was so pure it was almost white.

I slipped out of bed and padded to the window. A van was double-parked outside; a figure leaned over the steering wheel taking measured drags of a cigarette. The passenger door was open, as were the doors at the back. A stiff breeze jerked at the branches of the elm outside the window: chancy light spat through it onto the pavement where a shadow was growing. I moved back, out of sight, as the shadow was eaten by its maker: a slim, short-haired woman in a jumper and combats. The doors slammed shut, the engine started and the van moved away. Light, rapid footsteps died almost before they'd begun on the old, bare staircase. A shadow spoiled the strip of light beneath my door.

*he looks… just like his dad?*

I scanned the street. Nobody else seemed to be awake at this hour; I felt restless, inexplicably upset. Questions were queueing up at the enquiry desk in my head, which was blocked off by a sign that read: *Go Away, I'm Tired*, though I knew the chance of sleep returning was unlikely now.

*he looks... like he might shape up to be a proper little clever clogs?*

In the dark, I found a jumper and a pair of jeans in the suitcase and pulled them on. I was hunting for my keys when I heard another sleeping form stir: the house next door. For months there had been a tall, protective shield of wood blocking the entrance to the grounds and tanned men in protective headwear and jerkins with luminous flashes fussing around the exterior. I was used to the house's voice by now: the skitters and whispers that traveled up from the exposed foundations to whip around the interior like trapped birds.

*he looks... lonely, alone, and I never meant to leave you like this, my love?*

LONDON, THIS LATE AT NIGHT: PLENTY OF PLACES TO WALK to; nowhere to walk. Nowhere to walk *safely*. It was all about circles this late at night, a route to bring you safely back to point A. I never used to be this nervous about my city at night. But people were dying out there as if their lives depended on it. Yellow police incident boards were appearing on main roads with terrible frequency. *Did You See Anything?* Young men murdered for no greater crime than walking home late at night. Women robbed sitting in busy parks during their lunch hours. One day, a bus on its way to Waterloo from Highgate had to abandon its journey because someone on the top deck set fire to the seats.

Frustrated by my lack of options, I marched down Dartmouth Park Hill to the junction at the bottom where Tufnell Park Tube station lies sleeping and silent, collecting litter in the bars of its security gates. The roads around here were as black as a smoker's lungs, and at this time of the night unnaturally quiet, clotted with cars that all looked the same color under the sodium lights. London unnerved me like this. And I was in no fit state for it. I was feeling wounded, Morrissey-like. I felt as if I should consider developing an absinthe habit. I should start reading Polish war poetry and wear more black.

A month ago, Laura finished it. On her birthday. A present to herself.

I bit down on the inclination to brood, which was becoming more and more of a habit, and sucked some cold air deep inside me. Relationships were like rules: there to be broken.

The city seemed vulnerable and deserted: travel to the center, a couple of miles south, and I might find that its heart had stopped beating completely. A city shouldn't be like this. It wasn't normal. It should be full-on: people falling face first into their pizzas and fighting and fucking and dodging the traffic at all times of the day and night. A quiet London was a London untrue to itself. It was like being watched. It was like everyone but me knowing what the score was. Lately, London appeared to me more and more as an alien city in which I no longer felt welcome. Who was I if I couldn't get a handle on the place that was supposed to be home?

The moment passed. I hung around by the gates of the Tube, smelling the air—redolent of oil and sweat and a kind of restrained panic—that moved up through the lift shafts. The platforms would be deathly quiet now. Perhaps the only sound would be made by newspapers and drinks cans pushed gently along by that underground breath. Did they keep the lights on down there, and the cameras? Did they turn the escalators off?

I felt a deep vibration move through my feet. The moan that followed seconds later might have been human but for the hydraulic whispers, the shunting of buffers that couched it. Service trains, possibly, carrying men and women, maintenance staff, the fluffers and gandy dancers who swept the tunnels and platforms, or repaired tracks while London slept. But then I heard a voice, male, strident and breathy, as though its owner was in danger. Or trying to explain something, having just exerted himself too much. I couldn't make out any words, but I distinctly heard a wet, ripping noise and a shout of alarm. When a confusion of hardware sounds ordered themselves into the unmistakable noise of a lift rising, I moved on. Quickly.

I had been aiming to walk along Fortess Road before doubling back along Highgate Road, to complete a rough triangle along Chetwynd Road and Wyndham Crescent, thereby returning home. But now I hurried across the street and hunkered down behind the bonnet of a blue Tigra, eyes fixed on the locked gates of the Tube station. I placed a hand on the pavement to steady myself and felt the concrete, cool and cracked, against my skin. It was kind of a comfort. I thought I heard the thunk of the lift as it arrived at ground level, and the meshing of gears as its doors opened. Beyond the gates, the dark had no detail. And then, suddenly, it did.

A pale circle emerged from the murk like a bubble breaking the surface of a brackish pond. It hovered awhile, before two hands emerged below it, white as bleached bone, to grasp the concertina bars of the gate. They shook the bars lightly, testing them, and the sudden noise made me flinch. I moved further back, and my heels scuffed against the pavement.

The figure stopped shaking the gates. The circle shifted, rotating backwards, and I realized I was staring at the top of a head. What clung to the face below it was an object lesson in thinness. Apart from the eyes. The eyes bulged from that drawn, pallid rectangle of pain as though eager to escape and find a more accommodating skull. It was like looking at a still from the Second World War, a picture of someone liberated from Belsen or Dachau. I felt as if I ought to do something; maybe the person had locked himself in and was in need of help. Perhaps he was a security guard who was injured. But then I could tell from where I was crouching, as the ghostly color of his skin filled itself in against the darkness, that he was entirely naked.

And he was gazing directly at me. His gummy mouth was cross-hatched by saliva, his whitened tongue emerging; mummified, desperate.

I stood up, close to shitting myself. The figure returned my gaze for a few seconds and then his head slowly lowered until he was showing me his crown again. His hands found a more secure purchase on the metal and began shaking them again, harder, more insistently. A piece of metal sprang clear and jangled on the pavement. And another. A complete strut snapped off. A hinge popped out of the concrete with a little plume of dust. He leaned down, suddenly studious, and scratched at the pavement with nails that must have been six inches long: I heard the awful skrit skrit skrit of them against the concrete.

When he looked up again, a wash of saliva had turned his chin to glass.

I moved away, forcing my legs to do what they were there for, but seemed to have forgotten. I wasn't around to see if the gates came toppling down, but I heard a monumental crash of metal a little while later, which set off a car alarm. I didn't stop running until I got back to my road. And once I had stopped, I felt as though I was still fleeing: my heart might have been a die in a cup held by a child desperate to throw a six and my legs were twitching to carry me on, to forget the front door of my flat, to keep running, keep running. But I managed to cool down, relax. Nothing hideous was loping after me, I wasn't going to become a statistic, a body on the street replaced by a yellow incident board ignored by everyone.

Approaching the building where I lived from a new angle felt strange, not least because I had never seen a light on in the room above my own before. Despite my earlier unease, it was a relief that somebody would be living there. It would counter a little of the loneliness caused by living next to the dead building on the left. That building was as still as ever, seemingly crushed beneath the weight of night. Empty buildings always bore the dark so much more uncomfortably. On the fence surrounding the collapsing house, somebody had spray painted a strange sign:

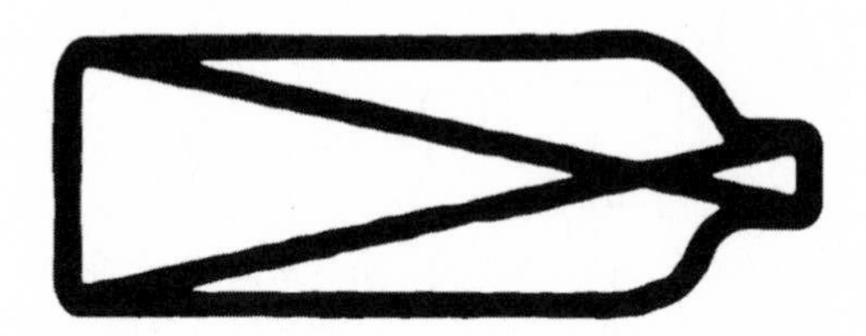

Studying it, I became aware that I had seen it before, a number of times, on bus stop shelters, underpass walls, other places. It called to me although I couldn't place the shape. Maybe it was some slick new advertising campaign, for some new breed of alcopop maybe, a series of teasers that would gradually be revealed to a public growing more and more curious.

Just before dawn, I found a shallow kind of sleep, despite the adrenaline whizzing through my veins, the kind that doesn't stop the outside world from filtering through. The city was rediscovering itself. Commuter traffic droned in the road. A radio blared as the hardhats arrived at the site next door, but nobody referred to the Tube station in the news. It was like a nightmare that had learned to exist outside of my thoughts.

WHEN I GOT TO WORK LATER THAT MORNING, I WAS FEELING hollow from lack of rest and still edgy from what I had seen, or thought I had seen, the previous night. I tried to ignore my irritated eyes as they persisted in gluing themselves together. The woman who moved in at such an anti-social hour had kept me from my much-needed sleep. If it weren't for her, I wouldn't have had the shit scared out of me.

I had checked the sign again, as I walked by, tracing my fingers along the rough lines of white paint as if in doing so it might somehow impart the secret of its code. There had been an engineer at the entrance of Tufnell Park Tube station, fixing the gates when I walked past. A couple of Underground staff were watching what he was doing, leaning in and talking about what could have caused it. I felt a tremor of panic at the sight of the warped steel, the gouges in the brick that looked like scratches made by strong, desperate fingers.

I seldom traveled on the Underground. I couldn't stand it. It was too crowded and hot in summer and too crowded and damp in winter. I didn't like the way some people appeared down there, as though they'd left their brains behind before leaving for work, or were this far away from snapping and massacring everyone in the carriage. Nobody wore an expression worth the name in the Tube. Nobody laughed, and there was no reason why they should. Down there, people acted differently. It was almost a social requirement that nobody spoke to each other, that misery or boredom surfaced on each face. You could believe by those masks that the people down there never actually went up top, that they threw away their tickets and kept to the trains. Perhaps popped up on the escalators occasionally to stare longingly at the ticket barriers and wonder how things were outside. I usually took the bus to work.

Work was one of two places. Daytimes I worked at Cherry's flower stall, on the wedge of land between Castellain Road and Warwick Avenue. Three or four nights a week I had shifts at The Pit Stop in Archway, pulling pints of gut-rot for men too old to give a toss about the quality of the beer or pubescent chancers too wet behind the ears to know better.

Cherry was in her mid-thirties, two or three years older than me. She wore her hair in bunches most of the time. Her clothes differed only slightly every day: jeans and jumper and Doc Martens, or jeans and T-shirt and Doc Martens. She was the kind of woman who was slim only because of the extent of her activity. She ate constantly: chocolate bars, crisps, quiches and cold pizza wrapped in greaseproof paper from her fridge; burgers and hot dogs snaffled at lunch, along with a pint of lager at the pub. If she stopped moving, fat would catch up. In a certain light, sometimes I thought I could see it trying her on for size, positioning a girdle of itself above her hips or showing me how her jowls might hang. But I knew that she'd be happy with that, if it ever happened to her. Cherry was that kind of woman: accommodating, fatalistic, agreeable. Nothing fazed her.

She had taken me on just when it seemed I would have to give up my dream of living in the city, and head back north, to the dull industrial town I had worked so hard to get away from. It was just a couple of days each week, but that, allied to the pub work, meant that I was just about able to afford the tiny flat on Dartmouth Park Hill. I was existing on little more than potatoes and tins of Heinz Soup For One, but it was better than the life I'd left behind.

I liked to think I knew a bit about plants. I wasn't Rachel de Thame, but I could say *Acer Palmatum Dissectum* before I knew what one looked like. My parents had allowed me a corner of their garden when I was a child where I could do as I wished: I spent a week digging the soil over, weeding, picking out the gravel, introducing a few worms along with a rockery and a pond. But despite my efforts, I couldn't grow anything beyond a virile strain of bindweed. I knew it wasn't the fault of the soil; feet away, Mum had cobbled together a mix of fruit and vegetables that would have satisfied the most vengeful of gods at harvest festival. It seemed I was destined only to look at plants and not nurture them.

But I didn't give up. I took to more unorthodox measures; anything to get a result. I talked to plants. I shouted at them sometimes, suspecting they'd benefit from a little tough love. I massaged stems, stalks, petals, buds and when that didn't work I furiously wanked them off. I watered and sprayed, invented my own composts after forays into mulchy forests to collect high-quality leaf mold failed. Whenever I quizzed my mother about these shortcomings, she would shrug.

"I just leave it alone. A bit of weeding, that's all. You can move your plot, if you like. Maybe we're just lucky with the soil on our patch, I don't know." This last was meant to pacify me, I was sure, but I was certain there was something more to what she did. Sometimes, I would imagine her gliding into the garden at midnight dressed in billowing white robes, splashing blood from her wrists onto the blossoms and offering up a prayer to the Great Garden God, Fison.

When she died, just after Christmas a couple of years ago, I lay flattened by the flu for three days, convinced that her magic would creep into me like the quiet attenuation of the sky as it gathers snow. I'd maybe feel a sappy thickening in my veins or a blossoming of secrets deep within my mind.

When I was finally able to get out of my sickbed, I wandered up on to Parliament Hill on foal-weak legs and watched the night fall. Below, London looked clean and emergent, Canary Wharf and the BT tower flirting with each other; jets banking over the city; the lights dangerous and expensive. I sat in the grass, something Mum loved to do, and thought about her planting lettuces or watering the lawn, hand on hip or fingers trawling through her hair. She was very beautiful. Old photographs of her resembled Sophia Loren: large, wide eyes and a full mouth. I liked to think there was something of her in the way I looked, but then, I would, wouldn't I? I liked to believe that some of her sensitivity for living things had passed on to me, but once I'd returned home and given the ivy a drink (keeping it in an environment where there was no direct sunlight and the temperature remained between 16° and 25°C) I knew that its famished appearance was not going to improve. In the same way, I was certain the aspidistra I bought soon after my mother's funeral (there were buttercups growing around her headstone these days) was going to struggle. The cast iron plant. I did everything you were meant to do: I left it well alone. It was dead within three months.

Slow, cold days—like today—I stood freezing in my overalls and watched people climbing or descending the steps at Warwick Avenue Tube station and guessed where they might be going to, or returning from. People appeared staggered emerging from the Underground, as if even a short period away from daylight rendered them amnesiac to everyday sights. I had seen young men halt at the top of the flight and look around, blinking like owls while the man holding a wad of *Big Issues* tried to break into their catatonia.

"Only a quid. Help the homeless. Only a quid, mate."

Some of the people I saw seemed to connect with me in ways I couldn't understand. Maybe it was a distance in them, a social flaw, which called to my own feelings of inadequacy. This man, wearing a thick twill overcoat, carrying a translucent carrier bag that rustled like tissue paper and contained a Sunblest loaf and something by Fray Bentos. This woman, her hair too consciously styled, her skin decaying under its fine powders and creams. Something in their deportment, or the lost way in which they scanned the road; it screamed out at me, in a way that this girl emerging with a padded envelope and a can of Tizer didn't. In a way that this man, with his briefcase and headphones, didn't. Whatever it was had an unknown frequency and I was tuned in to it.

There was a problem too with the flowers on Cherry's stall. They were, according to the reference books, unable (or reluctant) to open up. A number of people had brought them back to complain. Some accused Cherry of doctoring them to give this permanently fresh look. But a few people stopped on their way home, perhaps preferring the slim, gathered petals, perhaps not knowing any better. Cherry was at a loss as to their reticence, and I kept quiet about my apparent horticultural voodoo.

I concentrated on the flowers, wrapping them in cellophane and marking prices on cards with a gold marker pen. *Freesias to please you. Poppies to make you soppy.* What kind of hard bitch dumps you on her birthday? *Glads to make you... well, what do you think?*

While I was cursing Laura and myself for losing her, a woman stepped into my light, her eyes clouding, no doubt as she felt the change in atmosphere. I smiled and steered her away from the lilies. "They're past their best," I said, though they'd failed to bloom in the first place. Brown smudges were underscoring the petals and the stems looked tired. "Lilies to make you chilly," I said.

She smiled. "I'm looking for something colorful for a friend who's sick. She needs cheering up. How about some of those chrysanthemums?"

I wrapped her a couple of bunches in tissue paper and charged her for one, apologizing for the fact that I hadn't thought of a rhyme for them yet. I was often giving away too many flowers; all down to guilt regarding their parsimony. Once we had complained to the woman we bought them from wholesale at Covent Garden Market but she directed us to a flower stall owner in Holborn who had bought from the same batch. We couldn't see him for a tumult of buds. We tried changing the way we stocked them; moved the stall to alter the angle of light; loosened the bands that group them together. Nothing worked. Less a flower stall than flowers stalled.

Come eight-thirty, a series of small steam clouds at the Warwick Road Tube entrance heralded the arrival of Lucas, the *Big Issue* man, who always finished his sprint up the stairs with a little hop, a flourish to energize a day begun in a squat shared with about thirteen Kiwis in Kensal Green. When he left, at seven in the evening, the slope of his shoulders was so pronounced, it was as if his neck has been removed. He trudged back into the bowels on steps that might be made of thick toffee.

By mid-morning I had a headache. I switched on the radio because the chant of "*Big Issue?*" was getting on my nerves. When that failed to drown out the noise, I beckoned Lucas over and offered him a cup of tea.

"So how's it going with you, man?" Lucas wanted to know, nodding as though I had already provided him with an answer.

"All right, I suppose. Although I don't know if I'm coming or going half the time. Half the time, I don't know who I am, or what I'm supposed to be doing." I snapped my mouth shut and looked away. What a dumb thing to say. But Lucas didn't miss a beat.

"I know what you mean," he said.

"What about you?" I said.

"Tight. Cracking. You know?"

I guessed he hadn't been at this game for very long; he was too enthusiastic. Some of the sellers I'd seen on, say, Shaftesbury Avenue, had the wizened, defeated countenance of people who seemed to have turned to glass and can't get any attention unless they stand in the way of pedestrians. One seller on Berwick Street was so disenchanted with the whole game that he'd taken to a novel way of offloading his stock of copies. "Aw buy a *Big Issue* won't you, you miserable bastard? Come on, you grouchy old mingebag, open your sodding purse. Bitch." Whether he was frightening Londoners into buying his magazine I couldn't say. But it seemed to work.

Not that I felt I could transplant the practice here: "Step up and buy a bunch of daffs, fuckface. And you madam, improve your smell with a bouquet of tulips, why don't you? Twat."

Lucas sucked at the rim of his mug. "Used to see you get picked up round here of an evening. Tasty-looking Maude in a VW Golf. What happened? She run off with someone higher up the social scale, eh?" He laughed. "News vendor, was it? Sandwichboard man?"

I fiddled with the change in my pockets and swallowed the temptation to point out his position in the food chain. "She's on a lecture tour of Europe at the moment. I'm taking care of her flat." Why shouldn't I lie? I wasn't going to tell every toe-rag my ins and outs.

"Yeah? Why didn't you go with her? She could be being shafted *at this very minute* by all kinds of trouser."

"That's my girlfriend you're talking about," I said. But because it wasn't, it was a protest without muscle. I couldn't rise to the bait. I wished I could. But what was the point of defending something that wasn't there anymore? What was the point of defending a lie? I didn't know where Laura was, though my treacherous imagination was eager enough to show her in any number of sexual positions with hulking, shadowed strangers. And her face would bear the same shapes it had worn at the moment of her last orgasm with me: sealed into my memory, the look of a person fighting for breath after too long under water, and a confusion, as though she couldn't quite understand what was washing over her. All the times we had made love before that: I couldn't recall her expression from any of them. You don't, do you? You lose all that. When a relationship dies, that's one of the first things to parachute out of your head.

"Mmm, well I can't sit here with you all day, chatting about shit and everything. I've got a living to scrape. Thanks for the tea." And he was off, pursuing a woman along the zebra crossing. "Buy a *Big Issue*, Madam?"

One woman couldn't buy flowers from me without touching my forearm. One elderly gentleman brought me a small apple pie from his son's bakery every fortnight. I noticed, if they did not, that we looked at each other in a different way. As I handed them their change, their eyes lingered a fraction longer or they would smile more expansively, or force a short conversation. A difference, then; an aspect that brought a connection they didn't understand or hardly recognized. I wished I could speak about it, to Cherry perhaps, or Greg, or even Lucas, but I couldn't be sure I wasn't making it up, as some kind of compensation for what had happened with Laura.

The day wore on; a white sun failed to burn off the haze drifting up from the canal in Little Venice. For April, it was bitterly cold.

WHEN I MOVED TO LONDON, I TRAVELED EVERYWHERE BY THE Victoria, Bakerloo, Piccadilly and Northern lines. You could trace my movement across the capital with a web of cyan and brown, navy and black. Now and again I'd sample Central's artery or the lime and lemon of District and Circle, but those other four lines remained my staples. I used up my travel cards on London's secret country; as the trains muscled through the dark, I imagined nineteenth-century laborers churning through the unhelpful clay soil, tensed against the threat of collapse (either of the shored-up tunnels around them, or their own). I tried to imagine the suppressed panic they must have experienced, to know them, bodies streaked with sweat and mud, the alien underworld reek of gas pockets and rich, mineral earth. The endeavor. The sacrifice. I wondered if I could ever marshal my nerves enough to accomplish something so encompassing and revolutionary. But there was nothing but flowers and beer.

I dreamed of a crowd. A part of it was made up by me: my mass, filling a me-sized space. I was jostled and swept along as easily as a leaf on a breeze. Yet there was something centrally wrong, an intranuclear fault, and I realized that it was my otherness that was the cause. The crowd lost its oiled precision of movement; became aware of the buckled spoke and ejected me. The properties of each constituent body, though melded into a sinuous flesh current, were hallucinatorily sharp: polished buttons on a military overcoat; slivers of clear light seen edge-on in the orbit of an eye; a scab healing on a pale hand.

My features turned to water; my spine dissolved like ash in rain. The boxed snout of a train barreled down on me. I didn't belong anywhere, or to anyone.

"Are you all right, Adam?"

I came out of it a little, just enough to tell Cherry to break my fall. Then I was gone. Gone.

# CHAPTER THREE
## SCHEINTOD

It's in the tunnel, just standing out of the ring of light at Goodge Street, watching the suits on the platform. There are hundreds of them jammed together, pretending to be interested in their newspapers or their novels or the music that pours into their ears through their headphones. Ageless currents of cold air flap Its clothes and caress Its neck. London leaps away from It above the arch of tiles, a great mass of death and history mingling with the smell of scorched fuel. The smell plucks at Its muscles, the emotions, the sharp sweat, the tang of fear. The people on the platform wear wide eyes. They look at each other, assessing, sizing up: *Is that one of them? Could she be? Could he be a Pusher?* They just want to get home. Everybody in this city, in an ecstasy of to and fro. Waiting to be somewhere else. Never concentrating on the here. The now. Well then....

It watches as women at the front of the pack glance nervously around them. Some of them stand side-on, to reduce the threat of attack. A member of staff exhorts passengers entering the station to walk to the end of the platform where there is more space. The next train, he warns, is very crowded. Groans lift from the crowd. People relax a little, united in irritation. It sees the tension in their shoulders reduce a fraction. A strange Mexican wave of shaking heads ululates through the crowd, giving it the impression of singularity. Somebody laughs. Somebody else says: "You just can't give in to it. You mustn't."

The vomit rises in Its craw.

It can hear the train now, at Its back. It knows its speed by the special sound of the train's movement and the deep vibrations that move through Its feet. It knows to the second how long it will be before it is upon It.

Pressing against the nearside curve of the tunnel, It edges out, sinking into the dark beneath the lip of the platform edge. It can smell shoe leather and boot polish, hear the skitter of ferrules, the clack of a throat lozenge against teeth as a tongue shifts it from one side of the mouth to the other. Smells and sounds that fill It with hatred and despair.

Light on the tracks, slithering along them like brilliant snakes. It stops when the light splashes across the wall tiles and the clatter of the wheels explodes into the confined space. The brakes shriek. At least It thinks it's the brakes, but no, it's more than that. A collective sound, It realizes, as It lets go of the man's leg and watches him fall across the path of the train: a collective sound of horror, loud and shrill enough to crack the arched roof.

But not just horror. It scampers alongside the train, dipping beneath it and pulling Itself through to the blind side, then into the tunnel. Faster. Faster.

No, not just horror. Those screams had the flavor of rapture in them, relief that this time, it wasn't them. Relief that they had been spared.

"IT'S NARCOLEPSY."

I had said those words to maybe half a dozen people in my life and had received the same response every time: the same as Cherry's now. A look of sympathy mingled with incomprehension.

I read somewhere that for a doctor to be an authority in sleep disorders he or she needs just ten hours of specialization. I don't know if that's true or not, but what is certain is that nobody is certain about what narcolepsy is. And as long as that's the case, you can bet there's as much chance of a cure in the near future as there is of chimps living at the bottom of the Marianas Trench. There's plenty of debate as to what kick-starts this particular bastard of a disease, a list that is syllable heavy to say the least: baroreceptor hypersensitivity, ultradian or circadian rhythm disturbances, receptor abnormalities, immune response modulation defects, genetic defects, neurotransmitter abnormalities, neuronal membrane defects, neuroanatomic abnormalities, head injuries, tennis, blonde jokes, an allergy to semolina... I'm fisted if I know. Could be any or all for all I care. Fact is, I've got it and I'm stuck with it.

I don't take anything for it, which might not be wise, but the Ritalin I was once prescribed was as effective as a dog muzzle made from Pedigree Chum. Depending on the whims of the illness, I can have an attack as many as five times in one day. On good days, I'll have just the one. On really good days I won't even yawn. Lately, I've been fine. Not even the glimmer of shuteye.

Sometimes I know when I'm going down; I'll feel drowsiness pour through my body as though my blood's been substituted with syrup. Other times I can switch off like a light bulb. I don't hurt myself when I drop; everything relaxes. The worst injury I sustained was when I swan-dived into a bowl of oxtail soup and burned my face. It is not something you can resist. The narcolepsy, that is. Not oxtail soup.

I revived after a couple of minutes. It can last hours. Cherry's face was contorted with concern.

"It was like…" she struggled, her voice breathy with shock, "…it was like someone removed all your bones at once."

"That's what your beauty does to people," I said, shakily, trying to make light of the matter.

"You really should have told me about this," she said.

"I always meant to," I said. "I'm sorry. Sorry if I alarmed you. I haven't had an attack like that for months."

She gave me a sip from her can of Coke and asked me if I was okay. I nodded.

"I think I'll go home," I said. "You don't mind, do you?"

Of course she didn't.

By the time I got to Kentish Town, people were pouring out of the Tube and onto the buses. I moved my bag to allow someone to sit next to me. There was an announcement on the station platform, something about trains on the Northern Line being delayed due to an "incident" at Euston. It wasn't the only one. There were four other stations that had been closed. Four other "incidents."

On the bus, someone wearing a Walkman hissed: "Jesus wept." He had been listening to the radio. Apparently, the incident at Euston involved a woman being pushed under an oncoming train. And at Russell Square, Goodge Street, Bond Street and Holborn, the same thing. All of them at three p.m. Five people pushed under trains. It's not yet known how many survived.

It is difficult to die on the Underground, contrary to belief. Touching the live rail is not a foregone conclusion; neither is jumping in front of a train. Often, the driver will be traveling slow enough to stop, or the deep trench between the rails—the suicide pit—will prevent you from coming to grief.

I remembered a report on the front of the *Standard* from the previous week. A similar incident, involving a woman. She had been saved because the wheels snagged in her shoulder bag and acted as a buffer, pushing her along rather than slicing into her. Where was that now? Late night, St. James's Park? Already, there's talk that whoever did that acted as the vanguard for this spate of attacks. Already, there's talk that the incidents are acts of terrorism.

I thought of the pusher. I had the awful conviction that I knew him.

Soon, the rain had turned the windows into blurred squares and everything outside had a rilling, uncertain quality. There were so many people here. All of them borrowing London. All of them in transit. The thought of past civilizations—buildings, bodies, wooden toys, love letters, shit and tears—compressed beneath the thin crust that supported Kentish Town Road only made the edges of what I perceived as myself more blurred. My name and my me-ness seemed as fragile and as pointless and as limp as the flowers I was trying to sell.

It wasn't just this "terrorist," or the narcolepsy that was worrying me. There were other things too. Like the way the Tube seems to warp London, make it less real. Less reliable than it already is. London shrinks. It does if you've traveled on the surface here. On the Underground, time becomes this vampire that attaches itself to the back of your neck, tapping you of energy and the ability to relate space to movement. It's just you, and the clatter of the train, and the streak of black in the windows: between platforms, there's nothing there to offer any clue to how far you've gone. Sometimes you get the feeling you must have missed a station. Just motion. Just blackness.

Because there's nothing to look at, people immerse themselves in fiction or *Metro*, trying to keep hold of a place that is normal and human, using the immutable ink in much the same way that they use the handgrips that dangle from the ceiling. We fear the swift glide into tunnels, the jarring and jolting, MIND THE GAP and platforms choked with commuters, like rats congregated on a sewer ledge. Descending: it is not something we look forward to really, perhaps because we step nearer the place we ultimately wish to stay away from. It's a constant reminder of burial.

In the flat above mine, a fresh pair of lilac curtains hung in the window.

I checked the plastic label above the doorbell, which read: DEUEL. It was fresh ink, newly laminated. Inside, on the stairwell, music drifted down from her flat, but I couldn't identify the artist. It sounded incredibly strange: without any discernible rhythm or vocals. I was feeling a little better, so I put my keys back in my pocket and strode up to her front door.

I knocked and waited. A smoky voice behind the door husked: "Go away, H, I've got clients coming in an hour."

"Hello?" I said. "My name's Adam. I live in the flat beneath you."

She opened the door. Big green eyes, slathers of soft brown hair.

She was wearing a knitted cardigan that reached to the floor. "Oh, come in," she said. "Shoes off."

I heard the music more clearly. It wasn't music at all; it was whale song underscored by the lapping of waves and the odd cry of a gull. I slipped off my boots and went in. She had been busy. The living room smelled of freshly applied matt. A Moroso sofa in pale blue took up the space along one wall. On it sat a large black dildo. A tiny NAD stereo was positioned under the bay window. A Toio lamp and a chunk of flat, smooth glass supporting a large church candle in the fireplace were the only other accessories.

"I saw you move in last night," I said. "I just thought I'd come and say hi."

"Surely," she said. "I was going to come down and say hello myself, a little later. You aren't from around here, are you?" With her head, she gestured I should come deeper into the flat. "I mean, it's not just the accent—which, I should guess places you somewhere Manchesterish—but your manners. Most Londoners are too busy, even when they're relaxing, to go out of their way like that."

The hallway was filled with tea chests, cardboard boxes and tins of paint. A rough pencil sketch of a horse and half a dozen books—Graham Greene Penguins, a Taschen collection of erotic postcards, Matthew Weinreb's study of London architecture—rested against a wall. We went through to the kitchen where she offered me tea. Brand-new appliances gleamed subtly under fitted ceiling lights: Smeg, Bosch, Gagganau.

"Am I right about Manchester?" she asked.

"Near as dammit."

"Oolong? Yunnan? Assam?"

"Coffee would be better, thanks, if you have any."

"Go and sit in the living room," she said. "I'll bring it through for you."

The sofa was the only available sitting space. I considered sitting on the floor but it was dusty and anyway, she'd probably think I was a terrible prude if I didn't just move the dildo out of the way. But she might not realize that the dildo was on the sofa. She might be mortified if she saw it when she returned. I should hide it, in a box. But then she'd think I was prying if she was aware of the dildo.

I moved to the window and studied the putty in its frame. "My name's Nuala, by the way. Nuala Deuel." She handed me a mug of black coffee. "No milk, sorry."

"I could lend you some. Till you go to the shops that is."

"No, it's okay. I only drink soya milk and they don't sell that at the corner shop." She moved to the sofa and picked the dildo up, placed it on her lap when she sat down. She folded her legs beneath her as she settled. She had the kind of posture that makes any position seem comfortable. She was like a cat. One of the fingers on her free hand rubbed at the sculpted glans of the dildo; she did this with distracted skill, as if she were tickling a puppy's chin.

"I suppose I ought to go," I said. "I just thought I should say hi. See if there was something I could do for you. And your clients...." I drained my mug and put it on the floor.

"Well, actually, you could shift some of these boxes for me. They're very heavy. The clients thing was just a firewall."

I spent twenty minutes lugging tea chests, mostly filled with books, into different areas of the flat while Nuala followed me around, eating half a toasted bagel with Marmite and giving sporadic direction. The dildo stared at me, supercilious and Cyclopean next to a plate of sliced organic peaches she had brought from the fridge. In one box I saw a mass of buckles and straps and wedges of padded material. From another, an oddly-shaped cushion fell.

"What's this?" I asked, retrieving it.

"Oh, it's a womb-shaped stress reduction pillow. I have a very strong maternal side: I get in touch with it as often as I can. It lulls me."

"Mmm."

"Listen, why don't I cook you dinner tomorrow night, for helping me? I get a good vibe from you, you know? You'll be a good neighbor. I bet you don't eat meat."

"I'm cutting down. I don't touch red meat anymore, apart from the odd bacon sandwich. Too heavy."

She was regarding me with an expectant expression.

"But of course, I aim to cut out meat altogether eventually. Anybody who has owned a pet can't possibly live peacefully with themse—"

"For sure. That's all well and good, but do you want to come for dinner?"

IN THE CITY THE RAIN IS SOMEHOW MORE OFFENSIVE, THE sun dirtier, turning everything parched and dusty. Cold winds are channeled and intensified, filleting you with boning-knife precision. I watched the water collect in blocked storm drains and drip from arthritic branches. Traffic made mist of the road.

There was a telephone message from Greg. We hadn't spoken much since Laura had stopped seeing me: I thought it was a guilt thing but maybe it was just because Greg was busy. They went back years, had gone to university together. He wanted me to meet him for lunch, the next day at Mozart's. For the first time since Laura, I had consecutive meals sorted out.

I thought about Nuala. Could something develop there between the two of us? Other than the dildo? Could I become involved with someone who drank Rose Pouchong?

I placed a Nirvana CD in the player and waited for Kurt Cobain's scarred, pitch-perfect voice to find a way through. I lay on the floor and rushed to a place that roiled at my core, where the music simultaneously calmed and inspired me. Eyes open, I looked through the window at a sky that was sullen but trying hard to impress, like a shy kid at a party. When the screaming started, scraping against the edges of the melody and my spine, I felt I could disclose any part of my past to anybody who wanted to know. Slowly, my muscles relaxed and the music became so fluent that it was like liquid, pouring into my ears and bathing my brain. Womb-shaped pillow, indeed. Whale song, for fuck's sake. She should try "Very Ape." That'd blow her windows out.

I had a bath and tried to take a nap, but I couldn't relax knowing that I had to be at the pub in a couple of hours. It's the cruel irony of narcolepsy. Nuala was heavy in my thoughts too. She was nice. She was very nice. She had that kind of softness to her that you find in some people. A lack of angles or edges of any kind. You couldn't clash with people like that: you'd just slide off. You'd about as much chance getting bananas off a pear tree.

I lay on the bed, mentally prodding and poking her for half an hour, then made myself a peanut butter and apricot jam sandwich. It was easy to select that evening's clothes: you get your own Pit Stop T-shirt—bottle green for the male staff, white for the females—and you have to wear it with black trousers. I thought about ironing them, for maybe a split nanosecond, then pulled on my jacket and headed for the door. I was closing it when I heard a voice. I was moving at the time, and making noise—the keys in my fist were jangling and the old leather in my coat was creaking up around my ears—so I can't be sure where it came from, but it was either from the grate in my living room, or from beneath the door in Nuala's flat. I wouldn't have thought anything of it, but for the strangeness of it: *Pass the warning.*

I GOT TO THE PIT STOP AT A LITTLE BEFORE SEVEN. MEDDIE had been there most of the afternoon, replenishing the bottle stocks, sorting the empties from the skips into their appropriate crates ready for collection, ringing up staff to get them to cover for last-minute sickies. She was on the phone when I walked in. I clenched my jaw when I saw her. She had yet to change into staff gear for that evening's shift. She was wearing a khaki vest top that bore the legend *Urban Bitch* in a grungy typeface, tight cut-off jean shorts, cheap plastic flip-flops and a lapis lazuli bracelet. Her long brown hair was tied up in an elaborately plaited coil. She never wore it down.

I dumped my jacket in the kitchen and made a cup of tea. Meddie came in and brushed past me with a brief "Hi," to retrieve a roll of masking tape by the sink. She didn't look at me once. As she was returning to the bar, she said, "I'm going to see Saskia tonight. You should come."

It was the same every time. The first time I had fucked her, a bitter, grunting thirty seconds or so, was at a party at Saskia's, just after Laura told me it was over. It was as if there were no other venue worth the name for her in London. I asked her if she wanted to go to see a film once, and she looked at me as if I'd asked her if she wanted to cut her breasts off and use them for ear muffs. I didn't ask her again. It was her who asked me stuff. It was her who asked me if I wanted to go round to Saskia's. I didn't, but I did. Every time. I didn't know if her fondness for Saskia was because Saskia had a regular supply of drugs, or if it had anything to do with Iain. If it did, then why did she always insist on fucking me instead?

"Who'll be there?" I asked.

"Same crowd as per. You know. Don't come if you don't want to."

I didn't. But I did.

It was busy that night. It was always busy in The Pit Stop, even though the pool tables had been removed a few months back, and the beer had a greasy, metallic taste. Archway is one of those in-between places in London. You don't go for a night out in Archway. You might meet your friends there, before moving on, but the only all-nighters are the hardcore fifty-plus bunch who sit at the bar and scowl, their hair bearing the plow-marks of a steel comb; a triple-folded copy of the *Sun* or the *Racing Post* in their back pockets.

I made a few errors: poured the wrong drinks, short changed, long changed. I couldn't get the voice I'd heard back home from my thoughts. The telly, I thought. "It was the telly."

People were looking at me askance. I thought I might drop. I felt light-headed.

Sometimes, pulling pints, usually when I was feeling woozy like this, and needing something to concentrate on in order to fend off a narcoleptic attack, I'd get this incredibly strong feeling that I was drawing on something deeper than what sloshed in the kegs in the cellar; something that tapped into the juice below London, the very stuff that sustained the old city and allowed new layers to develop on top of it. Then the frothy mess would spill over my hand and I'd be dragged back into a world of beer that smelled thinly of detergent, ashtrays piled high like nightmarish open sandwiches and customers who looked lost, perpetually startled, trying to find a map home in the bottom of their glasses.

On my knees in the bar, bottling up after the doors were closed, I'd feel the last trains on the Northern Line thrum beneath the palm of my right hand, flat on the floor, balancing me. It was a different vibration from the stop-start rhythm of the generator that cooled the cellar; this was a steady, rising throb that reached its limit just as it seemed it might go on indefinitely; as it curved off into nothing I would feel a sense of loss that I couldn't begin to unravel.

All of my bases in London, I recognized, were governed by the presence of Tube stations or a proximity to their dirty magic. I hated them, feared them, but I was in awe of them too. My involvement with them was at a more attenuated level than I could understand, but it settled in my bones with the same compulsion as the urge to eat, or to make love.

Now another voice, one that I couldn't match to a mouth, said: "There's stuff underground you wouldn't believe. It's like another city, it's like London but *upside down*." I searched the crowd, but everyone's mouth was swilling beer, or vodka, or tongues. All the colors turned to ash.

And then I rallied. Just as Iain was walking in, and I thought: *fuck me, please let me go.* Lying spark out was infinitely more appealing than listening to that flapping knackersack.

Hair as slick as an emerging otter, he homed in on Ilse—another of Meddie's Saskia-centric friends, standing at the bar with a bottle of Moscow Mule—with smart-bomb precision. Ilse was dressed in a cropped white halter and white denim shorts. Tanned skin filled in the gaps: she looked like a humbug.

"Pint of Caffrey's," he said to me, without looking up from where a steel ring clung to the pitted knot of Ilse's belly button. My head was pounding.

"Name?" he asked Ilse.

She seemed to ignore him, continuing with her drink as if he were one step down on the food chain from a low-life, chivvying for a cup of tea on Regent Street. But then she said: "Ilse. Now fuck off."

Iain looked past me, checking his profile and full-on reflection in the mirror behind the bar. Ilse's friend, who I had never seen before, was clutching her handbag in a way that indicated she wanted to leave. She was glaring at Iain and tutting like a Geiger counter. Every couple of minutes I'd drift by to see how he was doing. Within half an hour he'd wangled her address and a kiss out of Ilse. Her friend had had enough and left. Light from the multi-screen videos bounced colors off the sweating plank that was Iain's forehead.

It didn't seem to matter that Ilse was pissed on Moscow Mule or that she persisted in calling him "Wankpot" rather than Iain. No matter that she'd rather eyeball the six-foot-fuck-off bouncer on the door with the questing pecs. He was in. Kind of. You had to give it to him.

"Is he for real?" I asked Meddie.

"Iain is a teddy bear," Meddie said. "You know that. He's soft as putty, really."

"He's a game bastard, I'll give him that," I said.

"Can I walk you home?" Iain was saying now.

Ilse: "Go myself. Taxi. Why don't you fuck off back to your mother, you sad bastard?" Iain laughed at this and leaned in, started gently eating her mouth. Ilse wasn't in any fit state to protest. She departed not long after. She wasn't up for a long night at Saskia's. Neither was I. But I was.

Suddenly, it was chucking-out time. Iain waited while Meddie and me collected empties, transferred the contents of ashtrays into buckets, shared out the evening's tips. And then we were walking back alleys, trudging through the drifts of chip papers, the bottles and empty cans of wifebeater, of electric soup, absently eyeing the graffiti and the dog shit.

"What's your favorite film?" Iain asked. He was always asking. And never listening to our replies. "Mine's *Don't Look Now*," he said, as usual.

"Really?" I said. "Fancy that. I didn't know."

Sometimes we caught a cab, but mostly we walked. At the flat in Crouch End that Meddie shared with Iain, we would have something unspectacular to eat before heading on to Saskia's. Yoyo was sitting on the steps outside when we got there.

"You tanked?" she asked.

"To the max," said Iain, and he certainly seemed pissed, but I hadn't seen him drink more than two pints all evening. "You?"

"Got any bacon? I could murder a bacon sarnie."

Yoyo was tall. About six-two. She walked with her head down and her shoulders rounded, looked up at you under her fringe whenever she said anything. She spoke in a whisper. It was as if every other facet of her life needed to be miniaturized in order to cancel out her size. She drove a Yaris. Somehow. She was never without a soft blue cricket hat with a floppy brim. Or a paperback stuffed into one of the pockets on her duffel coat. Always a different one whenever I saw her. Always something a little left field, a little cultish, that you never seemed to find in the bookshops. There was one there now. I couldn't see who the author was, but the title was *Paddington Bare*. A quote by David Lynch in white lettering across the top of the cover said: "And you think *I'm* weird?" I liked her. She was the only one of the bunch that I did like. I don't know why I persisted in hanging around with the others. It was just some ill-advised staff thing, that was all. Like going for a drink after work with the office dolts you wouldn't otherwise give the steam off your piss. Iain had that kind of psychotic edge that made you want to observe him, like a car accident in the making. Meddie was fit as fuck, and dangerous with it. It was as shallow as that.

Meddie—having consumed the best part of a six-pack of Carlsberg on the long walk back—attempted the maneuver that was Inserting The Key In The Lock. Dry cider ghosts wrapped themselves around us as we piled over the threshold. The hallway, briefly lit by a low-wattage bulb on a timer, revealed a rusting sit-up-and-beg bicycle without any wheels and a large pile of sun-faded *Q* magazines tied up with string. In the kitchen, Yoyo cremated a few rashers while the rest of us ate bowls of Rice Krispies and stared at an empty Pilsner Urquell bottle on the table.

Iain said, "That Ilse. That Ilse. I'd crawl naked and peeled across a thousand miles of salt and vinegar just to hear her tell me to go and shit up a pole again."

In Iain's bedroom, I shifted some dirty clothes and a bottle of Renovex from on one of his rickety old director's chairs and sat down, idly leafed through a copy of *Premiere*. Iain put on a purple silk shirt and too much Issey Miyake. Hundreds of issues of *Hotdog* and *Empire*, and older copies of *Photoplay*, *Picturegoer* and *Film Weekly*, were stacked in every available space. His walls were covered with posters of old films, silver screen classics rubbing shoulders with horror movies and skin flicks: *Gilda*, *Death Line*, *Deep Throat*. An old Bell & Howell 16mm projector stood in the center of a table next to some plastic reels, a splicer and a Kodak presstape. There were a couple of cans of film with labels stuck to them, written in an illegible hand. The wall next to his bed was dotted with the corpses of flies, midges and moths he had swatted over the years. He never cleaned them up. They were like the decals of downed enemy planes on the side of a fighter. He saw me admiring them.

"That Ilse," he grinned. "Ah, Ilse, how I'd like to swat something that crawled on you while I crawled on you. We could leave it there and get a tattooist to mark the spot forever. Silverfish on your thigh, earwig on your cleavage. To remember me by."

Iain Wild was originally from south Wales. Barry Island, I think. He had worked hard on removing his accent. But it was as if he had removed every other thing that supplies character alongside it. He had even excised his past. When I asked him where he had worked previously, before his current job, fixing old French cars at a garage in Ealing, he had pursed his lips and touched a finger to his nose, as if it were some great, terrible secret, as if he had been some kind of assassin, rather than a cleaner at McDonald's, which, according to Meddie, was what he had been.

He tended to wear outfits that were in differing shades of the same color. Half the time he looked like various areas of a Pantone chart. He ate meals that were color coordinated too. His favorite was pork chops, boiled potatoes, boiled cauliflower, and white sauce. On a white plate. Vanilla ice cream to follow. I said to him once, when the best part of a bottle of Bordeaux had turned me mean: "This isn't some fucking eccentricity that makes you mysterious or fascinating, you know. It's an affectation. It's an affectation that is dumb as fuck. It makes you look like nothing more interesting than a cuntist."

"Your trouble," he said to me, "is that you care too much about what's going on around you and not enough about what's going on." And then he touched his finger against his nose.

Getting on for one a.m., we caught a taxi up to Muswell Hill, and Saskia's place. She lived in a house filled with dressmaker's dummies and Wade Whimsies. She earned a lot of money designing corporate websites. Saskia. Jesus. As we walked in she was leaning out of the window blurting a soup of thin vomit and obscenity onto the patio roof below. She was far, far away. She said hi and air-kissed us all, but she might as well have been in Ulan Bator. I didn't know what was more distressing: the bump in her gut or the lack of color to her eyes. Saskia's baby went wherever she went: Hampstead Heath on a Saturday night, say, where she dropped gelatin strips of acid. The baby is well traveled, though it hasn't left London yet.

"You're going to give birth to Timothy fucking Leary if you ain't careful girl," somebody said, out of the smoky, syrupy dark. "You'll bear down and a fucking Blue Meanie'll fly out your twat."

Some drinking went on. As it does. Loud music. A complaint from the neighbors. A visit from the police. A quiet word. More drink. A dark room filled with chill-out music and rafts of reefer smoke. Another dark room filled with coats and fucking. Drink.

"Egg," said Saskia, glottally. She always wanted eggs when she was stoned. Scrambled, fried or poached. She had a thing for eggs. She lifted her top and ran her palms over the bulge. A papery sound—like the hiss of a hangnail against an emery board—turned my stomach. I started making my excuses. Before I left, a spill of light from an opening door ignited Saskia's swelling and I was convinced I saw, for a second, a blue, skittering suggestion uncoil in the subtle transparency of her flesh.

Iain had tried it on with every female in the kitchen and scored a grand total of 0.0. He ended up on his own in the bedroom, in front of the portable TV, trying to coax something from the beery collapse between his legs; he'd fallen asleep with saliva drying on his fist. I had to help him down the stairs and into a taxi back home.

"Do you have no fucking self respect?" I asked. He was asleep all the way. I kept asking anyway. I was asking myself more than anyone else.

# CHAPTER FOUR
## STORM WARNING

She survived, the first one. It read about it in a *Standard* It found fluttering around the tracks somewhere between Marylebone and Baker Street. Three of her fingers were severed, that's all. Her name is Jemima. It says the name to Itself over and over until it loses its meaning. Jemima. Jemima. Jemimajemimajemimajemi. Less of a name now. Just a noise. A shape made with the mouth. Which helps. The human things are what makes this so hard. It remembers seeing pictures of the Iran/Iraq war from Its childhood. Corpses on a road just outside Basra. The blank faces or the relaxed nonsense of their limbs weren't what affected It most. Rather, it was trimmed beards, or a bangle on a wrist. Moments of vanity.

It's standing flat against the curved wall, palms open, resting against the damp surface. Water trickles somewhere in the dark. Occasional gleams of light from the rail signals catch in the dusty curves of ceramic insulators. It breathes in. It breathes out. It breathes in. It breathes out. It breathes in. It breathes in. It breathes in. And holds the air inside It, all the atoms of forever permeating the membranes of Its lungs, being changed, becoming something else. Might there be air from Napoleon's lungs inside It now? Might there be the exhalations of Churchill, Nehru, Pol Pot, Boudiccea, Quetzlquatl filling Its chest, making its head thump?

*We are but dust, and a shadow.*

It is the dust. It is the shadow. The shadow is death. It is the shadow.

The scatter of sound along rails; the hiss and sizzle. A train chasing its own overture. It presses back against the wall, feeling the brick dust and moss writhing against Its clothes, Its skin. It exhales. It becomes a part of the dust and the shadows. And now in the dark It is less aware of Its face. That despicable signature. Hateful signifier. The thing that allies It to all the suits standing on the platforms waiting for trains to take them back to 2.4 and Sunday drives in the Mondeo for supposedly happy family lunches at the pub, but the food's shit and the beer's off and the kids won't stop squabbling.

Its legs shake as the train gathers pace, clattering into the bend a hundred meters away, lights scouring the blistered, scarred tunnel. The worm in its hole. *Its* hole. The tunnels feel like open mouths calling It home. The train barreling on, optimum speed, midway between Hampstead and Belsize Park. The Misery Line, they call it. Well, come on Misery, have at ye. Try some of this on for size.

It grins as the wash of headlights arc across Its face. *Look upon me and know true fear, look upon me as I do and understand what horror means.*

It peels away from the wall and raises Its arms as if to welcome a lover. It closes Its eyes at the screech of brakes filling the air. Thirty meters shy, the train hits the pile of sleepers laid across the track. The snout of the first carriage buckles and buries itself in six feet of earth, plowing through rails as if they were made of toffee. The rear of the carriage jackknifes and gouges a trail through the roof of the tunnel. Broken tiles and brick debris rain down. It steps back into shadow as the train crumples around It, mashed at impossible angles through the tunnel like potato forced through a ricer. Some of the panes, before the lights within the carriages stutter and die, become drenched in blood. An interminable time later, It picks Its way through the rubble to the rear carriage, which is half as big as it ought to be, concertinaed between the two walls, a giant vertical rupture splitting its center. A soup of limbs and oil and blood is bubbling out of it. People are screaming. For what?

It screams too, lustily apeing the sounds It can hear. Save us, save us from death so we might go back to what we wanted to kill ourselves to escape from.

It is over.

It is beginning.

THAT GREAT FUCK-OFF PANTHER CAME CRASHING THROUGH the undergrowth again this morning. It's a good job I keep a bag of cat nibbles handy or I'd probably be gnawed to the elbow by now. It's a mean looking bastard. Goes by the name of Marlon. I wouldn't be surprised if it had a bit of form: GBH, armed robbery, that sort of thing. Its meow sounds like a thirteen-year-old boy trying to keep his voice level. Before he was neutered, Marlon's bollocks must have been the size of satsumas.

I tried putting down a bowl of milk and scratching his head but he was looking at my arm like he was going to eat it, or fuck it. With Marlon you could never be sure. When I was with Laura, she'd find my magnetism towards cats amusing. The flat below her was occupied by a psalm-singing female tattooist who owned two ginger Toms that paid frequent visits and wrestled with me on the floor when Laura was too tired to. Another battle-scarred specimen used to delight in dashing through from the front window to the back, as if sent on a cat dare by its cat friends. Laura thought my reverence of these creatures a touch excessive but she humored me, even when I went on about how, if you send your love through your fingertips when you stroke a cat, it will feel it and trust you. It was a trick I tried with Laura when she hugged me goodbye for the last time. It worked like a malingerer in an office where everyone else has gone to lunch. But then Laura wasn't a cat.

"You know you're drinking too much," began Greg, loud enough for a pair of American tourists in pearl-colored shell suits to hear, "when you wake up in the morning and last night's unflushed piss has got a skin on it."

I seated myself opposite. Mozart's was filled with newspaper-reading middle-class men and women with floppy hair and oatmeal linen. We ordered. You get great English breakfasts at Mozart's, even at lunch-time. And you get music too. Mozart.

A notebook was opened in front of Greg. Ideas for sketches were scrawled upon it, along with pornographic doodles and cross-hatchings. He was putting together the pilot for a late-night sit-com he wanted to pitch to the commissioners at the major TV stations, set in a TV cookery studio run by Sicilian chefs with a mob background. It was called *Suck My Dish, Mothercooker.* Greg is nothing if not in your face.

I had first met him four years previously. He had come out of Lupo on Dean Street at a speed that made me suspect he had been forcibly ejected. He fell into me and we both went into the gutter, to the hilarity of the half-pint knobs spilling out of The French House. He picked me up and offered to buy me a drink by way of an apology.

"What is with birds these days?" he said. "What, you're not allowed to pinch their arses any more? Tell the fucking Italians that. Why do they get away with it and we don't?"

I was protesting that I had to get away, it really didn't matter, but he was having none of it. And it was a nice day, I was feeling pretty affable towards the world, I thought, why not? We walked up to the Dog & Duck on Bateman Street and I ended up buying the beers, spending the best part of twenty minutes waiting to get served at the tiny bar. I soon found out that when he was buying lunch or dinner for people, he took them off to the Eritrean restaurant in Kentish Town, or to Ed's Diner, or a Stock Pot. When other people were buying, he pressed them for a table at Mezzo or Quo Vadis, or Quaglino's.

I wanted to sink the beer and leave, but we ended up staying for a few more. Everything about him was my antithesis: the strategically crumpled Arnold Zimberg jacket, the lecherous way in which he sized up the women that squeezed past us (he felt totally justified in reaching out to squeeze parts of them, as if he were testing fruit: "But it's a gesture of respect, innit?"). There was something about him that fascinated me, and also worried me. His behavior felt somehow borrowed. He had it down too pat. It was like looking at a caricature of Soho man, right down to the surfer beard sticking out from beneath his lower lip, the Oakley Plates sitting on his scraped-back Beckham locks, the American Express Gold card, the cutting edge Sony Ericsson phone that spent the entire evening nestled in his hand, as if it had been glued there. It never rang once.

He lived off the Holloway Road, in some split-level flat that nobody had seen. He drove something fast and black with a soft top and then winked when you asked what kind of car it was. "I never said it was a car, did I? Did I?"

Our eggs arrived. I liked the way they add a little sprinkle of herbs to the top of the yolk, and the side order of sourdough toast. That's London, I suppose, in a nutshell.

"How's the script?" I asked.

He's always been a bit of a drinker (he waded through a couple of Bloody Marys while I sipped at a fruit smoothie) though lately it seemed he had increased his intake. But then, apparently, productivity was up, as was his social standing. Much of this was down to a Channel Four contact who had started taking him drinking at Groucho's. Being among the wolves gives you the illusion that you're actually a part of the pack. He still hasn't come down. Maybe he won't. This all seemed less weird than the fact that I still hadn't been invited round to his pad for dinner, or beers and footy on the TV.

"Getting there," he said. His face was as expressionless as the omelette placed in front of him. I set about my food, keeping my contributions to a minimum. If you're not careful, if you mention something out of context, he's liable to veer off on a different tack, which means he'll have two stories to tell you. Chip in again and, like a warren full of rabbits, you've got tales lined up all day, multiplying like hell. I consigned myself to the odd arched eyebrow, the occasional, demurring "Noooo" and "Hmmm," and *"Really?"*

He took an almighty mouthful of omelette—his first and last. Pushing away the plate, his meal already congealing, he lit a Marlboro Light and gusted a blue question towards me. "Sorry?"

"I accept your apology. Now, have you been getting any? A nation needs to know."

I shook my head.

He asked how I was. I told him. Laura's name came up. In a rather relaxed, non-obsessional way, it has to be said, but he was onto it like a stoat with a hare.

"For fuck's sake, Adam. You... you're like a bungalow. You've only got one story."

"Funny," I said. "Put it in your script." I had nothing else to say on the matter of my sex life. He knew that and so he didn't balk when I changed the subject. Give him his due, the bastard.

I asked him if he'd seen any of the old *Capital* crew. He hadn't. And he didn't want to, come to that. He had moved on. Moving on was a staple in his repertoire of things to say.

*Capital* was my first whiff of London employment, an outfit trying to compete with *Time Out* but proving to be an extremely poor relation. Greg edited its city guides for tourists and students new to London. He got me a job checking facts on the latest edition. I felt I could do a decent job on the subs' desk even though I didn't then know the difference between a running turn and overmatter; kerning and tracking. I knew how to spell and I understood when writing needed to be cut. An emergency lesson in the vagaries of QuarkXpress (which sounded like some kind of fast cheese delivery service rather than a piece of design software) on an office Mac one Sunday evening and I was thrust into a world of goatees and Gauloises Blondes, Evian face spray and Obsession. There were six people on the subs desk: India, Elspeth, Greg, Shaun, Claire and Elliot. I knew which of them I would get on with and which would be awkward bastards almost immediately. It's like going to buy a pet.

Elspeth came in at nine, before everyone else, so that she could leave at five, before everyone else. That she put the same number of hours in didn't matter to anyone: seeing someone collect their bag and flounce out an hour before the Real People's home time was enough to give you indigestion. She rarely spoke to anyone, and when she did it was with a barely concealed disdain, sarcasm filling her voice like effluent plopping into a river. I watched her more than the others; mainly because my desk was opposite hers but also because her head fascinated me. Her chin didn't slope upwards into her neck; it shot back at ninety degrees and was as flat as the underside of an iron.

When she talked, she'd collect cheesy deposits in the corners of her mouth and would later dislodge these nuggets with a specially unwound paper clip. She'd leave messages on her screen-saver such as *I'd rather be washing underwear* or *I'd rather be a rich man's plaything*. I often wanted to ask her why, if she was so transparently unhappy with her lot, she didn't pack up and find something else to do. But I kept shtoom; being the freelance, you never feel suitably liberated to be so upfront about such matters. Everyone else was all right, approachable, not so intent on the work that they couldn't enjoy a laugh now and then. But I was a little bit intimidated by Shaun, who was vegan, shaved his head and wore different badges on his bomber jacket every day: *I Hate Travis* or *FFC* or *Jesus Jones.* He had strange-colored eyes. A kind of pale brown, almost dark yellow. If I asked him a routine question, the kind of thing we always asked each other on the subs' desk, such as whether he'd copied a file from the server over to his machine without initialing the original file to let people know where it was, he'd wave me away with his hand without turning around. Once, I'd gone to make a coffee in the staff kitchen and tried to engage him in conversation. He watched me while I was twatting on about something, possibly hating Travis too, and had simply walked away, mid-sentence. He was astonishingly successful with women, apparently. They liked the challenge. They liked his pinched look, his expression of perpetual disdain. They liked his heavy-lidded eyes. They liked, when they asked how he was, how he answered: *In a state of urbane ennui.*

For a boy who had grown up in the north of England on a chiseled lexicon filled with lopped "g"s and dropped "h"s, it was a shock to find women talking like Radio 4 newsreaders. Those cultured voices made my chest tight with excitement. It became almost Pavlovian; I'd turn hot and gooey when India breathed the words "I'm off to the sandwich shop for a tuna salad. Anyone want anything?" I started to fantasize about her enunciating unlikely morsels such as "Marrakech" or "rapacious" and the surely unattainable "clitoral stimulation." If her lips and tongue could make her speech sound so good, what could they do when turned to other tasks? Sometimes I'd work myself into such a fever I'd have to go for some fresh air or suffer a headache. She could make "Good morning Adam, Jesus you look rough" sound like a come-on.

I was grateful to Greg for the work, even though it didn't work out. Offices and me. Went together as well as shit does with custard. I was grateful too for him introducing me to Laura. Even though that didn't work out either.

I paid for breakfast and asked him if he knew what had become of Shaun and Elliot. Shaun, apparently, had jacked in work to travel, disillusioned with London life, and Elliot was now Chief Sub.

I walked Greg to the bus stop where he did a very Greg thing and hailed a cab. And then asked me if I had any money to pay for it.

A WIND WAS GETTING UP BY THE TIME I RETURNED HOME, exciting the litter in the street. I felt bushed. The previous night's so-called party had left me edgy and dissatisfied with my circle of friends. I couldn't work out if I was tagging along with them, or allowing them to be a part of my life. I didn't know how hard it might be to quietly leave them.

A bitter flood of sunlight slashed at the window when I looked at it. If it could have made a noise, it would have been the cry of an unoiled gate opening. I took a shower and wrote a letter to Dad. While I was eating lunch I heard the wind coming up the flue to howl behind the fireplace in my bedroom.

And then voices.

I knelt by the hearth, carefully pushing aside the wicker arrangement of dried flowers my mother had given me years previously. Trapped in the gusts of wind came sudden, alien words, wrapped in diesel: "...enditohoff..." and "...urtcob..." and "...stardwan..."

It occurred to me that I was catching snatches of sentences, but the voices that uttered them were somehow inhuman: atonal and passionless. Perhaps they were being distorted by the movement of underground breezes. Perhaps they weren't voices at all, just the movement of metallic echoes through tunnels that, by some architectural fluke, produced vocal similarities. Laughter made a mockery of that theory, though. Thick and phlegmy, it hung like smog in the gutted heights of the house next door, at one point passing so close to the fireplace I thought the mouth it was coming from must only be inches away from me.

The rest of the afternoon I spent indoors, becoming more and more nervous about that evening's dinner date with Nuala. I flicked through gardening notes I'd made, wondering if we should go for something a bit unusual for the stall, make it less a flower thing and more a wild sanctuary for plants. A bit of Japonica, say, or Hoary Mullein, or Himalayan Balsam—something hardy, with a bit of clout that would attract attention. Hopefully, it would be tough enough to survive even my most savage bouts of care. But the color plates in my book could not touch me with their calming images of hedgerows and ivy; I felt restless and itchy, my skin somehow not right for the body it was containing, as if I'd bought it from a shop only to find it was a size too small. "...barramulch..."

There was nothing on the television, but I increased the volume for a bit of company. The sky's color was deepening. A cat loosed an unearthly cry somewhere out back. I imagined Marlon nailing some hapless female with his satanic cat penis. "...isphersprit..."

Footsteps gritted next door. What was going on? There were no vans or plant outside. No tea-breaks or wolf whistles. I was just nipping to the bathroom for a piss when the phone rang.

It was Yoyo.

"You have to come. You have to come. Can you?"

I could. I did. But I wish I hadn't.

THE TOWERS OF YOYO'S ESTATE CLOSED IN LIKE BUNCHED shoulders as I walked the few hundred meters to her flat from the bus stop on Edgware Road. The previous night's beer still wallowed in the greased confusion of my guts. The moon was an incomplete thumbprint breaking free of the tower block's edge. I could see Yoyo, mannish and gawky, stumping around the car park, her hand on her hat to stop the wind from taking it. I pulled the frozen lapels of my leather jacket around me and shouted her name. She trotted over and got hold of my arm.

"It's Saskia," she said.

"It always is," I said, thinking, I'm fucked if I'm coming all the way out here just to go all the way back to Muswell Hill. "What's wrong?"

Yoyo didn't know. She had received a phone call an hour previously but Saskia hadn't said anything. There was very loud music in the background. Raised voices.

"I heard someone say 'Pass the warning,' and then the line went quiet."

I must have winced when I bit my cheek because she asked me if I was all right.

I said, with a voice I barely recognized as my own, "Where's your car?"

She was too nervous to drive. I drew the driver's seat closer to the steering wheel and we set off. It started raining as I pushed the Yaris up through Marylebone, and by the time we had circumnavigated Regent's Park, the weather had deteriorated to such an extent that, even with the wipers full on, it was difficult to make out what was happening on the road just a few meters in front.

We were leaving Camden in the rear view mirror when Yoyo took my hand in hers. "I'm scared," she said.

"I can call the police if you like," I said. "If you're worried about what you think we might find."

"No," she said. "I'm probably just imagining things. Sas probably pressed a button on her phone by mistake while she was watching a noisy film. She likes horror films, doesn't she?"

She asked it in such a way that replying in the negative wasn't an option.

"What are you reading?" I asked, reaching out to switch on the radio. I found jazz FM. John Surman. Soothing. I removed my hand from hers, changed gear, and patted her leg.

She removed the novel in her pocket and cursorily waved it at me. "It's called *The Vanishing Road*," she said, as the rain found a new, impossible intensity.

"Apt," I said. She laughed. The tension unwound a little in that tiny space.

By the time we got to Muswell Hill I had the crazy urge to suggest to Yoyo that we go to the pub for a drink first, because whatever had happened to Saskia couldn't still be happening. And then I felt sick for thinking that, and for thinking that whatever might have happened to Saskia was too good for her, which reminded me of the sentence that I had heard on two separate occasions. Which made me feel even more sick. In the end I pulled over and *was* sick.

"Fucking hell," Yoyo said. "I mean, fucking hell."

All I could smell was my vomit rising from the gutter, the exhaust fumes and Yoyo's lip balm, a cloying strawberry. I felt too weak to try driving the car through more of this shitty weather so I suggested Yoyo waited in the car while I checked on Saskia, whose house was less than a quarter of a mile away. She protested, said she wanted to come with me, but when I started across the road, she didn't move from her seat. I looked back at her shape, spoilt by the cascade of water across the windscreen, and thought, right then. Right then.

I was sopping before I got to the end of the street, but I felt better for being out on my own in the cold. Hunched figures bore down on me, blind, steaming with beer, and I had to dodge out of the way of all of them. I put my hands in my pockets, fixed my eyes to the glassy pavement and walked hard.

Saskia's place was like a blacked-out house during wartime. I tried the door and wasn't too surprised to find it open. Inside I waited for my heart to calm down and the sounds of the house to make themselves known to me. A television was playing somewhere, quietly. More quietly than Yoyo had suggested. I checked the downstairs rooms but there was nothing out of the ordinary. Unless you count as extraordinary split bin bags and dozens of flies in the kitchen; a living room with three televisions and a massive framed film poster depicting Bruce Dern in *Silent Running* and a cork notice board in the hallway studded with Polaroids of semihard penises wearing colored condoms. Mildewed blankets hung from the banisters, slowly drying in the damp heat of the house. This is Saskia we're talking about. I don't find it extraordinary.

Upstairs in the master bedroom I found her fast asleep. An ashtray filled with roaches trembled uncertainly on her belly. There was nobody else around. I moved the ashtray and, as there were no blankets available, wrapped Saskia in a couple of cardigans from her wardrobe. She shifted slightly in her sleep. Reached out a hand and cupped my crotch, said: "Yeah, Pete. Yeah." Smiled. Disappeared back into the depths.

My thoughts folded inwards and the edges of the room followed it, dissolving to black, leaving only the trembling outline of Saskia, like a cut out. Through the loose-knit cardigan I could see how her blouse had ridden up to reveal her swollen belly. I saw the sleeping curve of potential within. It turned its head towards me and opened its eyes: ash trickled from them. Its yawning mouth carried no sound, only the rank, concrete ghosts of what it would become.

EVERYTHING WHITED OUT AND AS I SUCKED IN BREATH, SO the colors returned. I was in my bathroom and there was shaving foam all down my shirt. My razor was in my hand. I pulled myself upright and caught sight of my half-shaved face in the mirror. The strip light over it made me appear pasty and undernourished. Too many shadows. According to my watch I'd been out for about five minutes. I could smell strawberries and mildew. There was ash on the floor, but when I bent to touch it, I saw that it was just talcum powder, colored by the dust. My fingers left prints. Laura's talc; I never used it.

I WONDERED IF I SHOULD PHONE NUALA, OR POP UP TO TELL her I wasn't feeling well and that I couldn't go through with dinner, but as I was thinking this I was rooting through my suitcase for something to wear, and I could smell dinner drifting down the stairs.

Should I opt for a jeans and T-shirt combo, or go for something a bit more dangerous? I didn't own any kimonos or sarongs so I plumped for a linen shirt opened cheekily to the throat and a pair of slacks. I had half a bottle of Australian Chardonnay in the fridge but I suddenly had a panic that she might be tee-total so I took a few cans of Pepsi Max instead. And then berated myself as I waited for her to let me in for being such a twat.

"No wine?" she asked, when she saw my offering. "You might like drinking that liquid death, but I don't. I'll pass, thanks." She had progressed with her unpacking. The paint on the walls had dried, brilliant white throughout, and a Moïse Kisling nude was hanging above the fireplace. A vase on a Minotti table was tightly packed with pebbles from a beach. A battered bronze cat was being used for a doorstop. There was a bookshelf containing more orange Penguin spines, large coffee table books on photography and art, and dog-eared copies of *Wallpaper**.

"It's starting to look very welcoming in here," I said. "Very cozy."

She was wearing some kind of wrap, so tight she might have been poured into it. I could smell vegetables, ginger, garlic. She'd changed Whale Song to *Storm in a Rain forest.* At any moment I expected a disgruntled baboon with an arse like lava to come clattering through the bamboo drapes and make off with the olives. What was I doing here? Too soon. Too soon. Laura danced through my thoughts, a mischief that was as brightly compelling as a paper cut. Despite Nuala's simple, tasteful surroundings, I craved Laura's uncomplicated flat. She had a beautiful china tiger that stood under the window. A bowl in which she floated tealights. I wondered if the cards I sent her were still propped up on her groaning bookshelves.

Greg had leaned across in the pub and tapped her on the shoulder. "Laura. This is young Adam. Say hi."

She said hi. She smiled. Her eyes were blue, and almost ruinously symmetrical. At the end of the night she asked me back to her place for a cup of tea. I sat in her kitchen, waiting for her to put the kettle on. She sat waiting too. I thought maybe I should get some cups sorted out. She said, "You know, when a woman invites you back for a cup of tea, well, that's not necessarily what she means."

Over the course of a year, we fell in love and drew the city unconsciously into the bubble of warmth that enveloped us both; it's hard not to involve London at some level; it's almost an imperative. It regimented the way in which our time was spent, and it rushed us into spending that time, and of course, it sat there while we played in its belly. It was difficult to recall a time when we ever simply relaxed and chatted, watched shit television, ate pizza, slobbed out. Always we were bathing and dressing and making telephone calls, arranging cabs, dinner appointments. When bedtime came we fucked till exhaustion knocked us out. We made plans; talked of the house we would share. We even looked for it, pointing out likely contenders in St. John's Wood, Belsize Park, Marylebone. She told me she wanted to have a child by me. Always, there were little encouragements and reassurances; always, her hand in mine, her eyes brimming with me. The death of our relationship was my enslavement, her manumission.

London life is a race. A marathon with a sprint finish and a lap of honor. Woe betide if you get a stitch, if you lag behind.

"Hey. Reality check," said Nuala. "You've got a face as long as a pair of wet tights." She pushed a gin and tonic into my hand and told me to sit. I lowered myself onto a floor cushion. The black dildo peeked out from beneath it; I resisted an insane urge to sniff it.

"What's her name?" she said. "You know, I can tell you're uncomfortable. Something in the eyes. My eyes, they change color when my moods alter. My hair too. See, eyes blue? When I'm angry, they go really blue. And when I'm tired or sad they fade out, to a kind of soft blue. You too. She must have really meant something."

"I don't want to talk about it." I didn't, I didn't.

"You do, you do. I'm a great listener."

"I'm sure you are—it's just that I'm not a great talker. I can't talk about it."

"How long's it been?"

"How long's what been?"

"How long's it been since she finished with you?"

"She didn't finish with me. What's for dinner?" I moved to the kitchen, stepping over the item I'd seen stuffed into a box. It appeared to be a huge fabric bag but the buckles and straps indicated otherwise. Nuala was delving about in a compartment of her refrigerator, her words muffled.

"Oh come come come, Adam. You have to face up to these matters. It's no good tucking them away inside where they can hurt you."

"I'm sorry, but I'm not prepared to discuss my private life with someone I met just a little while ago."

She lurched from the fridge, a flare of lollo rosso shivering in her fist. "Why not?"

"Because I don't know you."

"Rubbish. You go to the doctor and tell him about your piles or pruritus don't you? I mean the generic 'you,' that is."

I knew I wouldn't be able to deflect her unless I walked out and I didn't want to do that. I was strangely fascinated by her. "It was a case of right people, wrong time. That's all. It's my problem, something I have to deal with. Talking about it won't help."

My heart sank when she yanked what seemed like an acre of coriander from a brown bag. Its ammonia smell filled the kitchen. I fucking hate coriander.

Nuala tore at the salad leaves with the aimless zest of a person trying to swat a fly. "But it will," she said. "Pain has substance. It sits here—" she pressed her hand against my solar plexus, "—and draws bad stuff towards it from your mind, stuff that you remember or feel or predict for yourself. It grows here and unless you drain it you'll end up making yourself ill. Drain it. By talking about it."

"There's no problem," I insisted. "I don't have any pain."

We sat down to eat, the atmosphere stiffening a little around us. But the meal wasn't as bad as I was beginning to anticipate.

The food was excellent, and I managed to steer the conversation elsewhere, for a little while.

"What do you do?" I asked her.

"I'm a hair stylist, if you mean how do I earn my money?"

"A hairdresser? But you look... you seem so... you appear to...."

"What?" Her lips flattened, pressed flush against a piece of aubergine before vacuuming it into her mouth. She seemed to inhale food, barely chewing before swallowing with such violence that I could see the cartilage in her throat spasm from the effort.

"You seem so unusual."

"I see. And what do you do?"

"I sell flowers. And I work in a pub."

"Well there you have it. You don't look like a flower seller. You look like you should be working in a record shop."

She tapped a button on her remote control. Apes shrieked. Warthogs truffled through the mud. Impala trotted across hissing pampas.

"What I mean is. This flat. Your decor...."

"Is too lavish for a person who trims hair? Well, I work from home and I have a very exclusive client list. And the hair I style isn't merely the stuff on your head. Follow?"

"Ah." I followed. "So who's on this client list? Anyone famous?"

She smiled, and everything felt better. "A couple of internationally renowned footballers. A rock star. An A-list actor."

"Get away. Give me names."

She gave me names. I had to fight to keep my mouth shut. "But he's a hard bastard, that United player. Don't they take the piss out of him in the showers? I mean... in the shape of a *love heart*?"

AFTER THE MEAL I STARTED CLEARING PLATES BUT SHE HELD up both her hands like a mime artist feeling the sides of an invisible box. The shadows of the candle flames slithered around the walls. Light glinted off the pictures, the spines on her bookshelf. Nuala's eyes, I now saw, were swirls of cobalt. I was drunk.

"No need," she said. "My cleaner will see to those tomorrow." She went to the CD player and stuck on another disk. Proper music for a change. I didn't recognize it but it was full of swirling guitars and a woman's voice that sounded as light as the air.

Nuala said: "Now, would you like to sex with me?"

LATER, SHE STUCK HER TONGUE IN MY EAR AND WHISPERED: "I noticed you didn't complain about the fact that we'd only just met." Her voice was redolent of coriander. I could bear it. "You fucked me like you fucked her. I know, shush, you don't have to disagree with me. You kept pushing my arms back over my head. She must have been very trusting to expose herself like that to you. Or was it just because you like the shape my tits make in that position?"

"Well, they aren't bad, are they?" I said. And then, "Who's H?"

"He's the missing piece in my jigsaw puzzle. He's the yin to my yang.

Or yang to my yin. Whatever it is."

I wasn't hurt by her candor but I was hit with a sense of déjà vu. Being with Laura, thrilled by the way she held me in such high esteem, had, at the time, given me a sense of worth, a belief that I was special to someone for the first time in my life. When, after our break-up, she confessed that she'd never quite got over the split with her previous boyfriend, Ed, and hadn't managed to put behind her the interim affair with James—who, she told me, she would have married within days of meeting him if he'd asked—simply left me feeling duped. I felt as though I'd been an experiment: the test to see whether Laura could proceed with her life in a normal way. Answer: no, not yet—so cheerio but thanks for all the hours you put in. I longed to be the soul mate that these others seemed to have been. How could she feel so deeply for them when she had told me they weren't keen on sex and treated her so shabbily? Ed, apparently, did nothing but curse and moan all the time and James relied upon her solely for emotional support. I was really attracted to her. I wallowed in her curves. We did things in the bedroom (and in the kitchen, on the lawn, in friends' bathrooms) that she'd never done before. I wrote her little notes and hid them in the fridge. I went down on her for the length of a Smashing Pumpkins album (a double CD, mind).

"Hey. Reality check, Adam. You're getting tense. Think of nice things. Think of amniotic fluids. Think womb. Here, snuggle this."

She handed me her special pillow but I put it aside and placed my face against her breasts. They weren't right, but they'd do.

"Love," she said. "It's like glandular fever. It takes a long time to get it out of your system and when it's finally gone, you're left feeling weak and vulnerable. Love fucks us something rotten, but we never fuck it. We worship it."

Towards midnight.... That song, still drifting, programmed on constant loop. It didn't get boring. I got up to see what the track was but Nuala called for me from the living room, distracting me. She was unpacking the thing with buckles and straps. I was wearing her dressing gown. I noticed, with some dismay, that it smelled of the same perfume Laura used to wear.

"What. Is. That?" I said, pointing at her.

"Oh, this old thing?" she said, flicking the shark's tooth that depended from her clitoris. "H bought it for me. He said my cunt was so greedy it ought to have teeth. I take it off, pre-coitus, as you know."

"I should bloody well hope so."

"Tiger shark. Makes me feel closer to the animal in me." She slid it out and began untangling the buckles and harnesses. "There we are," she sang, as she fitted the last strap and swung herself into the hammock.

Her feet slipped into a pair of stirrups and she yawned at me: just the right height.

"Oh," I said. "Oh, I see."

# CHAPTER FIVE

## THE WEB

Nuala dozed beside me, but I was too fitful to follow suit. Every noise made me start—from the slam of a car door to the rush of juices in Nuala's belly. And then, very clearly, I heard: "Not long now. We're almost through."

I'd known all along that the sounds were voices—not breezy indiscretions in the pipes. But hearing complete sentences, rather than snatches, helped cement my conviction. I rose and dressed quietly, not knowing what I was intending to do. Outside, a stiff wind was pushing a tide of filth before it down Dartmouth Park Hill. Dust, plastic bottles, empty tins, twists of paper; there was even what looked like a dead shrew in there but it was enveloped by all the other bits of grime before I could be sure. It snagged around the wooden hoardings and whispered there, a strange convolvulus daring me to do what I didn't know I'd already decided upon. Warm light flooded from Nuala's bedroom window. I ducked out of sight till her shape had diminished in front of it. At least, I hoped it was Nuala's shape. I really didn't want to have to explain my mad behavior to her.

There was a padlock on the door that would have let me through the hoarding so instead I climbed over the spiked iron railings at the side of the house, the corner of which marked the beginnings of Wyndham Crescent. All the while, I was muttering to myself: "Adam, what the *fuck* do you think you're doing?" The house was wreathed in shadow. A huge hole had been bored in the front garden, which I edged around, though not before I'd peered in and felt my legs turn to pulp. The depth of its blackness made it appear without end, but I also had the unpleasant thought that it was quite shallow and that, just beyond the limit of complete dark, people were huddled there, watching me intently.

On the front door was a warning sign: a white, expressionless face wearing a hard-hat against a red background. DANGER, it read. DEEP EXCAVATIONS. Beneath it, someone had scrawled: *You talkin bout yo mother?* Beneath that, the shape I had seen earlier on the bus shelter was crudely scratched into the wood. I pressed my hand against the door, expecting it to be locked. But I was hardly surprised when it sprang open, hinges wailing hideously. I waited there, eyeing up the block of revealed dark so carefully that I began to see tendrils of black tear off and curl towards me. I might have turned round and gone home then but for a single whoop from a siren in the road behind me. I stepped inside.

I've never been afraid of the dark. I just have a problem with what might be hiding in it. Once my eyes had grown accustomed to the gloom I inched forward, telling myself that the humanoid forms that loomed out of the thin pockets of gray were just workers' jackets hung up on hooks. I had one unpleasant moment when I looked up the stairs to the landing and saw a bulbous shape against the window. I didn't want to go and check it out, and the fact that it wasn't moving was enough to satisfy me, even if I was still uncertain of its identity. Something else wasn't right here, but I was too busy deconstructing the alien forms that emerged with every step to recognize it. Then I saw the reason for the warning signs. A chain barrier tapped my shins. Two feet further and the ground fell away. Joists of wood had been rammed into the earth beneath the concrete foundations and an aluminium ladder descended, severed by the dark beneath its sixth rung. The wind, or whoever possessed the whispers that had bothered me, was singing down there.

*Why not?* I thought, swinging my legs over the edge and trying to understand why this should feel like the most natural act in the world. The temperature dropped rapidly as I descended and I was in half a mind to go back for a jumper when the ladder ended. Solid ground was nowhere within reach of my probing toe so I clung there for a moment, looking back the way I had come but unable to see the lip of the hole I'd sunk into. I'd been on the ladder for a few minutes, but it seemed fair to assume that the floor was within leaping distance. And then I felt something bend inside my head and I fell anyway. Somehow, the darkness became even deeper.

HE HAD BEEN WALKING A MATTER OF MOMENTS BEFORE figures emerged from the gloom and approached him. They were naked and pale: a man and a woman. As the dark became known to him, so their detail increased. She carried a baby in a papoose, slung around her hips. He carried what appeared to be a spear. Close up, now. Close enough to see the small rat that was following them, that gnawed at a hard growth poking from the man's ankle. Close enough to see the candle wax color of their irises.

"Whofuck?" the man said. The spear was out in front of him, its blade—some crudely sharpened piece of flint—gleaming black in the darkness, like coal.

"I'm," he said, but found he couldn't follow the sentence through. "I... am...." He couldn't draw anything from his mind. He did not know who he was. "I am..." he said. "I forget."

"Monck," the naked man whispered, seeming not to notice the vermin chewing at him. His voice was cool and cruel, heavily sanded, perhaps by the grime that flew through the tunnels. "It's Monck, come back to us," he whispered. "Wherefuck? Lucky it weren't the soldiers come across you. Dead now, you'd be. A dead head on a pike, decoration for her Ladyship."

The woman laughed. The baby giggled and pawed at breasts swollen with milk.

Monck rubbed his head. He didn't feel quite right.

"Why fiddle with thy nut? Does thou suffer a dysfunction? Afraid of us, is it? And rightly so. Monck. *Monck*." The naked man laughed: blackened teeth oozed from beneath his lips.

"Tread soft, Mitre," the woman hissed. "He might be the one." The humor fell from his face.

"And he might not," Mitre said. "He might just be a fly fallen into the silk: fuel. Fuel for the final push. And a couple of sovs for us, finder's fee, like. You shouldn't be so jumpy, Herschell. They can't all be Gonebads."

"One of them has to be. Why not him?"

Mitre prodded him with the spear. Monck flinched. "You. Are you Gonebad? Or are you Surfacetype? Or are you thick with us?"

Monck rubbed his head some more. It seemed to help, though not with his memory. He felt more relaxed. He didn't feel under threat in any way, despite Mitre's weapon and Herschell's hostility. "I don't know," he said. "I think I fell."

"He's Surfacetype," Herschell decided. "Let's get him along to Vane. Let's have him processed and padlocked. The quicker the better. I don't like being around this Topside scum." The baby fastened its lips to Herschell's nipple; spilled mouthfuls made black tracks through the filth on her tit.

"I'll take him," Mitre said.

He prodded and poked Monck into some kind of narrow duct with loose floorboards underfoot and scarred tiling overhead. Sweating tallow candles showed the way at regular points, drenching the air with a claggy animal fug. The interstices were filled with shadows: one sinking into his feet as he passed beneath a candle, while at the same time another grew as he approached the next.

"Who's Vane?" Monck asked.

"Vane will have thee right as a carrot," Mitre replied. "And then we'll have you at the Face working like bastards, or wherever it is you're supposed to go." He laughed again, a sound that put Monck in mind of molten tar.

They emerged onto a platform choked with thick hives of litter. The line that served it appeared disused; mounds of filth had accrued between the rails; deep splits journeyed across graying enamel tiles. The station's sign was just legible on the wall, in white on a blue panel, surrounded by the familiar red ring: *Gospel Oak*. Why then, should it transmit to him only warning signals? Error messages? Something wasn't right. The electronic noticeboard stuttered, on the edge of total breakdown, its yellow letters and numbers glowing faintly, alerting him to a thin mist that folded through the tunnel. He couldn't read the destination. Something that ended with the word "Fields." Due in three minutes. Mitre waited with him, considering his clothes with unabashed expressions that moved between amusement and disgust. One of the hives of litter stirred: a young girl moved out from behind it and walked towards him. He took in the naked, wasted curl of her posture and made to reach out for her, worried that she might fall onto the tracks, but she was stronger than she appeared. She stopped short of him and pressed a piece of paper into his palm; smiled: the effort sent fractures through the caked skin on her cheeks.

"Hello again," she said. "I'm Coin. Well, it's Penny, but my friends call me Coin. I was told to give you that."

"Who gave it to you?" he asked, trying to read what was written on it, but the light was too poor.

"Oi, you," Mitre said, "sod away out of it, you little worm. Go fishing. We're in need of muscle down here, and you playing footsie with this shitehawk isn't doing nobody no good."

She left without speaking again, jumping down between the rails and scurrying into the tunnel. He glanced again at the train indicator board just as a large *CORRECTION* alert flashed across it. There was a blank next to the train's destination for a second or two, where the estimated time of arrival was meant to be, and then: *9 YEARS*. Thankfully, the text stuttered again before resolving itself as *@&*^$)*&*, which was somehow more comforting.

"What did you mean, just then?" Monck asked. "What did you mean when you told her to go fishing?"

"Thy knows full well," Mitre snarled, waving the spear in Monck's face. "Now lace up that cakehole or shitting hell, sir, I'll paste thee something chronic."

One of the benches was relatively free of refuse or human waste. He parked himself and sank his face into his hands. A faintly marine scent drifted from his fingers but he couldn't recognize it. Tears came, born of hopelessness and frustration. He felt hollow, his center stolen from him by something unseen that danced nearby, teasing him with its substance before snatching it back when it seemed he might gain purchase on who he was.

A metallic whistling drew his gaze to the tunnel. The walls deep inside the dark shivered with blue light. The bruised face of the train rattled into the station. The windscreen was heavily soiled—what appeared to be a bloody clot was smeared across the glass—concealing the driver, who was little more than a lumpen black shape. None of the compartments were inhabited. As soon as the train shuddered to a standstill, Monck stepped on and sat by the door. Mitre positioned himself opposite, his large genitals mashing beneath him as he sat. A hum invaded the carriage, punctuated by moments of static, as though the driver's intercom was primed. Monck studied the map of the line—the Fleet Line—and allowed the somnolent jostling of the train to seep into his muscles. He didn't know where he was meant to get off, which confused him, because he was sure he'd made this journey many times in the past. He noted the station names that succeeded Gospel Oak. Malden Road, Primrose Hill, Inner Circle, The Web, Urbania, Yerkes Way, Myatts Fields... names that managed to both excite and deflate him at the same time. His confusion was increased by the gathering pace of the train and the apparent depths it was sinking to. He swallowed hard to counter the pressure building in his ears, then stood up when the next station appeared in a blur, packed with bodies, their faces streaming, featureless orbs. So it was with the next station, and the next. Through the doors of the adjoining carriages, empty cars jinked and swayed. Mitre said nothing, choosing instead to run his thumb over the edge of his spear.

Gradually, the train slowed. The tunnel beyond the window grayed out and details—cables, switches, ducts—hove into view. Monck was able to read the station sign as it flashed by the windows: *The Web*. With a final lurch, the train shuddered to a halt. A voice, raspy and baritone, fluttered through the PA.

"This is The Web," it said. "Passengers change here...." It drifted away for a while and then: "Thank you for your attention. We look forward to the opportunity of serving you again."

Nobody, bar him and Mitre, disembarked. There was no one waiting to get on. Not that the train hung around long enough to collect any passengers; as soon as they were standing on the platform its doors hissed shut and it chuntered away. More of the hives of muck were clustered around his feet—he didn't want to see what they encased.

There were no signs hinting at a way out, but Mitre ushered him through the nearest exit and he allowed himself to be led by the point of the spear, while at the same time struggling to understand where he was.

At the entrance to The Web—a fence with a padlocked gate—Mitre barked a single word, *Almond*, and then left him. Water trickled down the walls here, and ran along an uneven path that was studded with rat droppings, crumbling brickwork and sopping tumbleweeds of hair, dust and grease. Monck took the time to study his own clothes, trying to understand why they looked so different from everybody else's. What had happened here? Had he been sleeping? Had he been ill? He felt much fresher for it, whatever the case.

Presently, a slightly stooped man appeared, jogging through the soup. His large, sad eyes glittered for seconds before his entire face was visible: they seemed to slope towards the frog-like spread of his mouth, as if his head was slowly melting. He might have been any age between twenty and sixty. His features were filled with dirt and fear: both had erased whatever it is that suggests a vintage.

"What's the rumpus?" said Almond, quickening from the dark, like the insects he liked to breed in his burrow, Monck thought, and then: *How did I know that?* Almond unlocked the gate and shooed him through. "You're lucky. Vane is free for the now. Plagued she is, usually with folk moaning for fruit."

As Monck pushed past him, Almond quietened, to the degree that Monck had to turn to see what was wrong. "What is it, Almond?" he asked, wondering why he should feel so familiar with this creep. "See something green?"

"Your smell too fresh, too clean," said Almond. "I don't like it. You skimmers, you waterboatmen, you sicken me. What makes you so special that you should be allowed to dip in and out of the above while the rest of us grow blind down here?"

"Lock your gruel-gate, prater," Monck said. "Stop gob-shiting me."

"I'll report your attitude. We all have to do our jobs. Without divergence. Monck! Come back. I'll have to report this."

"At your peril," said Monck, and: "I am doing my job." Yet he couldn't recall what his job was. Almond's words flirted with something recent in his memory that he couldn't solidify. The heavy, almost cloacal smells of deep earth; the dun, hemispherical uniformity of it all. Regiments of train sounds, all of them bass rumbles that, by the nuances their vibrations took, gave away direction and line. It was as close and as identifiable to him as his own skin. Another place away from here he couldn't begin to envisage, although somehow he knew he'd spent the greater part of his life on the surface. It seemed such a long way away. It took on the rippled nonsense of dreams; a nonsense of tall buildings and queues and the siege mentality of light.

Vane met him as she came out of her burrow. "Follow me," she said, giving him the once over. They sank deeper into the earth, the cold becoming something that clung, like wet clothes.

"Where are we going?" he asked, thinking he ought to know.

"We have to talk to Odessa," she replied. "About what should happen to you now."

"Mitre said I needed to see you because I have a headache."

"Mitre is a brain-dead fool. He'd fuck up a wet dream, that one. And leave it to me to say what you need to do."

It grew so dark that he had to catch hold of the woolen tassels on her cardigan in order to negotiate the winding path. Eventually, cold light seeped from a crook in the passageway, lazy as slob ice. Even the air here seemed tired, coiling heavily in his lungs; tasting stale, slightly burned, reminding him of uninvited kisses. Two women flanking a jet black fissure in the rock unwound themselves from hills of blankets. In the unflattering light, their eyes were milky orbs, ceaselessly motile, like flies' eggs. They wore vaguely recognizable clothes, like poor, ill-fitting armor that had become matted with filth and plates of mud.

"It's me, Zoffany," said Vane. "Let me by. I've brought Monck for the Queen."

He didn't like the way she said that, as if he were something to be served. The guards did not stand down. "Code me," said one, kneeling.

Vane lifted the stiff folds of her skirt and shot an angry squirt of piss into the guard's face. No further exchanges were made: Zoffany stepped away from the fissure. They went in.

Vane made him wait at the edge of this new dark while she disappeared into it. His breath came evenly, despite his not knowing in detail who lay ahead. He knew she was benevolent, of that he was sure, though he didn't know how. Sighting her would make everything clear, he was sure. Whatever muck was fogging his brain would be put right soon enough.

Something tethered by a thick rope clawed its way out of the shadows, snuffling at the ground a meter or so from his left foot. From the slant of its head, the greased sleekness of its hide, he guessed vermin as its root family, though he wouldn't have put money on it. There was a shadow of dog in that thing, if his eyes were to be believed. And—

"Monck."

He moved instantly towards the flat bark of her voice, a child to its mother's demand. The creature slunk back, baring a yellow tusk that writhed with mites. Monck was standing by the side of a collapsed chair upon which a moldering stack of newspapers were balanced. When the stack unfolded slightly, twisting to accommodate his approach, he felt his blood quicken. The chair was legless, or rather the legs that had once belonged to it were without shape, blended into the irregular ground on which they stood. As for Odessa, the closer he came to her, the more she seemed fashioned from the very stuff upon which she sat. Her face was oaken and runneled. Grainy eyes sucked at him greedily, taking in his substance as if she were starved of such visual sport. He couldn't tell whether the folds that swaddled her were fabric or skin, so gnarled were they, vague upon her shape and without any of the adornments that might give them away. She shifted continually, or rather, the muck piled against her did, like miniature tectonic collisions, re-configuring her posture into varying degrees of collapse. He stopped about three feet away, registering a smell of ancient things: he was put in mind of attics, of seeds in woods cracked open during wet autumn evenings, of classrooms filled with thin clouds of chalk dust.

She inclined her head towards him as his breathing calmed. A nictitating membrane wetted the surface of her powdery eyes; the papyrus scroll of her mouth fluttered. Though nothing of substance passed through her lips, he heard the words anyway, flirting in his mind, much like the echoes of long-departed trains vanishing through unseen tunnels.

"He walked among us once, Monck. This man who turns against us now. He will be our undoing unless we can arrest him."

"The Pusher," he said.

"Whatever moniker the linens have given him, yes. Here we knew him as Blore. We need to stop him, and the handful he has recruited, bent to his will, or he will reveal us. And that must not happen. An age of understanding has evolved here, Monck. A new direction. There are religions down here, philosophies born of the earth. If knowledge is observation, we have all the wisdom we'll ever need to survive here. Up Top, we'd be dust."

He watched the thick, furry coats of grime move against each other like wads of iron filings crawling on a magnet. He didn't think to suggest she'd achieved that status already. A dim flickering in the corner of the chamber caught his eye: a television, he saw, fighting to spray its cathode secrets past a static cling of grit. Its carcase was long gone; tubes and valves and wiring hung free like the innards of a gutted animal. He couldn't determine where its power was being sourced: it was being leeched directly from the abundant pool of electricity down here, no doubt. He sensed Odessa watching him with her chalk-dry eyes as he approached the screen, and Vane tensing. He crouched and wiped some of the dust away, revealing black-and-white images, alien shapes that only became recognizable at the end of their cycle of movement: two mouths, caught up in shade, meeting for a kiss.

"Monck," Odessa gentled, "Monck...." Her voice skipped through his mind like dead leaves on a pavement. For some reason, he found it crucial to be cautious around this woman, this Queen. Something in the kiss and the other-worldliness of the television called to him, plucked at a part of his being that wanted away from this place, that didn't understand its secrets and codes and protocols. And yet, all the while, he was revelling in the womb-like protection the underground afforded.

"Monck...." Again.

He waited for her to cap the sentence. She shifted on her chair, steadied by Vane's hand.

"I'll find him," he said finally, standing.

Vane studied his face. "There's word gone round that you've been spending too much time Topside." Vane whispered the final word, as if mention of it down here might be heretical. "That you're suspected of going native. Of becoming Surfacetype. You must know," she hissed, looking to Odessa for support, "we will do everything in our power to stop you, should that be the case. Our resources might be depleted, but we'll send someone after you." Her voice deepened with the implicit threat, as if it should inspire dread, but he was unimpressed. If there were more dangerous creatures than him down here, then why not send them after Blore? She appeared to mistake his impassiveness for nonchalance, and stepped back, suddenly apprehensive. Whatever his position down here, he knew two things: that people feared him, and that he was largely an unknown quantity. He didn't know if this was good or bad.

"I'll find him," he said again.

Odessa's hand rested upon his for a beat. Her touch felt like wafers of burned paper. "Don't become another Blore," she said. "Your link with Topside will be important in your search, but don't linger. Bring him back. To me. Dead if you must." Her face twisted into the approximation of a smile then lost its shape to a landslide of soot that clung to her brow. "Not that death could protect Blore from what I intend to visit upon him."

He left then, Vane in tow, hastening him back to the trains.

NUALA WAS SITTING IN HER KITCHEN, HER HANDS CLASPED around a mug of Russian tea, when I entered her flat.

"The door was open," I said. "I've got a headache. I didn't sleep at all well." I couldn't tell her about my narcolepsy. Not yet. I had come to across the street from my flat, next to a manhole cover through which,

I was certain, I could hear footsteps and somebody whistling a tune. My clothes were filthy, streaked with oil and grime.

She was reading a magazine; she didn't look up. "Wherever it was that you tried to sleep," she returned.

"Uh... meaning?"

"Meaning: it wasn't in your bed." Now she did look up and I could see real concern in her eyes. It touched me. I hadn't seen a look like that for a long time. "Where were you, Adam?"

I didn't know, that was the thing. "I went for a walk," I said, lamely. I could see she didn't believe me but then she threw up a barrier; the concern went from her face and she began turning pages. "Whatever," she sighed. "It's not my business. A few fucks do not a relationship make."

"I haven't been anywhere!"

"You're so hostile," she said. "Even when you're on the defensive."

"Oh come on," I retorted, and tried to force an incredulous laugh. "Jesus. I feel like I'm in the middle of a Woody Allen film."

"I know what's chewing you inside out. It's her, it's Laura."

"Will you please leave that alone."

"You know, you really should be more open with me. All this stress is ruining me inside."

"Nuala. It wasn't somebody else. I didn't go to see anyone else." The wrong thing to say, patently. She hadn't been thinking that.

"I'm not the jealous type." She put up her hands to ward off any further protests. "Please, Adam, no more. You're filling my kitchen with negativity. I've hardly moved in."

I went back to my place, hoping to find some clues to what had happened after my attack. There were three messages from Yoyo. I couldn't hear what she was saying in the first two, her voice was fractured by tears and traffic. In the third one, she was pissed, and had called from a silent room. She said, simply: "Saskia."

I twisted the cap off a bottle of beer and took it to the sofa by the window where I watched life drag by on the street. Prams, shopping bags, briefcases. Everybody carries something, or looks after something. What was I looking after? Who was I carrying? I couldn't even carry myself. A small child darted from behind a hedge and stood for a while, grubby face turned up towards the sun. She was smiling: even from here I could see her little, blockish milk teeth, her eyes squeezed tightly shut.

I guzzled the beer and fetched another. I put some PJ Harvey on the stereo and returned to the chair.

The girl had gone.

My attention was continually drawn to the fireplace and the empty bottle of beer. I couldn't get comfortable. That bottle. Something about its shape. Why were bottles preying on my mind so much?

# CHAPTER SIX

## SURFACE TENSION

What's this? The papers are calling It *The Pusher.* Belittling It, reducing It with a name they give to drug dealers. It reads the newspaper, a *Sun* It salvaged from a bin up Top early this morning. The headline screams TUBE TERROR, and beneath: *Cowardly Pusher Strikes Again—Police Vow to Catch Killer Soon.*

So she died, then, the last one. It wasn't what It wanted but it doesn't matter; It had rescued her and alerted everyone else to the quiet, creeping dangers It had once fallen foul of.

"Don't end up like me," It whispers, scrunching the rag and tossing it into the corner of Its living space. Something flinches there: supper, if It's not mistaken. Taking a stone from Its pocket, It closes Its eyes and launches the projectile after the noise. It recovers the limp rat—half a foot long—and with deft, sharp fingernails rips the spine from the flesh before shaving off its fur with a rusty old Bic. With a knife, It delicately slices through a thin web of subcutaneous fat to find the area where the stomach links the duodenum. This tube, thin as a hair, is severed before its pale contents are squeezed towards the anus, which is chopped off and discarded along with the tail and the feet. The meat is thrown into a kettle to be boiled later. It loves to suck those poached eyes from their sockets: like juicy capers bursting on Its tongue. Real food. Natural food.

Food. Warmth. Love. These were the things that people ought to crave. Not iPods. Not broadband. Not 0898. London was suffocating from the weight of all the crap being unfolded into it. All the packaging. All the crap. All the people. People were being crammed into London like hens into a battery farm. It was bad enough before the houses were gutted and repartitioned into flats. The thought of sleeping in a room with another dozen stinking animals breathing their shit all over the world makes It feel nauseous. How London has sucked the evil into itself. How It must try to unburden the city. Sometimes it seems such an impossible task. But things can be achieved. The mouse can scare the elephant.

The peace of Its surroundings creeps into It, subtle as a murmur, working the flints from Its muscles, reducing the core of fire in Its stomach to a manageable ember.

The roar of a train, eastbound Central Line, electrifies It, reminding It of Its love for this place and the task ahead. It feels the unhappy marriage on Its face between skin and bone, dreaming of its wet, crimson promise.

I GOT A LETTER FROM GREG.

No mention of his work, no reference to my own life. Perhaps it's better like that. Just a shallow, obscene letter about all the women he'd either fucked recently, or wanted to fuck. Or women from our working past that he had fucked or wanted to fuck.

*So we ended up snogging half the night and in the taxi home I had her tits all over the back seat and my tongue so far down her throat that I could taste what she'd shat out for breakfast three days ago—*

But something bothered me. It wasn't the letter itself, but the fact that Greg had never written to me before. Always used the phone or arranged a breakfast meeting. I had a feeling he wanted to tell me something. Or maybe I was just reading things into it, his last line: *Hope everything's all right.* Not in keeping with the general tone of the letter. Not in keeping with the general tone of him.

A reference to our days in the office together, and India specifically, brought a memory out of the file in my head marked *Days At Work You Wish You'd Forgotten.* It was one of those recollections where everything is razor sharp and you don't know why—probably it's due to your brain having a day when it's been miraculously spared of caffeine or E numbers and it feels pretty healthy, showing off—but here it was muscling out of the mud of my back brain like some barely vertebrate creature eager to evolve....

APPARENTLY, ACCORDING TO GREG, THIS IS A PRETTY incestuous office, or rather, it used to be: all the permutations have been exhausted, except for those including me—I don't know whether that excites me or scares me to death. Greg used to see Claire, who was going with Shaun and having an intense affair with him, or so the rumor went, after having a brief fling with Elliot during an office party. Elliot's now married to Jane in telesales but rumor has it he slept with India on more than one occasion. I fancied India—I'm sure you could have seen it in my eyes—but she had the hots for Harry, the editor, and he was kind of interested but then she slept with Rachel.

I remember India carrying a tray of coffees so the first I see of her is her slim, heart-shaped bottom backing through the swing doors, the zip of her skirt like a silver tear beneath a triangle of white where it's not quite fastened properly. She pours, as always, left to right: Elspeth, Greg, Shaun, Elliot, Claire, me. When India serves, I get the bitter tail of whatever's in the pot, which is so strong you could surface roads with it. "Can I have a spoon to eat this?" goes the joke. An office favorite that raises not a snigger. My stash of biscuits are locked in the bottom drawer of my desk. Anyone for a Coconut Cream? Is there buggery. Nobody likes them. Which is why I buy them. Another Sad Office Triumph. I don't like them either.

It's quiet. Our deadline has gone. In a minute, someone is going to suggest we pile down the pub for a swift one, precursor to the predictable all-nighter. There'll be murmurs of demurral from most but we'll all go along, even Elspeth, who, after a gin and orange, will slope off back to whichever room she sulks in when she isn't doing so professionally.

I'm happy to saunter along after everyone, even though I'm still trying to get past that initial new boy stage, a limbo between occasionally feeling involved and skating around on the edge of things. Part of the downer about being a freelance (or "temp" as some irritants are wont to call us) is the feeling that your time is owned, that you come into work and get your head down from ten to six or your number gets struck off the list. It gradually got to the stage where I felt relaxed enough to lift my head from the screen for three minutes and chat to someone in the kitchen while the tea brewed. I fell in love with India for making the effort to talk to me, when I was too shy to start a conversation. She had a big mane of wheat blonde hair that reached down almost to the point where those dimples on a woman's back sit, either side of her coccyx. The sacrum. Great name for it. Her hair was so thick and heavy, it would barely move when she walked, but for a deep undertow of shift, like currents tugging at the surface of a river. She'd lean back against the work surface and fold her arms under her breasts, assess me levelly with her striking blue eyes and ask me about my home town or my friends in London; how I knew Greg, where I went in the evenings. Tame stuff, but it helped me, made me feel like I had an ally; someone I could say good morning to without them looking at me as if I were some scuzzball drifted in from the street.

So it was that I latched onto her as we walked down to Quinn's on Kentish Town Road, just up from the tower block where the magazine was based. She'd been going on about her favorite baked potato fillings and had said the word "cottage" as in cottage cheese. Something in that thick, glottal word, the way she said it, didn't half give me the horn.

"How did you get your name?" I asked her, apropos of nothing more than the need to hear her voice again, and a desperation that she'd turn her attention to someone else if I didn't keep breaking up the silences.

"A mistake. My mum wanted to name me after Indira Gandhi but my dad fucked it up when he went to register it. Dad wanted to call me Hecate. For Christ's sake. Only reason he didn't was because he was pissed—probably didn't remember. Probably too pissed to realize what he was doing anyway." She laughed. I was smitten. Say fucked again, I was thinking to myself.

As soon as we entered the pub, I felt on edge and knew something unpleasant was going to happen. I'd externalized this hunch, saw threats in everyone else at the bar without realizing that the danger was radiating from our party and that I'd just felt that bristling, spreading as we moved among the crowded drinkers. If anyone else felt similarly, they didn't let on, although I saw Greg look at me twice in quick succession, a trace of unease on his face.

He went to the bar and bought a round of drinks. Elspeth had decided to hold court in that imperious, slightly withering way of hers. She was talking about how her neighbor's garden had gone to seed since the death of the wife.

"She used to go at that garden like a monkey having a wank," she said, taking her gin and orange from Greg with a curt nod. "When she shot her bolt, he couldn't care less. He just used to go out with his hands in his pockets of an evening and stare at the clematis. Grass was up to his knees in no time. It's a jungle. I'm telling you, it wouldn't surprise me if they found a live dinosaur in that mess. Or a Japanese soldier who doesn't realize the war's over."

"I like it that he doesn't touch the lawn," I said, instantly regretting my words. All heads turned to me; Greg was grinning. I took a restorative sip of my lager and shrugged. "Maybe he doesn't mow the lawn because he likes the idea that she was the last person to touch it. It gives him some natural measure of how long she's been away."

"Maybe he's just a lazy old giffer," Elspeth said, "who can't be arsed. I bet his bathroom looks like something that's overwhelmed an agar dish." As soon as she'd said it, her eyes darted around, eager to feed off any appreciative laughter, but whether her joke was too sophisticated or, as I suspected, too cruel, nobody reacted. The familiar, slightly puckered manner of her face returned. She drained her glass and stood up. "Got to be off," she said, "it's my turn to cook."

I could tell I'd made a few allies by what I'd said; India, especially, was favoring me with a warm smile. But I felt a bit guilty that my gainsaying of the office crone was the reason I'd been accepted. I was about to make amends, say something conciliatory and dumb like: "What are you cooking?" when the contents of a glass sprayed across her front, followed by the glass itself, which shattered against her chest, sending shards into her face. Her hands jerked to the pain: a surge of blood fled her cheeks, drizzling between her fingers. She remained shockingly quiet.

"Shit, Shaun, what are you fucking doing?" Greg got up, then sat down again when he saw the wildness on Shaun's face.

"I am just so sick to fucking hell, man," he said, though his voice was calm as a priest giving benediction. "Sick of all this fucking so-called social inter-fucking-course. Everyone's watching what they fucking say to each other. Nobody wants to step on anybody's toes and everyone's toeing the line. Yessir, nossir, three bags fucking—*stop bleating you fucking whingebag or I'll give you something to fucking moan about!*"

I heard sirens. The bar staff must have called the police. Since Elspeth had started keening, I could hear everything, every last drip from the beer taps, every anxious susurration of breath from the punters watching this unfold.

"You'd best scarper," I said to Shaun, I don't know why. He looked at me for a long time before heading out through the front doors, pushing past Elspeth who was being comforted by Greg, India and Claire as red slowly crept through the cotton of her blouse. Claire's mouth flapped open and shut like that of a beached fish. Her right hand moved to her breast and pressed there as tears silvered her eyes. Then the police burst in and introduced some welcome monotony.

# CHAPTER SEVEN
## BLUE

I received an invitation handwritten on expensive, watermarked paper. Saskia had signed it, and marked it with a lipstick print of what looked like a pair of nipples, her nipples.

*Adventure.*
*Find the blue car near Holloway Road.*
*First four to arrive get to go.*

I rang Yoyo.

"Have you seen this madness?" I asked her.

She had, and she was just about to leave her flat to be a part of it. "I need a break," she said.

"Come here instead, then," I said. "We'll stay in and watch horror films. I'll make hot chocolate. We'll order a pizza."

"No, Ads. I need to get out."

"Well meet me outside the Nag's Head shopping center," I said. "I'll come with you."

It was the last thing I wanted to do. But I hadn't seen Yoyo for a while and I was worried about her. No. That wasn't quite right. I was worried about her, but my reasons for needing to see her ran to more than that. I needed her, she was my barometer. She was my measure of how far from reality I was falling. I caught a cab outside and a couple of minutes later I was paying the driver outside the Odeon. I looked back the way we had come, along the straight thoroughfare that is Tufnell Park Road, and felt a strange tugging in my gut, as if being able to see, in the distance, the junction that I lived off from such an uncertain viewpoint was one mismatch or imbalance too many.

I trotted across the road and waited by the entrance to the shopping center while dozens of people wove around me, ducking into or coming out of the entrance, weighed down with plastic carrier bags. Kids implored parents for rides on a grubby motorized elephant as if their future happiness depended on it. A young woman who looked too thin to be able to withstand the spank of freezing wind was rocking on her haunches, copying a picture of Reggie Kray on to the pavement from a post card. The white chalk went down gray, instantly fouled by the grime. Next to her, a dog licked at itself half-heartedly. Somewhere, someone was playing very loud music, but I couldn't begin to guess where it was coming from; the sound was picked up by the wind and looped and fragmented even as it teased me with its identity.

Suddenly Yoyo was standing there, a still point around which everything was moving hard. Something seemed wrong with her, as if the color of the clouds, or the pavement she was standing on, had infected her skin. But the shadows passed when she smiled, and I kissed her on her cheek, which was cold, but a nice cold, a fresh cold, and her skin smelled of apricots.

We walked in the direction of Islington, checking side streets for this blue car Saskia had been on about. It was lunchtime, and people were going about their lunch hour business: sinking fast pints at The Litten Tree, sitting on walls with their overloaded subs and baps from sandwich shops that didn't sell anything that didn't have mayonnaise in it. People were walking along the street, eating, sitting in cars, eating, clustered around café tables on the pavement, eating. I wanted to do anything but, and if Yoyo was hungry, she wasn't doing anything about it.

There were a few false alarms, and no doubt Saskia knew that would happen. I could imagine her relishing being told about my approaching a metallic blue Ford Sierra and tapping on the window to find the driver trying to wipe blood off his hands onto his jeans.

"What the fuck was that about?" I said, breathily, as we hurried on. The guy had climbed out of his car and was looking after us intently, as if committing our retreating shapes to memory, so that next time he would be ready.

"Forget him," Yoyo said. "It was probably just a nose bleed, or he was wanking too hard."

I started laughing at that, and at Yoyo's serious face. "I wouldn't like to have a look at what's lying in his boot," I said. We approached another car, a pale blue Mercedes parked on Hornsey Street, but the middle-aged man with mirror shades in the passenger seat shook his head and mouthed *No.*

"What is it with blue cars, today?" Yoyo said.

"We've probably missed out," I said. "Four people have found a blue car and they're now enjoying an adventure that involves trying to rescue Saskia from choking to death on her own vomit on a cracked toilet swarming with flies. Meanwhile, we're going to spend the next five hours tapping on car windows until we find someone willing to shoot us through the brains."

"That's not funny, Ads."

"Where've you been, lately?" I asked her, carefully. "What have you been up to?"

"I don't want to talk about it."

"No?"

"No."

"You okay? I mean, you look a little peaky. Have you been ill?"

She sniffed. "I'm always ill."

"What are you reading?" I asked, nodding at the top third of a slim volume poking out of the top of her coat.

"The Rapture."

"The *Rupture?*"

She laughed. Yoyo had a great laugh. It was giggly, infectious. I realized that I hadn't been hearing it too much, lately. "The *Rapture,*" she said.

There was something in the day that didn't feel right. Maybe it was because the sun didn't seem to get above a height that was rooftop level, or burn with a color that was any fiercer than a kind of blood orange. Maybe it was the incipient mist, which never quite grew as dense as it was promising, or it could have been the spate of narcoleptic attacks I had been having: day swapping with night at the speed of a blink to the extent that I was never sure of the where and when. In all likelihood, it was my own nervousness, and in such cases, when you expect it, bad things tend to happen.

We found the blue car.

It was a dark blue Mark II Escort, parked up on the curb on Chillingworth Road. It was battered almost to the point of submission. A hole in the rear windscreen the size of a fist drew the eye, mainly because it was the only solid color that didn't gleam or glint. There was nobody in the car. Nobody hanging around it, waiting to go on their adventure. A note was tucked behind the windscreen wiper, along with a couple of parking tickets.

*Hi Yoyo and Adam.*
*Nice to have you along.*
*Now we are four.*

The beep of a horn behind me. I sauntered over, thinking, *Here's weird for you.*

The guy in the driver's seat of the Renault Clio wound down his window. He didn't look at me. He was chewing some kind of red gum with a strong, spicy smell. I caught wafts of it as he said: "Adam Buckley? Get in. And your girlfriend. I'll take you to Saskia."

"Where is she?" I asked. He'd switched off. Staring straight ahead, chewing, waiting. I asked him again. He responded by turning up the Snoop Dogg on his stereo.

Yoyo pushed by me and climbed into the back as if it was the most natural thing in the world. I followed suit. I asked the driver his name, but nobody was talking. It all seemed scripted. I played dumb.

The quiet driver dropped us off on Wattisfield Road, a busy little rat-run off the A104 at Lea Bridge. South Millfields Recreation Ground, which separated the road from Chatsworth Road, was host to a game of football that included more than three dozen players, a guy in a wheelchair and two dogs. Before he drove off, the quiet driver tossed me a door key.

"What's this for?" I asked. I should have saved my breath.

Yoyo took the key off me and was trying to guess which of the houses it would let us into. "It can't be those because there are toys in the garden," she was saying.

"Yoyo," I said. "Let's fuck off. Pubs were invented for days like this. This is madness."

I must have donned my cloak of invisibility—nobody was listening to me any more. I shook my head and followed her into the driveway of a semi that had the stripped-down skeleton of a Kawasaki motorbike sitting in a puddle of old oil. She tried the key and the door swung open. The door would have swung open had she breathed on it, it was so feeble. We passed into a sour fug of burnt fat and nicotine.

"Yoyo," I tried again. She turned to me, eyes wide, smiling. She was lapping this up. This was better than sitting in a flat watching flies mate on flaking window frames. This was better than turning the pages of novels that helped her escape not one jot. Or looking for places that didn't exist, and finding them.

She swept up the stairs and I trotted after her, thinking of how much I had hated treasure hunts when I was a child. Maps that weren't as good as the ones in my copy of *Treasure Island* drawn by dads who had had too much to drink at whoever's birthday party it was. X marks the spot. And the spot was the fridge. And the treasure was some shit with gold wrapping: a Crunchie bar. A Twix. For fuck's sake.

We found Saskia sitting in a bath with a razor blade in her right hand. Her left forearm was opened, a huge mass of sopping red toilet paper wadded into it, as if she had changed her mind when it was too late, or was trying to keep the mess to a minimum for the poor fuck who would have to clear up. She had scratched a pattern on her swollen stomach: a series of cross hatchings that looked like diamond link fencing. Keep out. Stay in. Some adventure. Some treasure.

Yoyo was staring at herself in the bathroom mirror, a three-quarter length affair that was foxed and warped, its edges permanently misted.

She said: "There's a little... gap... in the river. You can walk to it. You can walk to it over the water. There's this hard seam, like glass, you just walk along it and there's this gap."

I was looking at the blood. Such a lot of blood. I wondered how all of that could be contained inside someone so small. I thought, crazily, unforgivably: *She's bleeding for two....*

*THERE WAS SOMETHING IN THE DAY THAT DIDN'T FEEL RIGHT.*

And hindsight is a wonderful thing. But I had felt that at the time. I had felt the streaks of threat in the air, like the odd sensation of slow pain that reaches out in soft, arbitrary directions from a bruise when it is pressed. I opened my eyes in a bed that smelled too strongly of me and nobody else. I felt the shadow of a second hand slide slowly over my body and tick off another moment from my time. I never knew what I could be. What I had the capacity for. I still don't. London was meant to be my map, something that would reflect me, give me more of a clue as to who I was and what I could do with myself. But all of its streets were being dug up, or barricaded, or designated No Entry. Trying to better myself was turning into battering myself flat. I felt a tear, one of those that creeps out of the corner of your eye if you keep it open for too long, slide into my ear. I watched a brick of sunlight edge its way from one side of the wardrobe to the other. I was still here. Saskia wasn't. Saskia's unborn child wasn't. So close to a first breath, to a sizing up of a world there to be conquered, or at least got along with. So close. One terrible moment found me thinking that it was better off as it was, where it was. For ever on the cusp of being, having known nothing but senseless nourishment. I cried for the baby, and for Saskia. I mean, I tried to cry, to cry properly, but no more tears would come. I was dry as sand. I cried that uncry, that nothing cry, until the brick of light dissolved into the wall.

And then Yoyo phoned to tell me that Saskia had been found dead on the Fulham Palace Road, hit by a car as she was crossing with an armful of new toys for a baby that would never know what play meant.

# CHAPTER EIGHT

## CATAPLEXY

"There are many things that can cause it, Adam," Dr. Ferguson said. "You'd be surprised."

The cramped GP's surgery was filled with cigarette smoke. He liked a crafty drag in between the sore throats and pulled muscles and unmentionables.

"Laughter. Resisting an attack of sleep. Yawning. Sexual intercourse. Attempting to join in with a bit of banter, even."

"I know what causes it," I said, trying to not sound spiky. "I'm, like, you know, *there* at the time."

Fergie smiled and scratched something with his pen on a pad bearing the brand name Risperdal. It looked from where I was sitting like tombstones.

"What I need to know is what can happen while I'm out cold. I mean, how dangerous is it? How dangerous am I?"

I don't know why I had decided to make an appointment to see my doctor. I had been through all this, years before, when I had first been diagnosed.

But then Saskia flitted into my thoughts. I was doing this because of Saskia. Her death had spooked me. Death was inches away for all of us. It was in the shape of the cars that tore along the streets, only a curb and a bit of concentration keeping a ton of very hard from a couple of hundred pounds of very soft. It was in a poorly cooked chop, or a loose bit of scaffolding. It crawled on the fingers of a friend reaching out to shake your hand.

"I'm not sure," he said. "I could refer you to a specialist, but they probably know as much as I do, only with different letters after their name."

We sat staring at each other for a while. He took off his glasses, a pair of old-fashioned horn-rimmed jobs, and chewed meditatively on one of the ear-rests. "What is happening to you," he said, "is nothing to do with epilepsy, or anything like that, you know that, right?"

I nodded.

"You're suddenly finding yourself in a position that most of us find ourselves in after a few hours in bed. You're REMing, but you're awake, or rather, you're in a waking state. I don't think you're going to harm yourself, unless, you know, you fall into a tank of piranhas or something."

I nodded again. Laughed. The smoke and the laughter. All we needed was a pint and the sound of a darts match in the background.

"What about other people?"

"I can't vouch for other people. You're the only narcoleptic I—"

"I mean, what about me harming other people?"

"Oh, I see." Dr. Ferguson replaced his spectacles and went back to doodling on his pad. He wore a shirt with the sleeves rolled up. Braces. His jacket was draped over the back of his chair. There was something in his hair—Dax, Brylcreem—that made it glisten beneath the fluorescent strip light, made it seem more blue than black. There was a wave in it that made him look a bit more dashing than he ought to. He looked a bit Ted Hughes, a bit David Owen.

"I don't think you need to worry too much about that," he said. "You're not a violent person, are you?" He raised his eyebrows. I shook my head. "So there's no reason to expect you to start behaving like Biffa Bacon when the lights go out. You should tell people about it. So they know what to expect. A full-on cataplectic attack can be a pretty shocking thing to watch. Especially for children. Got kids?"

"No," I said. "None that I know of."

He smiled, capped his pen, pushed away his pad of doodles. "What are you taking for it at the moment?"

"Nothing," I said. He frowned. I told him about the ineffectiveness of the Ritalin.

"Popular with the Yanks," he said, dismissively. "I could put you on Anafranil or Concordin. Tricyclic antidepressants. They could help."

"Any side effects?"

"Of course there are," he said, and then, as if he was reading it from a label: "Can cause interference with the male sexual function."

I said I would think about it, and see how the attacks continued. I didn't like the thought of taking antidepressants. And the possibility of interference with the male sexual function sounded like something to avoid for as long as possible.

I was getting ready to go, feeling frustrated, unfulfilled, as if I had expected the doctor to unfold me and pick out all the bits of strange fluff in my creases, when he tapped his pad with his pen.

"Any strange dreams?" he asked. "Any nightmares?"

I thought about the vivid episode I had had involving Saskia. Her arms unraveling in the bath. I thought of the baby turning in her stomach.

"A few," I said.

"Try not to worry about it," he said. "Hypnagogic hallucinations. They can seem absurdly real, and affect all your senses. They're basically dreams that project into your wakefulness. Non-narcs can experience them too, but you should be aware, you should know that it's quite all right. Quite safe."

I left then, with him advising me to try to follow a regular sleeping routine at night, and taking naps throughout the day, if I felt I needed them.

Outside, everything suddenly seemed unreal, as if it were a scene being played out by a brain that didn't see things the same way as everyone else. The traffic followed the rules: there was no running of red lights, no illegal overtaking, no horns being sounded. A man dressed head to toe in blue stood in a department store doorway, as still as the mannequins flanking him in the windows. He held a phone to his ear but he did not speak once. Four police cars followed each other serenely towards Paddington, like an escaped theme park ride.

I walked around for a while, had coffee in St. Christopher's Place, had a look in a few bookshops, drifting, waiting for something to happen. In truth, I was waiting for an attack. I didn't imagine it would be any different from usual, but Fergie's words about hypnagogic hallucination were still fresh, and I wondered if I might identify something that would let me know if what I was seeing was real or otherwise.

I called Yoyo.

"Do you want to play out?" I asked her.

"Hi, this is Yoyo. It's cold out, I've got a mug of hot chocolate here, a new book, and some soundtrack music on the stereo. Insert the answer you think I'm going to give you when you hear the beep."

I managed to persuade her to meet me at Russell Square Tube, so that she wouldn't have to change trains anywhere. We had a look in Skoob, but she didn't buy anything. "Not when I've got a book on the go. I don't buy a new book till I've finished the one I'm on. Bad luck."

I found a nice copy of *The End of the Affair*, and bought it for Nuala.

"What now?" she asked.

"Food," I said. "Let me buy you something to eat."

The Brunswick Center was everything that Yoyo wasn't: low-rise and high-density. We walked along the public space between the residential blocks, away from the Renoir cinema and the book shop. There was a cheap café and we sat at a table outside because there was a big party of yabbering locals inside, drinking espresso, eating pastries and smoking like they were in competition.

Yoyo ordered a fried egg sandwich and I went for a toasted cheese and tomato. Big coffees. Someone in the tightly-packed grid of flats was playing old music. You could tell it was old, because it didn't last long, and it had a fiendishly infectious tune. We listened to it for a while, and Yoyo started swaying on her chair and clicking her fingers:

*Yesterday it rained in Tennessee,*
*I heard it also rained in Tallahassee,*
*But not a drop fell on little old me,*
*Cos I was in shu-shu-shu, shu-shu-shu, shu-shu-shu-shu-shu-shu Sugar Town.*

Three broken umbrellas jutted out of a litter bin, a sight that saddened me. Broken umbrellas are terribly depressing. Hobbling pigeons hung around, eyeing us nervously, their feet tangled up with twine, or clumped with chewing gum, or severed. The music had been switched off, replaced by the sound of the café's extractor fan and the muted sound of a football match on the TV.

"So," I said. "What are you reading?"

She slid the top half of her book out of its pocket.

"*Sipping Midnight.* Never heard of it. Any good?" She nodded, and then our coffees turned up, and she spent a while blowing on hers, her big, liver-colored lips sending kisses across the frothy surface.

I had never seen Yoyo read a word of these novels she carried around with her. I wondered sometimes if they were comforters, her version of a teddy bear, or a favorite blanket, something to hold near to her while all the weirdness and terror howled around outside. Some of them were fairly thick volumes. I doubted she could get through them unless she was spending all of her time reading, or at least skimming.

"How are you bearing up?" I asked. We didn't need to mention Saskia directly. I wanted to ask her about that day we searched for the blue car, but at the last moment I realized that it hadn't actually happened. That day had existed inside me. In a way, I was glad about that. Glad that Yoyo hadn't really seen what had turned itself inside out in the bath.

"I'm okay," she said. "A little jaded. I feel as though I've got a hangover all the time, regardless of whether I've been drinking." She looked tired. Her hair smelled of fresh shampoo, but it appeared lank and uncared for. The whorls in her skin where the sunlight glanced off her looked out of whack, as if this was her mirror image and not the original Yoyo sitting with me. She kept rubbing her hands together, maybe trying to get rid of some dry skin, or sticky residue. It seemed as if she were vacillating over a prayer.

"I can't think about the future too much," she said. "I'm scared of it. Scared of something that doesn't exist yet. But it's there, all ready to unfold, the days, weeks and years, all empty and superficial. Filled with nothing but books about other people, nowhere near here. I don't feel involved, at any level. I don't feel as if I'm a cog in the machine. I don't mesh with anything. Anyone."

"You mesh with me," I said. "I might only be a small machine, but you're a big cog in it."

"Thanks," she said, in the way people say thanks when they get a compliment they don't really believe. She bit into her sandwich and chewed slowly, ruminatively, as if she had a mouth full of gravel rather than soft egg and bread.

"I feel like an echo of everything close to me," she said.

"You need a man," I said. "Or a job."

"I haven't worked for ages," she said. "Give me a job now and I wouldn't know what to fucking do with it." She thought about another bite, but replaced her sandwich on the plate. She turned her attention to her coffee, and her book. Her fingers stroked the top edge of tightly packed pages.

"As for men, who wants to go out with Bride of Frankenstein?"

"Tall women are in this season," I said.

"Alas, ladders aren't."

We laughed, and drank our coffee.

She said, "Shall I take you to see something?"

A splintering edge of afternoon sunlight broke free of the concrete division of ledges behind us. Her face darkened and I had to shield my eyes to find its details again. A bright smile was hanging there. "Okay," I said.

We caught a Connex South Eastern train at Charing Cross. The Thames, as we crossed it, was listless and soiled, like slow blood in an over-tapped vein. The heat of the carriage and its motion sent me to sleep. When I wakened, seemingly seconds later—it was about ten minutes—we were somewhere I didn't recognize. A shopping precinct went by on the right. A snooker hall. A Bingo parlor. It was as if we had escaped the city to a provincial town.

Yoyo was holding my hand. "Where are we?" I asked.

"Lewisham," she said.

We caught a bus to Hither Green and, crossing the road, turned off onto a quiet street. The corner building seemed to be some kind of crêche; through the window I could see kids playing in a sea of colored plastic balls. Opposite was St. George's hospital, a condemned building, so quiet that it seemed to be sucking any noise from behind us into its walls.

"Where are we going?" I asked. Yoyo nodded ahead of us, and we passed through some open gates into a park.

"Mountsfield Park," she said. "Where I was first kissed."

It was a fairly run of the mill park, a bit of green to rescue you from the headache of the A205, and the ugly blot below it that was Catford.

"How long ago are we talking?" I asked. "How many years? Or was it some time last week?"

She kicked me, and tugged my sleeve as she peeled off to the right towards some shabby tennis courts. "Down here," she said. "Me and Alex Subton. October the fifth, nineteen eighty-five. We were both thirteen. He was wearing these black trainers, new on that day. Cruisers, they were called. And he had these stretch jeans, skin tight. And an Adidas T-shirt, one of those Ivan Lendl jobs. He had this gorgeous dark skin, he looked like he always had a tan. Soft, curly hair, kind of blond, kind of brown."

The trees moved; I caught a glimpse of the swollen urban snarl-up spilling away towards Bromley and Beckenham. I followed Yoyo into a dappled gap in the bushes. On the floor was a torn, pulpy mass of glossy pages from a pornographic magazine. Next to it, as if she had just discarded it, or been copying its poses, a woman was sitting back against a tree, her face scratched and scarred so deeply that no features remained. Her skirt had ridden up, revealing a naked crotch obscured by blue paint. One of her breasts had been cut away: the hole in its place had been stuffed with more pages.

I felt my legs turn to pulp. "Jesus," I heard myself hiss.

"He had this squint, you know, like a turn in his eye, only very slight, but he was so self-conscious. He'd look at you with one eye closed, as if he was staring at the sun."

Even when I could see that it was a mannequin, some plastic, red-mouthed, hard-nippled come-on rescued from a shop window, my heart wouldn't slow down; the force of my relief seemed even more shocking. Yoyo had stopped and was leaning back against a tree, her eyes closed, lost to a moment years old.

"He kissed me here. He pressed me back against the tree, he said my name. His tongue tasted sweet, like chocolate. Like milk. I could feel his dick poking my thigh. Our teeth were clashing, and there was a cut-off branch or something sticking in my back, but it didn't matter. Nothing mattered. It was delicious. I got home, and I was sopping."

Her eyes opened. She seemed glassy, not there. It looked as if the muscles that governed her face had all done something other than what they had been used to all her life. She was different, for a moment. Someone else. "Oh God, Adam. I'm sorry. My stupid mouth. It's just. I've been...." And now she started to cry. "I'm so lonely."

So instead of moving out of the bushes, and dragging her off for a beer, getting her to snap out of it, I moved to her and put my arms around her and hugged her. And that too became something else, and as she freed her breasts and they puckered in the chill, her face was hot against mine, her mouth kissing my ear, tonguing me. Beneath her breasts, the suggestion of her ribs were like echoes of themselves, like sandbars on a beach. Her breath was urgent, almost distressed. She said: "I've been reading maps. At night, before I go to sleep, I look at maps. You look at them for long enough, you see patterns there."

I felt myself thickening in her hand. She raised her skirt; she was wearing pale stockings with rubber tops that dug into her thighs. Frantically, she thumbed at her gusset, pulling it to one side. She was so hot. She was so slippery that I thought I would slide straight through her. The clumsiness of our movements went away, and fluidity replaced it as we found a rhythm. One of her long legs was wrapped around me, her right heel was tapping against my right arm. My face was against her breasts, being painted with the cold spit that I had slicked across them. Her hat had slipped forward and was concealing an eye. The other was shut, moving like that of someone in REM sleep. I thought of what Dr. Ferguson had said and suddenly everything began to tilt. Her mouth was open: a pink tunnel that I instinctively crammed with my fingers. She sucked at them, but I was losing my nerve, certain that something had been trying to come out of that tunnel before I blocked its path. I turned away and gazed at the sightless creature collapsed in the bushes. Again, a tilting, but the usual one: a moment of absence, when my body and mind felt detached by a sliver of alien heat. My thoughts folded inwards, to the sleeping curve of flesh in Saskia's tummy. As it had done last time, it turned its head towards me and opened its eyes: brilliant pinpricks, the headlights of trains, emerged from them. Its yawning mouth loosed the thunder of arrival: hundreds of tons of metal squealing to a stop.

"It's like *The White Album*," she muttered into my shoulder as I softened within and against her. "Like *The White Album* after the Manson murders. You know? Messages everywhere. Signs. You look at the maps and you swear there's something buried there for you. If only you knew how to look. Something coming through, like a shape you recognize in the clouds. Like faces in the fire."

I pressed my hand over her mouth and she relaxed against the cold bark of the tree. The lack of movement anywhere was as comforting as a thick blanket from childhood. I rested my head against her tits and listened for her heartbeat.

"Tall girls," I said. "You can't beat them."

# CHAPTER NINE

## VADE MECUM

God, how it hurts It to do this. Topside, the watery sun is still too bright for Its eyes. It spends half an hour cowering in the shade of a leafless tree, hoping for some acclimatization, not knowing how It's going to do what It needs to do. Still, there might be a chance—the traffic is very slow. And she is a doctor.

Just as It's decided she isn't going to show—that she must have gone home by a different route, or forsaken home for another appointment—she appears, hunched over the wheel of her car. She's belting out a song and suddenly it feels as though It wants to stop her more to find out what it is than to make any contact. It waits till she's bound to see It, then It walks straight out in front of her. Collapse.

She slams on the brakes, even though she's only doing fifteen tops. A couple of oncoming dolts have stopped by the pavement to rubberneck. There's already a tailback. Her door opens. Hmm, The Jam. *Going Underground.* The urge to laugh is almost too great.

She feels for Its pulse and loosens Its clothing. She's making soothing noises. She leans over It to check in Its mouth and It pulls her close enough to push Its tongue in before It bites her bottom lip. She makes a noise and tries to pull back but It's got her. Nobody can see what's going on. It pulls a metal spike from Its jacket and presses it against her windpipe. Opens Its eyes. It sends a message to her. It's very clear. *One false move....*

It hides the spike and she slowly stands up. It stands up with her, thanking her profusely, explaining that It just felt faint and that It's sorry It caused such a fuss. The crowd is already dispersing, disappointed at the lack of drama. It asks her if she wouldn't mind taking It home. She shakes her head, dazed. *Thanks awfully, you're really very kind and... do as I say. If I for one moment believe that you're trying something funny I'll rip your throat out and you'll have time to watch me feed it to you before you die.*

It's comfortable in her car. Cocooned, It relaxes and watches the streets blur. She's making a whimpering noise—not unpleasant. It copies it, pitch perfect. The traffic thins and she winds up the power in this little bucket. She selects third gear, veers onto the slip road just before the Westway takes off into the dusk, and It sinks in Its seat, imagining Itself as a fighter pilot skimming the rooftops. The sun is bloodying the horizon. It says *Chances are, you will not survive until morning.*

AFTER SASKIA'S DEATH, THE PARTY PEOPLE NEEDED A NEW distraction. Thanks to Yoyo's new obsession, they found it in London, or rather, they went about trying to find it in London. Whether it was a reaction to how Saskia had died, or something refreshed in them that needed to turn away from hedonism for a while, they took it upon themselves to discover oases within the rotten heart of the city. They'd heard—rumors in crowded bars, rammed Tube trains, endless bus queues—of places so clean and new that it was like being in a dream. Places that were like the ideal parts of your own interior, places you would never find in a lifetime of needing them. And they didn't mean Kensington, or Hampstead. Lost places. Pockets of wow.

I didn't fancy it. I didn't fancy it and I didn't believe in it. I didn't want to spend my spare time sipping halves of bitter in off-the-beaten-track pubs and saying, *This is nice, isn't it?* I decided it was time I had my break from the group, so I met them for lunch at a neutral venue and told them about my narcolepsy and that a doctor had advised I spend as much time at home resting. *As much as I'd like to hang around with you guys*, I said.

There was much in the way of sympathy, as well as an open invitation to return to the fold once I was feeling better.

"If you want to," Iain said, scrutinizing me, as if trying to see the narcolepsy in the shape of my nose, or the color of my skin. "Sleep on it," he said.

He was the real reason for my retreat, not Yoyo, who I would miss, or Meddie, who I was still going to be seeing anyway, at work. There was something about Iain that worried me. Something beneath the layers of bravado and abandon that smelled of violence, or madness, or both. I didn't want to be around when it surfaced.

The party people became pocket people, hunting the streets of London for their micro-Utopias. Over time I heard from Meddie about cemeteries and quiet parks they'd found, in the most unusual places, and I thought, yeah, right, so far, so *Time Out*. But over the coming weeks, things seemed to get more intense. Yoyo would tell me, when I managed to catch her on the phone at home, that they were spending more and more time on the hoof, clutching large, spiral-bound A-Z street atlases that were becoming less relevant by the day.

"You wouldn't believe the places we're finding, Ads," she said, in a small, uncertain voice that suggested that she didn't quite believe it either.

Meddie became less forthcoming about the areas they were searching, or what they did there when they found what they were looking for. I suspected that, despite happening upon their little pockets of calm, their group dynamic was anything but.

They were pranging themselves against each others' hard edges: away from the loud music, the rooms full of coats and plastic cups of cheap Bulgarian red, there was really little they had in common, and it was hurting them to find out. Meddie grew more solemn at work, and I noticed small bruises appearing on the backs of her arms, her calves. She took to wearing pullovers, and jeans. Her hair, which she never wore down, she wore down. It gave her a guarded look. She appeared hunted.

We had never spoken about Saskia since her death, and I was worried that now it might be too late to say anything. Meddie had changed. She had become more aggressively, more recklessly carnal, as if she wanted to atone for Saskia's treatment of her unborn baby by having one of her own. She would flirt with the men that came into The Pit Stop, as she always had, but none of the humor was there any more. Instead, she was coarse and direct. The four nights I worked there one week, a month after Saskia's death, she went home with five men.

By chance I bumped into her one afternoon in Tottenham Court Road, when I had decided to do something about my flat and spend what pittance I had on some kind of wardrobe. I was sneering at the expensive cherry wood chest of drawers in Heal's when I felt a hand press against my shoulder blade.

"Bit upmarket for you, isn't it?" she asked, but it was as if someone else was speaking through her. Her voice was stripped down, raw, mechanical.

"Are you okay?" I asked. I was expecting someone, a man, to materialize alongside her; she was so rarely by herself, but today, it seemed, she was.

"I'm fine," she said. She was holding a shopping basket that contained candles, soap, tea towels, a brown suede cushion cover. Her hair was down again and I had to resist the urge to lift it, irrationally certain, if I did, that I would find a necklace of rot eating into her flesh. She wore faded jeans that could have done with a wash, a tight white T-shirt, a red leather biker jacket that highlighted the red in her eyes. Her lips, which were a natural cerise—she seldom used lipstick—were pale, but their edges were sore, as if she had been rubbing them with a handkerchief. I felt suddenly desperate to keep her with me, at least for a little while longer. Already she was turning to go, and, unconsciously, I was mirroring her.

"Coffee," I said.

She shared my dislike of department store cafeterias, and we crossed the road to avoid the chains too. She had left her shopping basket by the bathroom accessories. "I didn't want to buy anything," she said. "I just like browsing, sometimes, and filling a basket with stuff that I'd like. But I hate queues so much that I never go through with it."

There was a small sandwich shop tucked out of the way at the north end of Whitfield Street and I bought lattés and a plate of tuna mayo sandwiches. We squeezed past a couple of builders too busy with their sausages and chips to help us get by, and found an empty table in the corner. I turned my back for a second in order to make the space I needed to shrug off my jacket, and when I faced front again, she had gone.

There was no reaction from anyone else in the cramped seating section, and for a moment I questioned my own sanity, thought that I hadn't actually seen Meddie at all, that I had imagined it all, but there were a couple of coffees here, and enough food for two people. I left my jacket where it was and forced my way outside. The cold coated me on the threshold. Nothing but pale roads stretching away from me. No sign of her, no sign of anybody.

I went back inside, and there she was, waiting for me, turning up the corner of a slice of granary to see what was underneath. I settled myself opposite her and stared into her eyes, waiting for some kind of explanation. When none was forthcoming, I said: "There are no bogs in here, and there isn't enough room under the table for you to hide, so where were you?"

Despite her evident distaste for the plate of sandwiches, she picked one out and bit off a corner. Through the food she said, "Don't, Adam. Please."

"Don't what?"

"Just leave it, for now. I'll talk, but not yet."

We ate the food and drank the coffee in a silence that I had not expected to sit between us. I tried to get her to open up, but this normally garrulous flirt had clammed. She was a different woman. It might have been acceptable to check that her name was in fact Meredith Purches, that she wasn't an impostor, that the real Meddie wasn't locked up in a walk-in freezer somewhere, slowly winding down. The woman in front of me looked undernourished, shivery—in any sense of the word—and intractable. She would talk when she was ready. When I had paid, and we were back on the street, she took my hand and led me west, along the streets running parallel to Marylebone Road.

"I don't want to go home yet," she said.

"Nobody's forcing you to."

"I'm fucking people in the dark, these days."

"What? Meddie, it sounded as though you just—"

"I did. Christ, can't we go somewhere for a drink? A proper drink?"

We wound up at the Marylebone Tup. I bought pints of lager, thinking, I should be at home with a screwdriver and a set of badly printed instructions. I should, at least, have my underwear stashed away by now. Meddie had secured us a table overlooking Marylebone High Street. Pedestrians walked by carrying Waitrose shopping bags. I noticed Caroline Munro peering into the window of a jeweller's, but I didn't think Meddie would be in the mood for celebrity spotting.

"I'm fucking people in the dark. I've never done that before."

"How do you mean?"

She nodded, as if she accepted that her statement was ambiguous. It was, as it turned out. She implied that she didn't remember doing it, as well as the more obvious meaning, and Meddie was no prude.

"It doesn't matter," I said, although I wanted to ask her about her current bout of promiscuity, whether it was fueled by anything, whether she was trying to block something out, or discover something about herself. Both options were disturbing.

"It matters," she said.

She had been switching the lights off ever since she had been at a party, the last one Saskia had hosted before her death. Some locals had crashed it and Meddie had been drawn to one of them, a tall, thin guy with braided hair, strong hands and skin the color and sheen of freshly laid bitumen.

"We went upstairs. The only free room was a spare bedroom being used for storage. There was no door. It had been taken off so a sofa could be squeezed through. I didn't care. You know me. It turned me on, the thought of people going to the toilet and seeing my tail going ten to the dozen. We got down to it, both of us naked, and he's hunched over me, and it's like... Adam, his eyes were lit from within."

I swallowed the mouthful of lager I'd just taken. My mind was on what Meddie looked like naked. Pretty nice, as I remembered. I hadn't expected her to suddenly stop like that, just when her story was hotting up. Expected less her look of inquiry, as if I might be able to decipher the nonsense she'd just uttered.

"Maybe it was a reflection," I said. "Maybe it was light from the streetlamps. Maybe it was true love."

"Fuck off, Adam, if you're not going to help."

"We're having a beer, Meddie. When did meeting you suddenly turn into therapy?"

"I'm pregnant," she said.

I put my glass down, my gut suddenly jumping, as if I must be the father. I didn't know what to say. Congratulations were clearly not invited.

"I can't be pregnant," she said.

"So have an ab—"

"No," she said, vehemently, and now it was her eyes that seemed to contain their own core of light. "I mean I can't be pregnant. I had a hysterectomy when I was thirteen."

Maybe it was the afternoon beers, or the smoke in the room, but I was beginning to feel nauseous. Maybe it was Meddie and Iain, studding my brain with little cloves of madness. I tried to claw my way back to a stable position, found my voice hoist up an octave, almost demanding for my explanations to be accepted.

"No, Adam," she said. "The operation was a complete success. They scraped me cleaner than a child with a chocolate pot. I had uterine cancer. They had to get it all."

We sat in silence for a few minutes, watching the late-afternoon crowd huddled around their tables, laughing, joking, smoking. It all seemed a world away, rather than a few feet. Nobody else was sitting at our table, despite it being able to comfortably accommodate at least six more, despite clumps of drinkers forming in the aisle between the other tables and the bar. The people on the edges of those clumps shuffled away from us. We were enveloped in a chilly pocket, in danger of infecting everyone else in the pub. You could see confusion in the eyes of the staff. You could see them shooting us accusatory glances, without knowing why they were doing it.

Meddie went to get more drinks.

I closed my eyes and I was behind hers, looking up at a dark shape that smelled of cinnamon, whose arms beneath mine felt like smooth, sinuous twists of varnished hardwood. Lifted my gaze and there were pale blue eyes, unblinking, staring down at me, almost too close together to be human. They glowed, like luminous paint on the cusp of fading. He opened his mouth and the smell of wet meadows, of lichen and rotten bark on dead trees fell from it. I came out of that too quickly, like a diver with the bends, his blood fizzing in his veins: I felt the shadows in the room quicken, as if they had sensed their chance was here, that they could consume the shapes that fed them. My own, I was scared to look into my own in case it had eyes that glowed. And then, as I was going down, my foot twisted under the table leg and the weird wrenching pain jerked me awake. People were looking at me, and that was fine, I was used to that. But Meddie was gone again. I stood up fast, sending our empties to the floor, and rushed outside, almost piling into a toddler in a red Mr. Bump T-shirt who was wagging his finger at his mum and dad, and yelling excitedly, as if telling them off.

I couldn't see Meddie on the main drag, and part of me thought good, good, thank Christ for that. I wanted to get back to Heal's and sneer at more furniture that I couldn't afford.

"I have something I want to show you."

She was standing to my right, a little way down Moxon Street. I followed her.

At the end of the street we entered Paddington Gardens, a small park straddling Paddington Street. I turned back but the toddler and his parents had vanished. Everyone was gone. The park was not as I knew it. The trees seemed to have increased in number and invaded the spaces meant for pedestrians: great boughs thrust up through the paths, splitting the paved areas. The grass here was deep and lush, combed by the wind into perfectly coiffured patches where it was usually strictly maintained. Its patterns up ahead were governed by the path of the breeze, at once dark, the next moment a curve of reflected silver, dancing away like a shoal of fish turning, as one, into a shaft of light. The air felt fresher, slower somehow, almost tangible: I could feel it deep and sticky in my lungs, cleansing me.

"Where are we going?" I said, though I knew as soon as I had asked. Meddie, despite holding my hand, seemed to be farther away than the combined lengths of our arms might allow. She suddenly appeared beautiful, as I remembered her from a couple of months previously, before this insanity began. Her skin was unblemished. Her eyes were as large as those of a cat, and dark, her mouth—even from here I could trace the individual crinkles and creases that patterned the flesh of her lips—bright with the color of black cherries. She opened her mouth to speak and more colors slipped out, but I recognized none of them.

A 747 measured out our madness in miles of white vapor. We sat in the grass.

"What was it you wanted to show me?" I reached out and held her wrist. Her flesh seemed boneless, soft as a pillow.

"Two things," she said. "First...." Like the meat of her arm, her lips felt unsupported by anything as solid as tooth or jawbone. Not that the kiss was unpleasant: there was firmness but it was supple, unlike anything I'd ever felt. When her tongue roiled against my own, it too felt unreal and almost unbearably tender.

It's because she's rotting, I thought. Squeeze her and she'll tear open, like a bin bag filled with rot on a hot day. Like a banana blackened by ripeness.

All of my senses seemed strung out, my nerves exposed like guitar strings resonating, waiting for something to show me what was happening. The texture of her mouth was both insubstantial and tactile like the weird repelling force felt through the fingers when you push two magnets together. The harder she pushed against me, the more an unbearable vacuum built up between us till I was convinced we would subsume each other. It was a remarkable kiss. She'd never kissed me like that before, even when we were shagging up against the kegs in The Pit Stop cellar.

When it was over, she stood up. "Come," she said, without a hint of irony. My mouth was filled with the taste of fruit on the turn. Cloying. Musty. I dumbly followed her, but the farther we went, the more she seemed to sag, though the terrain was even and pleasant on the feet. When the trees began to encroach on us, I glanced back, at the route we'd taken, at our footsteps creating tracks in the green. Already we had walked further than we ought to have been able. By now, we should have been standing in some room in the University of Westminster on the Euston Road.

The elms in front of us were stunted, their boughs filled with famished branches. Any foliage was brownish, pitted with scars, in stark contrast to the vital sproutings we'd encountered at the other end of the park. In between the trunks, crazily, impossibly, I could see parts of London that should have been miles away, but here they were, up close: mist drizzling into the bowl of the City; the winking tip of Canary Wharf; a scattering of bright canvas parasols in St. Christopher's Square; subdued light skipping off the roofs of cars on the South Circular. I noticed a tear in Meddie's combats; a bruise gave her leg an alien tinge.

"Things are happening," she said. "There are leaks. There are infections. These places we've found, they seemed to promise so much, but they're all fouled and fucked. Everything's fucked."

I felt the air go out of me in a sudden rush as she prodded around at the foot of the trees and came up holding the fly-blown corpse of a baby. There were others like it piled like firewood in amongst the boughs; someone was playing a gruesome game of hide and seek. Some of them had elongated faces, warped and alien as though pulled out of true before their skulls had time to harden.

Something gurgled.

"Meddie," I said, and my voice surprised me: it had taken on a flighty, fascinated whine despite what I was seeing.

It was dying. Its torso was clearly defined, yet somewhere south of its hips the flesh became milky and ill-formed, like chicken flesh seen through layers of polythene wrapping. It died quickly, before we could get to it—although I didn't know what I might have done to keep it alive had we reached it in time—its body flexing like a large muscle before slackening completely. Despite my revulsion, and feeling faintly dislocated, as though my hand belonged to someone else, I reached out and touched the area where flesh and form became mismatched. The cool, slightly fluid sensation continued beyond the body; I chased it with my fingers, reaching up as far as I could. When I pulled them back, they felt tight and shiny, the way skin feels after molten wax has been allowed to dry upon it. When I rubbed my palm, a layer came away, only to drift away to nothing in the air.

Meddie seemed to be unaware of this black magic; she was more concerned with the trees; the fan of grass at her foot that was unhealthily tinged.

"London's going off," she said. I might have laughed at that if she had said it at any other time, anywhere else. She swiveled her huge eyes and trapped me with them: a startled rabbit.

"And what about you?" I said. "You and Iain? And Yoyo?" My heart suddenly lurched. I hadn't heard from Yoyo in a long time. It seemed inconceivable that something should happen to her, but how could it not, if she were in cahoots with the others?

"What about us?"

"The bruises. I'm not stupid. What's going on?"

"We're infected too," she said.

"How?" I said. And then: "What with?" I wiped my lips with the back of my hand.

"I don't know. But it started when we unearthed all these little pockets of London. And it's getting easier, Adam. I'm drawn to them now; before I had to work at it. I was following hunches before. Now I'm like an elephant smelling water a hundred miles away. I know where to go."

"But look at what it's doing to you," I said.

No matter that her body was failing, or that it was doing things that a body in her state clearly shouldn't be capable of doing, I was jealous that I had not been able to unlock London in the same way. It might have been madness, a collective hysteria that was the only infection going on, but it had me like fever. I could see what they were seeing, but I couldn't divine my own little pocket. I wouldn't have known where to start. London was still being niggardly with its gifts to me. London was the lock on a safe that I had the combination to, but all of the numbers on the dial had been rubbed off.

She said, "I feel as though I'm slipping away, bit by bit. Fading. Falling through a gap in the world."

I closed my eyes and wished it all away. When I opened them, the sky had darkened a shade and the world had turned another couple of degrees. The trees were still there, the appalling carpet of grass and bodies too. But for the third time that afternoon, Meddie had vanished. I didn't try looking for her. I felt weak and sickly, as if some of what was cooking her had been transferred to me. I went home. On the way I called Yoyo. Her answering machine kicked in and I listened to her voice—pleasant, almost teasing—and I listened to the silence after the beep, not filling it, just thinking of what reasons she might have not to answer.

# CHAPTER TEN

## BRUISES

It's tied her tightly to the chair. Gagged her with the knickers she was wearing. It's shaved her head. She cried when It did that. Such vanity, it really amuses It. Even though she's never going to be seen by anyone ever again, she worries about her appearance. It holds up a mirror so that she can see what she looks like.

This is a beautiful flat. High ceilings, deep carpet. There's a wall filled with books and a small cabinet in which some smoky metallic box winks green light. A stereo, apparently, but the working of it is beyond It. There's a large desk in the adjoining room, upon which sits a ruby iMac and a framed photograph. In the bathroom, expensive-looking jars and tubes and bottles are clustered beneath an ornate mirror. Outside, there's a garden with a pond. A fountain plays its water music. Large silver fish move lazily through its fun.

It picks up the copy of yesterday's *Standard* from the sofa, points at the headline: THIRD TUBE DEATH IN A WEEK PANICS COMMUTERS, then points at It. Her eyes widen and she starts making short yelping noises around the gag. A frothy dribble escapes the corner of her mouth. Her breasts quiver like poached eggs on a plate.

Bored, It sits down and spreads Its hands. "Sorry," It whispers. It means it. She doesn't look convinced. "No, really. I am sorry. But it's all for a purpose. You dying—" She renews her yelping but then stops when she sees Its expression darken. "You dying will be for a good cause. Your death, all these deaths will prove a catalyst."

*What?* Her eyes beg.

"A slap around the head," It explains. "A wake-up call." It leans over and presses the grime of Its fingertips against her so pale, so cleansed, toned and moisturized face. Her un-face. "It's just all this shit... you know? How we live so close to each other and we never talk. I bet you've got people living in this house, in the other flats, that you've never spoken to. There are people we stand next to every morning on a platform or in a queue. We've stood next to them for years. They aren't strangers but we never talk to them. Ask them how they are. The only talking we ever want to do is on the telephone. Phones should be banned in the city. If you want to talk to someone, go and see them. It'll get so we lose the use of our facial expressions. It'll get so one ear is permanently flattened against the head, one fingertip flattened from all that dialing. How would you like to die?"

It leaves her for a while, goes into the kitchen. It doesn't mean to kill her. But It needs her to be scared, scared enough to go through with what It needs from her. It's choosing a knife from a block when It sees the pictures on the wall, pinned together as a rough collage on cork backing. Pictures of her with friends. A lot of boys. Popular. It carries the knife into the living room where It finds that she's turning blue, a gruel of vomit oozing from her nostrils.

"Oh. Not like that, doctor," It sighs, pulling away the gag so that she can be sick in comfort. If she goes like this, "I'll not be happy." Something other than the sight of her bound arms jerking as her body lazily spasms, her eyes bugging out of her stupid little head, irritates It. She's making a lot of noise. It claps her on the back with such force that It knocks the chair to the floor. It seems to do the trick. She's lying there, a professional woman, all her dignity gone. It can see brown smears on the crack of her arse. It hauls her upright and wipes the sick from her face. She's got slightly crooked teeth and a faint moustache of fair hair. She's got a mole right on the dimple of her chin.

She says, "I don't want to die. I don't want to die."

It says: "Maybe we can come to some sort of arrangement. But only if you'll agree to do something *awful* for me...."

WITH MEDDIE WITHDRAWING INTO HERSELF AND NEEDING strangers for the specific comfort she sought, and Yoyo incommunicado, I found I was forced to get in touch with Iain.

"It's been a while," I said, when he met me at The Beehive one late afternoon in November. The sky was molten anthracite. We were sitting at a table by the window; over Iain's shoulder I could see Baker Street, teeming with cars, and a queue at the Barclay's Bank cash machine on the corner that stretched almost up to the doors of the charity shop opposite the pub. There was a queue too at the Baker Street cinema, although I couldn't make out what was being shown: two buses were parked at the side of the road, hazards flashing, the reason for such a build up of traffic.

"Has it?" he asked. He was wearing a black corduroy jacket a couple of sizes too big for him, and faded black Levi's. An old, off-white T-shirt and a silver chain hanging over it. He had a large sports holdall with him, which contained a serge uniform. He hated wearing it before he got to work; the material could hardly breathe and before he started his shift he'd be pickled, his shirt in a mess. "I've got three shirts. All of them are rotting to fuck." His face seemed thinner than normal, and there were gray flashes in his dark brown hair. His eyes were the same, brutal blue flares.

"Doesn't feel as if you've been away," Iain said. "You've been up our arses ever since you gave us that sob story about the zeds. You wanted out, but you really wanted in, without the effort. Without having to talk to me."

There was no use protesting. He was saying it matter-of-factly, not offering his words as questions for me to bat away. He lit a cigarette and I noticed a pale bruise on his left hand, in the V between his thumb and forefinger. I got us a couple more pints and found my hands shaking as I received my change. Iain gulped back half his pint before I'd sat down. It seemed to have got darker inside the pub. The lights behind the bar, and those on the fruit machine, blazed more intently. The sky had lowered, somehow: its strange, heavy color was bleeding onto the streets, glossing them, giving everything a clean edge, a new shadow. There was rain in that sky, you could feel the weight of it, bearing down.

"What have you been up to?" I asked.

"This and that. Showing a few films at lock-up parties out Finsbury Park way. Some old stag stuff. Weird stuff. Underground stuff, mainly from the 1960s. New York. You know, Andy Warhol, Ken Jacobs, The Kuchar Brothers. *Blonde Cobra, Overstimulated, Sins of the Fleshapoids, Flaming Creatures...* you know that one?"

I shook my head, not really listening to him. It wasn't what I wanted to hear.

"How about this *new* hobby of yours?" I asked.

He snorted laughter. Smoke flew from his nostrils. "*Hobby,*" he said, slowly, as if trying the word out for the first time. He didn't say anything else for a while, just worked slowly at his Stella Artois. I didn't know what else to say, and knew that if I opened my mouth to offer anything, it would sound desperate, the sound of a man trying to fill an awkward silence. All I wanted to ask him about was the places he'd found. I was curious, I wanted closure with the group, but the only way I was going to have it was being let in on their secrets. I needed to know that what they had found was less about secret pockets in the middle of London, and more to do with their sense of who they really were. Truth be known, I wanted in on it.

Iain seemed to sense this. I could see it in the insouciant way he tapped the ash from his cigarette, and the half-smile that curled one side of his mouth.

He said, "They do good burgers here."

"Want one?" I said, glad for something to say. He raised his eyebrows briefly.

"With cheese," he said, as I set off for the bar again. While I was waiting to be served, he said: "What must it be like, wanting for a burger and having to eat salad instead?"

I turned and looked at him quizzically.

"That's you, isn't it?" he said. "Losing some fat. Living carefully. Everything in moderation. Nibbling cress when you could be gorging yourself at the fucking table we found."

"I want it," I said, hating myself. Fucking hating myself.

"It'll cost you," he said. "And more than a measly cheeseburger." He swept up his cigarettes and his lighter and he was outside before I had chance to tell the barmaid that I had changed my mind, I didn't want to order any food after all.

IAIN HAD DUMPED HIS GARAGE JOB IN EALING IN FAVOR OF security work for a firm called Barrier, a pissy little outfit with an office in a business park behind Kentish Town Road. They took the work that other firms didn't bother tendering for because of the high risks and low pay involved. "They're prawns sitting around the outflow pipe with their gobs open," Iain said. He earned £3.50 an hour patrolling building sites in the less salubrious areas of the city. When I asked him why, he said he'd had it with routine and was attracted to the unsociable hours and the silence offered by security work. He was sick to the back teeth of Swarfega and Citroëns. One night around five a.m., when it was just him and Sir, the Alsatian, doing the rounds in the car park of a new petrol station being built on the Seven Sisters Road, he'd stumbled upon couples fucking in the open air, in a small park adjacent to Manchester Road.

"It was real meat and potatoes stuff," he told me, his face slashed to ribbons of gray and orange by the streetlamps along Camden Road. There was me and him on the top deck of the 253, and a couple of students who'd got on at the stop outside Sainsbury's and were tearing into their economy packs of Malted Milk. "These girls, thin and white, prozzers they must have been, three of them, bent over and getting their insides pulped to fuck by guys, I don't know, on their way home from the pub, nipping out to take the dog for a walk. And they were quiet as graves, even though they were banging away like their lives depended on it."

I didn't know why he was telling me this. How could it have anything to do with the project they had been involved in over the past couple of months? Had they all seen this, or were they falling into their own individual territories? And what was it with the bruises? I gritted my teeth, knowing that to start asking him questions was to put a lid on him for a while. He didn't like being interrogated. He gave his information when he was ready to give it; it didn't matter if you thought it relevant or not.

"Where are we going?" I asked, despite myself. He replied by turning to watch the scenery pass us by. Holloway prison, the traffic at the Holloway Road junction, Finsbury Park. When we were motoring up past Manor House Tube, he looked back at me, and his face was like that of a child's, moments away from its birthday surprise.

"Next stop," he said.

We disembarked on Amhurst Park. A couple of the streetlamps were out; the one directly above our heads flickered, dissolving Iain and then stamping him back into true. I grabbed his arm, nailing his reality, and hissed: "Where the fuck are we going?"

He led me into Bethune Road past ranks of rusted, broken-down and abandoned cars; a fridge with its mouth open wide, gasping for breath around the pounds of litter that were choking it; a mattress half folded out of the gateway of an uninhabited house, the brickwork of which was failing: large wooden beams held its face erect. A pregnant dog regarded us dolefully from the mattress as we passed. Her mouth was open to show us her teeth. It was only when we got downwind of her that I smelled the death pouring off her and realized the swelling in her belly must have been rats.

We kept walking. At the bottom of the road, a park bench supported two towers of matted clothing filled with things that might once have been people. They were tossing each other off and drinking from bottles of Thunderbird. Before we reached that far, Iain took a sharp left, into the gap between two dark houses. A tiny gulley flanked with yew hedges gave on to a small crescent in which a café was nestled. Polished, wedge-shaped cars hunkered against pavements that seemed dust-free and uncannily level. The car interiors gleamed dully; I could almost smell the soft breath of leather. Rain-bright slates trapped the sun and cast fractal greens and blues into my eyes. The trill of pastel-colored birds was everywhere. The lack of bustle panicked me for a moment. I didn't feel right. This didn't feel right. But I couldn't find a way of voicing it. The coffee shop sucked us in. We took seats by the window. The warm vinyl impurities of a Sam Cooke song accompanied the pleasant sounds of an espresso machine chuckling in the background.

And then the free-floating anxieties that had settled on me over the past few years seemed to slip a little, as if I'd suddenly found the knots that bound them to me and discovered a way to loosen them.

"Iain, bonjour. You've caught a little of the summer," said the waitress, slipping into the seat opposite him and gesturing vaguely across her face. "Freckles. No, don't pout. On you they are quite appealing."

Her eyes were unblinking yet full of humor. Green flaws nestled at the edge of an iris like flecks of mint in a round of bitter chocolate. Her sandy-blonde hair was scraped back from her forehead, tied into a ponytail that heightened her jaw's sweep and the tidy bow of her mouth. A plastic badge bearing the name *Monique* was pinned to her lapel.

"Robert sends his regards. He's unwell today but he hopes to chat with you soon. Just a sore throat but he milks it, you know? If I step into his room to see if he wants a little tea he'll beg me to stay and talk. It's like he loses his sense of being and needs it reaffirmed with a conversation."

"I can understand that," Iain said.

Monique's eyes widened. Her skin was so clear it seemed to deliquesce in the pale light seeping in off the street. I felt as if I had diminished, become tissue-thin. I felt as if I wasn't there.

Monique leaned over to fill his cup. Beyond the V of her blouse, her breasts curved into shadow.

Iain said, finally, "This is Adam Buckley. He's a friend of mine."

Monique smiled at me, and then nodded her head, almost imperceptibly, as if confirming something she had on her mind. "What would you like?" she asked.

"Can I see a menu?"

She smiled. Iain smiled. I smiled.

"We don't have a menu. Just say what it is you want."

I shrugged, and said, "Okay, I'll have a corned beef and sweet pickle sandwich. And a cup of tea."

In the street, the cars were beginning to shimmer. The windows of the houses were cold and empty. Now and again I thought I saw oily shapes moving beyond the glass but there wasn't enough light to be sure. Slowly the crescent began to fill with life, all of it immaculate. I felt like an intruder; at any moment fingers would point and we'd be undone, me and this threadbare security guard with a poorly shaven face and swollen eyes. But it didn't seem to matter. The square jaws and frosted pagodas of hair strolled by, almost like figures filmed in slo-mo. Some of them smiled at me, all luster and silk. I nodded, raised my hand. A woman in a black dress filleted at the sides waved at me and blew me a kiss, her eyes concealed behind vast shades. Iain checked his watch.

Our food arrived. Iain was having egg and chips and a glass of milk. The sandwich was excellent: two slices of corned beef with some Branston in the middle. Lurpak butter on two pieces of Sunblest thick. The tea came with a spoonful of sugar added, how I liked it, even though I hadn't asked for it. And I would swear blind it was PG Tips, the only tea I really enjoyed.

"This is weird," I said. "My mum used to make my corned beef sandwiches, and my tea, just like this, when I was a nipper. I mean, exactly like this."

"Same here," Iain said. "Good, isn't it?"

"This is part of it, isn't it?" I said. "This is part of what you've found."

He nodded. "What I'm getting at is this," he said. "You have to be able to see the moments of depravity as moments of beauty, before you can see the extraordinary in the everyday. I was searching all the time, and seeing things that, ordinarily, you'd turn away from. All that fucking in a park full of dog shit. The discarded condoms. The prozzers grinning with their wet mouths, wearing a little something over their tits, quim-skimmer skirts, high heels and little else, pumped full of drugs to deal with the cold... you have to accept it. You have to see the positives. And in a way, it was a beautiful moment. All that rank carnality going on under a sky that was filthy black until you really stared at it, and then it was chock full of subtle color: swirls of purple, deep blue and bottle green. I saw it, in all that sloshing flesh, I saw something that was like art."

I swallowed tea. I really fancied some Battenburg cake. "And this is your reward? A café with a sexy waitress, a meal that reminds you of home?"

He was ignoring me. "At first I found little impressions that leaked light when it was dark, until you got up close and found nothing. Holes in fences. Cracks in walls. I thought I had a brain tumor. I heard weird things, sounds coming out of stuff that shouldn't have carried sounds at all: classical music from a vacant demolition site, a discussion about brass in an empty bus terminus, a typewriter clacking away in a disused church. And then I saw turnings off main roads where, on the map, there shouldn't be any. I rang the council and they denied it. When I followed the roads, they petered out, or became dead-ends. A few days later, when I tried them again, they reached deeper. Until they finally led somewhere. I sat in a tapas bar at the top end of Eversholt Street for an entire afternoon, watching to see how many people would turn into Cable Lane, this new road that had gradually excavated itself out of the buildings opposite, between Cranleigh Street and Aldenham Street. Cable Lane, NW1. Nobody did. *Because only I could see it.* You won't find it in the A-Z."

He was mad. "And this place. I won't find this place either?"

"You can try," he said. "On the map, where we're sitting, it should be someone's back garden. We should be right on top of some poor bloke trying to assemble some decking and worrying about the cat from next door who keeps pissing on his begonias."

I was dissatisfied with what I was being shown, and convinced that he was keeping something from me. I said as much.

He said, "And what about you? What makes what you're looking for so special?"

I opened my mouth and shut it again.

"We all need something," he said. "Saskia needed something and when she found it was too much for her. At a certain hour of the night, Yoyo has found deer roaming around one street in SW1. Meddie plays cards with pirates just before dawn on a jetty off the Albert Embankment."

I said, "Fuck off, Iain."

"You owe me," he said. "Stick around, and allow yourself to be convinced." He opened his bag and slid a battered ring-bound AZ across the table, opened at page 50. His dirty fingernail rested against the white strip delineating Bethune Road. Square 1E. No crescent opposite St. Kilda's Road. No nothing. I felt the floor fall away from me, and for a moment I was staring across the Formica into Iain's face with a sense that we were tumbling through millions of acres of cold space. If I blinked and lost the connection with those flat, reptilian eyes of his, I'd be lost for ever.

"Everything okay?" Monique's voice pinned me back to where we were, and I gulped and nodded, waiting for the colors to sink into the surroundings, waiting for focus, waiting for Iain to speak and so reassure me as to why I was here. She handed me a small plate with a slice of pink and yellow sponge on it. Marzipan. Apricot paste.

Before I realized it, we were on Stamford Hill, caught up in a thrash of sweaty bodies hailing cabs and throwing violent glances at watches. A woman sneezed into her handkerchief but failed to prevent a staple of snot from fastening her lips together. A girl with a patch over one of the lenses in her spectacles buried her sad face into an anemic pie. Buses clattered by, filled with cheesy, featureless orbs.

My mind slowly and mournfully readjusted itself to the hubbub around us. Iain was saying something else now, but I couldn't hear him. My pulse was filling my head, and the traffic was too dense. I thought he said, but I hoped he hadn't: *I've never set foot in that coffee shop before in my life.*

I WANTED TO GO HOME, BUT I FELT HONOR-BOUND TO SEE through my half of the bargain. We arrived at the building site in Hackney just before midnight. I was trying to work out why I had thought it was daytime at the café but the heartbeat in my head had segued into a nasty little ache and I knew there was no point in asking Iain questions.

Not just because stubbornness wouldn't allow him to answer, but also because I felt sure that he didn't know, any more than I did.

The security guard he was relieving was a monster called MacCreadle. Six foot plus, sprawling beard and limbs so large it seemed the serge suit he was wearing could only have been handmade for him. I imagined he could wear nothing off the peg. A red bandanna was wrapped around his head. He was sitting with his feet up on the table, leafing through a copy of *40+*. His black cowboy boots were scuffed; his spurs had turned the table-top into a grand doodle.

"Mac," Iain said.

MacCreadle grunted and pushed away from the table. He removed the clip-on tie from his collar and stuffed it into his pocket. He almost filled the Portakabin and had to hunch over so his head wouldn't knock against the broken neon strip light.

Iain said, "Any trouble?"

They moved to the doorway and surveyed the building site. The foundations for what would be a new daycare center had been laid: before them stood a forest of scaffolding and small hills of breeze block and brick, not yet released from their stiff plastic packaging. The estate opposite was like a child's attempt at construction: simple brown rectangles punched with slit windows—a prison without bars. A sneering pub sat like a creased and shabby piss-artist against the crippled elms that separated its beer garden from a barber shop. The only other places in our sightline were a post office and a chip shop, its entrance obstructed by a pile of bin bags.

"Jus' kids," said MacCreadle. "Fuck'n kids. Tell you man, if I was quick enough to catch 'em, I'd fuck'n fuck 'em." He spat a great loop of phlegm against the bowl of a cement mixer and inspected a sore on his hand.

Iain asked, "So, what are you up to tonight?"

MacCreadle grinned, his molars creeping into the open like foraging black slugs. "You don't really want to know that," he purred. Picking up his rucksack and helmet, he strode to the Harley Davidson that was hidden behind the Portaloo. "Tomorrow," he mouthed, and roared away, blazer tails flapping in his wake. He hadn't even looked at me.

We sat in silence for twenty minutes or so. My mind was still stuck in the place we'd left behind. I could still smell melted cheese in the Breville toaster; the peonies in their little vases. I could still feel the blue-checked gingham and the slow breath of ceiling fans. Monique had been all eyes and cleavage and Amarige by Givenchy. I sat in a torn PVC swivel chair waiting for Iain to put me in the picture, and delved for her lyrical voice.

Iain lit the gas burners on the wall, flinching when they popped into life. He tuned the radio till he found the sports bulletin but the football match he wanted to listen to had been abandoned because of a pitch invasion.

"This business, security," Iain said, "is anything but. The whole business has more bent people in it than you'll find in a rheumatology ward."

I sat and waited and wished I had something to drink. Across the road, a light came on in the opaque window of a bathroom. Someone walked into the frame it provided, long hair, naked, judging by the amount of pink blur. Her shadows and curves bulged and elongated as she fussed with her hair, piling it on top, maybe teasing it into ringlets. I could even see, through the distorted glass, a twinkle or two from her earrings.

A shout turned her head; mine too. "Eggy! Eggy, ya wankah! Rock and roll... Rock and fucking roll!"

Violence has its own timetables and schedules. Its nature is cyclical and swift; tonight it had made an appointment with this particular urban stretch. Something in the way the air moved, or a posture in the buildings and streets that I hadn't noticed before, told me to watch out. The night was sticking its chin out, daring someone to put a fist in it. So when a figure came sprinting out of the dark, chased by a pack of lads cackling like hyenas, Iain snuffed the lights and we watched, Iain holding his flask like a comforter between his legs.

They caught up with "Eggy" outside the entrance to the pub. The pack leader grabbed hold of his hair and, like an Olympic hammer thrower, swung him around before depositing him on the curb, where they kicked him until he stopped making little grunts of pain. A tide of bodies spewed from the pub, where, apparently, a privileged few were enjoying a lock-in until the noise disturbed them. Glasses smashed. I could watch no more. There was more shouting and pleading before the sirens arrived. Bodies were either dragged off into vans or stretchered into ambulances.

When I remembered to look back at the bathroom, the woman was gone, replaced by a man with his arms locked behind his head. I saw him relax before throwing a punch at someone unseen—perhaps the woman—which brought a black splash to the window just as the light went off.

By the time Iain's boss, Nathan Troake, arrived in his soiled Jag, the area was studiedly calm once more. I could almost see the nervous faces beyond the blocks of curtain, waiting for it all to kick off again.

"Want some pips, start shaving properly. And who's this cunt? Your girlfriend?"

Iain told me later that Troake never began a meeting with "Hello, how are you?" It was all business—cut, thrust, me first, me second and if there's anything left over, me again. He also said that the only pips he wanted were Troake's and he'd like to retrieve them himself with a rusty knitting needle. Being an inspector in this line of work was even more of a grim experience than guarding. You earned two different species of abuse: the usual civilian kind from those who called you a "fascist" for not allowing them to eat pork pies in stationery shops, and the resentful kind from your former peers who were now no better than dog shit—and all because of those silver nipples pinned to your shoulder. But Iain wouldn't say as much; that was like saying he didn't want to work in security. Apparently you had to look keen to please Troake.

Hot nicotine scorched my nostrils as he leant over to shake my hand. He wore a black beret tipped forward across his eye. The collars of his coat were batwings concealing his neck. When he moved back his collars shifted; I saw a damp gray bandage at his throat with a core of yellow. He took a silver cigarette case from the folds of his coat. Opening it, he pressed it against my chest.

"Snout?" he said. I shook my head. "Any trouble?" he asked as Iain passed him a mug of tea. His voice was ragged and scarred, as though formed from the stuff he was dragging into his chest. Perhaps it was. His cigarette was finished already; he flicked the butt into the mesa of dog-ends in a tinfoil ashtray. I watched it land, and by the time I'd returned my attention to him another cigarette was smoldering between his lips, a cold, blue helix of smoke winding around eyes so pale their color might have been borrowed from between the bricks outside.

"Not here, no. Other than a bit of a scrap outside the pub."

"So there was trouble. Iain, security is all about observation and anticipation. You aren't just a deterrent you know. You are the wedge, the bolster, the thin red line." He sipped his tea. "So, is there trouble elsewhere?"

"How do you mean?" It was interesting to see Iain like this, cowed, not in control. It wasn't just the difference in rank, though. Iain didn't have any respect for hierarchy. I had the feeling he felt threatened by Troake in some other way.

"You see, Iain," Troake was saying, "I'm trained to read between the words, to note the nuances mid-letter, even. The way you punctuate speech, lad—God, you might as well underline and italicize with a great big sad black pen. You said, when I asked you if there was any trouble, 'Not here, no,' which implies that there are wars being waged in another part of your world. Am I right or am I very right?" He smiled, and his bottom lip spread out like a discarded piece of hamburger pressed under the heel.

Iain shrugged.

Scoffing, Troake pushed his mug away and stood up, shoveling a fan of papers back into his briefcase. He paused by the door, looking out at the night, which seemed to be coagulating in the sky, its darkness somehow softening, like dust on a sable coat. There would be frost the next morning. I couldn't feel winter in the air, but I was shivering anyway; even the thought of warm air scooting through vents in the oak panels at the café didn't help. The way Troake's hair was mismanaged at the back of his head—tufted like some duck's plumage—made me feel sorry, despite his aggressive manner; this was a man who rose alone in the morning, ate alone at lunch and perched alone in front of *EastEnders* with his microwaved lasagne.

"I might pop round tomorrow," he said, and then looked at me. "Want a job in security?" I shook my head. He shrugged. "Your loss. And remember, Iain," he said, as he slid behind the wheel, "you are the thin red line."

"And you're the thick red prick," Iain murmured as he waved Troake goodbye.

"So how do I get involved?" I asked. "You said something about cost."

"You've already paid," he said. "Open your shirt."

In the warm glow of the gas lamps, the constant flicker of shadows, my skin seemed as complete as ancient paper. Darkness moved across it, dappling my chest. One area of black over my heart remained still. I touched the bruise and felt its dull pain deep inside me.

"It goes right through you," Iain said.

"How?" I demanded. "What made it?"

He shrugged. "That we still need to find out."

He admired the bruise, and his hands went to his arms, his chest, where bruises of his own hung in the skin like fruit that has turned bad on the vine. "They don't go away," he whispered. "They never go away."

# CHAPTER ELEVEN
## SECURITY

It wasn't so bad, in the end. It had craved the pain, had felt it settle across the boss of Its skull like known fire; a necessary pain. But pain was all it was, and pain is always manageable, eventually.

While It knelt before her, she had worked the knife almost tenderly, despite her fear, not wanting to slice too deeply lest she severed any nerves and angered It. But It didn't care. It had nerves to spare. She was going too slowly so It had to take her wrist and force her to carve with more urgency. It kept hold of her even when she was working at a pace It approved of, because by then there was a lot of blood drizzling into Its eyes and It could no longer see her clearly. It didn't trust her not to plunge the blade through Its throat, given the chance.

In the end, she held Its face in her hand the way a child will hold a sugar cube out for a horse: outstretched, fingers so splayed they bend backwards slightly, the palm tight and shiny in its offering. It tried to speak—*Keep it,* It wanted to say—but the blood and the loss of Its lips meant that all It could manage was a moan, a spray of vermilion spittle.

It rose. Everything felt clearer, even as the blood and lymph clogged Its eyes and trickled down Its throat. Its own smell, the freshness of Its life, astonished It. Its face sang.

It looked down at the woman in the chair, her legs still bound together, sweat pooling in the V between her thighs. Shock was painting her own face white. It tried to lick Its lips and laughter fell messily from Its mouth when It realized It could no longer do that. Carefully, It attempted a few words. It said: "I... owe... you."

IAIN HAD CALLED ME, SICK WITH A MILD BOUT OF GASTRIC flu, and asked if I wanted to make some hard cash by covering for him at the building site. Troake wasn't bothered who was wearing the uniform. It was a little nerve-racking. I mean, I'd never done a night shift before in any capacity, and despite Iain's sureties that little ever happened, beyond the odd drunken fuck in a sandpit, or kids playing in the empty rooms, I was a little jittery as I climbed on board the bus in his suit, a size too small, the serge itchy and smelling of wet dogs, Wrigley's Spearmint and Mandate.

Something seemed to be wrong with the roads the buses were traveling along. They were peeling, scrofulous, as though suffering from some sort of skin disease; they bulged and tore, suggesting that the thoroughfares were too wide for the surfaces that glued them together. But that might have been something to do with the fact that I hadn't eaten since the previous evening. I felt good though, honed, on edge, super-attentive. The blood in my head felt thin and hot, I was pumped up. If any night was right for chasing the insane, it was tonight. I felt mad enough. Iain enough. I was determined to try to find my own secret place, my own pocket.

And, really, I had no choice in the matter. It was nothing to do with Meddie, or Iain, or Yoyo. It was me. It was the bruises. I was convincing myself that I could see my internal organs through them, as if the skin were becoming so thin as to be translucent. My heart resembled a child's fist, gray and shocked, being shaken in rage. If I was sustaining bruises, then I must be able to access these blackspots. Fuzzy logic... but it was all I had.

The 253 was deserted. I sat at the back, remembering my first time on a bus, on my own, my mum seeing me off, my dad in town, waiting for me to arrive. I'd been on my way to get a haircut, and a new PE kit. I remember my mum receding in the window of the bus and a scattershot of panic in my stomach as it hit me that I had never been on my own among strangers before. There was always mum, or dad, or mum and dad. This was how things would be when they were dead, I thought. The panic, and the not knowing, and the strangers. A destination that didn't exist until it was reached. An in-between that was unbearable, yet inescapable. Grown-ups eyeing me with suspicion or indulgence. Predators. Guardians. Strangers.

And then Dad at the terminus. And the haircut, a new pair of shorts and a T-shirt. A toasted tea-cake and a milkshake at the Golden Egg and everything forgotten. Everything all right. Me, a big boy now. It was always said: "Who's a big boy? You're a big boy now." As if, in the saying of it, it became so.

My thoughts fell upon Laura, as they often did when I was focusing on other times, other events, and I thought how nice it would be to be able to enter her flat while she was still asleep, to slip into bed alongside her and enjoy her warmth for an hour or two before she had to get up. Before she realized I was there. I could let myself out again before she was aware of me. She might have my ghost in her thoughts. She might contact me. Try to make things right between us. If not mend things, at least make things right. How I would sit naked on the bed, filled with croissants, drained of semen, watching sunlight paint the down on her breasts; edge the moist O of her mouth gold as she snoozed. A soft, amorphous time when there was neither consolidation nor diminishment, before her way towards me had soured, our language turned vituperative, her enthusiasm palled to indifference. It was easy to watch the seams fall apart.

Lights stuttered; the bus rocked. Suddenly there was someone on the top deck, some bleary-eyed dragon sipping from a can of tramp-brew and reading the Bible. I stepped off at Manor House into a draught redolent of diesel and the previous night's kebabs. I sensed people checking out my uniform, hostility coming off them like heat. MacCreadle was sitting on the steps of the Portakabin when I arrived, drinking from a West Ham United mug. "Keen fucker, hey?" he said. "Not that I'm complaining. Just don't expect me to turn up half an hour early tomorrow morning. Is that injurious to your good humor? Where's rat-boy Iain?"

"He's ill. I don't mind taking over. It's just one night."

"A lot can happen in one night."

"Hopefully not though, hey?"

MacCreadle shrugged, emptied his mug on to the floor and eased his boots on over feet so large that to put shoes over them appeared unnatural. He ought to go barefoot. He ought to be wearing nothing more than animal skins and tribal tattoos.

"Last night there was more of the old ultra-violence kicking off outside the pub. Some of it spilled over here. I mashed a few noses, cracked a few skulls, you know how it is. They might have revenge on their minds tonight."

"I'm no hero," I said. "I'll be a mile away before they set foot on this building site."

"It can be a beautiful building site, this, if you look at it in the right way."

I eyed the big man. "You been drinking?"

He smiled. "The bricks and the plant and the breezeblocks. The bags of cement. The unlit windows. It fair bristles with potential, this place, don't you think?"

"You have been drinking. It's a building site. It's a shithole."

"You should spend a bit longer looking at places like this," he said. "Even the girl with the harelip deserves to be kissed now and then." He gathered together his things and somehow folded himself through the doorway. He half-turned and his beard altered the shadow of his face into something that crawled.

"Troake'll be along around ten. Best if you stick your tie back on and have your brow furrowed. He likes his staff to look on the ball."

The engine of his Harley starting ripped the night in two. People came to their windows to watch him leave, as if relieved, as if they needed a security guard to keep them safe from the security guard. "See you later, masturbator," he called out, as he accelerated away.

I drank some strong coffee and tried to work out where the time wasn't going to. Two hours till ten o'clock, and Troake. Another half-hour after that before I was able to slope off and start divining.

Across the way, the pub was filling up. I could make out shapes in the window, throwing darts. Other faces were underlit with brilliant, ever-changing light: a fruit machine, or pinball. Light caught on a million glittering fragments of glass in the car park, transforming it into a beach of diamonds. The rest of the estate behind it was all chewing gum whites and graffiti, painted wickets and goalposts on splintered garage doors; the people I could see walking between the stairwells looked like shabby pigeons cadging titbits, gray and misshapen with crusty, dazed stares and scarred faces. How had Iain described them? Pondlife on the take. The kind that steal from their mothers and display utter apathy when someone pulls a knife in a brawl. The kind of people who aim low and still fuck up. The underclass. Scum.

A man in a V-neck sweater pushed a woman in an A-line skirt up against the wall of the pub and went at her face like he was bobbing for apples.

I thought Iain was being a bit harsh.

By ten o'clock, the pub was jumping. A crowd had spilled onto the street despite the cold, and loud music was pouring out of the doors, along with laughter, shouting and billows of blue smoke. The gas in the heater ran out so I buttoned up my overcoat and decided that if I was going to freeze I might as well do it properly. I stalked about the site trying to follow the progress made on the building since the previous night. Black stains—piss, oil, blood?—decorated one of the partially erected walls and an empty plastic liter bottle of cheap cider stood next to them. Someone had clearly been using a few of the undeveloped rooms to camp in. There was evidence of fires: soot up the walls and on the ceilings. Presumably the builders had cleared the remains of the fires away, but their smell remained, somehow damp and sour, persistent, like urine.

There would be none of this on the roads around the café, which sprang into my thoughts, unbidden, or perhaps perversely encouraged by the dearth of positive images that were currently being filtered through them. It was as if the roads around the café were self-cleaning. I thought of Monique and the slope of brown skin under her blouse. Her sing-song voice.

I mooched around a little longer, keeping an eye on the pub in case it should disgorge someone with a sudden lust for a bit of bloodshed. I was finishing a slow circle, and returning to the Portakabin to make some tea and listen to the radio, when Troake's Jag turned onto the building site, the beams from its headlights jerkily arcing over the infrastructures and cement mixers until I was fixed within them. I raised a hand to shield my eyes and at that very moment he killed the engine and the light died.

"Adam, isn't it?" he said, as he got out of the car. "So you do want a job in security. Iain warned me you'd be filling in for him tonight. I'm grateful. It's rare that we get cover as quickly as that, if at all. How's it going? Had any adventures yet?'His face emerged from the murk: a flat oval underlit by the intensifying coal of his cigarette. He was wearing some flash overcoat right out of the pages of *GQ* magazine, dark and soft, something with a cool, smooth lining and a label to raise eyebrows. He smiled: a butter-colored scythe.

"No," I said. "But then, isn't security supposed to be the most boring job in the world?"

"Do you find this boring?"

"It's hardly taxing to the old brain, is it? And the money doesn't help much."

"Anything else in your life?"

I looked at him, trying to make out if he was taking the piss. "Plenty," l said, at last.

He dimpled. "Some people don't. For some people, security is, well, security. It's a friend to them when they don't have one. It's money—shit money, sure—but it pays the bills and puts food in the kids' mouths. It's kept some men straight, this job, even though most of the chaps we recruit are bent as bastards."

"I don't need the job," I said. "I've got work. I'm doing Iain a favor."

"Iain," Troake said, as if the name was new to him. "He needs the job. He'll say he won't, but he does."

"He wants it because it offers him something you don't get in an office." I said. "No routine. Mobility. It's probably saving him a fortune in hemorrhoid cream."

Troake smiled again. It was an unnerving smile that failed to shift the skin above the corner of his mouth. It was shark-like. Ungenerous. "I don't think so, son," he said. "I think he needs the job because it's the only solid thing in his life. Even Iain himself, he's diminishing."

"Diminishing?"

A huge cheer, the kind of ironic noise you get when you finally sink a ball in pool after about a million misses, flew up from the pub and turned to ice in the air. There was something unpleasant in it. I felt all kinds of bad lifting from the static and living things positioned around me: everything had its own, incipient menace. Everything conveyed a threat.

"That's right," Troake said. He lifted a hand and rubbed at the bandage on his throat. The sound went through me like the squeal of a fork on a plate. "He's like water, that boy. A long stretch of water. Tasteless. Bland. You could look right through him. You know, he told me this job was all he had. He was hanging everything on it. 'Pack up, I crack up,' he told me."

"Whatever that means."

"He doesn't feel as though he's connected to anything. He feels lost."

"He does now. He's gone too far. The things he's found. It's as if he's unraveling. The others too. And me...."

Troake frowned. "What's this he's found? What are you talking about?"

"I don't think you want to know. It's dangerous, what Iain's been getting up to. There're after-effects. Side-effects. Something."

He seemed to be smoking constantly, blue ribbons rising from his face, gray bands striping the air above him, although I couldn't see a cigarette in his hands. I almost laughed. He was like Valeria, the Fenella Fielding character in *Carry on Screaming.* Smoke made solid.

"Maybe, after all, it's linked with Iain's need for this job," I said. "Maybe he sees it as a possible way to reinvent himself, reintroduce himself to the world." What I was saying sounded tacked on, badly thought out. Words from someone trying to patch up a mistake.

A glass smashed. Everything grew very quiet, as if we had somehow emerged into the eye of a storm, just before the other side of hell came to rough us up.

"We all have a capacity for re-birth, son," he said, so softly I wasn't sure I heard him correctly. Danger radiated from him like vapor, like smoke. "People make the mistake of waiting till they die before attempting it though. It can happen now. There's a womb and we all slumber inside it: blind, stupid, smothered by our TV comforts. Nobody ever strives to escape it, nobody wants to better themselves."

He dragged on a cigarette that materialized between his fingers. I thought he would make it vanish again, push it into his ear, pull it from his nose. Swallow it. His eyes were pits of amber. The smell of diesel poured off him then, as if he were keeping some in his pockets, or washing with it. His stench was of the underground. And I felt my mouth water for it at the same time as everything became hazy and insane.

The noises from the pub turned ugly. I heard someone shout, very clearly: "You. Are. Fucking. Dead."

Troake said: "Fancy a pint?"

I looked at him. "I'm on duty."

"Bollocks," he said. "You're sacked. Now you're off duty. Let's have a drink."

"Over there?" I asked him. "You're joking aren't you? MacCreadle said—"

"I don't give a fanny fart what that overgrown beard said. It's safe. I've supped pints in there a thousand times and haven't so much as had my change placed roughly in the palm of my hand. Let's go."

The pub didn't even have a name. The sign hanging over the door was split and rotten, warped like a flag that had frozen solid. Whatever paint had existed there was now scratched away, or obscured with pigeon shit.

Inside, the heat was tremendous. The serge suit began to prickle against my arms and legs. Heads turned our way. I took off my clip-on tie. I took off my cap. I kept my eyes on the sawdust and floorboards until we were at the bar. A woman with an amazing figure but an old face pushing through the pancake pulled us a couple of pints of Spitfire.

Music lifted from a corner of the room. Bass, drums, guitar, vocals. I didn't recognize it. It sounded raw and unmannered, but there were so many people between me and it that I couldn't tell if it was from a jukebox or being played live. If there was a band over there, then they were being studiously ignored by the punters. Troake nudged my arm and nodded towards the opposite corner.

We sat at one of two tables. A woman in a tight T-shirt with the word Lush written across it in pink glitter was sitting on the other, flanked by two men. She had drinks queued up in front of her: half pints of Guinness and black as far as I could tell. The men wore plain, dark suits with colorful shirts, one in maroon, one in electric blue, open to a depth of three buttons. They sported identical French crops shot through with some expensive-looking product that shone dully in the nicotine light: moisturizing wax or putty. A bank of perfume separated us. The woman was saying drunkenly to maroon: "I mean it. You get it out, put it on the table. I swear I'll kiss it."

"This your local?" I said to Troake, downing half my pint, and hoping he wasn't expecting a session to develop.

I could just make out, through the scrimmage at the bar, a fat man in Puffa jacket and jeans with six-inch turn-ups yelling at a woman whose face was lowered over her glass. She might have been crying. Hot red spots bloomed on his cheeks above mutton chop whiskers. His eyebrows were arrowing into the center of his face above a pair of mirror shades. He was pointing at her and pointing at the way out. She hadn't yet got the message.

"What do you think?" Troake asked. I turned to him. His mouth was poised over the rim of his glass. Thin foam squiggles formed a code on its sides.

"About what?" I said.

"The Pusher, hey? All this pushing going on. What do you think?"

"I think he's a mental fucker who wants to get caught."

He took a sip and placed the glass on the table. Names were scratched across its unvarnished wood: *Bri, Merce, Barnesy.* The woman at the next table said: "I don't know about the both of you. Not at the same time, anyway."

"You think he wants to get caught?"

"Well, no. It's a figure of speech, isn't it? Like 'he wants his face slapping.' Or 'she wants a good talking to.' "

"Figure of speech," Troake said. He hadn't tapped the ash from his cigarette. It curled off the end like a horn. It looked much harder than it was. I hoped the same could be said for Troake. He was fidgeting now, and licking his lips. We were sitting a comfortable distance apart, but something was being exuded through his skin that was like an affront. It crept into my personal space, jabbing its fingers into the nerves at the center of my gut. I raised my glass and it trembled.

The guy with the whiskers was prodding the girl in the chest. She looked up at him. Her face was white; her opened mouth turned it into a Japanese flag. I saw her say please. I saw him show her an open hand. I saw him make to slap her and then hold back at the last moment. Somewhere, someone said: *And I'll fucking slaughter you and all.* The woman at the table next to ours put her hands beneath my sight line and kneaded her companions. There was no height for the heat to rise into. It was so intense it was causing itself to sink to its knees. The music turned into a howl of feedback that would not end. The barmaid was turned away from the gaggle of customers waving fivers at her. She was peering into a mirror, digging at something in her face with long, false nails.

"The Pusher," Troake said. "He wanted me to give—"

I stood up and launched the glass at the fat man. It caught him behind the ear but did not break. It ricocheted backwards and smashed against the bar. A woman shrieked. Obviously not a regular. I moved out from behind the table and shoved it back against Troake as he tried to rise. Then I drove my fist into his face and vaulted over the bar. Lots of pushing was going on now, around the fat man. I saw the girl he was with back off, concern shutting her face down. Someone swore. Someone raised half a snooker cue and brought it down hard. The barmaid was at my back asking me just what the fuck I thought I was doing. I ignored her and nipped out into a private corridor. Boxes of crisps, piles of cardboard peanut displays. I could hear footsteps on a set of carpeted internal stairs, hurrying down to start ejecting people before the police arrived. By the toilets was a door leading into a yard. A generator was droning. Pale blue skips, like high-sided bath tubs, were lined up by the door, ready for closing time, and the empty bottles. The gate out to the street was locked, but I climbed it easily enough, driven by the adrenaline flushing through my veins. Seeds of black sowed themselves across my vision. The taste of wet earth filled my mouth. Something had crunched when I punched him, but fear wasn't allowing me to feel any pain. I hoped it had been his nose, and not my fingers. I took off and didn't stop running until I had put a good mile, and a lot of twists, turns and streets, between me and the pub. I waited for a while on the corner of Stoke Newington Road, watching the traffic, waiting for him, and then began to jog north.

By the time I arrived at where I wanted to be, I felt lost, which also felt right. What wasn't right was the lack of warmth, something I couldn't just attribute to my panic. A mist slithered into the streets; through it I could make out dark lumps on the pavement, but something about the fresh constrictions around me—in the air, the buildings, the shut-in movements behind curtain and door, and somehow *inside* me—warned me that they might not be anything as innocent as litter. The deeper I went into the narrowing thoroughfares, the broader the canvases of urban decay: boarded windows; stultifying graffiti; shivering, sunken-eyed dogs. The café should have appeared by now. But there was only a wall where the turning should have been. No smells of hot chocolate or the pleasant sound of tomatoes being chopped on a wooden block. No Sam Cooke. The place reeked of Troake. The bastard. He'd followed Iain here, in his search for me. He had infected the oasis.

Now I could hear the Jag crunching through low gears as it nosed this way and that in the streets behind me, sniffing me out. It wouldn't take him long to catch up, what with this disorientation sitting fat in my mind.

Gastric flu. Iain didn't have anything of the kind. I imagined him turning to pulp behind closed curtains, a failing light bulb sending gleams along the wet lengths of his limbs.... It didn't for one moment strike me that the disease, the damage they were causing themselves, was as likely to exist as the Crescent itself, that it might all be a confection produced by the narcolepsy. I had to continue as if this was real, because somewhere, at some level, things *were* real. I just didn't know what, where and who anymore. Something somewhere would no doubt heal itself and at some point in the future I might level out and find it.

Me. I'm real. I'm real. Keep hold of that, if nothing else. I'm real. I *am*.

I headed west, crossing Green Lanes into Brownswood Road, heading roughly for the Tube station at Arsenal. I was almost at Gillespie Road, the bull's-eye sign for the Tube station a target within reach, when his Jag drew up alongside me.

"Jump in," he said.

"Fuck off."

"You've got me all wrong, Adam. I'm trying to protect you. Get in the car. It's warm. And Iain needs us. He's in trouble."

I stopped. His face was edged with pale yellow from the dashboard. Smoke leapt from the open window as if the interior was on fire. He turned off the engine and got out. Spread his arms as if to show he was harmless. He walked around the Jag, and I mirrored him, but in the other direction, keeping the car between us. He retrieved a long metal rod with a curved spike from his coat and inserted it into the slots of a manhole cover. With a grunt, he lifted it clear.

"Come on," he said. "It's really not so bad. We could use a good man like you. Come now, and there'll be no threat to you."

"What are you talking about?" Steam rose from the manhole and laced him. He was flexing his fingers, one by one. I slowly moved away.

"Walk, and we will find you, Adam. *Monck*. You'll not bring us down. You won't bring *him* down. I won't allow it."

At least I thought that was what he said. I could no longer hear him very well as I sprinted to the Tube entrance, the wind in my ears, scouring his threats away.

# CHAPTER TWELVE

## CHAIN REACTION

It knows this dark. It knows its moods and vicissitudes. It knows its geography; It knows that the dark can be mapped. It isn't something to get lost in. Panic gets you lost. The roads, the streets, the tunnels are all the same in the dark. People. You get lost in people. You lose yourself to people. People are different in the dark. And in the middle of the brightest day, all people are in the dark. Blind. Stumbling. It knows this as deeply, as intuitively, as It knows the constellations of glass studded into the ceilings of the chambers It moves through. It knows this, as It knows the city. Its people, its histories, its crimes, its failings.

In a short while It will go and find the woman. She is in the dark too. She is lost in panic. But first It needs to spend time here. It needs to spend a little time here, every day.

It reaches out and touches Him. He is all around, but He is here most of all. It can see Him in the dark. It is His dark, as well as Its. More so. He made this dark. He breathed it. Fed it. Enlarged it. His blood and sweat and piss steamed in this dark. His teeth gritted in it, for it. His muscles bunched in it, under it, against it. His seed was nourished by this dark. By extension, so was It.

In the dark, Its fingers trace the flat contours of His face. In a time of happiness, of hope. Before His face was taken from Him. Before He became a part of the dark.

I STEPPED OFF AT ST. PAUL'S AND TOOK THE ESCALATORS UP to the exit. Outside, I felt the same lurching sense of diminishment I felt whenever I exited the Tube. Down there was all about suffocation, enclosure; the compression of air, time and space. Then suddenly you found yourself thrown into the space of the big city, with the sky jetting off in every direction above you. I also felt slightly sick. I don't like it. I don't like it. The crush. The people breathing on you. The weight on the tunnels. One day it will all pile in. It will all collapse. I can see it. I experience it every time I'm down there. The underground knew about death. And I knew about death on the underground.

In 1999 fifty-four people had been crushed in a stampede into an access tunnel at Nyamiha station in Minsk. Rush hour on a February morning, 1975, at Platform Nine, the southbound terminus at Moorgate station, a train failed to stop and slammed into a dead wall, killing forty-three. Ninety-seven dead at Malbone Street, New York, 1918, when a driver lost control of his train. Line two of the Paris metro, 1903, eighty killed in an electrical fire that started in a driver's cab. This year, last week, fifteen dead when a train was derailed in the tunnel between Hampstead and Belsize Park. Death queued up with everyone else at the ticket booths. It hung around the platforms like a busker without any tunes to play. Sometimes it picked a train to travel on, with no particular destination in mind.

The dark seemed pegged back by the street lights; that enhanced my feelings of disorientation for a few moments, until I gathered myself and climbed the steps of Panyer Alley, which formed the entrance to the ghost complex of St. Paul's Shopping Center. Almost instantly, the sound of traffic behind me was sealed off, as if I'd pierced a bubble and was now protected from the outside world. And I knew something was intrinsically wrong, although I couldn't understand what. The black, chipboard barriers of condemned shops pressed in from the walkway. From the sodium lights that worked, only a thin, grainy relief was offered. Ahead, ravaged shrubs in perishing rubber pots rustled as breaths of wind swept into the open air sections of the complex. A figure wrapped in black clothes stepped out of nowhere, making me flinch. As she passed by, I saw her glance at me and pause as if to say something, but I didn't pay her too much attention, not when her face glistened like that.

I hurried on into a space adjacent to Paternoster Square. Although I felt smothered by the proximity of so much featureless concrete, the sky reared away from me, a paradox that made me feel even more desperate. A pub—The Master Gunner—sat squat and ugly to my right. Smeared shapes moved beyond the windows. I couldn't make out any faces that might have been watching for mine. I could smell piss and stale roast beef. One sign was left on the deserted shop fronts, grimly informing anybody who could be bothered that *Stage Door of Drury Lane* had once done business here. I was trying to work out if the shop was a hairdresser's or a florist's when I heard footsteps—a woman's footsteps ringing shrilly on the paved expanse beyond this last section of Panyer Alley.

I moved forward, bothered more than I should have been by the bulky swaddles of blankets tucked into the corners of landings on brief flights of stairs that seemed to go nowhere, or wadded beneath benches. To my left, one of the large paneled doors of St. Paul's Cathedral was rendered chalky and indistinct by spotlights. Bells in the clock tower pealed the hour. I felt utterly alone and exposed as I stepped into Paternoster Square. The owner of those determined footsteps was nowhere to be seen. The Square was host only to a few tired pigeons settling down to roost and one or two couples, too far off for closer inspection, heading towards the main streets, perhaps for a late after-work drink. Because I'd been striding so purposefully since disembarking, the lack of any discernible object to project my attentions upon—the necessity of waiting—made me realize the dislocation of my surroundings. I didn't know what to do. The cathedral was awash with ice-blue light. Though it was a major landmark, it had little influence on my bearings. The Square was a no-man's land bleached by arc lights. Beneath my feet, as silence crept through the courtyard, trains rumbled. It proved little comfort. I checked the note in my pocket. *Midnight, Paternoster Square.* I tried to remember where the note had come from, but my thoughts were too glassy. Every time I thought I was settling on something, it reflected my scrutiny back at me. Something wasn't right.

"Something isn't right," I confirmed to myself, and started to back away. The empty, black panels of glass that gave Bancroft House a punched-in, drained appearance took up the dead light from the globes scattered around the square. Denuded coppery nets hung limply from their posts on a dismal netball court that didn't seem capable of supporting the fun of fourteen laughing girls. It made me think of gallows. It made me think of bodies in abattoirs being opened up and left to bleed. A blue polythene bag rustled, trapped high in winter branches.

"I don't want to die here," I whispered to myself, as the top of a head became visible on the steps leading up from the cobbled path of St. Paul's Churchyard. For a lunatic split second I thought it must be a clergyman with his rosary beads, reciting the Paternoster Prayer. The head had been turned black by the backdrop of light. Hair created a wild halo that fussed with motes. As the arms cleared the top edge of the steps, I cleared my throat. "Nuala?" I whispered, hopefully. But of course it wasn't her. Nuala wouldn't mean to visit harm upon me. Nuala wouldn't be naked from the waist up, her breasts gleaming as if they carried their own light source. Nuala wouldn't be carrying a long, thick coil of chain. It couldn't be her.

I ran.

Clattering down the steps, I almost collided with a car—it wouldn't stop for me; there were no taxis or buses. I chanced a look back and found that she wasn't around, but I didn't want to wait to discover whether or not I'd imagined her. Across Newgate, I headed towards the gutted remains of Christchurch and crouched, hoping that I'd be invisible in the pool of dark between two rows of lights studded in the mulch by the pergolas.

When she appeared, a fluid spine of moving night, trickling down the steps towards me, my nerve broke and I backed away, stepping through the archway that brought me out onto a small path by the side of the Royal Mail sorting office. I thought about making a break for it, into open air, and just legging it down the main drag till I found life, hoping she wouldn't be able to catch me. Instead, not knowing where she might now be approaching from—I didn't want to find myself sprinting into a mouthful of whipped steel—I slunk back into the shadows tucked beneath the church's tower, folding myself into the spaces between moss-covered chunks of carved stone that had long been separated from their parent building. I hid my face. She came.

At one point, I could hear, along with the jangle of those chains against her scuffed leather trousers, her breathing. It seemed too even and self-conscious, almost as if it were regulated by something other than flesh and blood. I chanced a look just as a blur of black silver thrashed into the masonry by the side of my face. I saw sparks, felt a hot bite against my jawbone, and as she raised her hand again to take surer aim, I dived beneath her arm, scrabbling to my feet, at any moment expecting the full weight of that deadly loop to come crashing down on my skull. I glanced back as I moved away, which saved my life. I was able to move my face away from the strike, though the links bit into my shoulder, turning the entire top right quarter of my body into a fiery mass and dragging a yell out of me. Her grip on the chain relaxed and it coiled at my feet. The space in front of my eyes fogged over and I thought I was going to faint. I couldn't see her face. All I could see was that she was painted with oil, or grease, her hair plastered back from her head so that it resembled a helmet. I managed to stagger away, accelerating as my vision cleared, until I reached a corner of shade. She was collecting the chain into great swatches, swinging it lightly, giving it a rhythm that made me feel ill. It thumped against her thigh. I saw her crouch and put her hands against the ground, her face rearing back to look at the sky. Her breasts were covered with sweat or water and something else, tribal signs, swirls, something I didn't know, something utterly alien. Christ. It looked like she was sniffing the air for me.

Slowly, slowly, I crept from my corner of shadow and disappeared down the path up which she'd originally come. I started running, ducking into the entrance to the Royal Mail sorting bays and crossing into the car park next to St. Bartholomew's Hospital.

I hit Giltspur Street at full tilt, bearing down on Smithfield Market with an unbidden image in my mind of flayed red corpses twisting on their hooks, their shrieks and the squeal of chains canceling each other out. I didn't stop till I'd reached Farringdon Tube. Passing through the ticket barrier and feeling drawn down into that musty warmth, I closed my eyes and imagined I was insubstantial as smoke, inhaled into lungs, where I lost my shape and color and just became a part of something greater. The comfort I sustained from this depth surprised me, although something about it unnerved me too.

I didn't look at anyone else. I tried to think about the flowers at the stall, but, like them, my thoughts wouldn't bloom. Nearing Camden I started to get edgy, so I got off and stood at the fork in the road that separated the routes to High Barnet and Edgware. Going home seemed too dangerous.

She answered on the third ring.

"Will you meet me?"

"Sure, Adam. Where are you?"

"I'm in Camden. You know Elodie's? The wine bar?"

"On Pratt Street? For sure."

"There. Come quickly."

"But Adam... what's wro—"

I hung up.

ELODIE'S WAS COLD AND UNWELCOMING, ALMOST EMPTY. The light was subdued. A few office types were emptying a bottle of champagne and drunkenly pondering their mobile phone screens. A barman with a ponytail checked his face in the mirror once or twice a second and ran a cloth over the spotless bar, tidied a small column of beer mats, shook peanuts into dishes. On the odd occasion that somebody approached him for a drink, he looked utterly out of his depth, as if he'd been casually asked to perform a tracheotomy. I decided to screw him up completely and complained about the floaters in my glass of wine. While he was dithering over whether or not to talk to the manager or pour me a fresh glass on his own initiative, Nuala walked in.

"Make that two," she called out, which threw him even further. I had to laugh, but it had too much of an edge to it. Nuala didn't know me—or rather, didn't know my laugh well enough—to pick up on it.

"Hark at you. On the phone you sounded like someone had been holding a blowtorch to your groin. Or is that just your charming telephone manner?"

"I need to talk to you. To a friendly face." Now she recognized the strain in my voice and all the mischief in hers vanished. We took our drinks back to my table, which was as far away from the other drinkers as possible. Maybe it was this distance, or the state of my voice (and my appearance too—in the bar's mirror I looked as pale as the mayonnaise that came with the chips) that triggered her questions. I held my hand up to stem their dizzying flow. I answered the last one before going on with my story.

"No, I'm not sick. Someone tried to kill me tonight."

"You are joking, of course." Her own expression answered that one for her.

I told her everything.

"Are you sure she wanted to kill you?"

"Come on, Nuala. She was carrying a fucking weapon. She was there at midnight as specified on the note. She came after me. Swinging a chain. Look at my face." I pointed out a thin red weal and some tiny black specks, which must have been caused by the sparks when the metal impacted against the stone. I showed her my shoulder, which sported an ugly red track of small ovals, already turning black.

"Who was it?"

"I don't know. I couldn't see her face. God, I'm not even convinced she had one."

Her expression didn't change. She was obviously still skeptical, despite my wounds. I drained my glass and went back to the bar without asking her if she wanted another.

The barman did a good job this time. I was mildly concerned by the urge I had to pan his face in though. I grappled with my frustration on my way back to the table. Nuala had lit up a menthol cigarette. I could see the spine of a book peeking out from the lips of her bag. *...ing The Commotion of an Inner Traveller* I read. She fiddled with a friendship ring on her finger. Yin and Yang glittered in her earlobes. God, did I want to fuck her so badly.

"Believe me," I said. "This happened. This is real. Somebody wants me dead."

"Come on Adam. Don't get down on this. It was an isolated event. She was a mugger, you were in the wrong place at the wrong time. Think yourself lucky you got away." She shook her head and blew out some air to illustrate just how lucky I'd been.

"Naked. She was fucking *half-naked*."

"She was on drugs. She's insane. I don't know."

"So you're saying I'm imagining things?"

"I'm not saying anything," she said.

"For someone who isn't saying anything, you're flapping your lips quite a bit."

Silence. Silence. Silence.

I wanted to apologize. Instead I said, "But she wanted me there. The note—"

She gestured: *let's have a look at it then.*

I fished the crumpled fragment of paper from my pocket and smoothed it out on the table for her to read.

"Who gave you this?"

"Initially, I thought it was you. I thought you'd slipped it into my pocket after we fell out yesterday. When I was filling your kitchen with disagreeable humors."

"We didn't fall out. You might have fallen out with me but I certainly didn't fall out with you."

"Whatever, Nuala. Look, that isn't important...."

"Oh, it isn't impor—"

"Well of course it's important, but we aren't talking about that at the moment, are we? The truth is, I don't know who gave me that note. I just found it in my pocket and thought it was you put it there."

"Somebody gave it to you, the night you walked out on me. Wherever it was you went."

I stared at her blankly. That night was still a dead spot in my memory. A cold ripple moved through me.

"Maybe," she said gently, "you went to Laura's house—I know you deny that—and just blocked it out of your mind. Too painful." Laura. Laura. The name made about as much impact upon me as an ash bullet. Laura. I forced memories of her through my head. Playing chess in the nude as slivered summer sunshine flashed through the blinds; getting stoned out of our heads and nipping out for a curry that took us about three minutes to eat; wrapped in a duvet sharing the same heavy cold and the same Patrick McGrath novel throughout a weekend of rain.

"I don't care about Laura. Well, I do, but not in that way. Not anymore. She means absolutely nothing to me any more." I meant it. I couldn't understand why, remembering the dread I felt every time I re-enacted her dismissal of me.

"Oh Adam, that's an absolute lie."

"It isn't. Honestly. I think of her and it's just... I could be thinking of a plate of cold porridge."

"You're in denial. It's okay. It's natural."

"I'm not in denial. Look, I've got narcolepsy. There, I said it. It's out. I've got narcolepsy and I don't know what the fuck is happening to me at the moment. I've got black spots. Dead gaps in my memory. Great chunks of time go by when I don't know where I am, what I'm doing, or who I'm with."

More silence. I felt as if we were collecting it.

"I can't go home tonight," I said. "It's too dangerous. She might know... Jesus, she *must* know where I live. She could be there now—"

"Enough. We'll go to mine." Her voice had softened. It didn't calm me.

"But that's my place too, practically."

She reached out and held my hand, stroked the skin on my wrist. "It's okay," she said. "It's okay."

I wanted to hug her. And then I was, hugging her tightly, like I used to hug my mother when I'd hurt myself, or hurt her.

We went outside and she hailed a cab.

"Nice uniform, by the way," she said. "You look like a piece of shit on its way to an interview."

I couldn't stop laughing. I laughed even as she bundled me into the taxi and headed north. Before long, Nuala was laughing too. And the driver. We laughed so much.

# CHAPTER THIRTEEN

## OUBLIETTE

"What do you hate?"

"Pardon me?"

*"Hate."* H said the word as if it had only recently been introduced into his vocabulary. His voice rushed out of the receiver and into my ear like a torrent of clicking beetles. I looked over at Nuala and she shrugged, smiled, mouthed: *Humor him.*

We were sitting on a thick blue rug in the center of her living room. She had put on a Harold Budd record and gone to make a pot of jasmine tea when the telephone had rung. Light seesawed languidly upon the walls, reflected off the turning vinyl. Old orange Penguin paperbacks were spread across a coffee table, along with a clutch of CDs: Four Tet, John Parish, Stina Nordenstam, Bill Laswell.

I tried to imagine what H looked like, just from the sound of his voice. I saw sleepily intelligent eyes, a large mouth, plump lips, Jack Palance cheekbones. His soft voice was mesmerising. A cat shifted from beneath the droop of a yucca leaf. Arching, it considered me imperiously before slouching towards the kitchen.

"Manchester United," I said. "People who use the phrase *mea culpa.* People who put those bull bars on the front of their 4x4s. People who drive 4x4s. Coriander. Call waiting. Public transport. England in a penalty shoot-out. People who smoke when I'm eating. The Americanization of this country. Old people paying for groceries at the supermarket till with small change. Nearly Nude nail varnish. Ewoks. Having to pay to use a toilet...."

"Okay," he said, and his voice sounded suddenly clear, free of static, as if he was sitting at my shoulder. I actually looked behind me. Nuala was standing there with a teapot. She had undressed and was wearing a large white T-shirt and lots of leg. "Now," he said. "What do you love?"

"My parents," I said, coming right back at him. And then I halted, my mind blank. In my mind I studied his face again, the narrow nose with the flared nostrils, the wolfish mouth, the Slavic sweeps of bone and soft, feminine eyes. Lots of white. Lots of eyelash.

"See?" said H.

I couldn't see. I didn't know what he was getting at. I was surprised he was so animated at four-forty in the morning.

"I'm just proving how negative everyone is," he said. "It's easy for us to reel off what we hate, what gets our backs up. Not so easy to list what we care about. Mainly because there ain't so much love going around."

He sounded like a DJ, nothing but soundbites and tenuous links. I kept expecting him to say: *Okay, it's twenty before the hour, let's have three in a row from Sting.* I was too tired to argue, but I didn't need to; Nuala protested on my behalf, taking the phone from me and replacing it with a white china cup the size of a chamber pot. I sipped my tea and signaled to the cat, but its face was planted in a bowl. Nuala was saying "no" repeatedly, her face becoming more and more drawn. "I can't," she said. "Not now. Not yet."

Embarrassed by what appeared to be an intimate conversation, I found myself drawn to the fireplace, even though it wasn't lit and there was nothing of interest there, beyond a porcelain phrenology head. I think it was the dark; its sooty promise of warmth and camouflage. I sprawled against the rug, straining towards the clinging nests of dust and grime on the intricate scrolls of ironwork. They gleamed like clustered spiders' eyes. I slept there, haunted by flashing images of windows backlit by white and stained by trapped figures, burning, trying to escape the thin barriers of glass. Tubes and tunnels and caves vanished away beneath me to similar ink-spots of infinity, all of them vying to suck my dangling shape into their eternity. The perfect meld of steel wheels on track spat blue ghosts into my eyes. At once, this was the most alien place of my three-decade span and the most comforting. I heard the chunter of carriages and couldn't tell if it was echoing the sound of my heart or vice versa. Looking down, I found that the skin of my arms was peeled back to reveal a juicy knit of veins and muscles. From the core meat of both, an artery snaked, plugged into the scorched cables that fled along the Tubeways. We sustained and weakened each other with each beat. I belched and farted clouds of black oilsmoke. Sparks wept from my eyes. I came a torrent of marbled electricity. The walls and wires grew slick with mucus and blood. When the trains arrived, powering towards me from all sides, we impacted to nothing: a universe folding in on itself. I came out of sleep mewling like a newborn, my wrists married, thrust forward as if I were imploring someone unseen to drive needles into them.

The living room was empty. A stiletto of morning sunlight impaled the floorboards by my feet. I could hear Nuala's voice in her bedroom, murmurs streaked with the same urgency she had displayed the previous night. I knocked lightly on the door and wiped the sweat from my face. Nuala was sitting cross-legged on the bed, stroking the cat. They both looked up at me when I entered, indulgent expressions on their faces as if I were a little boy they'd allowed to stay up late. Nuala killed the link and tossed the phone on to the pillow.

"I'll be off then," I said. "Thanks for letting me stay."

"Where will you go?" Nuala asked. "Do you think you might go to the police?"

I didn't know where I was going to go. I shrugged, wanting to ask if she'd come out for breakfast with me. Wanting to get onto the bed and remind myself just how long her legs were. She leaned back and the T-shirt rode up her belly. She was wearing a plain white thong. Through the sheer fabric I could see she had trimmed her pubic fuzz: no topiary; just a neat little short, back and sides. She smiled at me. Turned over. The white string split her plump, smooth bottom into two perfect halves. "I could do with a massage," she said.

"Who am I to argue with that?" I said, shrugging off my jacket.

ON THE WAY TO THE FLOWER STALL I WENT OUT OF MY WAY to walk past Laura's house. Her car was parked on the street but my heart didn't lurch at the thought of her sitting topless behind those blinds, maybe drinking a glass of orange juice and eating toast, reading a magazine on the floor. I considered knocking on the door and saying hello but it was all still a little too close; she might have thought I was coming to beg that we get back together. But I was healing. I was coming back from the brink.

The flower stall was as I'd left it: shuttered up, a sign on the front saying CLOSED. Cherry had left me a message: "We sold our entire load of geraniums despite you and your *geraniums to wow your cranium.* And the fact that they are all, without exception, buggered to buggery. Well done that chapster."

Lucas, the *Big Issue* man, was drinking coffee from a Styrofoam cup. He waved when he saw me. Even though I hadn't seen him for a couple of days, there was something about him that seemed new. Something new but deeply familiar, like seeing your dad wearing a tie that you'd only ever seen him wear in old photographs. It put me off my guard for a moment, and I wanted to call his name, but another name, one I couldn't articulate, leapt to my lips.

I bought a *Big Issue* from him and he asked me if I wanted to go to a party. I recognized something in the way I was looking at him in his own appreciation of me. Something a little bit desperate. I said, sure. He told me where to meet him and at what time. I said I would see him there. And then I ducked down into the Tube before I realized what I was doing and caught a train home. In the carriage, I suddenly felt safe, certain that my attacker wouldn't be here. And even if she had been, she couldn't do anything in front of all these people. At Tufnell Park, I pushed my way through the passengers to the doors and was standing on the platform when I saw two further instances of the logo I had first seen the night Nuala moved in. One was scratched on the glass of the carriage I had just vacated; the other had been painted with green nail polish onto a poster advertising mobile phones.

Back home I retrieved a warm beer from the cupboard and gulped it in front of the window. The slow bleed of light across the rooftops at this hour really was lovely, I decided. The next thing I was aware of was lying on my bed, the telephone insistent. I checked my watch, fearful I was late for Lucas' party, but it was only six. It seemed terribly important that I go, even though it was just a party. Just Lucas. I reached out and pulled the telephone down beside me. It was nice there in the dark.

"Finally plucked up courage to head back to the nest?" Nuala asked. Her voice seemed nearer than it ought to be.

"Yeah," I said. "Wasn't such a great leap though, was it? I'm sorry for being such a pussy."

"Forget it," she said. "It was nice to have you stay."

"H wasn't, you know...?"

"Jealous? No. I think he gets off on the idea of me and other men. I think it's all a big effort for him, a distraction, and the more help he gets, the better."

"Look, I'm going to a party tonight. Want to come?" I didn't really want her there but the question blurted out. I knew I was asking her because she had this kind of charmed effect on me, like some celestial bodyguard. I had the feeling that nothing could happen to me with her around.

"What? Last night almost dead, tonight let's have fun?"

"Why not? If you can't go to a party to celebrate surviving a murder attempt, when can you go?"

She said that if she was going to come along, she'd meet me at the party. She wasn't promising anything.

I could handle that. I put the phone down and sank my head into the fluff, the Toffo wrappers and the empty cans of Kronenbourg on my carpet for a few minutes. Thoughts of getting sticky with Nuala, nice though it was, even without H's periodic insertions, didn't do anything for me. Everything that had once excited me was losing its sheen. I wanted nothing, looked forward to nothing. Except sleep. And the places I went to when I dreamed. The places everyone else went to seemed so much brighter than mine.

Somehow I got to Shepherd's Bush, although every changed Tube train, every wait on a platform found me huddling deeper into myself. It was as if I felt I needed to be anonymous, needing to bury my conscious self as completely as possible before I could function. The light was too great; the babble of voices around me too constant and invasive. Nevertheless, I was recognizing a change in me. The Tube no longer repulsed me, scared me as it had once done. Now it seemed to be the safest place around. Its warmth and closeness were something to be embraced, rather than avoided. Suddenly, all the space and choice that span around up top was too great. It seemed ludicrous that small bodies should be allowed to exist in such an expanse. It didn't seem right. Being down here with the worms now made much more sense.

It took about half an hour to get to the party venue. Lucas was waiting outside, in a dark blue fleece: his eyes glittered like turning shreds of silver inside his hood. "Made it then?" he said, unnecessarily.

"Looks that way," I returned. Equally dumb.

"Shall we?" he asked, nodding his head towards the library on the corner of Pennard Road. I couldn't hear any music.

"Rude not to."

He led the way into the street, the houses of which backed onto the market beneath the railway bridge. Halfway down, he slipped through a gate and rang a bell. There were no lights on in the house. I looked around in case Nuala had decided to make an appearance, but the street was filled only with nose-to-tail parked cars. The small of my back grew cold and sticky. After a long time—I twice stopped myself drawing him away in favor of the pub—a figure coalesced in the dimpled frost of the door's glass panels. It stood there a while, gently seething, and I tried to make out the pattern and sex of its face, then the door was swinging open—a female smiling and beckoning us in.

"I'm Maureen," she said. Her fingernails scored blue-white light in the grainy dark of the hall: stray light catching on the steel hoops shot through each cuticle. She smelled of mint, grass and burnt milk. Or was that the house? I was too intent on following Lucas' feet to work it out.

At the end of the hallway we turned sharp right. Maureen pulled back a curtain and ushered us through into a cubbyhole beneath the stairs. I went, not because I was comfortable with the situation but because the other option, moving into the kitchen, was a no go: three shapes huddled around a table eating very loudly in the dark. All I could hear was the scrape of cutlery on plates and wet, mulchy sounds. I felt faint, but kept it together.

Maureen bent and fiddled with something on the floor and I was jolted out of my queasiness as a large disc of wood swung up, the gap it created immediately filling with a shaft of smoky light. Now, music... thin, bitter and wintry, skittering out of the hole like a host of spiders. We went through the floor via an aluminium chain-link ladder. In the basement, I felt much more comfortable; the mystery was over: it was just a party after all. A ragged sofa spilled sponge and people out of its sagging middle. All eyes turned to us as we moved into the small crowd. There was an equal spread of men and women; every now and then, as we approached the makeshift bar—a plank of wood resting on two beer barrels—I thought I recognized a face or the way someone spoke, or the way a person moved his or her head. Again I searched for Nuala, but half-heartedly. I doubted she'd come in without me, or a direct invitation.

Lucas passed me a beer and we moved towards the sound system, stepping over people or ducking the outcrops of masonry. A woman drinking from a bottle of cider frowned almost imperceptibly when I caught her eye. I smiled at her and she smiled back, then withdrew into the black stole wrapped around her shoulders and the man who held it.

"Who's she?" I asked Lucas.

"Dunno, but she looks familiar. Maybe she reads the regional news on TV. Come on, let's see if we can get some more beers that are colder than this piss."

"Do you know anyone here?"

"Of course. How would I know about it if nobody invited me? Relax, will you?"

Lucas had a word with the DJ, who was standing behind his turntable and speakers like someone from an underground organization about to make a speech. His face was as stiff as a mask as he put on some more of the brittle, discomfiting music—which I now recognized as Triangle—that only helped to increase the oddity of the atmosphere. There was a large metal bathtub behind the DJ filled with ice. Bottlenecks poked out of it.

"Someone tried to kill me last night," I found myself saying to Lucas, even though I hardly knew him. The compulsion to do so came from a tricky part of me that wanted to gauge his reaction, almost as if I suspected him for the attempt on my life.

He didn't look shocked, but some people never do. He swigged on his beer and suggested I paid. I handed some money over to the DJ and took a long pull on my own bottle, relishing the cold that somehow helped to push back some of the strangeness of our surroundings. Just a cellar. Just people. No reason to feel so edgy.

"People get killed every day. I could take you to meet friends of mine, in this city, who have witnessed murders."

"Sorry," I said, not exactly sure why.

He nodded, then shrugged. "S'okay," he said. "People die. I need to go to the bog. Look out."

I watched him snake through the tight knots of bodies towards a misted patio window. Then he was gone, into the basement garden, which I could see nothing of, though I could hear a fountain splashing into a pond.

I finished my beer and paid for another and then went for a wander around. Everyone was air kissing everyone else. Or exchanging business cards. Or whispering. Whenever I tried to make inroads on someone's conversation the three or four would move closer together. One guy wearing a bandanna and reflective shades and a goatee even apologized before standing right in front of me.

Lucas was taking his time.

I was looking at the non-existent pictures on the wall when I felt someone grip my arm. Before I had chance to turn and see who it was, she was drifting back into the shadows, her hair in her eyes but her eyes unblinking, upon me like chips of slate buried in ice.

I went to her—it was the woman in the stole—and she took my hand. Hers felt clammy and unclean. I looked down and it was coated with dust and grit. Her hair too was streaked with grime. I thought she must have crashed the party. Or just crashed.

"Raglan got you here, then." She pressed something cold and metallic and heavy into my hand. "You left this behind," she said.

She'd only given me a knife. A big bastard. "Behind where?" I asked, but she only shook her head. She kissed me on the mouth, so savagely it was almost an assault.

"Do the job," she said. "Get it finished."

The man she was with was chewing something. Gum, maybe. Maybe his own lip. "Vane! We have to go. Now."

"Get it finished," she said again, and: "There's rumor going round that he's using the dead zones when he's not pushing. Check them all. And watch out for his followers. He's recruiting more and more. At least a dozen now, that we know of." She smiled. Touched my face. "Don't stay up too long." And then she hurried away with her partner.

I made to follow, confused, scared, but Lucas was back, telling me to calm it or we'd get thrown out. He bundled me into the garden and sat me by the pond. In the light from the underwater spots, I could see the word *Monck* inscribed on the wooden handle of the knife. The name tickled at something at the back of my head. Monck. Monck. I knew that name. The knife was an ugly thing with a fat, serrated blade. It was designed to kill things, simple as that. You didn't dice carrots with this fucker.

"Yours?" asked Lucas.

"It is now," I said. "But I don't want it. You want it?"

"Got my own. You should keep it. Self defense in case your friend has another go at you."

"Who was that woman?" I asked again, feeling with a warm thrill how the handle of the knife melded itself to my fingers, as if it had been fashioned with them in mind.

"I don't know," he said, and then: "but I kind of think I do. If that doesn't seem too weird."

"Me too," I said, noticing the way my pulse was tripping madly through my wrists. "Does the name Raglan mean anything to you?"

"Jesus," he said. "Yes, of course it does."

"What?"

He blinked. Opened his mouth. Shut it again. "I don't know. It feels like something half remembered. Like a word you know, on the tip of your tongue, but it won't come. It won't come."

I said: "Do you know a guy called Troake?" I don't know why I asked him that. How could he? Troake was from a different circle to Lucas', and the two weren't part of any Venn diagram.

"What's his real name?"

I stared at him. "What do you mean by that?"

Lucas laughed, somewhat scratchily. "I don't fucking know." We started drinking heavily then, partly to stop us from getting too weird with each other, but also to try to achieve a state in which we might be able to understand what we had been talking about. I certainly hadn't been dreaming the previous night, although I connected with Lucas' vagueness, remembering the night I'd spent with Nuala then gone for a walk, after which I couldn't remember a thing. Blaming it on narcolepsy didn't seem to be good enough anymore.

We split up at one point and I didn't see him again that night. Inside, the clusters of people had become warmer and more migratory and I moved among them, stopping here and there to make small talk.

"Hello. It's a hummingbird," said one girl. "I'm Pia. As in Zadora."

"As in Pakistan International Airlines?" I offered and, give her credit, she didn't tell me to fuck off.

"Don't I know you?" she tried, ladling on just the right amount of confused recognition to faze me utterly. Maybe she did and she was genuinely trying to fit a name to the face. Maybe she didn't and she wanted to fit her face to mine.

"Don't know any Pias," I said, thankfully binning my witty coda: *unless you count Brighton.* How much had I drunk? It obviously wasn't enough.

"I didn't ask if *you* knew *me*."

"Well," I said, losing my temper, "how am *I* supposed to *know* if *you* know *me*?"

"Good question. And I'm going to answer it by doing something I don't usually do."

"What?" I said. "By talking some sense?"

She kissed me. I saw her as though through a fisheye lens, her face enveloping mine: her eyes thick with kohl, growing concave and vulpine, her brownish mouth running to a slit, gumming at me like a fish at the hook. In the last moment I saw it broaden, her tongue slide forward as she moved against me. I felt her breasts, hard as rocks, crush against my chest. I went to raise my bottle to my lips, but my addled brain took some time realizing that they were already being used for something else.

When she'd finished, she moved away, her expression even more confused. "I *do* know you," she said. "I just can't place it. I've kissed you before. In the dark too. Which clubs do you go to?"

"I don't," I said. We laughed politely.

Something in her tenderness had struck a chord, but I was sure I'd remember such a full-on kiss as she'd just given. I felt more like somebody else, as if someone were borrowing my skin and I was a cipher for their experiences. She reminded me of someone, although she seemed removed from my immediate recognition of people. She was like someone I'd known many years ago, or someone I'd invented in a dream.

We talked a while longer—shared a few bottles of beer—and then she said something strange that nonetheless pressed a few buttons with me.

"I feel like I'm in a way station," she said.

"I know," I nodded. "But I don't know what we're supposed to be in between."

She laughed and kissed me again. Lucas still hadn't come back. Half-moons of filth were crammed beneath her nails. She was vampire-pale.

"Somebody gave me a knife," I said.

"Why doesn't that surprise me?"

"Not sure," I replied, a new wave of alcohol breaking itself upon the tide-worn shores of my head. "But it surprises the tits off me."

The party went on and people smeared into each other. I lost Pia to the stream of bodies. I thought I heard conversations about faces and rogues but when I merged with a group of intent-looking guests, they seemed to lose the thread of their involvement with each other. They looked suddenly lost, as if I were a fresh integer come to unsettle their code.

I heard the doorbell above the clamor and wondered if it was Nuala. I watched the hatch for signs of new arrivals but nobody came. I decided to go and investigate; if it wasn't Nuala, then it was time to go anyway. As I was climbing to ground level, the lights went off. I heard Pia's voice behind me: "Be careful, Monck!" Again, I experienced a strange little bend inside my head. I knew Pia, or at least I knew her by another name that I couldn't now place. I felt as if I knew her more deeply than I was letting on to myself. As if I had been involved with her—was still involved with her—at some secret level. And then I was in the hallway, and it was empty. Nobody shrugging off a coat and handing a bottle to the host. No sounds of drinks being prepared in the kitchen. There was a creak on the stairs.

I tried the hallway light but the power was still out. Beyond the opaque glass in the front door I could see the cut had reached further than this house. Car horns blared in the distance.

"Nuala?" I whispered.

Another creak. The sound of a door handle being turned. Footsteps on a carpet. Springs on a bed realigning themselves to the weight of someone sitting. The rasp of a match. Silence: the sound of someone waiting.

I was halfway up the stairs, my eyes becoming accustomed to the murk—framed photographs on the wall followed the angle of the stairway; a white dressing gown was hanging over the banister—when another, momentary, unmistakeable sound, that of a length of chain clinking against itself, unspooled across the landing.

I stopped and put out a hand. Smooth, cool wallpaper and the thrum of traffic, of cars and underground trains, moved through it, into me.

Without turning, I took a step back down the stairs. Beneath me I heard the hatch shift. More guests leaving, I hoped. "Monck," came the voice, crippled by the stuff it was drawing into its lungs. "The inbetweeners. There aren't that many of us around. The ones you met tonight: Raglan, Pia, even Vane, they're weak. This is your last chance."

I took another step. Stopped. Began to descend.

He said, "As you can see, it is easy to find you. So easy. It isn't just me looking for you. There are others. Think about that. Do you want to spend the rest of your life looking over your shoulder?" He said no more.

I lurched downstairs and stumbled over a couple having sex against the wall. I knocked over a telephone table. A plate smashed. Keys and coins rattled across the floorboards. I headed into a room next to the kitchen and stood still, trying to let peace return. But it wouldn't. Danger pressed in, as if this was some weird film set with collapsing walls. One moment I was standing in the center of a cluster of coats and murmurs, the next, I was

SCAMPERING ALONG THE TUNNEL, MONCK IGNORED THE litter ghosts rising on currents of warm air, the rats, the distant thunder of trains. His senses were primed for other, more subtle signals. His knife was out, though he couldn't remember where he'd come by it. He seemed to have been running for an age, but his lungs were up to it. The burn in them was a comfort to him. It meant life, after all. He'd stolen a ride from Lancaster Gate, train-surfing the Central Line to Holborn, where he had switched to this abandoned offshoot of the Piccadilly Line.

"Blore," he whispered, then louder: "Blore!" The name ricocheted lazily off the dirty, curved walls. There was no answer. He'd heard rumour that one of his lairs was down here, somewhere along the disused portion of tunnel that terminated at the dead station Aldwych. The only illumination came from the lamp clutched under his arm, filched from a worksite somewhere around Queensway; it spilled a manic, inaccurate clown light that picked out movement in the walls where Monck reasoned there could be none. His boots gritted in the dust-packed mess between the rails. He checked each emergency duct, each ventilation shaft. Most of them were tightly locked or nailed shut. Others had become nests for rats; he could see their baleful eyes fixing him when he stepped too close. It was unnerving, seeing such creatures display a total lack of concern for him. He hoped they would not be the only ones.

After another ten minutes of fruitless poking around, he was ready to give up on the tunnel, when he reached a short platform. The bull's-eye Tube sign on the wall read *Strand.* The platform was strewn with paint pots, brushes and rolls of masking tape. A ladder, a spirit level and several large plastic buckets had also been left behind. It looked as though the platform was still being used by Underground staff testing new finishes for Southwark station: a section of the naked wall had been filled in with *trompe l'oeils*: columns and freshly painted backgrounds with that station's Tube sign featuring predominantly. Part of the platform floor had been retiled with primrose and blue diamonds; part was a dark, military gray with pastel shades hop-scotching randomly through it. Something about the Tube stop's stillness, its unfinished appearance, its inbetween-ness, made him hang back awhile; he didn't like it. Blore's smell was all over the place.

Monck doused the lamp and allowed his eyes to become accustomed to the fresh dark. Stealthily, he leapt up onto the platform, removing the lamp from his shoulder and leaving it by the mouth of the tunnel. He edged forward, head cocked for new sounds that might alert him to Blore's presence.

Always moving, he left the exposed stretch of platform—buffers signaled the end of the line up ahead—and entered the corridor that led to a stairwell up to the surface. A door to his left swung on its hinges. The grime-encrusted sign on it read *Sub Station.* Inside, every surface was piled with about an inch of dust. A newspaper from 1979 celebrated the FA Cup final win by Arsenal over Manchester United. The walls were adorned with pictures of nude women with their names scrawled beneath in lurid green typefaces—Roberta Pedon, Uschi Digart, Janet Lupo—heavily breasted, heavily made-up, their hairstyles thirty years out of date: delta sweeps, held viciously fast by hairspray. *Does she or doesn't she?*

At the other end of the room was another door leading into a narrow corridor that rose at a steep angle to a walkway over the tunnel. The ceiling was spaghetti: defunct wires and cables that had once carried power. Without pause, he delved into the corridor and followed its path until his breath came in white gusts and his fingers turned numb. He could smell violence in the air. At the end of the corridor was a junction. He turned left and after fifty meters was met by a great clutter of folders, files and dented cabinets, chairs with broken casters, cracked desks. He doubled back and found himself flanked by large grilles that looked onto the tracks. He was standing on the ceiling of the station. Bending over, he found the desiccated remains of small mammals and doodles that had been scratched with chunks of glass into the paintwork of the corridor. Blore had been here, he knew it. But it was old Blore he was smelling. Smart man—he'd moved on.

In his anger and frustration, Monck pulled the knife from his waistband and drove it into the mesh. The squeal of metals greeting each other shivered away down the tunnel.

I CAUGHT THE TUBE TO ARCHWAY, GAZING OUT OF THE windows, as I usually did, for a glimpse of South Kentish Town's disused station as we rattled north, or maybe even the Fleet river, which the Tube stop straddled. Three figures, palely lit—maintenance men I assumed—watched the train go by the foot of a stairwell. I saw only the shape of their bodies: their heads had been twisted off by the dark.

There were thirty or forty of these limbo stations beneath the city. Lonely platforms, dead staircases, gutted lift shafts. Places that had once known thousands of feet a day now knew none, none that were human at least, beyond the plod of staff, or the occasional guided tour. This is how it used to be. This is how we were. How many more souterrains were there? How many more secrets could a city keep before it collapsed under the weight of them all? How strong could a city built on a honeycomb be?

Thinking about Tube stations had led to me thinking about Greg. Greg was an irritating traveler to accompany. He ran everywhere when he was underground, possibly to show off his knowledge of the labyrinth. He never consulted a member of staff, or a Tube map. He always knew which carriage to stand in front of at one station in order to be nearest to the exit at his destination. He trotted up and down the escalators. He never took a seat, either on the platform or on the train, even if the carriages were empty. He charged for trains when their doors were closing. I had been left behind on many occasions.

I'd been worried about Greg ever since receiving that letter from him. It seemed too jolly, too over-the-top excited with life. He hadn't called me for breakfast, he hadn't called to crow about his experiences at the Groucho with producers and celebrities. I was beginning to miss his crude humor and the hilarious air of other-worldliness he carried about him.

I ascended into the clamor and mess of the busy intersection outside the Tube station, reminded that I'd never been to visit Greg at his flat before. It didn't feel right to just drop in on people in London. You tended to wait for an invitation: the distance you traveled to a friend's was too great to risk when they might be out.

The Archway Tavern sat like a toad in the center of a polluted millpond; Highgate Hill was abuzz with traffic. The Pit Stop was quiet, and I thought about popping in to see if Meddie was around. But Greg was filling my thoughts, and I had to see if he was okay. I would see Meddie at work soon enough. I crossed the street and headed down Holloway Road.

Maybe he'd never invited me because this wasn't Islington or Hampstead or Chelsea. The thought of him stepping out in his Oakley sunglasses and Hugo Boss shirt seemed absurd here, where an ironed T-shirt and jeans might turn your head.

His flat, I saw, was above a fish and chip shop. You had to nip down a dingy side-alley to get to the entrance. I buzzed him and waited. The swine was out, it seemed. I was about to leave him a note when his voice chirred through the battered intercom:

"Hoozit?" He sounded slurred, drugged.

"Greg? It's me. Adam."

"Adam? Oh God, Adam." Silence.

I might have left him alone; he sounded drunk and lonely, as if he was having a few bleak moments of a much-needed reality check. But there was a ring in his voice that I didn't like. He was close to an edge of some sort, I could tell. I pushed against the door, it was flimsy as hell, so I kicked at it until the Yale lock burst from the wood. I climbed a narrow staircase clogged with junk mail and free tabloids. Food had been trodden into the carpet, deep red stains—wine, I guessed—splashed up the walls. There was a butcher shop smell: mealy and rank.

He was at the frosted door at the top, peering around it. The grainy stink of whisky powered off him.

"You okay?" I asked.

He didn't reply. He left the door open and shuffled back into the shadows.

"Hey," I said. "You didn't need to clean up on my behalf, really."

You had to get through the kitchen to his living room. He'd traversed it pretty quickly, despite the state of him, but I was a little more circumspect, stepping over plates against which cutlery was fused by weeks-old food. Mold rioted in the wash basin. Empty glasses on tables were furred with dust and tinges of dull color. A clutch of drained whisky, wine and vodka bottles stood open-mouthed by the entrance to his bathroom. I daren't look in there; the smell drifting from it was cheesy and intense. I stepped into the living room. More of the same in here. Cartons and pizza boxes had replaced the crockery, which must have run out days before. Greg was perched on the corner of the bed, dressed in his bathrobe. His left leg he lifted gingerly a few inches off the floor every few seconds. On his bedside table lay his mobile. Its face was peeling off: plastic, a toy. Net curtains swooned sluggishly against the open windows, caked with street grime. Everything seemed brown, including my friend.

"Are you all right?" I asked, wishing for a sound other than the traffic outside. I doubted we'd be able to enjoy any music from the radio or a burbling TV. I was sure there'd be a stack of unpaid electricity bills among the unopened mail downstairs.

"Not really. Stood on a piece of broken glass the other day. You wouldn't have a look at the bastard for me, would you?"

"Yeah, sure. Lie back."

He reclined on the bed and lifted his foot towards me, grunting with the pain.

"Jesus fuck, Greg!" I said. "Why didn't you get this seen to?" The sole of his foot had become swollen and was turning black. A large jagged wound was dribbling pus. It reeked of sour rot.

He started to cry.

I swallowed and went to the bathroom after all. The toilet was blocked and brimming. He'd taken to shitting in the bath. Christ, what was wrong with him? The mirrors on the medicine cabinet over the sink were smeared with grease and blood. Inside there was a bottle of kaolin and morphine; time and disuse had separated them off into a thick white silt-like deposit and a clear liquid. Behind that was a box of sticking plasters, a pot of Nivea hand cream and a small bottle of Dettol. There were some bandages in a small compartment. I took them back and drew some water from the tap into a bowl, added a few capfuls of Dettol and soaked a wad of bandage in it.

"Greg, mate, this is going to smart like fury. I hope. If it doesn't, you're up shit street." I pressed the bandage into the wound and Greg's head nearly came off. I cleaned it as best I could, then dried it on some more bandage, and wrapped it in the last few clean lengths that were left.

"What's happening to you, Greg?"

"It's not what's happening to me," he said, almost violently. "Take a look at the street out there. That's supposed to be sustaining us. The city. Our foundation. What hope have we got, our puny bodies, if the stone and cement and concrete of the city crumbles? It's all shit."

I stared at him. "Is that from your latest script?"

He balked. "Tell me you don't think I'm right."

"I don't think you're right."

"Then you're in an even worse state than I am."

"Yeah," I said. "I'll not be staying long. I've got to get home and have another dump in the washing machine."

He was crying again, although he didn't seem to notice. "I haven't made a dent in anything I've ever tried to do," he said. "I couldn't finish my script. I couldn't even start the fucker. The agents I talk to don't want to know. I've never... *I've never been to Groucho's!*"

"What about the girls?" I said, trying to find him a fillip. "All those girls?"

"There weren't any girls. I made it all up."

I knew that, and I almost said that he'd fooled me, that his fiction couldn't be all that bad.

"This isn't a fucking comedy, you know," he spat. "I'm opting out. I'm sick of the rat race, the constant pressure to succeed, to prove yourself. All your life people expect things of you. Teachers, employers, parents, lovers, friends. Religion, for fuck's sake! Thou shalt believe in God Almighty or you're fucked good and proper, son. Well fuck it, that's what I say. I'm canceling my subscription."

"Still, Greg. You've got to clean yourself up. You're in a hell of a mess."

"Why? Why do I have to clean myself up? Because in order to be a respectable, respected member of society I have to look clean and smart?

Because if I don't, I'm somehow less of a person?"

I didn't say anything. This wasn't going as I'd expected. Greg had knocked me for six with all this talk, with all this squalor. He was suddenly someone I didn't know very well.

"So be it," he said, absently picking at a scabby patch of dried fluid on the mattress. "I'm a social leper. Great."

I sat down on the corner of a table. Paperbacks oozed from a cardboard box by the bed. Empty bottles of Lamot lager were lined alongside the radiator, lots of them. I wondered how long Greg had lived his charade, and tried not to judge him too harshly by it. My life was hardly better. The thing was, this was the person who had shaped my London life, who had turned an urbane cheek whenever we dined at a Michelin-starred restaurant or tried out a Thames-side bar. I'd be thinking hello, how metropolitan, when he'd be inclined to comment upon how boring it all was, how contrived.

I made to go. I didn't know what else I could do.

"Adam," he said.

"What?"

"Leave the city, before it claims you. Before it sucks you under. Before... before it hurts you."

"Yeah, yeah, yeah."

"Adam."

"Yes, Greg?" I wanted him to ask for help, to at least ask me to go to the offy and get him a bottle of Absolut. His face was wobbling. He looked afraid.

"Claire's parents were killed in a car crash last week. The funeral's tomorrow. Will you go?"

"God," I said. And then: "Why don't you go?"

He made a frail gesture at himself. "*I can't*," he gargled, shaking with anger, with his impotence.

"I'll do it," I said.

I THOUGHT GREG WAS BEING UNFAIR.

I loved the city. I loved the way it could surprise me. Once I'd driven along Burnt Ash Road, miles south of the city center, and seen Canary Wharf in the dip of a hill between the trees, like a portentous tower in a fantasy novel. Another time I'd stepped out of an Indian restaurant on Westow Hill and, looking north along Beardell Street, I'd been startled by the bowl of the capital and the gray template of the buildings within it. I loved the eccentrics and the rare, visceral promise of danger. I loved coming back from a long journey and seeing its ghostly towers become solid on the skyline. I didn't love it unconditionally. Sometimes it tried my patience; its traffic, its arrogant or diffident citizens, its stink and clutter. But then there'd come a day when I'd pull back the curtains to see an odd light spilling out of the clouds and into the city's heart, making everything fresh, innocent and welcoming. Drivers would smile at you as they waved you across the street. If you were lost, someone would stop and ask if they could help.

London was like a tightly curled cat. Stroke it in the right places and it would open itself to you.

I HADN'T TALKED TO CLAIRE FOR YEARS. I HALF EXPECTED her to say "Adam? Adam who?" when I rang about the arrangements. But no, she remembered me with a genuine happiness that made me feel better, despite the circumstances of my telephone call. She told me where the funeral was to be held and I said yes, yes I knew where that was, even though I didn't have a clue because I had to get off the phone fast. I was crying and I didn't want to have to struggle through the awkward quiz show of her giving me directions.

She was so nice, Claire. We used to send each other mock insults on the Quickmail, a daft game to rescue ourselves from the monotony of the office. She spoke about her parents often, as I remembered. Her father, Dennis, had been a mathematics teacher who never concealed his disappointment that Claire had been born a girl. It never really stopped him from trying to coax her into the spheres he'd missed out on as a child: he bullied her into playing tennis from the age of three. She'd been good, good enough to play for her county, but even this had turned out to be a disappointment to him. Her mother, Karen, had been softer, more acquiescent. She'd harbored a quiet wisdom where Claire was concerned, had known that she'd finally rebel against her father's ambitions for her and go her own way. It happened, too, although Claire would tell me that she hadn't been able to make a complete break, that she was somehow destined to follow her father into teaching. Well, now she could do it without suffering any indignation on his part.

I splashed cold water on my face and went to the fridge. I gazed at the beer there, thought of Greg, and opened one anyway. Marlon jumped on to the windowsill and looked at me in such a way as to suggest that if I didn't open the window for me, he'd headbutt it in.

"Come on then, big lad," I said. He wore an expression of psychotic calm, like the guys you see leaning nonchalantly against the wall in a nightclub, eyes sleepily waiting for violence. All Marlon needed was some gum to chew. He muscled by me, granting me a glance at his puckered bum hole, before giving my living room the once over and looking back at me, surprised and disgusted that I was still around. Or that I hadn't offered him a Grolsch.

I tried to sit him on my knee but he wasn't into that idea. I think he was keen to try it the other way round. He took a swipe at me—claws retracted, nice guy—and wandered off to sniff the cuff of my jacket before leaving me alone in the living room. I did some bachelor stuff, just to get the practice in. Switched on the television, fetched another beer, spread the sports pages out on the floor. Farted prodigiously. I swore a few times too, for good measure.

There was a natural history documentary showing, all about parasites. I watched some guy delicately winding a guinea worm onto a matchstick, teasing it from a hole it had bored out of his leg, which it had done in order to release larvae. The guy was saying that he could only pull out a little each day and that, if the worm broke, its head would remain embedded in his leg for ever. Some worms were as long as 120 centimeters. I turned the television off, suddenly queasy.

A few beers later, I pulled out a photograph album from the bottom of my suitcase. Me and Laura. Laura and me. Me and Mum. Mum and Me. One of the pictures—Laura sitting behind me on one of the cannons on Gun Hill, Southwold, her arms loosely clasped around my neck—didn't seem quite right; it bulged out slightly. I peeled back the protective film and a note fell out from behind the print. It seemed half finished, unsigned, as if she was writing a draft for something more substantial, a dry run for the way it would all pan out.

It said: *I love you, but I can't see how this will work. You're there, but you're not there. There's no depth to you.*

# PART TWO

## INNER CITY

Egnaro is a secret known to everyone but yourself.

It is a country or a city to which you have never been; it is an unknown language. At the same time it is like being cuckolded, or plotted against. It is part of the universe of events which will never wholly reveal itself to you: a conspiracy the barest outline of which, once visible, will gall you for ever.

M. John Harrison, *Egnaro*

⇨ ⇨ ⇨

We run through the unknown, among the foundations of the city. At first we are buried in thick darkness, then we see for an instant the dim light of day, and again plunge into obscurity, broken here and there by strange glowings; then between the thousand lights of a station, which appears and disappears in an instant; trains passing unseen; next an unexpected stop, the thousand faces of the waiting crowd, lit up as by the reflection of a fire, and then off again in the midst of a deafening din of slamming doors, ringing bells, and snorting steam; now more darkness, trains and streaks of daylight, more lighted stations, more crowds passing, approaching, and vanishing, until we reach the last station; I jump down; the train disappears, I am shoved through a door, half carried up a stairway, and find myself in daylight. But where? What city is this?

Edmondo de Amicis, *Jottings About London* (trans)

⇨ ⇨ ⇨

Everybody's saying that hell's the hippest way to go,
Well, I don't think so,
But I'm going to take a look around it...

Joni Mitchell, *Blue*

# CHAPTER FOURTEEN

## WRULD

Orange and blue in the streets at this hour. This sorry hour. I'd decided to borrow a car. Nuala complied, tossing the keys from her window, a curtain wrapped around her, her shadow swarming behind in the light of a candle. It was far too big for one person. I guessed H was knotted to her, making imperceptible lunges, thinking of higher planes, Karmic bliss, cricket scores, burning babies....

I hadn't really expected Nuala to own a car, being such a friend to the environment. But she'd agreed soon enough when I asked her from the freezing cold of the pavement at dawn.

"It's parked down the road, opposite the pub," she said, her eyes shut. She licked her lips expansively. "It's green."

No surprise there, then.

I was expecting something acquiescent; Nuala was no more likely to succumb to road rage than to start harpooning whales. A 2CV, I thought. A Mini. A rickshaw.

There was only one green car parked by the pub, although I had to squint to make sure in the thin light. Everything appeared monochrome. But no, it must be this one. A squat, predatory Beemer. I slipped the key in, half-expecting an alarm to knock me off my feet. Inside, I felt like a little child who had wandered off from his parents in a shopping mall and got lost. Everything was so big.

Once I'd worked out where all the important buttons and switches were, I gunned the engine and flipped through the road map, relaxing as warmth eased into the... well, it seemed like a cockpit. I thought I should request permission for take-off. And then Nuala was at the passenger door, looking beautiful and sleepy inside a monster woolen jumper. There was something angry in her eyes.

"I'm coming with you," she said, flatly. "Wherever we're going."

I was thrilled. Her smell settled over me like a well-loved cat. I had to ask. "H? Conjoinment?"

She pressed her lips together for a moment. "Drive the fucking car," she said.

I WANTED TO TELL HER HOW GLAD I WAS THAT SHE WAS WITH me, but I knew I'd end up gushing and make her uncomfortable. I restricted myself to picking up her hand and giving it a friendly peck. The arch left her eyebrows. She seemed to settle even deeper into her woolens. I imagined climbing in there with her, everything pink and warm and impossibly soft. I kept hold of her hand. She didn't take it away.

"Where are we going?" she asked.

"Warrington," I said. "Where else is there?"

"Fun-ny," she sang. "What's in Warrington?"

"What *isn't* in Warrington?"

"I won't be if you don't give me a straight answer."

"There's a funeral in Kendal, a bit further north along the M6. It'll be fun. It'll brighten the place up a bit. My Dad lives in Warrington. We can stay with him."

The M1 was knackered. We were getting snarled up in traffic every ten minutes. Cones lined up along the outside lane.

"Who died?"

"The parents of someone I used to work with."

"Why are you going?"

"A favor for a friend." Up ahead, blue light flashed in the mist. My stomach tightened. This was the only reason we were going so slowly. Rubberneckers crawling by, checking for carnage.

There were three vehicles involved. One had shunted the other and then a third had piled into the middle one, concertina-ing it. There were firemen positioned around the car, cutting the door open. The boot and the engine seemed to have met right where the passenger seat ought to be. I didn't want to be around when the car's occupants slithered out all over the Tarmac. I put my foot down and the BMW responded, taking us into the pack of accelerating cars that obviously hadn't taken the accident as a warning for their own safety.

"That's one hell of a neg zone," Nuala said. "They should bring some kids here, let them play on the accident spot for a while, try to rescue it."

"You want to see kids playing in the fast lane of the motorway?"

"They could cordon them off, or something."

"Jesus."

We traveled in our own pockets of silence, the almost inaudible drone of commentators on Radio 4 the only intrusion until we reached the outskirts of Birmingham, where the traffic began to seize up again. We crawled, until the suck of the city diminished, cars filtering off to the surrounding districts.

Nuala put her head against my shoulder.

"Has anybody tried to hurt you, since I saw you last?"

"Marlon the cat," I said. "He tried to have my face off last night. For no reason other than for kicks. Apart from that, no."

"What I meant," insisted Nuala, although I could tell that she was becoming more good-humored, enjoying the games I was playing, "was: has somebody, you know, tried to kill you? Again."

"You still don't believe me, do you?"

She was quick to put out a restraining arm, although I hadn't lost my temper. "No, I do. I believe that somebody gave you a maximum spook the other night. It doesn't matter what happened. I'm concerned. It might happen again."

"It might, but I'll be ready next time." I had the knife in my pocket, the knife the girl had given me at the party. Lucas didn't know who she was when I described her to him. He didn't know an awful lot, Lucas. He didn't know where he'd gone to when he buggered off. Not to worry, I told him, we were pissed. I don't remember where I got to either. I might have had a narcoleptic blackout. I didn't know. I was that trousered.

As we drove through the gray channels that swept through the center of Birmingham, it began to rain. Very soon, water had collected on the Tarmac and was being sprayed into the air by juggernauts in the left-hand lane. Where the sky's ceiling existed, a whitish blur extended, rubbing out a view of the road beyond. I had to believe there was something to drive into when I overtook the lorries, had to have a blind faith in what lay ahead: more road, hopefully empty. While I gripped the wheel, Nuala slipped a cassette into the player; Billie Holiday singing "Georgia On My Mind." It calmed me down a little.

"You might try switching the wipers on, Adam?"

I did so. Sunlight staggered across the industrialized piles of the Midlands, igniting the mist of rain and casting uncertain spectra above the motorway.

"Now that's what I call pretty," I said, trying not to clench my jaw. "The spray of petrol-stained water, dancing with color, against the muddied arse of an Eddie Stobart wagon."

"It's okay, Adam," she said, rubbing my leg. I felt a crazy urge to grab her, smell her fingers to see if traces of H lingered. "It's only a squall. There's clear sky up ahead, see?"

She was right. Nevertheless, as we escaped the borders of the storm, it took Nuala's coaxing—her gentle massage of my arms and legs—to help loosen my white-knuckled grip on the wheel. We were doing almost a hundred and twenty. I forced myself to relax, to slow down, and noticed that my heart had been beating madly, the hundred miles we'd traveled since joining the M1 at Hendon.

"What's wrong, Adam?" she pressed. Checking the mirror, I saw that I was ashen, with a light coating of sweat on my forehead and cheeks. The skin around my eyes had turned gray. It had nothing to do with the funeral, or the storm. Or H making love to Nuala.

"It's because we left London," I said. She didn't scoff.

I explained everything to her. And once I'd exhausted all the panic involved with leaving Laura behind in the past, my odd interaction with the city, my mind's blackspots (especially the blackspots), I told Nuala about my feelings for her. I occasionally spotted my face in the mirror as I let it all come tumbling out and I was surprised to see no masks there, no attempt to conceal the raw emotion.

"In London, it's like putting a belt on and trying to kid yourself that it will go one notch tighter. You end up walking around feeling constricted all the time, unable to loosen yourself in public, always sucking in your gut and pretending to be impenetrable, unassailable."

I wasn't sure what I was saying anymore, but Nuala was nodding.

"In the few years I've been here, I've got caught up in it. I've started running for buses, even when I know there'll be another one along in two minutes. I go out with a scowl on my face. Shit, I've even started drinking London Pride."

I listened to Billie Holliday singing "Romance in the Dark." For a second, it was just me, Billie, the long, long road and London somewhere in my rear-view mirror. The city was a long-gone explosion of sunshine on the horizon. I felt like I was in one of those bulb-shaped glasses used in yard-of-ale competitions. I could imagine people getting indoors, shedding their coats, throwing their *Evening Standards* onto the sofa, peeling away their poker faces to reveal a tragic rictus. How they break down and cry.

"It's not the people that get me in London, although they have their own strange agendas, I'm sure of it. It's the buildings. It's the massive weight of history that hits you, the history in the dust that shifts around your feet when, oh, I don't know, when you go for a walk through the City at the weekend or find yourself on Waterloo Bridge at sunset, or a park when there's nobody else around. I wonder, sometimes, what's in that dust, *who* is in that dust."

"We're only going to Warrington for the day."

"I know, but... it felt like I'd been in the city too long, that it had got its claws into me."

She was trying to understand, but I could see she was having trouble cottoning on. Me too, for that matter. Fair enough, I was talking pretty weird stuff. I was talking, as Greg would put it, shit.

We stopped off at Keele Services for coffee, edgy from the long drive. Everyone looked half-alive, aghast, as if they'd been brought out of the oven ten minutes early. The enervation of non-arrival.

"So enough about me. What was your problem when we left this morning?"

"I'm problem-free, my sweet," she said, arching her eyebrow and looking directly at me, as if to say *What, do you want to make something of it?*

I decided I did.

"You had a face on you as grim as a wardrobe full of tank tops."

She huddled beneath the acreage of her jumper. Light color fled across her cheekbones. She mumbled something and then turned her attention back to her coffee. I felt bad, and considered asking her if she'd like something to go with her coffee. A doughnut, perhaps. But she'd have shot me down because of the E numbers, or monosodium glutamate. I got her one anyway, and she bit into it. Congealed jam oozed out of it. Her chin was trembling as she chewed; I reached out and touched her hand. She put the doughnut down and came round to my side of the table, where she held me and sobbed against my neck. Tears trickled under the collar of my T-shirt. I didn't mind a jot. The pale, half-eaten doughnut bled its innards across the plate. It looked like a poultice failing to staunch a wound.

"He wanted to come on my tits," she was saying. "He wanted to spray all that wonderful power away, instead of channeling it into me, where I could use it."

It would have been easy to laugh, but I was too busy wishing I was H and looking at the soft globes of wool beneath which her breasts would be warm and thick with the smell of her.

"Who is H?" I asked. "What does his name stand for?"

"Oh, God, do you know, I haven't a clue. He's always just been H to me. H Glaber."

"Glaber?"

"Yes," she said, "I think it's German."

"Do you feel up to getting back in the car? I'm worried we might be late."

She nodded. And then she said: "It's not everything." She looked uncertain for a moment, then she bit her bottom lip and seemed to come to a decision. "There's more I need to tell you. I can tell you. When we get back to London."

"I hate that. Tell me now."

"I can't. I have to show you something. It'll be easier for me just to show you."

THE FURTHER AWAY FROM LONDON WE GOT, THE MORE comfortable I felt. It was like backing away from a fierce bonfire.

"I had these friends," I said, thinking of Meddie and Iain. And Yoyo. It seemed strange to refer to them in the past tense. "People I worked with, really. But okay. Well, some of them were okay. Kind of okay. Kind of friends. They were London nutty for a while. You know, trying to discover the real London, the skull beneath the skin. One of them, Iain, used to poke around old churches in the City or have a day in Hackney or root around the library in Kentish Town in case he discovered some lost text, a key that would unlock the city's underworld." I glanced at her to see if she was listening; she had a sleepy smile on her face. The light was being kind to Nuala; it lit up her green eyes, the softly angular lines of her nose and jaw.

"The three of them went out to Mudchute on the first day's hunt. Later they split up and went off on their own, but first day, all mates together. There's a farm and a park near the DLR station. They went in, Iain clouted his head on the kissing gate, slipped on the mud walking up the path and landed on his arse. Two seconds into their first search, he's covered in shit and his eye's swelling up. Iain doesn't even notice, twittering on about the view and the aeroplanes banking overhead as they take off from City Airport. Then it started raining. "

We'd just passed Knutsford services. Twenty minutes away from Dad's.

"Sounds like a nightmare. Why did they go all the way out there?"

"Have a guess?"

"Not just the view. Pigs and sheep?"

"No." My arse had turned numb from all this driving; my right foot had contracted, I don't know what the affliction might be called—accelerator ankle?—due to the constant dipping when we'd been crawling along. Five hours it had taken. We seemed like different people to the ones who had moved through the darkness of north London all that time ago.

"They wanted to see the center of London or, as he put it, the omphalos. The true center. Apparently, there's a ley-line runs through the farm. He thought that if they found the line, if they stood at the heart of London, something would be revealed."

"What?"

"I don't know. Maybe the strange places in the rest of the city. The places they ended up finding later. They had all these maps. They didn't need any of them, in the end."

"So did they find something at this, what was it? Hephalump?"

I laughed. "Omphalos. No. A few drains, some tractor tires. Lots of cow shit." The Thelwall Viaduct hove into view, possibly for the first time this century uncluttered by traffic. We were really here.

"But didn't they feel energized?"

"You weren't the best person to tell this story to, with hindsight."

"Oh Adam," she chided, and I was glad that old joshing tone had crept back into her voice. She seemed more relaxed, the incident at the service station forgotten, or rather buried, for now.

Thinking of the others made me feverish for a while. They were in London, unearthing treasure. And I was up here, going to see someone bury it. London seemed the most magical place on Earth. But then I thought of Lewis Carroll, who had been born in Daresbury, just outside Warrington. I thought of Alan Garner's Alderley Edge. Ramsey Campbell's Merseyside. There were glittering cracks in reality around here too. There was magic in the moors, the Pennines, the old industrial towns.

I peeled the car off onto the M62 and stayed in the nearside lane, the filter for the A49 and Warrington. Dad would like Nuala, I guessed. And she'd fall for him, just like every girlfriend I'd had. Something my mum told me when I was younger: *He could charm the leaves down from the trees.*

North Warrington's outer limits unfurled before us as we cruised the dual carriageway. It was an ugly place, especially at this end, with its corrugated "sardine-can" business parks and anonymous estates. We saw the obligatory stray dog; the gang of kids crouching by a large yellow GRIT container; a tanned blond man in a tight black T-shirt filling up his Cosworth at the petrol station while a tanned blonde girl in a tight black T-shirt waited inside.

I turned right, past the former gasworks and under a tiny bridge, upon which foot-high letters had been painted: *WELCOME TO DALLAM.* A new housing complex being built at the other side were all boarded up. Kids on mountain bikes ripped through the building site. We caught a sliver of choice language, coated in the Warrington tongue, a hybrid of Scouse and Mancunian:

"Oi, Benneh, put that fuckin' brick down *now*, right, or ah'll fuckin' *drop* yoh, yoh fuckin' *wankoh.*"

Nuala fidgeted beside me. I patted her knee and swung the car down Lilford Avenue. Allotments sprang up; a field ran away to the horizon, where it lost itself to a small wood. An old house winked at us between the trees.

"Did you grow up around here?"

I nodded and dropped down a gear, took the car around a sharp curve into Lodge Lane. I parked behind my dad's old Toyota and smiled at Nuala. Approaching the front door, I glanced towards the garage. Through the window I could see the dull red glint of Mum's Fiat 127. Dad had never sold it, never driven it, after she died.

There was no answer when I rang the bell. We walked round to the back garden and I knew where he'd be, almost knew what posture he'd be taking, when I smelled wood smoke, saw its thin color drifting across the lawn. I wasn't wrong.

He was in the waste patch of land by his shed, sating his desires for compost and combustion. Mrs. Munro next door was flapping around the washing line, taking in her whites before the smoke from the fire could ruin them. Dad already had a good blaze going, and was leaning against his beloved garden fork, looking deep into the fire's core. He became an unreliable figure in the mist; that moment before he turned smudged the age from him—he could have come from any chapter of my childhood. My fear for him rose in me—it always did when I was around him—a strange, switched paternal concern, as if he had always been my charge, rather than the other way. I was reluctant to call him in case he was startled and fell into the flames. But then he turned and saw us.

"Hello there!" he said, and picked his way through the rubble towards us. I was gladdened by his enthusiasm. A picture flashed behind my eyes: me walking into my parents' room to find them in bed, watching TV, holding hands.

As always, the most acute feeling that I missed my dad consumed me when I was standing a mere foot away from him. "What do you know?" He nodded at Nuala, who smiled awkwardly in return. "Come on, let's get you inside. Want a coffee?"

"What about the fire?" I asked.

"It's okay. It'll just burn itself out."

I remembered one night in high summer as a boy, waking when it was still fairly light outside, the fumes from burning matter scorching the back of my throat. Dad had incinerated some newspapers and a broken old bookcase and left the fire to die once it had turned the wood to embers and the flames were gone. Mum spent a good hour pouring buckets of water over the majority of the back lawn, which was steadily smoldering. He couldn't admit that he'd been wrong, pointing out that the lawn would benefit from a good burn and claiming it was something he had been thinking of doing for a long time. "Scorched earth policy, Frances," he'd said to her from the back door as she did her thing with the buckets. "The lawn'll come up a treat and a half."

Something he'd once said, forgotten till now, leapt unbidden into my head: *Hey, Adam, what's the best way to get rid of rubbish? Burn it.*

I shook my head and followed him and Nuala indoors, where he set about making mugs of very strong instant coffee.

"Do you want something to eat?" he asked, nodding towards the breadbin. If I did, I'd have to make it myself. He was like that, Dad, charming and effortlessly hospitable without any application. "I'll take Nuala away and entertain her with my collection of insect carapaces. You'd like that wouldn't you?"

Nuala looked at me, wide-eyed, unable to see that he was joking. I made a plate of cheese sandwiches. When I got back to the living room, Nuala was laughing at something he was saying, her body language locked onto him, everything turned his way, open, at ease. Dozens of thriving plants vomited thick, waxy green leaves at me from earthenware pots and broad wall baskets, as though taunting me for my impoverished attempts back at Cherry's stall. I thought about the stall, filled with desiccated flakes of brown and gray. The soil was always better here.

"What are you doing up here?" asked my dad amiably, as if just visiting him wasn't enough.

"Funeral," I said, suddenly realizing that I hadn't brought any suitable clothes. "You don't have a black suit I could borrow, do you?"

He nodded, and I knew it would be the suit in which he'd seen my mother's coffin slide out of view on the short journey to the crematorium. I'd wondered after that if his appetite for fire might wane but it seemed to have stuck around. His smell—of charred things—filled the room. A cat wandered in and looked at us then walked out again.

I told him about Claire. He asked me about work, if I had any news, what the weather was like in the city. He asked about my narcolepsy and I told him I was taking medication, that I had it under control. We ate the cheese sandwiches. Dad asked Nuala what she did for a living. She told him she was a hairdresser.

"Really?" he said. "You should take some clippers to my old wig. I need a good trim."

I went up to take a shower, trying to keep a lid on the insane laughter that was trying to spill out of me. Nuala could stay with my dad for the afternoon; I needed to do this on my own. She didn't object too strongly, and anyway, she didn't have any black clothes either.

When I left, it had started to rain. Fallen leaves had turned into a brackish porridge on the wet windscreen. I sat in Nuala's car for a few minutes, conscious that they might be watching from the window but not having the nerve to stick the key in the fascia, to commit myself to beginning the journey, because that would mean I'd have to end the journey. Not going anywhere was a safe option. Temporary, but it helped.

At last I got underway. I drove through the center of Warrington, hardly recognizing the place where I'd grown up. All the pubs looked alike, neon and chrome jobs with huge signs for karaoke and Sky. The one-way system fed me into a traffic jam by Bridge Foot. I could smell the Mersey, thick and rank, through the fans in the car. It took me back to a time of riding my bicycle to Wally Rez for a swim with school friends, picking brambles off the hedges, trying to nonchalantly play football in the park while girls sat around and pretended not to watch while we pretended not to notice them.

I took the road through Grappenhall and joined up with the M6. I listened to music on the way to Kendal—Curve, Heathrow Browns, Starlover—in order to distract my mind from funerals, friends, narcolepsy. London.

I arrived at the church and parked the car, self-conscious because nobody knew me and I could see people muttering about this flash bastard in a BMW. I stretched, walked to the gate and smiled at a few of the mourners who were standing around, having a cigarette. One of them nodded; the others turned away. I heard someone say "London" as if it were a dirty word. I felt two hundred and seventy miles of bitumen tugging at me, sucking me back to the oily heart of the city. The sunlight filtering through the trees, the little stone church, the child clasping its hands together and smiling beatifically... it all made my teeth ache.

"And you are?" said a voice, a reedy, Lancastrian whinge. It was the smoker who nodded at me.

"Adam," I said. "Adam Buckley. I'm a friend of Claire's."

"Course you are," he intoned, dragging deeply on his cigarette and flicking the stub towards the gravestones. "Course you fucking are. Everyone's a friend of Cuh-laire's."

I felt intimidated by the sly coil of his words and his face, a hastily stitched affair without a pattern. His nose had been broken on many occasions. Or else he was just violently ugly.

"Do you play rugby?" I asked. His eyebrows joined and crept down the bridge of his nose.

"You bein' fresh, chief?" he asked. "You poncey-arse southern fuck."

"I'm from up here," I protested. "I'm a northerner."

He nodded. "You sound like a Cockney to me." He leaned in close. I smelled Marmite and Old Spice on him. "Twat."

"Look, why don't we leave this till after the funeral? It's not exactly respectful to the dead, is it?" I was wondering whether or not to get a pre-emptive strike in, to clock him one and then leg it, forget about the funeral altogether. And then Claire stepped in and pushed him away.

"Get lost, Dom," she said. "You're not being very helpful today. Go and lick a plug socket or something."

Dom sloped off, but not without mouthing the word "Later" at me.

"Who was that?" I asked, angry that I was shivering from fear at his threat and his wrecking of my re-acquaintance with Claire. "What brought all that on?"

"That's my baby brother. Seventeen years old and spoiling for a custodial sentence. So he can be like his mates."

"Seventeen?" I spluttered, my fear dissolving. "But he just near enough promised to put me in the hospital!"

"Hot air, Adam. And it's his way of dealing with all this. Come on, calm down, tell me what's been happening to you."

THE FUNERAL WENT QUICKLY AND I WAS HORRIFIED TO FEEL myself dropping off just as the coffins were being conveyed through the plush velvet curtains. Once out in the fresh air again, I revived a little and made my way over to Claire, who told me to follow the cortege to her grandparents' house, where there would be a buffet and a drop of something to warm us all up.

I was stuck behind Dom in his Nova on the way to Claire's. He would sneer at me when we got to traffic lights, or give me a V-sign, or perform an airwank.

The house was part of a small terrace that looked as if it had been squashed by its neighbors. Inside, there was a faint naphthalene odor, coupled with a fustiness, that I associated with my own grandparents. I sat on a sofa in the living room, along with two other people: it was a tight squeeze. The armchair by the window was already occupied by a grim-looking man with a hawkish nose and tufts of baby-fine white hair who I guessed to be Claire's grandfather. He was gumming at a sandwich but couldn't keep his mouth closed. He worked at it for minutes, turning it into paste, before swallowing. Noticing me looking, he gave me a solemn wink before returning to his ham and pickle.

I met a few of the relatives, and was aware they were studying me, not without hostility, as if I, a stranger, was somehow unsettling the familial coziness of their grief. A couple of them were friendly enough, but I could see I wasn't welcome and knew that the longer I stayed, the greater was Dom's chance to commit some form of violence with impunity. I couldn't blame them. I wouldn't have liked a stranger making me feel self-conscious at such a time.

I was about to make my excuses when I saw Claire standing by the window, slowly losing it. Her grandmother was trying to get her to have some Harvey's Bristol Cream, to distract her from her misery, but it wasn't working. Her face was crumbling like a sandcastle at high tide.

She shook her head and disappeared upstairs just as Dom drained his glass and made a beeline for me. It was the only encouragement I needed. I slipped into the tiny culvert between kitchen and living room and, pulling back the grimy curtain across the stairwell, climbed into a thick, airless gloom, my shoes echoing on the thinly carpeted risers.

I wondered later—especially on the long, silent journey home, when I was aware that Nuala was gearing up for her own unlikely revelation—whether Claire had heard me coming after her; certainly the house was not an ally of stealth. The walls were thin, the woodwork noisy.

She was standing in the sister bedroom, the door partly open. I could see in the dressing-table mirror her body as she slipped out of her clothes. The scars looked like heavily embroidered belts of purple and whitish pink wrapped around her: she looked like an escape artist ready for action. They did not reach above her chest or below her thighs. Her arms were clear. The ragged coils were smeared with light where the shiny, fatigued skin had stretched. Between these harsh borders, the no-man's land of her flesh was pockmarked with half a dozen ugly craters, as if she'd been punctured. Her buttocks had been slashed and knitted into a grotesque weave. A substantial section of her pubic patch had not grown back because of the shiny red weal carved deep into her crotch.

Maybe she heard my ragged breathing, or had known I was there all along, thinking it right that she should calmly acknowledge my presence at that moment. I went to her. It didn't matter that she was naked. It didn't matter who saw us. We were in our own little pocket, protected from the outside world. She cried so hard that the V between her breasts, where she was pressed up tight against me, collected a pool of tears.

"I miss him," she breathed.

MY FATHER HAD GONE TO BED WHEN I GOT BACK. I COULD see, through the living room window, Nuala alone, curled on the sofa with a mug of something hot, steam making uncertain the reflected, dead light on her face from the TV.

I didn't want to see her then. I needed to remain alone.

I let myself into the garage and shut the door behind me. Something scampered among the old wicker fishing baskets in the corner. There was a smell of old things: oil, grass cuttings, sweat. Mum's Fiat was dusty, smaller than I remembered it. I got in and sat in the driver's seat. Positioned the mirror so I could see her in the back. Her wheat-colored hair, her beautiful big hazel eyes. I talked to her for a long time.

DRIVING BACK, I SAID LITTLE TO NUALA ABOUT HOW THE funeral had gone. *Like a funeral,* I'd said, when she asked me. *Only with-*

*out all the usual gut-busting laughs,* I'd said. Snapped, more like. But she accepted it, kept quiet, rubbed my hand a little.

Claire's scars wrapped themselves around my focus.

It was a beautiful day. Very cold, with a sheet of corrugated cloud roofing the towns and villages and factories as we swept along the M6. A jet moving against its patterns looked as if it was slipping unnaturally from its trajectory.

They clung to her like jeweled snakes, these scars—there was something beautiful and compelling about them that kept broadsiding my revulsion. Her skin seemed dull and tired compared to these lustrous strips, these brilliant wounds. They swarmed across her upper body, biting into her breasts where they defined a new shape for her. Their architect had been careful. His had been a strategic cruelty.

She told me how Shaun had begged her to marry him, even while he was carving her into separate territories, the borders of which would be defined by the barbed-wire ghosts of thick sutures. I tried to imagine the faces of the nurses at casualty who saw her come in, clutching the pieces of her stomach together, wondered how they swallowed her story of an attack at the hands of a gang of anonymous lads outside a Morecambe pub.

She'd fled to a safe house in the north, close to her parents. Shaun never tried to follow her. At the time, we had all thought it was because she was homesick, had gone home to retrain as a teacher. That was the line trotted out by the chief sub, anyway. Claire told me how she was sleeping less and that her insomnia had started up when she thought about Shaun with another woman.

"I almost went back to him then," she said to me, a retreating look in her eyes, "just to stop him from doing this to someone else."

But she'd persuaded herself to stay put, reassured herself that he must have acted the way he did because she was in some way unfit, that she deserved to be brutalized. He would probably enjoy a stress-free relationship with the next one along.

"I was there," I said aloud, and Nuala jerked out of her reverie. She turned to me. I saw the reflection of the radio masts at Rugby sliding across the bonnet.

"Where?" she asked, frowning.

"The day Shaun asked Claire out."

"Claire? The one who just said goodbye to her parents? So who's Shaun?"

I explained who Shaun was but I didn't want to tell her what he'd done to Claire. It felt too private, too close a horror to share. And then it was tumbling out of me anyway, as if I was no more in charge of my mouth than a doll with a speech-cord attached to its back.

"It was at this magazine I worked at. In London. Where Greg—a friend of mine—got me in. I'd been there about a week, hadn't really talked to anyone. There'd been a slew of new recruits around that time and the company were getting a bit worried that there'd be claims for RSI—you know—if they didn't get somebody in to teach them how to sit at a desk properly, and hold a mouse the right way.

"I was scheduled to sit in with an instructor with a bunch of other people; some of them had been there a fair while. You could see they were potential RSI cases because they walked like crippled apes. This guy took us, looked like he was fresh out of business school. He really had a strut about him. Crisp, white shirt. Power tie. Close shave. He looked like he should have been called Dirk or Garth, rather than Roger. He had an overhead projector and a big notepad that he wrote on with a fat felt tip.

" 'Okay,' he goes, clapping his hands. Big on eye contact, big on remembering and using first names. 'Okay, what happens to us when we're stressed?' We came out with a few suggestions. Heart rate increases, sweat glands juice up, nervousness.... He's nodding all the while, saying 'Yep, that's good, what else?' We dry up. 'Some of us do this,' he says, writing SWEAT MORE on the pad. 'Some of us do this....' SMOKE MORE. 'Aaa-and *some* of us do *this*....' DRINK MORE.

"Made me feel really guilty, that did, although I only had the odd pint at lunchtimes. Shaun sat next to Claire and was whispering stuff under his breath, making her laugh. Roger kept casting them glances but he didn't say anything. I saw Shaun... I was the only one who saw this... I saw Shaun reach out and trap Claire's nipple through her blouse with his fingers—he kind of had his arms crossed on the desk in front of him so nobody would see. And he nodded down at his groin. Claire was already reddening but she looked down too and went even redder.

"She came into work wearing the same clothes the next day. And I saw her wince whenever she sat down. Everyone noticed but nobody said anything. I think it was because we didn't want to embarrass Claire but really, now, I reckon it's because we didn't know how Shaun would react. He was unpredictable. I know that sounds ominous now, but we didn't attach anything unpleasant to it then. He was a bit of a nutter, that's all. Every office has one. 'You don't have to be mad to work here' and all that. Claire left when he left but she didn't look mad keen. She lingered near the Art department but when he looked up from the door, she went. It was like he was drawing her towards him. She was trapped as early as that. He'd take her home and use her as a canvas for all of his anger and frustration and she'd never say a word. And none of us knew about it. Until the funeral."

"Why are you telling me this, Adam? Why do you want to frighten me this way?" Nuala's voice was tiny and brittle. I looked at her and blinked. I hadn't even realized we were still driving. My eyes had frozen on the industrial sprawl on the horizon as I battered down the silence in the car.

"I'm sorry," I said, squeezing her leg. "I didn't mean to scare you. I had to tell you." I turned my attention back to the road. It was gradually filling up as the tributaries fed it. London was less than twenty minutes away. I could feel its suck; it was a starving, ruined baby, looking for nourishment from any quarter. Defiled, indiscriminate, blind. It devoured us all, digested us in its poisonous juices for years and then spat out the bones.

BACK IN NUALA'S FLAT, SHE DREW ME A HOT BATH AND ADDED some lavender oil. She poured me a big whisky and put John Lennon's *Look At Me* on constant loop on the CD player.

"No animals?" I asked, smiling. "No chittering weevils performing Sinatra? No cane toads belching Burt Bacharach?"

*Look at me. Who am I supposed to be? Who am I supposed to be?*

She didn't protest at my ribbing her. She just smiled and stroked the hair from my forehead, and sadness settled badly into her face like cheap moisturiser.

*Who am I? Nobody knows but me....*

She rubbed me down and led me to the living room. The window was open and a cat was sitting on the ledge, washing itself with the kind of intensity that could at any moment convert itself into the need to chew leaves or rake a claw down a curtain. She pushed me gently into a chair and went over to a cupboard behind the television. Inside was a large red safe box. She unlocked it and pulled out three video cassettes.

"I said I had something to show you. Well, here it is."

She gave me the tapes and left the room. Then she came back in again. "No," she said, holding up her hands as if I was aiming a gun at her. "I should be in here with you for this."

"I should play these now?" I said. There were no labels to tell me what was on the tapes.

"If you want to. If you can stand it."

I slotted the first one in and pressed the play button on the remote. Immediately, the screen was filled with a wet-wax image of lurid colors. It took me a while to work out what was going on, and then a while longer to work out that it was Nuala lying there doing it, along with three permed, heavily bearded men. Tinny music warbled in tune with the thrusting and the grunts. When Nuala's mouth was free for a few seconds, she clearly said "Fuck me," but the tape was dubbed into some Scandinavian language and some breathless female voice took over. *Nukken me! Slap me an daf!*, it sounded as though she had cried.

"Jesus," I said, "who is *that*?"

"The one with the tattoo? His name's Eric. Known in the trade as The Baguette."

"And the other one, the one whose lips are drawn back. The one who you're, um...."

"He's Joe. Pokin' Joe Longhorn."

"And the short guy?"

"Graham. Footsie."

"Footsie?"

"Yeah, Footsie. His—you know—was a foot long."

"Right. And what was your trade name?"

"Martini."

I watched the film. I was getting a hard-on, as you do. I tried to watch with as much detachment as possible, knowing how tough this was for Nuala, knowing how much she must think of me to be able to share a secret such as this. I offered observations and asked questions too.

"That has to smart," and "Did you have to do exercises to be able to do that?" and "Woah, you did *that* in one take?"

Nuala cried a little, but then she started giggling when I made some funny comments and she could see how relaxed I was about it. I made her feel okay about it. It was in the past. It didn't matter anymore.

Later, she slipped my boxers off and in my excitement I sprang out and hit her on the chin. "Martini," I said, stroking her head. "Forget The Baguette. Meet Croissant Man. Meet Mr. Finger Roll."

I DREAMED I WAS SITTING ON A FOOT-WIDE PLANK SUPPORTED only by a few rotten trestles, a hundred feet above the ground, inching my way along, my arms filled with the fetuses that would become my friends and family. If only I could make it to the other side, a couple of miles away, I could plant them and enjoy a rich life of love with them. A strong wind, filled with freezing rain, made the plank swing; I could feel the tenuous grip of my sodden denims upon the grain of wood giving way. I could let go of these almost humans, these blueprints, and save myself. When I looked down, they had decayed in my arms. I let them go and put my hands out to grip the wood at the precise moment the whole fucking mess gave way.

I OVERSLEPT IN THE MORNING, BUT I STAYED IN BED FOR A while, wondering about the past few days, thinking how unreal it all seemed. Claire's scars seemed *Dr. Who*-ish, as if she might now be peeling them off, pleased that she had fooled me.

I rolled over, but Nuala wasn't there. Her note told me she'd gone to buy some muesli and yogurt for breakfast. I picked up the phone and dialed Greg. No answer. I felt I had to tell him about Claire, although I felt very strongly that he would not respond, that he didn't care or wasn't surprised or already knew. Maybe he would be able to help me find Shaun. His answering service wasn't on, so I ditched the receiver and got dressed. The memory of my dad's insultingly healthy plants had imbued me with a determination to wring any murmurs of life out of my stock as soon as I possibly could. I left a note for Nuala, signing it *Crouton*, then went out into the late morning.

# CHAPTER FIFTEEN
## THE FACE

Sixty feet under. The foot of a lift shaft. It might be midnight or mid day. The dark is utter. What might be lying between It and the surface? Dinosaur bones? Roman coins? The sweat and tears of forgotten, unrewarded toil. The bodies of those who gave everything in the name of life, of living, and are now nothing more than a scratched name in a register. A profound memory for the son or the daughter, a fleeting distraction for the grandchild. Dead for ever, after that. In every way.

Seventy years since the trains dirtied up this place. Down Street. Great name. There's dirt here, though. Sit long enough, It might become coated with the dust of all those ghost passengers from the 1930s as it blows around and resettles. It shifts on the step in the circular space, the darkness unbroken by even the palest suggestion of light from the Piccadilly Line. Tunnels snake away from the shaft; noises creep into it. The passage of trains is deafening, the shaft filling with the roar so great it seems that all the noise in the world must have been funneled into this space at the same time. As the trains move away, they suck air from the shaft, dragging it through the baffles of reinforced concrete, creating a shriek that sounds almost human.

And then the distant hum of electricity. And the darkness and the dust.

Concentrating on the noise helps to deal with the pain.

It raises a hand to Its face and feels the tacky lymph drying against the exposed surface. The jagged nubs of bone at the bridge of what had once been a nose pricks Its fingertips. Cold air hisses in and out between gritted teeth, drying and cracking the gash where Its lips used to meet. And my, what big eyes. It never realized how much It might miss blinking. Perhaps It should have kept Its eyelids.

It cocks Its head as she moves again. Another attempt at flight. The third since It brought her down here. It waits until It hears her footsteps on the metal bridge over the sump in the shaft before rising and wearily pursuing her up the spiral staircase. Their steps on the aluminium make *ting-tang* calls to each other.

"I won't kill you," It said. Its voice skips and scatters across the tiled walls. An underground whispering gallery. Someone on an active platform in another station many hundreds of meters away laughs, and the sound falls around him, as if mocking his promise. Speaking is difficult: the lack of lips, the swelling of tissue around his mouth makes the forming of words painful, almost impossible.

"I won't kill you."

"Leave me alone," she calls back. There is terror in her voice, but it is tired, her spirit almost broken. She stopped screaming an hour ago. Another hour and she might be begging It to take her life. Desperation can do that to a person. Desperation can betray itself.

"I need you. You're my insurance." Pronouncing an "m" is so agonizing it brings tears to Its eyes. "It's him I want. It's Monck. You can go when I have him dead in front of me."

HEATHFIELD ROAD WAS STUFFED WITH TRAFFIC WHEN I finally came to my senses. I didn't remember stepping out of Wandsworth prison or returning to the main drag in order to find a bus back to Clapham Junction. The howl and grind of engines met the numbed meat of my brain and shocked me into life. I sucked in a few filthy lungfuls of air and watched the shoppers sloping along the battered pavements. I decided not to rush back and instead ducked into a pub that was packed for lunch. Over a pint of lager—as I tried to rid my mouth of a dead taste—I recalled the meeting.

Shaun had sat there behind the mesh of the cage, shaven-headed, wizened. A decrepit Buddha, smiling serenely, perhaps touched that I had gone to the trouble of booking a visit. It could have been dope that smoothed him out so completely, but I didn't think so. Drugs were just another part of life's routines that he had grown to hate. It was almost funny that a person who had railed against convention so blatantly was now cooped up in a place that couldn't function without it. Three years, he'd been given, for a road rage incident in which he'd driven over the legs of a man who demanded his insurance details after a minor collision. He'd built up a bit of form, since I'd last seen him. GBH, wounding, affray. It was no surprise to me.

"I understand what he's playing at," he had whispered to me, after we'd been sitting there for a while. "I see the point."

The air in the visiting rooms was stale with ancient cigarette smoke and BO. I had found myself craving a drink.

"I know too," I said. I remembered that I had respected Shaun at first, because of his utter separation, but that was why I never really got close to him either. Who did? Claire tried and look where that landed her. Thinking of her stiffened my resolve. I was talking to a cunting bastard of exceptional quality. "That's why I thought it was you. A person off his rocker who thinks that society is evil. A person who doesn't like being told to 'Keep Left' and can't abide double yellow lines. Who doesn't agree with taxation. Who walks against the red light."

"Hey, so what? I'm just one in a long, long queue. Someone who doesn't jump when the system expects me to. Someone who doesn't put his hands on his head, even when, *especially* when, Simon says. Respectable people fiddle their Inland Revenue forms, respectable people keep guns, respectable people rape and kill. They go off the rails. Some people never go off the rails. They do everything that is expected of them. They are pillars of the community. They are salts of the earth. They are rocks. My dad worked forty years for the same company and got a carriage clock at the end of it. A fucking carriage clock. He died three years later because his work had been his life. And for what? A semi on the outskirts of an industrial town. A piss-poor pension. His name on the Employee of the Week wall. Big wank. The biggest crime he ever committed was putting his vest on back to front. He used to see someone toss a match into the gutter, he'd turn to me and say, "He's just committed an offense." He was so straight I was surprised he could sit down for a shit. People are pissed on in this country. And then they're forgotten when they slide off the plate. I go to that factory now, and ask the pair of braces sitting behind his big desk about my dad, he'll say, 'Who?' You get a job, you become the job. And the job kills you."

"Save it for your parole officer," I said. "Write a fucking book."

"So what are you here for?"

"I want to apologize," I said.

"Oh really? Why's that?"

"Because I thought you might have been behind this underground terrorism. Pushing people in front of trains. I thought you were involved. It was wrong of me and it has damaged my conscience."

He smiled. "No need to apologize. I might have got involved, if I'd thought about it. I think it's pretty smart thinking. So what? You looking for advice about him? My thoughts on a kindred spirit?"

"Do you know anything? Have you heard anything in here? Do people talk about it?"

He sat back and looked around him. "You know they had a gallows here until recently? Only dismantled it in '92, because they thought they might still need it if anyone topped the Royal Family, or committed piracy on the high seas. The Cold Meat Shed, they called it. It's a TV room now. Some of the shit they put on that box, half the time you're wishing for a noose to come and rescue you."

I thought of Claire and bore down on my urge to assure him that if he had a noose I would help him into it and pull any levers that were around. He rolled a thin cigarette, lit it, and let it go cold in a cheap, faux-Bakelite ashtray on the table. I sipped bitter tea from my polystyrene cup and waited.

"The answer to your question is yes, they are talking about it in here, when they're eventually let out of their cells. When they stop talking about overcrowding, and how nice it would be to have a shower, or use the phone to call home. Some say they can hear voices at night, coming from under ground. Or the Common. Or the tracks to Earlsfield. Sometimes they hear screams. There's talk around here the Pusher is a woman."

"What?"

"Yeah. Looks a bit like your mum. Likes getting reamed out on the buffers. You know."

I felt the hard plastic edges of the seat biting into my hands. I couldn't get to him, so even though my rage wanted to fly out of every pore, I tried to relax, knowing that he wanted a reaction and that if I gave it to him he would have his little victory.

"You must love it in here," I said, and the calmness of my voice surprised me. "Got a gripe with the world outside, it must be magnified tenfold in here. You've got to ask permission to empty your arse in here. Me, I'm off to the pub for a few pints next."

He shrugged, re-lit his roll-up. "You're missing the point with the bloke who's doing all this. Pushing people off the platforms."

"Am I?"

"God yes. Just a little bit. He's fucking insane, Adam. There is no cheese on his cracker. There are no beans on his toast."

"Insane," I said. "That's very interesting. Let me tell you about insane. I visited Claire recently. And I saw what you did to her."

He stood up and walked away then, but not before I had seen a look of shock on his face. Maybe I'd done the wrong thing, saying that. Maybe he was undergoing therapy for it, and my mention of his past—a past he was no doubt trying to block out—had driven a wedge into the treatment. Well, sorry Shaun, but your recovery is coming on a whole lot faster than Claire's. Relapse away, cockwipe.

At the door he turned to me, and some of his swagger had come back. "If you talk to her, pass on my regards," he said. "I promise you, tell her where I am and she'll write to me on perfumed notepaper. She'll send me photographs of herself masturbating, if I ask for them. She'd visit me, first chance she gets."

"I hope you have to share a cell with a wrestling leper, you cunt!" I shouted as he was ushered away by the guard. Heads turned. That's when they turfed me out.

I FINISHED MY LAGER AND HAD ANOTHER. BUZZING, I CAUGHT a bus back to the flower stall and talked to Cherry about how good things weren't going, until Lucas appeared at my shoulder.

"Lucas, hi," I said. "Business good?"

"Fair to middling," he replied. Then bowed his mouth. "Actually, bollocks to shite would be more accurate. I've sold one copy since three o'clock yesterday afternoon. I'm right pissed off. I think someone should just take this city and just... just flush it down the fuckin' toilet."

"Me too," I said, searching his face all the while. He was looking as distracted as me. Staring into my eyes with a kind of charmed fear. I said, "My crysanths are fucked."

"Adam?"

Seeing her there, completely removed from our usual zones of contact, was so unbalancing that for a second I didn't recognize her. She seemed like someone different, unknown to me. Her skin was the same color as the clouds. Her eyes were too large, too deeply shaded with their own color, as if she had been crying, or drinking.

"Adam?" she said again, as if she wasn't sure either.

"What's wrong?"

"I need you to come with me. Now. I need you to come with me. Will you come?"

"It's okay," Cherry said, with a little smile. "It's not exactly the Christmas rush going on here, is it?"

I told her I'd be back soon and descended with Nuala to the southbound platform, where I grew calmer. There weren't many people around at this hour, and the incipient threat I had been perceiving in the Tube was absent. There were no cracks in the ceiling; no shifty-eyed shadows waiting intently for a train. I thought I might persuade Nuala to come with me to Edgware Road, where I knew a nice café, but as soon as I was in the warm/cold currents of air, I felt guilty about not being back up top, clearing out the stall and making a list of the flowers we were going to order.

Nuala seemed to have settled into the new environment with gluttonous satisfaction, as if she were feeding off the claustrophobia, the hum of the electric cables and the unnatural light. Her confusion and reticence had vanished. She leaned into me like someone a little bit tipsy. She squeezed my arm.

"Better down here, hey?" I said, feeling a little odd, without my usual antipathy towards the place. A few late-start commuters arrived on the platform, with their newspapers, rucksacks and briefcases, but it felt like the entire tunnel's length was ours to plunder alone. When the train came, the two of us walked quickly along the platform until we found an empty carriage. We grinned at each other from opposing seats.

"Let's forget coffee," she said. "I want to show you something."

"Okay."

She seemed to sleep, or at least withdraw from herself a little, then. Her face, usually so animated, sucked the expression from itself till it was a flat area of pale planes, curves and angles. Her eyes closed. I wanted to lean over and smell her, run my hands over her head. Feel her through that cable-knit sweater, her bootcut jeans and Merrells. I wanted to open her mouth and run my tongue over hers, see what she tasted of, what she'd been eating. I wanted to place my ear between her breasts and listen to the codes of her heart. I wanted to breathe the warm odors of her cunt. Everything about her carried an immanence; there were messages and signals in every shred of her, from the contour lines in her thumb to the golden wisps of babyfine hair that followed the line of her jaw. Her hands were dry and flaking, the skin around the webbed curve between thumb and index red and sore-looking. I closed my eyes too and allowed the special jolts and rhythms of the Underground to sift into me. At Embankment, she nudged me awake and cocked her head. Her eyes were so large it seemed they had been transplanted from a smaller person. We caught a District & Circle Line connection to Victoria, where I followed her to the surface. The languor and intensity of the Tube seemed to follow us out, thin coatings of its ever-expanding and contracting journeys protecting us against an infinite leap into the blue above our heads.

Jesus, did I feel

strange

"This way," she said. Monck nodded and followed his slight companion as she padded across the road, jinking this way and that around the buses in the terminal. Across the busy Wilton Road they went, moving ever more swiftly as the vertiginous swirl of Topside swung around them. With Victoria Street stretching before them, Monck hung back, feeling greatly exposed, and craned his neck back towards Victoria's ornate entrance.

"It's okay," she soothed. "We'll be Under again soon. Don't worry. Come on."

It began to rain. The north side of Victoria Street as far as Kingsgate Parade was wrapped in scaffolding and green brick netting, like a giant Christmas parcel; three 1960s office buildings looking forward to a facelift. In Palace Street, cranes bent their elbows to the lifting of girders and concrete blocks. Seventy thousand square feet of contained turmoil unfolded around them. Nobody saw them slip through the barriers and shadow the perimeter boards to a quiet corner filled with shrink-wrapped tiles and a cement mixer. The traffic was muted now, it made the sound of a mother hushing her child to sleep. The tower of Westminster Cathedral darkened to burnt orange under the layers of rain.

He could see commuters crisscrossing the roads outside the building site, eyes dead ahead, intent on their meetings, their hirings and firings. Coffee. A fumble in the stationery room. High heels sent sharp echoes bouncing around the open space; a low, throaty cackle of thunder rolled away south. She squeezed between stacks of large blond wood planks steadily darkening under the rain, her jumper growing wet and heavy, hanging off her body and making her seem much larger than she was. She beckoned him in and they squatted, her eyes trained on the opposite side of the site, where a JCB digger was parked, its befanged mouth empty, its chin on the ground. Monck looked nervously around, almost expecting the walls of the site to start scything inward, like an iris diaphragm, trapping them.

"What are we waiting for?" he asked.

She raised a hand. "A signal."

There were messages scratched into the planks of wood; all of them seemed loaded with meaning, even the ones he couldn't understand. JAG VAR HAR MA-96 seemed straightforward enough, but HUR STÅR DE TILL? defeated him. Another graffito was written in black indelible pen on one of the containing walls: WE MAKE SAUSAGES YOU CAN TRUST. There were messages everywhere. Everything was a page.

Rain pelted *into* him, it seemed. His hands were cold, so cold he couldn't push them past the rough edges of his denim pockets because of the pain.

"Now," she said, and moved out of the poor shelter of timber. Here, behind the detritus of demolition, a community had grown in spaces forgotten, or ignored. They kept left of the rank of blanket tents and half-concealed boxes, the struts that supported them, the buckets and sleeping bags and ropes. Deeper still, a man was moving his hand from a small hessian sack to his mouth and back to the sack's lip with a distressing rhythm. Monck tried to see what it was that he was eating, but then he was bustled into a bivouac with its roof pegged against the wall.

A space about four feet by three feet was occupied, with their introduction, by four adults, a baby and a dog. The dog, a bull mastiff, seemed the spitting image of the child: both wore straining, drool-washed chops. There was a woman whose head was cradled by a sling made of stout, grubby fabric fastened to a hook protruding from the wall, which was concealed by a collage of notes, maps and sketches. She wore a drugged look and her skin was heavily scored by fatigue. She seemed in great pain. Her swollen cheeks and chin resting in the brace were discolored badly. Sores had erupted on the flesh where the material dug into it. One of her eyes carried the pale seed of a cataract.

"This is Sloe," said the woman he had traveled here with, whose name was now lost to him. He hunted for it, confused, while nodding at the people he was being introduced to. "And this is her boyfriend, Reef. He's blind, deaf and mute. He's also got a serious bowel problem, so excuse his interruptions, okay? They're sentinels. We've got thousands of them. Most of them fucked, physically. Chances are you see a tramp sitting outside a bank, or in a subway, well they're sentinels too. Keeping watch. Keeping our people safe and sound."

Monck pressed his hand against the dog's flanks; the animal responded with a grunt, rolling over to expose his belly. "What's up with her?" he asked.

"Someone broke her neck. That's why we're here. You're going to help me get her over to the Face. Where the nurses can help her."

"Why isn't she in the hospital?" Monck asked, clearing a space among the debris and sitting down.

The two women swiveled their eyes towards him. Even Reef shifted his head. "What is with you, Monck? Have you forgotten yourself? We tend to our own. The doctors are too dangerous for us." She held his gaze for a few seconds, and it felt to Monck that she was perhaps trying to read something in his eyes, but then she dismissed him with a flap of her hand.

Sloe was in a bad way. There was an empty phial of dextromoramide and some syringes scattered around the floor. Her vest was damp with sweat. A tear in the cloth disclosed a scar, an arborescent pattern, on her chest, as if a fern had been pressed into her skin. The skin he could see twitching with the beat of her heart. Even in this extreme state of incapacity, he could see she was lovely.

"We wait till it's dark," his companion said. "We can't risk anyone seeing us on the way to the tunnels. I'll fetch us a stretcher."

When Monck moved to follow, she raised a finger. "I'll not be away long."

Monck folded himself into a corner. Not wanting to enter into any dialogue with Sloe, he patted the dog and tried to make sense of the notes on the wall. There were pictures of tunnels. Sketches. Schematics. Calendars. A photograph of a woman, naked, her ruined body cabled together with thick sutures. A map of their Underground, and the way it secretly fed and interlinked with the tunnels used by the Topsiders. Documents in an illegible hand were signed and stamped with a red mark: an arrow pointing down with an eye on the top. All of this was both unsettlingly familiar and alien to him.

"Monck," she gurgled. "You. Are in. Such danger." Here she closed her eyes and swallowed, gritting down on the pain now paling her cheeks. "Mistral is going. To kill you."

"Mistral," Monck said.

"Your friend. She will. Do For. You. She has already tried. I was. Sent to help her."

"Why are you telling me this?" he asked her.

"Because I'm tired of the... separation." She frowned as she swallowed. Monck was getting impatient but he bit down on his demands that she continue. Clearly she was struggling to speak and probably wasn't meant to be talking at all.

"I want to see us pulled inside out. I want it all to collapse. Mistral. She's trying to draw you in, trying to get you to trust her. She's going to take you to Blore. She's. Protecting him. From. You." She frowned and coughed, her head jouncing alarmingly on its supportive hammock. She spat twice; the second packet of phlegm contained a bloody core. "Christ," she muttered. "Go now," she said. "Get Under. She'll be back soon."

"What about you? We need to get you to the nurses."

"I'm dead anyway—"

Reef severed her words with a spray of wild laughter. Before he left the tent, Monck snatched the wad of notes from the wall, stuffing them into his pockets. He fled just as he heard Mistral's boots gritting across the demolition site, a scrape of metal as she dragged the stretcher behind her.

He feared dropping into the Tube again, knowing he was being fed to a trap, so on Horseferry Road, he followed his nose to another redevelopment site, and passed through into the warren of tunnels beneath where the old bomb-resistant rotundas had existed, housing government officials during the war.

He closed his eyes and took off, allowing the dark to flood into him, to coat his senses with its rich mystery. He plowed through service shafts, broad, dead tunnels, refuse chutes and ventilation ducts. All of them as intuitively known as the vessels and fibers shot through his own body. He stopped when he heard the sound of industry. And opened his eyes.

In the immense chamber ahead, voices clamored around the noises of hardware, like lost birds. Lit by hundreds of candles, the walls seemed to pulse and shiver, wetted by the coolant jetted into the teeth of the drills as they ground a path through the clay, earth and rock. Monck watched the labor with fascination, as though for the first time. He was not alone; the work space was crowded with children, their faces pressed between the crooked wooden slats and iron webs that formed a fence around it. He saw a slick routine in progress, at odds with the archaic tools and harsh language. As far as he could discern, the workers were divided into a number of groups. Those at the Face, the "chiselers" he discovered they were called, hacked at the jagged wall of rock with edges and staves, cold chisels and pickaxes, sledgehammers; oil-lamps and candles cast frenzied shadows across the uneven walls and ceiling. Behind them, the nurses swept to and fro, offering the chiselers tit milk, if they were lactators, or if not, sugared water. Maintenance teams tended to minor wounds or ensured the tools were kept sharp and functional: a white-blue tongue rasped in a dark corner as a man in a protective mask welded a new handle to a hammer head. Transporters darted between the drones who packed the rubble into oilskin parcels and dragged it into the tunnels to be dispersed. It was tiring to watch, but invigorating too. All of the workers were white-skinned, thin but wiry. None of them looked to have seen the sun for years. Their expressions weren't worth the name: they all looked screened off, closed down, absent.

Monck forgot why he was here, until he heard the echo of boots spiral around the walls behind him, the *schrang* of steel as Mistral's weapon tripped across rock. She had sniffed him out. She was good. She was very good. Quickly, he stepped onto the wooden planks that formed a pathway through the mud to the Face. Picking up a tool, he pushed in between two flushed, sweating chiselers, Coffey and Rathlin. They grumbled hellos and a third, Mitre, slapped him on the back and said: "Goodstuff having you back in the fold, Monck. You've some muscle to apply, though, if you want to catch us up."

"Think of it, Monck," urged Coffey, leaning into him, his cracked lenses on fire with the reflection of greasy flames. "A matter of feet and we shall be finished. The Doorway opened."

Monck kept quiet, not sure he fully understood what Coffey was telling him. He went back to his work, hacking at a great split in the rock with new vigor. Coffey shrugged, frowning, and followed suit. Mitre took him to one side.

"Are you well in that secret place of yours?" he asked, gesturing towards Monck's head. Mitre's face was barely recognizable under a thick mask of grime; his eyes shone from it like pearls pressed into dung. "Only... you smell of Fresh to me."

Over his shoulder, Monck saw Mistral move into the workplace. From her hand hung a steel rope that split into four long wires, each tipped with a flashing, spinning razor. "Listen," Monck said. "I've been chosen...

Odessa selected me for a task. She wants me to hunt down Blore. The man who threatens all this. Who might stop you from what you're trying to do. She wants me to drop him before he exposes us to Topside."

"And you are the best man for this task?" Mitre looked him up and down as if sceptical. "What marks you out as different from the rest of us?"

"I... I don't know."

"It's because he's a Topsider too," snapped a woman, one of the nurses, as she passed by with a part for the lathe. Monck stepped back, and felt the cold, rough rock face press against him. "Quiet, will you?" he begged her. "I'm in danger."

Mitre rounded on the nurse. "Let him speak, Amhurst."

A small group had formed around Monck now, and though it meant his concealment was improved, he was aware too that Mistral might be drawn.

"I can't say what I am." He struggled to speak sense of his position. "I don't remember. I don't think I've been Topside. I don't know. Please... I'm trying to help. I'm in danger...."

A chisel hit the ground beside him, sparks flared. Monck saw Mistral look his way.

"You'll be in danger, Freshman, if you don't speak up," Amhurst yelled.

"Odessa," he pleaded, as if the name alone should pacify everyone. Mistral was closing in, her hand lazily turning the steel rope. Monck could hear the gentle whickering of the steel blades as they cut the air. Her face was a torment of confusion, as if she too was struggling to understand what motivated her. "Odessa has sanctioned this work," he said quickly. "I have to track down the Pusher. I have to find Blore. This is beneficial for all of us. Don't you see that?"

"Blore is a Topsider too," called a Drone, his empty oilskin sac slung across his shoulder like a deflated body. "You're in cahoots!"

Mistral was pressed up against the rear of the pack but she could not yet see Monck, who had shrunk into the shadows provided by his interrogators. He was considering trying to start a brawl that might give him some space to make an escape when a cry clattered around the cavern like a confused bat.

"We're through!" it said. "We're through! We're *through*!"

All heads snapped up and whipped left as the gravity of the message sank in. An isolated cheer bleated from the pocket of chiselers who had breached the Face, herding momentum until the cave was filled with a returning tide of applause and whistles. Forgotten, Monck went with the surge of the crowd as they piled towards the fissure; he melted away into the dark, keeping his eyes fast upon Mistral, who was running alongside the revelers, ducking and leaping as she tried to pick Monck out.

*I have you now,* Monck thought. He waited until Mistral appeared satisfied that Monck was not among those now working frantically on the break in the Face. He watched her move back into the tunnel. When it felt right to do so, he moved after her. Soon, his tunnel senses were singing again, his eyes sucking in every particle of light and swapping it for detail. He was fleet enough, and wily enough, to track her without making a sound, his feet gliding across the disused tracks of adjoining tunnels, navigating the rockfalls and drifts of litter, sprightly as a goat. The sensation of familiarity welled in him to the extent that he was able to close his eyes and feel his way after his quarry, confident that Mistral would never look back and sight him. A Topsider indeed! He was Underman to the core. The dark fed him and drew him on; the tunnels were extensions of him, they sustained and accommodated him as comfortably as the arms, the mouth of a lover.

It was another twenty minutes or so before he recognized a change in the air. He pulled up, ducking behind a shelf of rock at the opening to a disused station. Mistral was ahead of him, levering herself up onto a short concrete platform. A pack of rats scattered. Monck heard a voice dip down from the ceiling, where thick crisscrosses of steel peeked through the rotting tiles.

"You finished him?"

Monck thought he saw something move across the grille, shifting to gain a better view of Mistral perhaps. Mistral shrugged, the steel whip in her hand chinking gently against her leg.

"I lost him, my sweet," Mistral said. "There was pandemonium at the Face. They've broken through. The door has been opened."

"I don't care about doors. I care about Monck. I want us to make wetwork of him. I want these walls here decorated with his blood. I want a brawn of his head, served up to me on toast. Now... *find* him. And bring him to me."

Mistral seemed to diminish before returning towards the tunnel she'd just exited. Monck edged into the shadows, watching as she sped past him, heading back to the Face. Then he waited, certain that Blore was still watching the platform.

"Monck?" The voice sifted down through the scarred ceiling. Monck felt himself rise to reply but silenced himself and waited. The skin at the back of his neck tightened. Minutes passed. A figure stepped into the tunnel at the opposite end.

*I know him,* Monck thought as he shrank again into the dark, his heart fluttering like a dying bird. And then: *can he see me?*

Blore was leaning against the mouth of the tunnel at the other end of the disused platform, hands deep in the pockets of his black overcoat. His head was cocked to one side, the white clenched teeth flashing brightly through the filth that had been powered into him by the subterranean weather, the gusts of wind and the constant fine rain of dust; the black sun that tanned with its grime: an accumulation of decades' worth of sloughed-off skin.

Monck might have made himself know then, had it out with him—he was straightening, bunching his hands into fists, trying to control the racing madness of adrenaline—were it not for something that he at first took to be an illusion. The glints in the earth, the scintillas of silica or quartz or glass, seemed to be unstable. He saw the flints of reflected light spilling lazily out of the tunnel behind Blore, as if they were part of some slow-motion landslide. It was only when the ghostly shape of a reaching hand, like a badly drawn star, emerged from the dark to rest against the wall of the tunnel just behind Blore's shoulder, that he recognized the lights to be reflections in the curves of about a hundred pairs of eyes.

He felt the pressure in the air behind him changing, increasing, though nothing was moving there that he could see. But then he heard an impossibly faint noise, the slightest tap of an aglet on the end of a shoelace, perhaps, brushing a rail, and he knew he could not go back.

From where he was standing, Monck could see a cross passage linking the remaining sections of the platforms. They were illuminated by a single yellow bulb. The old maroon panel that read *East Bound Platform* was partially covered by one of the new designs, listing the major Piccadilly stations north. Ceramic insulators were stacked neatly beneath two large black-and-white fire extinguishers. Keeping to the shadows, he moved towards the passage, past the ubiquitous cables, the chalked graffiti and No Smoking signs, a single length of rusting rail. A cartouche on the wall bore an ornate arrow above the faded words TO *THE TRA*.

Blore remained standing like a statue, a creation of other people, peering into the gloom as if following Monck's progress. He was the Tube's history, all its energy and desperation. He was its blood and sweat, its disease, its tears. Monck found himself moved by the sight of him. Blore was somehow a link, the connective tissue between Topside and Underground. He was London made flesh, a cipher between the living and the dead.

Blore said: "During the Second World War, some of the goodies from the British Museum were stored here for protection."

Monck stopped; the sister platform was visible now, safety mere feet away. Blore's voice was lazy and sharp. It was not difficult to see how he had recruited his followers, inveigled their minds, got them to do what he wanted.

"Not a very safe place now though, is it?" he continued. "This astonishing little outpost, where good men sweated and hurt in order that people might be more convenienced. And then they closed it. Not that long ago. Why? Money, of course. Money drives us all, doesn't it? Well, most of us. They closed it because the lifts were falling apart and they didn't feel it was worth stumping up the millions to get them right again. The last train was full to bursting, for the first time in the line's history. Funny isn't it, at the point when things are on the edge of extinction, how everybody gets interested. Rubberneckers. That's what we are. Ghouls at a car crash. We don't want anything to die when death is at its closest. We love tradition, when it's under threat."

Monck heard his footsteps, softly approaching, no more than ten feet away. He saw his shadow bleeding across the entrance. That voice had thrown a cloak over his movements.

"Monck?"

Monck closed his eyes and dropped silently between the rails, scampered into the shelter of the tunnel, where he waited. He felt his body cool, his heart turn sluggish as a lake thickened by ice. In this torpor, he barely heard Blore turn on his heel and flee into the veins beneath the city. It took the best part of an hour for him to come out of his trance. By the time he had climbed the dead escalators and bypassed the decaying ticket barriers, picked a way out of the sealed station entrance, he emerged into a quiet side street

and God, I was so tired that my mind wouldn't work properly. I didn't know where I was; all the light appeared to have seeped into the sky and left the houses and pavements gray and matt for as far as I could see. A cab cruised me, the driver's eyebrows raised. I nodded and climbed in, mumbled my address and shrank from the windows, trying to make myself small inside a jumper that smelled of oil and death.

Back home I ran a bath, ignoring the urge to bang on Nuala's door and ask her to perform herbal brain surgery upon me. I needed time to think about what was happening to me. These fugues were occurring with increasing frequency, yet my ability to glean information from them had not improved. I thought about the people in my life at that time, how both Nuala and Greg were detached from the reality in which I saw myself. Was I looking for a way out? Was that why I was making connections with them? Did I, deep down, identify with their dislocation? Nuala might seem in control, but in her lifestyle I saw evidence of an escapee. Her past had exposed her as something of a chameleon. If she had spent the early nineties in two-a-penny skin flicks, and the rest of the decade smelling flowers and practicing *feng shui,* what other guises had she assumed that she wasn't telling me about?

Greg too needed a cover for him to exist alongside people. Thinking of him made me uneasy, especially since my last visit had proved that his patience with his own deception had worn out. If people didn't have a mask for their identity, what became of them? How many of us were true to ourselves anyway? How many of us were ever totally natural? When we finally get to be on our own, could it be that long hours of projecting, of society's conditioning, dilutes us to a point where we can never regain ourselves? The thought shook me. I'd never considered myself to be anything other than just me, but now I could think of dozens of minor incidents where I had chipped away at, or gilded myself, in order to make an impression on someone else. I had thought Greg and Nuala poorer for being so blatant in their deception, yet they were handling this problem of identity better than me. They had acknowledged what they had done; I was still coming to terms with it.

I tried to think of someone I knew who was totally genuine but I couldn't. People reinvented themselves for different occasions. They dressed in different clothes to combat certain challenges. They wore make-up or had their hair styled. Everyone was constantly making a statement. But it wasn't so much: *This is me* as *This is how I want to be seen.* Who could lay claim to being an authentic person? Babies? But they soon learned how to use people for their benefit. Loners, then. People who didn't work, never socialized. But they would have had to skip school, escaped their parents at birth, keep themselves isolated while the real person evolved within them. What nonsense. People become who they are because of other people. In order to be ourselves, we have to mix with others. We need human mirrors. So while we're busy bouncing off other people and trying to find out who we are, what we mean, we're constantly fooled into believing we know ourselves.

Jesus, no wonder so many people suffered from crises of identity.

I dried myself and dressed. Maybe this was Shaun's failing. He'd tried the conventional route—work, pubs, relationships—and found it wanting. That he'd done what he did to Claire was difficult for me to grasp, but I was able to just cling onto the coattails of his desperation. I was able to understand the frustration he felt. Just a little bit. It didn't mean that he had become trapped on a treadmill that was leading him deeper into violence. It didn't work that way. Shaun was someone who lashed out; his anger was incendiary, igniting and almost immediately snuffed. It was probably a healthier way to live your life than to keep the resentment locked up. The only problem was that Shaun's violence was very, very bad. Controlled too, so that even in the conflagration of his fury, he was able to channel the wildness to cool, almost creative ends. He had *worked* on Claire, not simply laid into her.

Greg wasn't answering his phone again. I was about to put the receiver down, having endured a dozen rings, when a voice cut through the static.

"Is Greg around?" I asked.

"Nah, he's sick. In the hospital. I'm the landlord. He owes me rent too, bloody swine." I heard him suck his teeth. "Sorry."

"Which hospital? What's wrong with him?"

"If you saw all these bottles you'd know what's wrong with him. This place is a tip, y'know? Anyway, he's in the Royal Free, innit. Man, if you is going to visit, you put him in disguise, cos I'm mighty enraged."

I put the phone down and went to the window. The street was tooling along as it usually did. Nothing looked out of whack. Yet I felt hunted, as if I was under constant surveillance. My mother had told me, not long before she died, that she would sometimes wake from her sleep thinking that someone had been in the room with her, watching her intently. It was almost, she had said, "like being chased, but by someone who was as still as I was."

At the time I thought she was talking nonsense. Not now.

"I know what you mean, Mum," I sighed. "Me too."

# CHAPTER SIXTEEN

## EVENT HORIZON

I couldn't raise Iain, and Meddie hadn't been to work for days. I even popped around to The Pit Stop first thing because she sometimes slept over in the spare room if she had stayed after hours for a lock-in. She had her breakfast in the bar while the cleaners hoovered around her. Bacon sandwiches. Tar-strong coffee. Marlboro Red. *Heat* or *Hello!*, *Time Out* or *Take a Break.*

*No, we ain't seen her for ages, my dear. What are you, her sweetheart or what? She deserves a sweetheart that one. Lovely lass.*

I even called Ilse, the girl Iain had tried to get off with in the pub, but she was sick of the sight of all of them, especially that Iain twat—*Doesn't he get the message?*

I called... there was nobody left to call. That was it where Meddie's sphere of influence lay, at least the one that I knew of. Early evening I caught a bus over to Yoyo's. She wasn't answering her phone either, but I was happier chasing after her than I was Iain.

Low sun turning the cement of the high-rise a dark amber. You get off the bus and the smell isn't of the city at all, it's of clean air, fresh and cold, the kind that puts you in mind of a childhood spent out of town, in woods and fields, hunting for conkers, chestnut-picking, a Sunday morning playing football at Cherry Tree Farm where the smells of wintergreen and mud on football boots is somehow a part of the magic. It's a smell that the city borrows, magics out of nowhere, maybe once or twice a year. It broadsides you, along with the paintbox sunset, and you suddenly feel the city's power, its beauty, its pull. Every city has its pull. Every city is a black hole, drawing you in, drawing you towards an unknowable singularity.

I climbed the stairwells until I came to her floor. Graffiti—amateurish tags, silvers, bombings—tongued the brickwork, robbing it of its natural color, all the way along the corridor. I stopped in front of Yoyo's door and listened. An argument was raging in one of the flats next to hers, and someone on the floor below had a stereo ramped up: Siouxsie and the Banshees. "The Last Beat of My Heart." The bass thudded through my feet. It didn't exactly help me to relax.

I knocked on the door three or four times over the next five minutes. Waiting, listening. The argument stopped, to be replaced by the sounds of repeated slamming against the door, a man grunting and a woman coming. I shuffled my feet and knocked again, bent over to have a peek through the letterbox. Unopened post scattered on the floor. Deeper into the flat, grainy darkness, but at the center of it a pale oval, a lamp, maybe, with a very low wattage bulb.

"Yoyo?" I called to it. Light, shade, light again. Someone was inside the flat, moving through it. "Yoyo?"

I turned, looked out towards the Paddington Basin. The sun had disappeared beneath the rim of the city and the sky was a bruise of blues and purples, even greens. The woman stopped moaning and a few minutes later there came the sounds of plates in a sink. There might have been none of what I thought was happening actually going on: it could just be a single occupant listening to a CD called *Domesticity.* Track 1: *Argument;* Track 2: *Fucking;* Track 3: *Washing-up.* I quite fancied a spot of washing-up at that moment. Washing-up seemed like the most wondrous task imaginable next to what I was doing.

I knocked again.

Yoyo said, "Go away." Her voice was tired. Suicide tired. I imagined her sitting alone on the sofa, daydreaming of Saskia broken open on a wet road. How long would you have to go, how lost would you have to be before you found that attractive, desirable? How tired?

"Yoyo," I said. "It's me. Come out to play. Come on."

"I can't, Adam. I can't."

I smelled stale pizza, stale curry. Delivery life. I smelled the kind of air breathed into and out of a person who hasn't known any fresh for days, maybe weeks. I wondered when she had last stepped out onto this corridor. When had she last eaten something she didn't dial up for?

"I'll buy you a steak," I said. "Steak and salad and a big glass of red wine."

"Adam."

"Ice cream. And then we'll go for a walk. Hyde Park at night is beautiful. Because you can't see the dog shit you're treading in."

"Adam. I can't."

"Then what?"

A beat. "Then... wait."

I waited. Darkness came on. The paint-sprayed nonsense on the brickwork faded to gray gleams. I heard footsteps on the lino. Slippered feet.

She opened the door. Her face in the crack: one eye, the corner of her mouth. She was wearing one of her floppy hats.

"I'll walk with you," she said. "But nowhere busy. I don't want people."

"Then let's go for a drive," I said.

She was painfully slow leaving the flat. She had lost weight. Her duffel coat seemed to weigh her down. Beneath it she wore pajamas stained with gravy. She had not changed out of her slippers. There was a book, of course there was a book, peeking out of her pocket. I caught a picture of a woman standing before the sun, lifting her arms to it, a great mane of black hair cascading down her naked back. A title: *Goodbye Girl*.

I drove. She said, "I was in the bath earlier. I found the mouth parts of an insect embedded in the flesh of my thigh."

That nearly had the Yaris into the back of a Bedford Transit van before I'd made third gear.

She said, "You know that on Earth, there are about one and a half million species of animal that we know about? That we've named? A million of those are insects. Thousands of new species of insect are found every year. There could be up to thirty, that's *trente*, that's *dreizig* million species still undiscovered. They reckon that the number of insects in one square mile equals the world population. People, that is."

I kept quiet, concentrated on the traffic. I didn't know where to take her, like this. I felt we should walk somewhere, but in London, where can you walk where there are no people? Sometimes it felt that there were more people in London than insects in a square mile.

"Just think," she said. "In summer, my windows open, I might have the insect equivalent population of London in my living room."

"What bit you?" I asked.

"I don't know," she said, her voice full of interest, as if we were discussing the plot of one of the books she was reading. "Wouldn't it be great if it was an undiscovered insect?"

"Yeah," I said. "Smashing."

"I can't get it out. And I don't know how long it's been in there. It could have been there for years."

"Maybe you should see a doctor. Maybe it could go bad. Infect you. Jesus, you've got an insect's mouth, its filthy mouth in you. What was it eating before it ate you? Jesus."

"Oh stop it, Ads," she said. Humor, strength was coming back to her voice. She was looking around her, at the lights and the people on Park Lane. She wound the window down. Fresh air, still that magical hit of fresh air, even here, in Toxic City Central. "I looked it up in an encyclopaedia. Insect mouth parts. I saw the mandible, the labrum, the maxilla. No glossa, though."

"Glossa?"

She turned and stuck her tongue out at me, waggled it lasciviously.

"Jesus," I said again. "Still, it could be worse. You could have an insect's arse trapped in your skin."

She laughed. "Do you want to see it?"

I shook my head, took the car into Mayfair, towards Piccadilly.

"Let's go to the river," she said. "I want to see the river." So we turned south.

"HOW DID YOUR MOTHER DIE?" SHE ASKED.

I'd parked the Yaris on the south side of Waterloo Bridge. Now we were standing on the South Bank, in front of the National Film Theatre, watching the flux of lights in the Thames. Behind us, people were crammed on to the tables outside the café. Someone was playing a violin. From further away came the clatter and cries of kids skateboarding.

Although it was the first time I had told anyone, it felt as though I had never said anything else. It felt scripted. And maybe it was, by me, at some deep level all that time ago.

"Aneurysm," I said. "Right in the middle of her brain. Congenital. Nobody knew about it until it was too late. Not that it could have been operated on anyway. She was in her bedroom, and she was wearing a pair of Gloria Vanderbilt jeans and one of my dad's extra large Ted Baker shirts. Her hair was tied back with a pencil, you know, through the knot, however it is that women manage to do that. She was barefoot. She wore a silver band around one toe, a present from a friend who had been to Bali. There was a glass of homemade lemonade next to her. It was a Sunday afternoon. She was listening to *Sing Something Simple* on Radio 2. She was writing a letter to her sister, Ursula, who was living in Australia at the time. Perth. They were slowly arranging a visit. Her there, or Ursula here, I can't remember. This letter. I've got it. It begins *Dear Bear, I hope you're well, was able to escape from the nasty cold you said was making its way around your neighbors. Robert is well and as we speak is in the garden setting fire to whatever he can lay his hands on. Adam is fine too, reading lots this summer, he looks*

"And that's where it happened. Bang. It did what it did and she died. Dad found her sitting upright in her chair, the pen still in her hand, poised over the space next to the last word she wrote. It must be one of the tidiest deaths ever. Typical Mum.

"I've spent so much time, too much time, trying to work out how she was going to end that sentence."

Yoyo opened her duffel coat. "Come here, friend," she said. She wrapped me inside it and we hugged each other for a long time.

And then... Then we were out on the water.

"See," she said. "I told you. There's this seam. You can walk along it. From the bank it would look as if we were walking on water."

A barge glided past us, twenty feet away; its wash dashed against my legs. "Yoyo," I said, "we *are* walking on water."

"Imagine the shit swimming through this," she said, and pinched my arm. "What if something was attracted to my insect mouth? I don't fancy walking around with half a fish sticking out of my leg."

"Do you have bruises too?" I asked.

She nodded and lifted her pajama top: a ring of black, fist-sized rounds—as if she had been bitten by some immense mouth and then spat out again—looped across her breasts. "They don't hurt," she said.

"I know," I said, and showed her the fouled part of my own chest. "It feels tender though. It feels like bin bag plastic stretched too tightly. It feel as though it might tear if I press too hard."

I looked down at the water. Where my legs ended at the ankle, the venerable old river took over. It was as if it began at some point on me, in me. As if we were part of the same body. The lights jinked and skittered across the oily surface, idiot patterns that seemed to signify meaning: fizzing neon ideograms. One of them, I thought one of them said *come on in*. Beyond them, I thought I saw real movement, physical activity unfolding in jerky stop-motion cuts.

I saw something blast through rock, a sliver of light for a fraction of a second: and then the river jolted around us and began to pour into the center of the world.

I said, "I can't think of anywhere I'd rather be, anyone I'd rather be with."

Yoyo said: "It's freezing out here. Let's get some hot chocolate."

# CHAPTER SEVENTEEN

## CHTHONIC BOOM

The tracks sent their snake messages of oncoming traffic. Blue light slashed across the tunnel's lip. I imagined my feet positioned on the faded yellow D and G of the MIND THE GAP sign, tensing as the electronic voice reminded me to do what I was standing on. People crowded me, jostling at my shoulders. The air changed in the second before I was pushed in front of the squared-off snout of the train, racked with forces that sucked its stale presence from my mouth. I registered the shock of the driver as his hand flew from its grip on the dead man's handle. I plunged towards the suicide pit, arms pinwheeling when the train struck me and mashed me into the rails like a slab of sausage meat under a rolling pin.

"You, Adam," came Nuala's voice, sinking out of the hot shadows above my duvet, "are a tripwire man. I can't say anything, touch you anywhere, reach out for you without some skewed connection taking place, some switch being thrown that turns you into raw meat. It's as if you've been flayed, your soul exposed, you're being rubbed out with every breath of air."

"Do something to help me then," I said, my voice like the tremble of an onionskin page. "Bash me round my superstition nodes with your karma chameleon, why don't you?"

"Come on," she said, pulling my hand. "We'll get you some fresh air."

It was just shy of 2 a.m.

I'D VISITED GREG EARLIER, AFTER I'D ESCORTED YOYO HOME, and been shocked by what I saw. He was hooked up to an IV but all the tubes and flickering LCDs weren't the problem. Neither was it the thick dressings covering both wrists, the faint crimson bloom that was beginning to spoil their starched whiteness. It was the way he resembled a little boy. His hair had been combed in a way he never had it, side parting, long hanks tucked behind the ears. He looked utterly un-Greg-like.

"Why, mate?" I asked.

Greg's eyelids fluttered and lifted to reveal clouded marbles. "I don't know who I am," he said. And drifted off again.

I sat with him for half an hour, wanting to touch his arm but worried that it might cause him pain. I became too aware of the acute lighting, the ammoniac rape of my nostrils. I had run from the ward, imagining the skin of his face slackening as a boning knife turned his forearms to bloody strips. He had needed something to help him on his way: Suede's "The Hollywood Life" at full blast on a constant loop. The landlord, living below him, had broken the door down and walked in on a bath full of mince. Part of me hoped that it was some kind of sleep trick I was playing on myself, in the same way that I had imagined Saskia's death. But there were no jolts to suggest I had wandered off the real road. No coming to in gutters with the freezing rain dashing into my eyes. No alternatives.

God knows how Greg survived.

I LOST THE SENSE OF HAMPSTEAD HEATH HAVING ANYTHING beyond the prettifying border of trees at the edge of Parliament Hill. London was framed by their tops, a black, glassy streak of light and jeweled color. I could feel the life rising off that skyline like a heat haze. I imagined human interaction coming into play in all its sick, fascinating, glorious manifestations. I grew dizzy imagining configurations of metal, concrete and human beings. Cars driven by sacks of offal dressed in Alexander McQueen and Zara. Men and women meeting appointments in squalid high-rise cubes, mating on newspaper-covered floors while dogs whined in corners. The innocent sleep of babies in windows looking onto railway tracks where midnight Tubes ferried deadheads dreaming of a chemical homecoming.

"Better yet?" asked Nuala, sitting back on the grass with me.

I sat dead still, hair in a crazy dance, trying to force myself to calm down. I was struck, looking out at the city, by how everything we did was governed by surfaces. We went through life clinging to the scurvy skin of the Earth, or more, burrowing under it. We were insects, building hives. There was so much sky I felt vertiginous, agorophobic. Seventy years of inhabiting alleys and caves and you were allotted your own little hole in the ground. Just like all the billions that had gone before you. I groaned and lay back.

Nuala moved over me and dropped her mouth onto mine. We were alone on the hill. On the other side, trees hissed like a black tide spilling against the shore. She fumbled with my zip; I got a brief impression of her grinning in the sparse moonlight before she moved down and slowly drew me into her mouth. Lying there, staring up at the dead bowl, I could almost believe that the city had disappeared. My senses were torn between the growing pool of heat spreading from my center and the howling mass of nothing spinning away from my eyes. With nothing to focus on, my eyes fed on the aimless dark. I was using dead eyes to stare. I imagined following their trajectory, wondering how many millions of miles I would have to travel before I hit something. Couched by the earth, the city's heart mere miles away, I was cast to the other end of my neurosis, suddenly aware that there were more gaps than solids. I closed my eyes as Nuala worked me, and shuddered as I came, as she created a vacuum, another miniuniverse at my core.

"HAPPY?" SHE ASKED.

I felt a little better. You can't help it. It doesn't matter how low you get, how depressed. A beautiful woman snacking on your nerve center just because she wants to counts as one of the better experiences you can hope to have. I could no longer see Nuala, she wasn't even a vague black shape against the restless grain of night.

"I want H to move in with me," she said, with all the gravity of a shopper mumbling the next item on their list. "I want our genes to get gooey. I want to get zygote positive. I was hoping that maybe he does too."

I didn't feel as crushed as I thought I might. We weren't really compatible, me and Nuala. Not in the way that life partners need to be. But the knowledge that she would remain my friend was an overwhelming relief.

"What are you going to call your offspring? I hear 'Nut Cutlet' is coming back into vogue. For girls, of course."

She kicked me. "I'm worried about you, Adam," she said, after a while. It was getting cold up on the hill. I had been staring so intently at the scatter of light it was beginning to liquefy and lose all suggestion of shape and form. "I understand you feel unattached, in more ways than one. Sometimes, I think, the best way to reassert yourself is to go back to where you started off a new chapter in your life. Make some peace with old connections. Make a clean break where you feel there's something holding you back. Otherwise, you wrestle with demons all the time in your back brain. You can never let go and move on."

"You mean Laura, don't you?"

"You said it. She's on the tip of your tongue all the time. Spit her out."

I tore at the ground with anxious fingers. A murmuring couple moved past us in the dark, their feet swishing through the grass.

"She isn't coming back, Adam."

I knew that. I knew that. But it still scooped a cold little hole from my heart to have it confirmed by someone else. I suppose I'd kept a part of me alive for her, a warm place that would always be ready to take her back into my arms and heal the rift between us without a moment of doubt. But she wasn't coming back. The thousands of hours I'd spent with her seemed to rush through me without anything for me to catch hold of.

One day, though, I remembered clearly. So much rain had fallen that the pavements were like glass. The color of streetlamps and Christmas lights bled together and disappeared into the gutters. We had been drinking red wine since the early afternoon and decided to go out for a walk. In this kind of dark Laura's face was gray and soft. She was wearing a hat. As we reached the end of her street the rain began again, lighter now, like a mist furring the skin. She had remembered to bring an umbrella.

She was songs by The Cure; perfume on the collar of my shirt; hot chocolate fudge cake and strawberry lip balm. Her eyes were soft and friendly. Cars hissed by in the rush hour. She kissed me. I remember the two of us sprinting across the road as a bus roared towards us. I remember shadows behind fogged windows and thinking that none of the people on there knew about the woman walking alongside me. Thinking what sad lives they must lead.

*Quick,* I said to her, *put the umbrella up, I'm getting drenched.* The mist was turning into proper rain.

*All right, all right,* she said, laughing as she tried to find the catch to release the canopy. When she laughed, she lost control of her legs and weaved all over the pavement. She persevered with the umbrella even though it was in a sorry state. The handle wouldn't extend properly and the fabric was worn ragged; the spokes bent like the legs of a squashed spider.

I said to her *I can't believe you're standing under that thing, it's much drier out here where I am.*

She laughed harder, almost staggering into the road. The door of a house opened opposite and an elderly couple stepped out. A pair of spacious umbrellas—spectacularly patterned—flew up, rampant against the sky. This set her off again; she leaned against me for support, her breath catching in her chest. The wind found its way beneath the edge of the ragged tartan and sucked it inside out. She clung on, laughing so hard that it looked painful.

Soaked, we slipped into the all-night shop at the petrol station to buy condoms and chocolate.

The cashier was reading a Mills & Boon novel. She took my money, her fingers stained orange by the open packet of Wotsits on the counter.

She looked at the umbrella as if she had never seen one before.

*Wet tonight, isn't it?* she said, handing me my change.

*You'll be lucky,* Laura replied, pushing open the door.

We swapped pieces of chocolate on the way back, heads squeezed together under our sagging umbrella. Her cheek was cold and damp when I kissed it. Her nose was cold and damp when she kissed mine. Looking up, I could see the sky through holes as big as pennies. The light splintered and died away as we drifted away from the main road. Laura squeezed my hand. She sucked chocolate from my fingers.

Before we closed the door on the night I nipped inside for my camera. I took a photograph of her standing in the rain, smiling, the umbrella falling around her ears. Later there was some wine left, and warm towels. A Cocteau Twins album and melted Mars bars with vanilla ice cream. Later still, in the darkness of her bedroom when she was a warm curve sleeping in my arms, the beat of rain on glass stopped and the bad weather went elsewhere. Now all the buses I caught seem to have misted windows.

I said to Nuala: "I see a lot of broken umbrellas in the road."

"What's that?"

"Nothing," I said. And then: "Laura fell for me because of who I was. But by the end, she was beginning to hate me for who I was too. How can people cope when they see two versions of the same person?"

"I know what you mean," she said, leaning her head against my arm. "I don't know. But I think it's damaging to try to understand it. It's just magic, Adam. It's all just magic."

"Bad magic," I said. "What gets me is that I see that in myself. I feel as though I'm two people in one zip-up skin. I sometimes wake up when I clearly haven't been asleep. I'll be walking along Kensington High Street, say, when I come to, having last been aware of myself and my surroundings in a pub in Holborn the night before. It's not just the narcolepsy. I'm sure it's not."

"You should be careful," she said. "London is no place for sleepwalkers."

We sat huddled together for a little while longer. Tiredness unwound in me. The hill grew busier, despite the hour. People from parties on the wane, in need of fresh air; the post-club brigade; loners scouting for company, desperation rising from them like the shimmers of a mirage. Someone launched a kite, a great bat-winged thing that glowed in the dark. Candles were lit, a radio was switched on. Laughter broke out in pockets, as if it were something being juggled and tossed between each group. I wondered where Meddie, Yoyo and Iain were tonight.

Someone close to me started to light candles and the pale light from them picked out the back of a bench facing the view. The logo that I had been seeing everywhere had been hacked into the wood.

"Nuala," I said, "Have you seen that?"

I saw her nod before the match died and we were plunged back into darkness.

I said, "What do you think it is?"

"It looks like a bottle," she said. "A bottle lying on its side." And then, whispering: "Seek closure, honey."

"You should be wearing a pair of wings," I said.

I WOKE UP AT AROUND 9 A.M. NUALA HADN'T STAYED WITH me. I hadn't asked. How's that for adult? I tried Laura on the phone, and then on her mobile, but I only found two versions of her answering service. She often ignored the phone while she was working at home.

I was going to catch a Tube from Tufnell Park, but Nuala had given me her car keys before kissing me goodnight, saying that I had spent too long underground. It took about forty minutes to drive to Maida Vale; I didn't mind, because I like driving in London. It totally rejigs your perception of distance and there's an adrenaline rush there too, if you take pains to drive with a certain degree of recklessness.

Maida Vale was bathed in the kind of sunshine that makes dog shit attractive. I sat in the car, listening to the engine tick over as a slow, liquid beat slinked from a speaker tied to an upstairs balcony. I could hear someone washing dishes too, an impossibly lovely sound. I imagined Laura, glasses perched on her forehead, drinking a G&T, flicking through the latest *BMJ* and listening to Messiaen. I had no dread about her reaction when I rang the doorbell. How could we have a bitter scene when there were two cats sitting side by side watching clouds roll across the sky? How could we rekindle the bitterness when an ice-cream van moved through a street nearby, playing *Greensleeves*?

No answer. Her window was adjacent to the doorstep, but I couldn't see beyond the wooden blinds she liked to draw if the sunshine was too intrusive. I tapped on the glass. "Laura?"

With a sickening wrench, I imagined her in bed with someone. Before I could stop myself, I had shaken her key free of the bunch in my hand and let myself in. I stood in her hall, disoriented. I could hear no moans from the bedroom, no breathy exhortations to *fuck me harder*. She had changed things around. There was a painting on the wall opposite the door now. A spider plant in a big blue china pot sprawled by the telephone desk.

"Laura?"

My feet tapped on the bare wooden floorboards as I moved right, towards the kitchen. I had fucked her in here, while she sat on the edge of the worktop over the washing machine. An omelette burning in the pan; the wine in the glass in her hand sloshing onto the floor.

A copy of the *Independent*—the previous day's—on the dropleaf table. In the sink, a dish with a few salad leaves clinging to it. I was still pinned to her notice board—a photograph of me she had taken outside a pub in Dover, on the morning of a journey to Bruges the previous year. Next to me was a picture of some grinning stranger. Blond crop-top, rugby sweater with the collars turned up. Tosser. I ducked my head into the bathroom. Same collection of Clinique bottles on the shelf. A framed photo of a dolphin making an arch over water. Old copies of the *BMJ* on a wooden, paint-spattered stool by the tub and a red pen resting on top.

I felt dreadful, snooping around. I felt like an intruder, although this had been my home for so long. I had been more intimate, more natural here than anywhere else. Unhappy and wishing I'd stayed with Nuala, I trooped back to the living room, and that's when I found a room redecorated with blood.

I couldn't look at the chair in the center of it for longer than it took to recognize that the red handprints on it were tiny enough to be Laura's. I moved around it, looking instead at the books in the bookcase, the new throws over old sofas that had taken my weight for so long and knew me no more. I studied the rose and the cornice and the color of the walls. I kept moving: the only player in a silent game of musical chairs. There was a lot of blood. Some of it was as bright as a child's balloon, tacky, but still wet. Some was dark and dry. Something lay on the carpet, like a discarded surgical glove, but with tufts of hair attached to it. I didn't look. I couldn't look. I grew colder. I grew older. I got out.

And all I seemed to notice were the cracks in the pavement, how the whole street was filled with cracks that fled along the roads, up buildings, so many of them it seemed they must transfer to the perfect blue of the sky. Some of the trees along Laura's road were listing badly, their roots exposed through the pavement as it fragmented. I ignored Nuala's car and walked, feeling vomit creeping into my craw, and the colors and lights reducing all the time, as if everything had been dipped in bleach.

Up ahead I saw an old woman in big rubber booties standing at the center of a jagged pile of paving slabs. She was raising her hand to steady herself and looking round her in a bewildered fashion. I hurried over to help her out, but I was in no fit state. It was me who needed her help.

"Yes," she said. "Yes, it just happened like this. I don't like this one. Yes, it just happened and yes."

She wasn't hurt, but even as she made off, more cracks followed her, like a graph plotting her route.

I walked until the familiarity of Maida Vale's streets were behind me. I had no location in mind, I just let myself be carried. As long as it was away, I didn't care. I didn't think. I didn't look around me. All my mind wanted to show me were the fractures in the pavement and a red froth covering Laura's lips, a hole in her chest where her heart used to be. Knives, thick with blood, as if someone had overdone it on the jam for his toast. Blood on her hands. The blood. That thing, on the floor. I squeezed my hands into fists until my knuckles were white. She wasn't there; she might still be alive. Hold on to that. Hold on.

About half an hour later, a strident car horn snapped me back to the here and now: I had wandered onto the A40 at the point where an elevated roundabout connects it to the West Cross Route. Brought to my senses by the growl and hiss of traffic on the Westway, I moved into the glare provided by the powerful floodlights ranged around a synthetic football pitch and a series of artificial climbing walls; giant splinters of textured cement thrusting out of the ground. A game of eight-a-side was going on down there, a red tide of players advancing on a blue team's goal. I watched one player dance around the ungainly lunges of the defence before letting loose with a twenty-yard left-foot shot. The goalkeeper, in his bright yellow jersey, dived gamely but the shot was too powerful, too accurate. He looked up at me with brilliant eyes, having retrieved the ball from the back of the net, shrugging animatedly. A thin rash of slow hand-clapping.

I thought, sluggishly: *I ought to go to the police.*

It was then that I heard, or rather, felt, a deep vibration, moving through my body like the charge of bass through large speakers at a rock concert. Traffic around me veered and slewed at speed across the Tarmac. The road was tipping; I was spilled against the barrier overlooking the drop on to the Astroturf. There were sounds of consternation as the players sprinted for safety.

Three feet away from me, a Sierra slammed into the barrier. A woman behind the wheel followed up her expression of shock with one of panic and pain as a double decker coach piled into the back of her car. I watched as the Sierra folded in two, the woman's head smearing across the windscreen like a lick of red paint.

I ran.

The roundabout crumbled behind me, vast cracks splitting the road in two, carving a path towards the opposite end, which I was endeavoring to reach. The crest of the climbing wall rose above the level of the road; I clambered onto the barrier, which was warping badly now, and flung myself through the air. A pocket of calm, a split second without tremors, afforded me a glimpse of the road as it collapsed on the carriageway beneath it. The sounds of rending metal tore at me as I hit the climbing wall and managed to grab hold of some of the pre-laid pins. It didn't prevent my fall, but it arrested it; by the time I crashed into the gravel pit below, my body was sliced up like a joint of pork scored by a butcher.

I lay there for a while, scared to move in case the pain was a mask for something even more serious, and listened to the death of the earthquake. Sirens already moved through the creamy morning; I could hear them through the settling tonnage of concrete, Tarmac and steel. And human shrieks.

Cautiously, I rose. Managing to pick my way through the newly configured concourse, I tried to see into the sandwich of roads to see if I could pull out any survivors. Cars inside had been crushed; their passengers had no chance. An intense flare of fire lifted into the sky towards Shepherd's Bush. Smaller explosions thudded around me as the ground discovered fresh levels to settle into and gas pipes ruptured and ignited. A great chasm yawned nearby, sucking in cars, lorries and a Hammersmith & City Line Tube train. The lights went out everywhere. As they did so, a great tide of sound rose from beneath my feet, like a rush of gritty air forced through tunnels. It took me awhile to realize that what I heard, but did not see, was a crowd of people cheering. Awhile longer and it dawned on me that I was making the same noise.

It took a long time to reach unspoilt pavement. Near Paddington Station, where the Ranelagh and Westbourne bridges had buckled and twisted like the deformed spines of dinosaurs, I paused for breath and made better time over a relatively level surface. I padded down onto the road, surrounded by a new topography of urban mesas and buttes created from mangled traffic and the erupted complex of the Paddington Basin; a horizon filled with crippled buildings. Fire swarmed through it, settling like strange scavengers on anything that would burn. Occasionally I saw bodies and had to turn away, but my shock had not yet reached the plimsoll line of my tolerance; the sight of blood in Laura's flat had inured me.

A skein of military helicopters arrowed in towards London's center, searchlights scouring the wreckage. The clatter of their rotors cut across the sounds of the disaster for a while, so that when the screams and the crackle of fires, the collapse of timber and masonry, finally returned, they startled me. The ground was level only for another fifty meters or so. A flattened stretch of land, like a demilitarized zone, had separated me from the rest of the city. Cracks in the ground fell away, sucking the light out like something with a great hunger. Paramedics tried to get stretchers down the trenches to people who would have been better off being carried away in several small jam jars. Policemen stood around ineffectually, jabbering into radios, utility belts jangling with so many impotent accessories. I picked my way by them, wondering where I was going. Nuala. That's where. Hopefully she was all right; hopefully she hadn't been folded into the ground by the tremors that even now were still shaking London like a pair of giant hands panning for gold in the sieve of the city. I wanted to tell Nuala what had happened to Laura. Like that really mattered now. Like that was headline news.

I laughed bitterly until I vomited. Once I had wiped away the crud from my nose and mouth, I felt somehow lighter, unblocked. It meant I could cry and cry, out here in the daylight, clinging to the shattered remains of Paddington Police Station.

Feeling sick, feeling dizzy, I lay back into the soil, wishing it would suck me down too, and thought: *Laura.*

# CHAPTER EIGHTEEN

## TUBEWAY ARMY

It was getting dark as I traipsed back along my street, picking a way through the eruptions and collapses, somehow knowing that I lived here but finding no feature to distinguish Tufnell Park from the demolition behind Marylebone Road or the mess that was now Camden Town. My long trek home had been punctuated by a brief adventure in Regent's Park, where London Zoo had been leveled by the quake; wild animals were moving through the twilight in a daze. A giraffe galloped as if in slow motion, something graceful among the madness. I almost screamed with shock when I saw two lions scything through the grass after a wide-eyed eland, and stood petrified until they vanished behind Regent's College, to the north of the Inner Circle. By the time I had reached Albany Street, I was being sedately pursued by a camel and an Indian elephant. They were soon impeded by the range of broken cars, buses and lorries piled up along what had once been the main road. I had kept on in a vaguely northern direction, drained and papery-mouthed with shock and exertion. Every so often I stopped to laugh or cry, or try to make sense of the violent new landscape as I made my way through NW1.

But finally, I was there. I had long given up any hope of seeing Nuala. I had a feeling that if she hadn't been buried under twenty tons of rubble she'd have escaped somewhere a little less spiritually taxing.

I shook my front-door key free of the bunch, pocketing the whole lot again rapidly when it transpired that I no longer had a front door. I went in through a failed wall of half-bricks and plaster dust, tearing away a few lengths of splintered timber to gain access to the hall. My flat had been looted already; my TV and stereo were gone. Someone had Blu-Tacked an old A-ha CD to the bathroom wall and written *OH DEAR* in shaving foam beneath it. I thought fair play to them, thieves with a sense of humor, and stood giggling at it until the mobile phone brought me out of my hysteria.

It was Dad, asking me if I was all right. He'd seen the news and had been trying to get through to me for hours. The land lines were down and the mobile networks were overloaded with people trying to get in touch with relatives.

"It was like the first time you moved down to London," he said, his voice fading in and out, so crackly I could hardly tell it was him. "I couldn't get in touch with you for ages."

"What are you talking about?"

"It doesn't matter. I'm talking to you now. But I was tempted to come down there and find you."

"I'm fine," I said. "My place is a little scuffed up, but not as bad as the city center."

"You've been to have a look?"

"God, no. It's too dangerous. But I can see it from here... what's left of it. The BT Tower's gone. But it seems fairly localized."

"Jesus, Adam," my dad whispered. "You sound so laid back about this. There's been an earthquake, for God's sake. London is *trashed.* You could have been killed."

"I know," I said, "it must just be shock. I don't know what to do."

"Come home," he said.

"I would if I could, believe me. But it would take me two days to walk up to the M1 to cadge a lift. It's an obstacle course, this place."

I continued to assure him that all was well, even when he asked me about Nuala. Hearing her name refreshed my concern for her. I gabbled a goodbye and slipped the mobile into my back pocket. I navigated my way through the small hills of rubble but couldn't see anything of Nuala. I tried calling her name but nothing came up from the ground save a gurgle from broken drains. Whatever was underneath all that devastation wasn't coming out alive.

I realized I was flailing for human contact, a spinning top desperate for something to bounce off, something to slow me down. I stood in the street for five minutes, waiting for a bus that would never come. Anyone I might have been able to talk to was half a day's march away.

Unless I used the tunnels.

Just thinking about them brought me out in a cold sweat. But I didn't have an awful lot of choice. I dived in at Tufnell Park Tube and stumbled through the collapsed ticket barrier. In the deserted office I found a torch, which I pocketed as I approached the escalators. I managed to pick a way through yards of warped steel and get onto the Southbound platform, where the damage wasn't so bad. At least the tunnel was relatively clear, although a portion of the arch had fallen into the entrance. The air down there, thick and muggy, made me feel sick. I bit my cheek

hard in an attempt to stop myself from fainting, then
Monck hopped down into the suicide pit and jogged to the tunnel proper, where he vaulted onto the track and headed into the darkness. The beam from the torch jerked around the curved walls as he ran, making what he saw seem soft, unreliable. He didn't know why he was carrying the torch—he didn't really need it, able as he was to navigate by sound and smell in these tunnels and ducts that he knew inside out—but he kept it on anyway, enjoying its play of light.

He made good time and, but for a few minor collapses, didn't run into any serious impediments. The tunnel moaned around him, taking the strain of the quake on its fragile shoulders. He wished he knew its language, could find a way of communicating with the earth and its beautiful souterrains, to reassure them, urge them to hang on.

At the fork of Camden Town, he changed onto the Edgware branch and set off north, but a hundred meters in he saw that his good luck had run out. A substantial portion of the ceiling had been downed, partially crushing a train. He managed to worm himself through the first few feet of wreckage, trying hard not to see the bodies that had been sheared apart in the accident, or the gouts of blood splashed across the interiors, but he soon realized that if he was to progress, he would need to get inside the train and walk through it, where space was more generous than outside. This he did, smashing in a window with handfuls of concrete, and pulled himself into the lap of a headless woman. The book she had been reading was still firmly clasped between her hands. A phone number was written on the back of one of them. Among the blood on the page he read a line of text: *Things which are too big to forget.*

He moved slowly through the carnage, trying not to step on the soft parts that had collected in the aisle. Blood ran sluggishly along the grooves in the wooden floor. He saw no survivors.

It took twenty minutes to reach the front of the carriage; there was a window already smashed for him to climb through, broken by the force of a male body that had been slammed against it and remained, partially within the frame, a belt of shards almost halving him.

He heard voices once he was back on the track, skating down at him from a distance. He waited until they had disappeared and struck north once more, looking back at the driver's cabin and training the torchlight upon the roof, shattered by countless tons of rock piled on top of it.

He shuddered, picked up his pace. At Belsize Park, not quite knowing why, and grimacing as the poor, granulated air coated his throat, he skipped onto the platform and took the steps two at a time, filling his lungs with fresh oxygen, as he sought the
surface

where there was chaos at the Royal Free. The doctors and nurses went diligently about their duties, flitting like soiled butterflies through a quadrangle of calm. Debris had been shoveled into one corner. Bodies needing attention were laid out on mattresses; emergency packs of donated blood bobbed in a bath of dirty cold water. I stopped one of the nurses; she was wearing a bloodied bandage on one hand. Her pale red hair, though pinned back, was coming loose, like errant strands of sugar on a candyfloss pile. The map of her face was spoiled by contour lines of stress and exhaustion.

"Sorry to bother you," I said. "But I have a friend here. He's a patient. Greg Noon. I need to know if he's all right."

"Which ward was he on?" she asked, looking back at the shattered building. One half of it was dust. I got the message.

"Never mind," I said. "I'll find him." I pushed past her and negotiated a path through the rubble, overturning ruined beds and cupboards when they blocked my way, halting and listening for voices despite the pleas by the nurse that I return. Occasionally, as I rose on the surface of the mound, a piece would give way, causing me to slip. It was treacherous going, but I wasn't really going anywhere.

"Oi, idiot!" came a harsh voice. A doctor in a grimy white overcoat came flapping up at me over the bricks, a stethoscope swishing about her neck. A paper mask concealed the lower part of her face, but her eyes were wild blue, pumped with adrenaline and concentration. "D'you think we haven't enough casualties around here without you trying to get your legs broken?"

I stood my ground and shrugged. She caught up with me. She smelled heavily of soap and soil. A plug of something viscous, blood-streaked, clung to her coat pocket, from which a half-eaten Topic bar protruded.

"I'm worried about my friend," I said, kicking at the bricks and sending a plume of dust over her shoes.

"There's nobody here, clearly," she said. "If he was in that wing," she pointed at the powder that remained of the hospital, "then he's dead, I'm afraid. There was a big explosion. A fire. Nobody could have survived. He'll have been moved elsewhere."

Elsewhere turned out to be the morgue. The doctor—Dr. Massey—explained that much of it had collapsed, precipitating the need to lay out the bodies on the stairs. Ahead, in the grainy half-light, I could make out pale wooden joists where they had been wedged up against what remained of the morgue ceiling.

"We begin here," Dr. Massey said. "Or rather, *you* do. I have to get back. I have to suture a wound *this* big with a needle *this* small. Jesus."

I called after her. "You have no idea where he is in here?"

"All the filing, the records, they're shagged."

"What about ethics?" I shouted, my voice breaking as I tried to argue my way out of the task. "You're happy to let me wander around here on my own?"

She was ascending into the light, her back to me. "They're shagged too. Just don't eat anything or fuck anything and I won't mind what you get up to. Everything's shagged. Earthquakes do that." She stopped and turned around. "Look, nobody's forcing you to do this. If you've got the heebie-jeebies, forget it. Eventually, when we've sorted ourselves out here, you'll discover what happened to your friend."

But I had to go on.

With every shroud I turned back, I half-expected to see Laura's face staring back at me, the blood at her mouth like strange lipstick. But all I saw were ranks of calm, fixed bodies, as though carved from wax or soapstone. Death had made relatives of them all, a breed of silent, serene creatures. I could almost sense a kinship with them, as though in the ruin that patterned their bodies, there was something meant for me, a riddle that only I could solve. I closed one eye and the imbalance within myself deepened—the uncertainty of who I was—until I felt on the verge of being bisected.

And then a crumbling of soil behind me. I turned to see a child looking at me through the wall. She was blinking like some large, mutated mole.

"Monck," she sang.

I opened my mouth to answer, though I wondered what she meant.

"Coin," I said, in spite of myself.

"There's movement," she said. She looked thoughtful for a second, then grinned. "Strange things are afoot."

"Someone close to me has been kidnapped," I told her. "Someone I... loved. She might be hurt. She might be dead. I need to know where Blore is."

"The dead zones," she gurgled through a sudden torrent of phlegm. She spat a black wad of it against one of the shrouds. The sputum slid slowly down it like a man shot. "You know that. There's one at Belsize Park. Let's both go."

"It's no work for a child," I said, wondering how I knew her, how I knew that I needed to find a man called Blore, how this all didn't seem quite as weird as it ought to.

Coin shook her head and smiled. "You know where to look. At least, you would if you came down here. Where it's warm. Where it's safe. Where you ought to learn to belong. Stop fogging your mind with all this Top shite." She wriggled backwards and was gone.

I went after her, grabbing hold of her leg when it seemed she was getting away. She laughed and then squealed, sank her teeth into my hand.

"Hey," I shouted. "Cut that out. You and me are going to have a talk."

She jutted her chin out at me and raised her fists. "Talk to this," she said, and swung for me. I felt the air move in front of my face. Up close, in decent light, I saw how she wasn't as young as I had initially believed. She was bird-like, her figure boyish. Her dirty blonde hair fell about her shoulders in clumps and tangles. She was maybe thirteen or fourteen. The expressions on her face wouldn't sit still; they shivered between a taunting impishness, petulance and flat-out anger.

"I need help," I said.

"That should make the news headlines," she said, a sly smile flirting with her lips. "I don't think."

I gripped her arm again and pulled her closer. "Stop fucking around," I said, suddenly remembering, *realizing*. "That note you gave me almost got me killed. Who put you up to it?"

Confusion pulled her face apart. Her eyes widened, her mouth opened. She said, "He said he wanted to help you. He's helped you before. He saved your life. He wouldn't—"

I shook her hard. "Who?" I said. "Fucking *who*? What are you talking about?"

"Down here, we know him as Griste. You'll know him as—"

"Greg," I said. "Greg." All the fury went out of me. I had to sit down. "What did he say to you?"

"He gave me the note. He told me to give it to you. He said he thought it would lead to you having a purpose. He wanted you to be a part of things. He said releasing you from the Face was the worst thing he had ever done. He was trying to make things right for you."

"I nearly died," I said.

"He couldn't have known that. He thought he was saving you. Saving you again."

"What do you mean?" I asked her. "Why do you keep saying that? The closest he ever came to saving me was getting me my first job in London. I met him by chance. He was kicked out of a pub. We got talking...."

As I was saying the words, I could see how that first meeting might have been contrived. "But he feels as though he has nothing," I continued. "You should see him. He tried to kill himself."

"Sometimes the people with the best skills become numb to what it is they're doing," she said. "It becomes so second nature, it's like drinking water. Like breathing. They suddenly see beyond that. It can be a shock."

"I bet it can."

"He was your guardian," Coin said. "He taught you the art of Inbetweening. You would have been missing for ever if it wasn't for him."

"Missing? Who's missing?"

"You were. Once." She came and sat by me, tucking her hands under her thighs, unselfconsciously topless. There were faint tribal markings coiled around the burgeoning curves of her body, like those on the woman who had come to kill me and not, as Greg had ostensibly believed, come to take me into the fold.

"What do you remember of your first days in London?"

I opened my mouth. And then closed it. I said: "I remember getting on a train, arriving, getting off the train...."

"You were picked up by sentinels in Monck Street. They noticed that you had banged your head. You were walking around in a daze, up and down the same patch of road. You had a bag with you. You looked lost."

"Monck," I said. "I'm Monck."

"Those photographs you see in *Big Issue* from time to time. Their *Missing* page. None of them are missing. Not really. They're all down here. Lending their muscles to the Face."

"Kidnapped?"

"You could put it that way. Odessa prefers to say 'acquired.' There are people from decades ago down here. They've become blind. They're pit ponies is all they are."

I sat and rubbed at the chain-link bruises on my shoulder. The densely packed soil walls around us glistened like coal. Part of it fell away into a deeper darkness. In the distance, a pale, oyster-colored light trembled. I thought of the creature I had seen at Tufnell Park, shaking the gates, his black eyes like open mouths, silent screams. I thought about the person, the family, who might be sitting at home with his photograph. Wondering when—if—he would return. My head pounded as this and other torments dawned on me. My narcolepsy—was it even deserving of the word? Was I simply tuning out of one level and into another? Maybe that's what narcolepsy was, after all. The doctors I had sat in front of over the years had all chewed the ears of their glasses, or steepled their fingers, and said words to the effect: *Research is ongoing.* Which means *fucked if I know.*

I said, "Thank God I wasn't picked up on Cock Lane."

SHE SAID SHE WOULD WAIT FOR ME WHILE I SEARCHED FOR Greg.

I emerged into hard sheets of rain. Men and women in overalls struggled to raise tarpaulin onto hastily constructed struts to shelter the wounded and the dying. I saw a man being tended by a whole posse of surgeons. He was bleating, frequently: "I'd really rather have a cup of tea, if it's all the same to you." A thick length of timber had skewered him through the center of his chest. I saw Dr. Massey gauge its width with a tape measure. She swore. Another day I might have joined her. Not today. My surprise gland had been removed and was currently in a bed with a sign reading *Do Not Resuscitate*, down at the gland hospice.

I managed to get back to the quadrangle without incident, where I continued my search for my friend. In the corner, where the rain was piling in unchecked, I found a sleeping bag with a piece of damp paper attached to it. The name Greg Noon was written on it in ink that was bleeding into the wet. The bag was zipped all the way up to the hood; it was a foul, brown affair torn in many places and scattered with dust, or tiny mites that bounced off the fabric in droves.

I unzipped him and his head oozed from the aperture like something eager to be born. I tried to grab it before it rolled away but I scuffed his scalp with my fingers and it landed in the channel between his sleeping bag and its neighbor with a loud crack. One of the other patients saw this and started to wail. I joined him.

There was a note driven into Greg's throat with a nail. It read: *Know who you are at every age.*

I knew it was meant for me. I had a feeling that all of this was meant for me.

A door slammed in the distance, its echo moving through the remains of the hospital like a tortured, ghostly heartbeat. I gritted my teeth and withdrew the nail from Greg's throat, wincing as it squealed against cartilage and bone. I put his head back in the sleeping bag and sealed it. As I stood up the lights in the ward and all across the hospital went out.

Through the window I could see a figure advancing in one of the corridors. Its shadow moved languidly, like the slow movement of blood filling a syringe. I could hear something heavy and metallic being dragged in its wake. I didn't hang around to see who it was. It might only have been a porter carting some important filing cabinet from one place to another. But I didn't think so.

I left the ward and navigated a way through the collapsed filing cabinets and storage cupboards that were now making an obstacle course of the corridors. I ran and stumbled for what seemed an age and then halted, listening for signs of him, or her. The sound of metal clinking against cool stone was still there, like the pulse of a robot. I took off again, desperate to find some stairs or a place where I could hide. I was disoriented and in the dark I couldn't see any of the signs that might point me in the direction of a fire exit or a passage to the main entrance. A fire burned lazily on the horizon. The clatter of emergency helicopters with nowhere to land came and went, a strangely comforting, tidal sound.

I fell into a room, when it seemed the noise of the chains was directly on top of me, a room filled with screens, a maze of them, the kind a patient might undress behind, before the doctor conducts an examination. I carefully forged a route through them, and was barely concealed by the nearest one to me when the door whispered open and I was no longer alone.

I stood still, maybe halfway into the room. The light cast long, looping shadows against the panels of canvas. I only hoped that they didn't show through the material. Slowly, I retreated, moving left to right until my back was against the wall. I couldn't see anything to use as a weapon. Among all the rooms filled with surgical instruments or caustic compounds, I had to hide in the one where they stored the screens.

I didn't know which way he would come for me. He might even simply wade through the center of the room, barging the screens out of the way as he wielded his chain. But his silence told me that he was still cautious. He thought I was in here. He didn't want to steam in, in case he lost me.

Crazily, I recalled a piece of writing I'd subbed on shopping psychology. It dealt with how, when a potential customer enters a shop, he or she tends to veer to the right, so that was where retailers displayed old stock that they wanted to shift or brand new lines to tempt the shopper. This was no shop, but I guessed my pursuer was anything but conventional, so I tiptoed to my left and began the slow return journey to the door, hoping that I might be able to somehow lock him in here. At some point, I knew, we would pass each other, albeit on opposite sides of the room, with any luck. I prayed that he would be too occupied with the care of his own progress to notice mine.

And then I realized that he *was* a conventional shopper after all. I was within two feet of him, a single screen separating us, when he announced himself to me with the slightest squeak of a leather boot against lino. I swiftly edged to my right, sweeping soundlessly along the rank of screens just as he stepped into view. I got a glimpse only of tattooed biceps and a face swathed in bandages. Black, scuffed boots. And that chain, as I passed into the rank that he had occupied moments before, slithering along the floor. Without looking back I slowly shifted towards the door. I was through it and sprinting even as he let loose a roar and began carving a route towards me.

HURRYING THROUGH BELSIZE PARK, I MADE MY WAY TO SWISS Cottage where the surroundings seemed less affected by the tectonic activity. I found a car abandoned by the road at the end of Eton Avenue, its keys hanging from the fascia, attached to a ring bearing a picture of Buzz Lightyear from *Toy Story*. I got in. Things caught up with me. I thought of Laura and Greg, who had both helped me become settled and comfortable in London, and who were now, themselves, anything but. I thought of being moments away from a terrible death at the hands of a man who was stalking me for reasons I was only beginning to understand. I thought of the earthquake and how many people must have died, or were dying now, while I struggled to keep it together in the driver's seat of a Renault Clio, staring at Buzz.

I thought of my mum, dying on her own in the house while me and Dad were outside throwing a ball to each other because he had found one while he was mowing and we were both a bit bored of Sunday afternoon telly. I remembered, as we came inside that day, the first spots of rain fizzing out of a sky that had bruised with storm clouds, thinking when we found her and Dad started this strange noise at the back of his throat as I went to phone for an ambulance.... I'll chin the first cunt who says to me: *At least she went quickly.*

She had loved azaleas and had meant to grow a great sprawl of them all along the back fence. Me and Dad did that for her eventually, but they never grew quite so well. Nothing ever did, if she hadn't planted it.

Gunning the engine, I took the car south, almost retracing the route I had taken earlier, until I was forced to get out as I approached Gower Street. An elephant was tapping at the windscreen of an upturned ice-cream van. An anaconda sleeping on the bonnet of a car tightened its coils more securely around itself. A tiger licked its paws at the entrance to Euston Square Tube.

Nuala had told me that H lived on Charlotte Street, above an overpriced Italian restaurant. I hoped that she had made her way here... if she had been able. The thought of her packed down under hundreds of tons of debris turned my throat dry.

I headed towards Tottenham Court Road, keeping an eye on the tiger and getting ready to sprint for a car if he launched himself at me. He looked too sleepy for an attack though, and his muzzle was already pink with dinner. I didn't hang around to see what it was he'd been eating.

I ducked into Grafton Way and clambered over the teeth of the road where it had burst upwards. What remained of the BT Tower was a jagged column, threaded with fractures, like a stick of rock that someone had just taken a bite out of. The aerial tip I saw as I reached Fitzroy Street. It had smashed into the landscaped part of Fitzroy Square, shedding its satellite dishes like scales. I turned left and hurried along the road until Charlotte Street took over. Most of the buildings here had escaped serious damage. Nice place, Charlotte Street, I had thought when I first came to stay in the city. Laura had taken me for chicken and frites at Chez Gerard on one of my first nights with her. We'd stepped out after the meal into a warm, well-lit street thick with lazy summer music. There was the lamp-post where I had steered her into a long, deep kiss. The lamp-post looked like a snapped pencil now; its business end disappeared through the window of a flat.

I headed for one of those café/restaurant jobs with a gaudy, faux-Italian façade painted green, white and red, the only obvious Italian in sight. Tony's, it was called, for a change. Only one of the nameplates on the panel by the entrance was blank. I rang the bell but after a minute or two I decided it wasn't working and tried the door. It fell inwards, moaning as it wrenched free of its hinges. The darkness swooped towards me like an effect on a cheap fairground ride, carrying with it the smells of groundnut oil, hibiscus and something that reminded me of cold Ready Brek. The reek of garlic came at me in waves from the walls. It seemed that the place hadn't had an airing for weeks.

"Hello?" I called as I reached the landing. I heard movement, a slump of noise, like a bag of laundry falling over. A huge crack had bisected the wall, culminating in a split that made a mockery of the heavy system of locks meant to keep H's inner door secure.

I was about to force my way in when I heard a noise behind me. I looked down the stairs to see Troake breaking open what looked like a shotgun and slotting two cartridges into the breech.

He said, "You know, fucker, if this was up to me, they'd be live." And then he raised the gun to hip level and fired both barrels straight at me.

MEDDIE HAD BEEN CONVINCED THAT WE ALL LEFT THE WOMB as established murderers.

"All that crap," she had told me, on a quiet stint—just a few dour pool players and a woman in a Kappa tracksuit top who kept putting Nirvana's "Come As You Are" on the jukebox. "All that crap about us being born as clean blackboards to be gradually sullied as you grow up... it's all crap."

There was just me and her. I was leaning back against the cold shelf, happy to watch the afternoon wend its way along Archway Road and wondering how I could have spent so much time cultivating Work Related Upper Limb Disorder in bad-tempered offices filled with photocopier dust and cheap coffee and feature writers who couldn't spell.

"In the womb, you know, it's a sheer bloodfest bucket of barbarity and slaughter. Chances are, you committed murder in your mother's belly while she slept soundly in her bed, anticipating your cherubic features doing all that 'kajagoogoo, aren't I cute?' bollocks."

Meddie's teeth were of an unholy—or even American—whiteness. She was wearing a tiny cropped T-shirt from Morgan to show off her buff tummy and the tiny bolt through her navel. Her breasts were exquisitely Wonderbra'ed so that they seemed to perch on the deep V of her top like proving dough. She was speckled and smooth as rare eggshells.

"You'll have dominated any twin in the coliseum of the cunt..."

"Steady on, mate..."

"—and absorbed the tiny bird-bones he or she was developing. Sometimes, though, parts of them escape you. You'll be born with a foetal head grafted onto your neck, or the mortuary men will cut you open when you finally slide off the plate and find a little cluster of hair and teeth grinning up at them."

She was like that, Meddie. Gruesome to the point where I think she got off on it, which pretty much nipped in the bud any possible romantic involvement between us beyond the occasional animal rutting session we rushed through in the cellar.

"That's why I think most of us are screwed up. We don't know ourselves because we don't know what we're made of. Our constituent parts, they're all cannibalized. We take a piece from Mum and Dad, have a chaw on whatever's lurking in the uterus, and before you know it, you're born, some patchwork creature. Some fucking evil, shat-out Prometheus."

"Meddie!"

She seemed to share my affinity for the skin of the city, that papery epidermis that separated us from all the weird sluices and sewers and gutters and ginnels, an alien civilization beneath our feet. This was before she went a little mad, preying on men, trying to extract secrets from London's shadowlands. Late-night shifts, she might stay behind when the punters had been kicked out and help me with the bottling up. In the cellar, the cold would tighten the skin and draw ghosts from between our lips. Bottles were massed before us, like a glass army. Meddie's T-shirts became even more interesting to look at.

She'd help me load the crates with the evening's drained bottles of Bud and Beck's. Sometimes the trains would surge beneath us, like wakening monsters. On one occasion, Meddie tugged me back against the giant kegs of lager and pressed her Rouge Pulp lips against mine, dunking her tongue for a second as her thigh slipped between my legs.

"Nearly dead, down here," she whispered, as I tried to scrabble away from her. "Deeper than the buried bones of thousands around us. I feel different, don't you? I feel... as though my skin has been peeled away."

Mostly, she was all right. She talked about the way London's underbelly had been manipulated by its human inhabitants over the centuries. How its secret rivers had been diverted or concealed or bested, turned into ditches; the bodies that had been claimed as the Tube network was tunneled. The hidden scars carved out of the city, a crude, ongoing liposuction.

"I feel different too," I had confessed to Meddie. "I get headaches when I'm in the cellar. It's as though, a few feet under, I lose sense of who I really am."

"No, you've got it arse about tit. You're being drenched in reality. You're losing all that surface cosmetic when you go underground. You're who you really are. Glory in it."

I sucked the chill air deep into my lungs and felt close to understanding the strange ciphers and signals as they creaked, rumbled and burped around the whitewashed walls, embedded in the ancient soil cradling us. Her smell was earthy and rich. I pushed her against the plastic crates, unwrapping her breasts and holding them gently as they threatened to overspill the span of my hands while I slid into her from behind, displacing her moisture, painting me with it. She thrust and ground against me until I withdrew and came onto the cellar floor. Watching it, as she hurriedly dressed herself... watching it soak into the unknown tissues of the city.

She said: "I won't be around for ever."

I CAME TO MY SENSES, FULLY EXPECTING TO SEE A GAPING hole where my guts ought to be and a trail of offal strewn upon the ground behind me. The concretized ramparts of the South Bank rose around me. What was I doing here? I tried to stand up but the pain was excruciating, as though somebody had gathered all the loose skin on my abdomen and fed it into a mangle. At least I was whole. I tore my shirt from the waistband of my jeans and inspected my stomach. Two large purple dinner plates had bloomed there, just below my heart. Rubber bullets?

My head felt tender too, a lump rising from my crown where I had banged it on falling. I felt exposed, played with, as though in its leveling London had been turned into a giant safari park and it was open season on the lesser-spotted Buckley. There was still much I had to do, but I realized I was better off traveling by the tunnels, at least until it was dark.

I had to get to Troake. It was he who had shot me and transported me across the capital. But why? Why not kill me and have done with it? What was he playing at?

I took in my surroundings. For some reason I had been dumped at the South Bank. The Thames was a strange color, almost purple, and its currents were disturbed by the collapse of Waterloo and Hungerford bridges; gray spume lifted off the water like dirty soap bubbles. One of the Connex South Eastern trains that crossed that bridge departing

Charing Cross was sticking vertically out of the river. A cluster of pigeons were roosting on top.

I shuffled over to a park bench that faced the river and Victoria Embankment. Cleopatra's Needle had snapped in two. A Japanese tourist took a photo anyway. Then he creased up. Even from here I could hear his hysterical bleats, but I couldn't tell whether he was laughing or in tears. St. Paul's was a punched in eggshell. Cromwell, Shakespeare and Lauderdale—the three residential tower blocks at the Barbican—had disintegrated; well, one had, the other two had managed to fall against each other, forming a giant, inverted V. Through the razed surroundings behind me I could see that Canary Wharf had become Canary Dwarf.

Sitting down, I noticed a dirty sack of clothing at the other end of the bench, slumped over, snoring. The tramp wore a filthy long coat, seemingly made more of dirt and grease than cloth. He smelled of burned oil. His head was obscured by an open tabloid newspaper. As much as I craved some human interaction, I let him sleep and closed my own eyes, trying to cleave together the disparate elements inside my head.

*Why was I Monck? How could things come to this?*

Hadn't I always suspected, or feared, that I might be someone else? But doesn't everyone suffer the occasional gap in their memory, a lacuna that can be sourced back to drink, or drugs, or madness, if it can be sourced at all? Lonely people, or mad people, or sane people even, trying to gee themselves up... sometimes we talk to ourselves as we would to another person. We might be single creatures, but our minds don't think that way. The physical, tangible parts of us contained a symmetry; why not the mental, the untouchable parts of us too?

It was momentarily heartening to consider these questions because perhaps it meant that Nuala was all right, that she too had the capacity to withdraw into another zone of being and was now drifting, like me, through the city, trying to find somewhere or someone solid enough to cling to.

On the tramp's face, the previous day's *Evening Standard* riffled in the wind. I leaned over and perused the front page, more to help nail me back into reality than anything else. There wouldn't be a *Standard* today, even though there was one heck of a lead story. Thoughts of dual personalities dissipated. The weirdness went away from me, for a while. What could be more normal than resting awhile, on a bench by the Thames, reading the newspaper?

The headline: *PUSHER RAISES STAKES.* Apparently he and his cronies had upped the ante in recent days and were forcing up to a dozen people a day onto the rails, despite the huge increase in security cameras and guards on the platforms. They had varied their methods a lot, changing lines and causing huge delays. The extra security outfits were unable to pin anybody down because The Pusher and his team vanished into the tunnels as soon as they had committed their crimes. They were opting to strike the busier central stations now that the number of Tube travelers was dwindling rapidly. The best surveillance equipment in the world and a crack team of security guards weren't going to catch anyone when a couple of hundred civilians were stampeding for the exits. Still, there would be no more pushing, because there was no more Underground. The Underground was overground now. In a day, the Pusher had been made redundant. Then again, I thought with a jolt, so had I. I had been charged with the task of finding Blore, before the world beneath ground was exposed. And I had failed. The authorities would be swarming through the tunnels as soon as the disaster scene had been made as safe as possible. Odessa, Vane, and the rest of them would be under the glare of the media spotlight within days. There was nothing they, or I, could do about it.

Something about the report I had just read bothered me.

The tramp was making glottal noises that percolated through the newspaper and the hood concealing his face. I thought he might wake up, or shift and spill the newspaper, but he settled down again. I pored over the reports once more.

The story continued to guard its secret from me. I read testimonies from some of the witnesses who had claimed to see The Pusher at close quarters:

*He smelled of diesel,* said one.

Who didn't? My own clothes were streaked with the stuff.

*He moved through the crowds like he wasn't there. Like smoke.*

Something wasn't right. I stared at the accompanying photograph, a grainy shot taken by the closed-circuit TV on a platform at Victoria. It showed a shadowy figure leaping into the mouth of the tunnel, clothes flapping about him like strange wings. A stationary train and a gaggle of commuters, faces twisted with shock. One woman with her hands at her face, howling.

*A dozen victims a day.*

"He knew the quake was going to happen," I said.

A tear in the newspaper filled with color. One brilliant blue eye swiveling in its black socket: a burnished claw clutching a jewel. And then a shift of movement and a great hole of black was opening behind my eyes. Any panic was swiftly doused by pain, and oblivion tried to pull me down. I bit down hard on my cheek and reality swung back into focus. Reality was the tramp, a great snake of large-link chain unfurling from his cuff, wading in to give me another crack.

I hunched forward, my head butting against his stomach as his arm came crashing down. He still managed to strike me but, his weight transferred, all the power was gone. I took a light knock against the small of my back and scooted out from under him, shocked by the way he repositioned himself so quickly. Before I was upright he was coming for me again. He shrugged away his coat: a skin sloughed off. His hood too peeled back, and I barked a syllable of shock. I recognized him, though he had done everything he could to rid his face of features. His nose was gone: a ragged pair of black holes were punched into the center of his face. His skin had been pared away from his face. Dust clung to it like a bizarre beard. His eyes seemed sunken into his head; an absence of eyelids and brows made him appear startled. But the mouth was worst—what was left of it. The teeth were gritted at me, a white curve of enamel. His face seemed trapped in a constant rictus of pain. Perhaps it was.

"H," I said.

IT SMILES DESPITE THE PAIN, RELISHING THE PAIN. IT SMILES *into* the pain, liking the look of shock. The shock says: *I met my match here.* The shock says: *I might die.* And then the shock is eclipsed by a gamut of expressions, chasing each other across the bruised angles of his face: anger, hate, determination. That's good too. No fight worth its salt was ever conducted without a bit of passion.

And he comes for It, more powerful than It expected, raining blows upon Its head as the faces of the dead swim up in the mirrors of Its eyes.

It's trying to manipulate him back towards the river. Perhaps, if It gets him off guard, It can push him into the mud, where he'll become stuck. It can finish him off at Its leisure then, or wait for the tide to take him.

*Where's Laura?*

"Safe... for now," It purrs, ducking under his arm as he tries to thrust his fingers into Its throat.

*Why did you do this? What's the point?*

"Why do anything? What's the point of anything?"

He's moving backwards, to the shattered railings that guard the walkway from the drop to the river. The ferocity of his attack is waning. He's tired. He wants an explanation more than he wants blood on his hands. That will be his undoing.

*But all the people you've killed... mutilated. What does it all mean?*

"Well exactly. What does it mean? Not a great deal. But then, what does it mean for the sheep that have spent years yo-yoing from home to work, doing the same tasks every day? All those jobs, those lunches, those briefings and pre-meetings and meetings and post-meetings. What are they worth now?"

*Didn't you ever consider that people might want that? Might rely on it?*

"People don't know what they want. They need to be shocked out of themselves, into new selves. Shock is what we need."

*Dead people... you can't shock someone who's dead.*

"I never intended to kill anyone. Death isn't the point to all this. Life is. One woman I pushed, she lost an arm. I read about her. She was a data inputter for a law firm in the City. She was suffering from RSI, she was paying through the nose for a tiny flat in Holborn. Now she's looking after sheep on an island in the Hebrides. She's happier now than she ever was."

*Maybe. But how can you be sure she isn't still waking up at all hours of the night, seeing that train carve her up on the tracks?*

"That's so negative. She sees the train as an emblem of her new life. She's no longer a slave."

*And what about Greg? Why did you kill Greg?*

"Because he got too close. As you have done."

WE WERE GASPING AT EACH OTHER, EXHAUSTED BY OUR physical and verbal exchanges. Both of my arms had been torn by the chain. I was holding my blade and it was smeared with his blood. Stab wounds on his hip and shoulder made the oily stains on his clothes seem darker.

Behind H, I could sense movement, as of a group of people milling. When I dared to confirm this feeling, my jaw almost fell off. Surely there was only so much I could take before my brain packed up and could deal only with my scrawling on rubber walls with crayons.

Spilling out of the rent in the earth came a torrent of naked, malformed bodies. Picked out by the sun, they were anaemic, pathetic figures, so thin that I could see the flutter of their organs through transparent skin. H was distracted enough by my expression to join me in this viewing. We stood there, drained, as these phantoms staggered around, their faces upturned, smelling the air, their useless eyes merely darkish nubs in their heads. Some were too weak to continue their trek beyond the rim of a world they had believed they would never see again. Undernourished but muscular, their limbs deformed or stunted, they panted on all fours, too exhausted or frightened to move. They were free. They were back in the city they had once known. But every one of them was still missing. Would they ever truly return?

H was away, shambling along the embankment. I took off after him, trying to ignore the hairless, pale forms streaming along the roads on the other side of the river.

Just before H dashed into a pleat in the ground, he turned to me and drenched himself with liquid from a bottle he'd slipped from the depths of his trousers. "Here's fun, Monck! I'll set fire to myself unless you follow. If I die, you'll never know if Laura is dead or alive! Come now, sharpish! We're at play!"

When I reached the spot, fuel vapors hung in the air, the shimmers of which seemed to contain his shape, his ravaged face, the petrol blue of his eyes.

# CHAPTER NINETEEN
## DEPTH CHARGE

He led me a merry dance, that harlequin. That H. That *Blore.*

I chased his ghosts all under London, in the stinking, moist darkness of its souterrains, on a feverish tour of the dead zones of the capital. Along the exposed banks of the Fleet, the Westbourne, the Effra, Counters Creek... Lost ministerial bunkers, cellars and safes. The deep-level bomb shelters, the sewers, Kingsway's underground tramway, the Rotundas in SW1, all the forgotten labyrinths that punctured London's bowels. His bloody fingerprints were on the rheostats and fuse boxes in the Plant room at Belsize Park's deep-level air-raid shelter; his sour body odor pervaded the air at the bottom of the Down Street lift shaft. And everywhere was the smell of petrol, and the hideous cackling that was his teasing laughter, always ahead of me, leading me on, leading me deeper. Sweat and the gasping of my breath as it fell in stitches from my burning throat. Footsteps ringing and gritting and splashing. Monstrous shadows slashing across walls furred with salt bleeding from bone-dry rocks.

Occasionally I happened upon more of those ravaged, deracinated souls as they drifted like smoke through the ruins of the city. They shrank from me, into the shadows, and I was grateful. I was too tired to fight anyone else. Part of me hoped and feared that I might come across my mother, that she hadn't actually died, but was merely lost. She was missing from my life. That was enough to fill me with optimism.

Nausea beat ceaselessly at me, and not just because the odor of petrol was even more overpowering in the tunnels. Laura might still be alive, but I couldn't help feeling that I'd let her down, that I was in some way responsible for what had happened. I could have prevented her abduction. And what about Nuala? She had obviously fallen under Blore's spell; she wanted his child, for God's sake. If she had survived the catastrophe, how would she react when she discovered that the man she loved was a monster?

After countless hours of scurrying, I started to get seriously worried. Not only was I unsure as to how I would overpower Blore when I caught up with him, but I was also entering territory that I didn't know so well. It was colder here; lighter too, but what light there was contained a pale green tint. I couldn't trust my feet as well as I had previously. Pieces of machinery were beginning to mount up at the edges of the wall: cogs, gears and pistons; broken, scavenged engines wounded with rust. I heard laughter up ahead, spinning around the caverns, mad, unfettered.

I stopped when I became aware of my feet splashing through puddles that weren't made of water. The petrol. The petrol was *everywhere.*

He'd led me to a graveyard. Great hulking carcasses of dead engines were twisted upon each other. The mess of rolling stock resembled a crash. This was where the trains came to die. We must have been fairly close to the surface, for slivers of natural light were slicing into the main cave. I had no idea where we were, whether we were in London's center, or on its periphery. The inner compass in me had been cracked by so much flitting about. My legs ached, my arms and back were swollen with chain marks, my chest was on fire. I needed a bath, a beer and bed.

I could hear water. And motors on the water. I could also hear the low, steady thrum of traffic, and the occasional trundling weight of a train, but not a Tube train. An overland express. There were voices too, and music: the thump of bass from ghetto blasters. Bhangra, hip-hop, jungle. People were clinging to their lives, their routines, a balm to protect them against the shattered city.

I sidled up to the first of the carriages, my blade slippery in my hands, and crept inside. The seats shrank away from me. Graffiti formed thick black webs that clung to the glass and fabric that had managed to escape the punishment of time. I walked the central aisle, listing slightly against the slanted position of the train, waiting for something to lunge for me from the shadows. At the end of the aisle, I slipped the catch on the interlocking doors and passed into the next carriage. The damage here was more extensive, and twenty feet along a rent almost separated the carriage into two parts. Rats had made a nest by the fracture; they teemed through it like a steady stream of oil.

I edged past them, feeling my skin bristle when, as one, they halted and turned their glistening eyes upon me, as if Blore was somehow controlling them. Into the next car, and the next. I could sense Blore nearby and wondered if he too was stalking me now that his bait had proved successful. I had to abandon my carriage when I was halfway through the train. The gangway had tilted too far to enable me to walk stealthily and the adjoining door wasn't going to open anyway, as it had become mangled within its frame. I slid out through one of the gaping windows and dropped softly onto the ground. More trains were stacked before me, rolled and wrecked, their snouts cracked and bludgeoned and covered in soot. I moved among them, growing more confident—or rather, reckless—as I proceeded. I wanted this over. I wanted Blore finished and I wanted Laura safe at home where we could both start trying on new lives for size. I wanted—

The sound of metal against stone. The shift of rubble underfoot.

I angled back towards the sound, the black windows of parallel trains flanking me like hellish paintings in an art gallery.

Up ahead, partly revealed by one of the slashes of light, a figure knelt. Its head was consumed by the dark. It straightened, almost languidly, as a thin blue ripple in the air wrapped itself around its shoulders.

"Blore?" I said. "*H?*"

As I neared, I could see that it wasn't H. The figure was much slighter. But my study was interrupted as it jack-knifed, a muffled scream turning to a dull reverb that moved flatly around the cave. The blue ripple flared orange as it consumed the figure. I lunged forward but the flames were spreading, folding over each other in plumes in their eagerness to find other fuel. The air was burning.

I dug my heel into the dirt and spun around, scrabbling to gain purchase on the uneven ground so that I might launch myself into a sprint. I felt heat on the nape of my neck and the hairs there start to curl. I was never going to make it, and it struck me that maybe that was okay because it meant I would never have to fret over who it was I had watched being torched.

Flames danced at my ears. I felt my clothes singeing, my skin begin to catch and melt. A frame of brilliant yellow closed in on my vision as I rushed towards the network of tunnels that had brought me here. My breath burned in my chest as I pulled on air that was itself on fire. And then—

"*Monck!* Quick, in here. *Quick*!"

I could barely see her, my eyes were so tightly squeezed against the heat. But she was there, her shaggy pile of dirty blonde hair thrusting from a fissure in the tunnel. Coin.

"Down here. Hurry!"

I don't know how I managed it. I dived and slid and scrambled, collapsing through the rupture in the wall just as the full force of the fire went howling down the tunnel behind me. Coin was on top of me in a moment, slapping at my clothes and hair, trying to stop me from going up in a blaze of my own.

"I'm okay," I said, after a while, without knowing if I really was. I just wanted her to stop slapping me. I got hold of her and hugged her. "Thank you," I said. "Thank you."

"YOU AREN'T GOING TO SCAMPER OFF AND LEAVE ME AGAIN, are you?" I said, as she led me by the hand deeper into the maze. I was hopelessly lost.

"Don't fret your noggin, dear, I won't leave you," she said, looking up with a smile on her face. When her eyes met mine, her smile faltered. I must have looked pretty rough. I badly needed medical attention; I could no longer feel my face, there were blackspots of numbness there. Pain had left me as easily as if I had turned on a tap to let it out of my body. I didn't dare look at my hands.

"You're in shock," she said.

The following hours dissolved into a feverish no-time. Sometimes I was convinced we were still walking, Coin and me, through the labyrinth of the underground, her forging ahead, hand buried in mine, tugging me onward. But other times I would blink and shake my head and be looking up at the shivering ceiling of a cave, lit by candles, as I lay on a rough bed of recovered Tube train seats. The bitter, tallowy smell of the candles was relaxing, as was the fluting of distant winds over the cracks and shafts that joined this world with the outer. The seats were slashed, lumpy and stained, but even razor blades would have been comfortable. Coin would dart around like a hummingbird, hovering long enough to trickle some water from the corner of a soaked cloth, or a few morsels of soft meat, between my cracked, blistered lips. I tried to ask her what the food was but my throat was too swollen and sore.

"Hush," she said, rubbing something fatty and soothing into my hands, the sorry skin of my face.

I don't know how long I spent drifting like that—her face or the coal-black walls swimming into focus—but it felt like days. By the time I was fit enough to sit up and take a cup of water from her hands, it felt as if I was wearing three or four days' worth of beard.

Coin was tired. She had attended to me throughout my recovery and had suffered for it. I ordered her to rest for a while, and as she slept I mooched about in the cave, which seemed more like a factory basement. The ghosts of tram tracks wove across the floor. Dirty yellow struts supported a low roof crisscrossed with riveted iron girders. The floor was scarred with mold and damp.

Nearby was a meager scattering of what I supposed were Coin's effects. There was nothing here to signify the presence of a teenager; no make-up, no cigarettes, no stereo, no photographs, no ticket stubs from the cinema. No mobile phone. There was a small shoebox, however, and inside it were dozens of newspaper cuttings. Many were like the article I had read in the *Evening Standard*, telling of sightings of The Pusher, but there were others too, in which other sightings had been made, of shadowy figures fluttering around the Tubes, observed by passengers in mid-journey through windows or on CCTV long after the stations had been closed. These articles were recent, but became more frequent in the days leading up to the quake. Some of the text had been highlighted and initialed: *O*. I didn't know how important this text must be, but I could at least ask Coin about it, when she revived. She'd not escape from me again.

I spent a few minutes examining my injuries. I couldn't see my face, but my fingers retained enough feeling to inform me that the hair on the back of my head had been scorched to stubble. The skin there was tight but had escaped serious burning. My hands, where they had blistered, were raw and tender, but again, I had been lucky to sustain only superficial damage, and the unguent that Coin had smeared on them had helped immensely. My clothes were damaged beyond repair but they had been substantial enough to save my body from harm. I shuddered when I thought of that rippling wall of orange-blue. And the scream that had seemed to power it.

Hours later, I put together a little meal for Coin, made from more of that strange, soft meat and a few crumbled biscuits. I poured some water into a plastic beaker and carried it over to where she lay. I stroked her hair gently and she opened her eyes. She was looking directly at me.

"Sleepyhead," I said, and offered her the tray.

"Thank you," she replied. She nibbled on the biscuits and drank some of the water, rubbing her eyes clear of sleep.

"What's this?" I said. "Are you vegetarian?"

"No," she replied. "I just don't like cat food."

"Great," I said, quietly. "Just beautiful."

She hid her mouth behind her hand; somehow, a laugh found its way out of me too.

"Do you feel better?" I asked.

"Much. You?"

"As well as I'll get, until I see a doctor, I suppose. Where are we?"

"Camden," she said. "The catacombs."

"What?"

She told me how the tunnels here were a relic of the 19th century; they served the Round House, the old locomotive turntable that prepared trains for their trips north. The tunnels shadowed the Euston mainline for a while, and were hemmed in by the goods depot at Primrose Hill to the north, and the Regent's Canal to the south. Blore knew these places as instintively as he knew the insides of his own eyelids. He knew them all. Better than I did. He had been the needle drawing my thread through the fabric of the city. He had tied me in knots.

"I need to go soon," I said. My voice fell against the damp walls like something executed. "I have to find Laura and Nuala." I searched her face to see if she recognized the name. There was something going on in those little blue eyes.

"Mistral," she said. "A fine assassin. Odessa called her a killer of rare ability. She was a great asset to our family, until she deserted us too, for him. We'll miss her."

"Excuse me?"

"You were referring to Mistral."

"No. Nuala."

Coin nodded. "Mistral."

I sat down hard. "Assassin?" I said. "She wouldn't harm a fly. She wouldn't harm the *bacteria* on a fly."

Coin shrugged. "Still," she said, and shrugged again.

Her words caught up in the sludge of my brain. It was like being in a canyon, and hearing the tail end of an echo.

"Wait a minute," I said. "Wait a minute. *Deserted*?"

Coin explained how Mistral had been Blore's partner in the underground, his bodyguard too, before he became a Gonebad. She had disappeared, the moment the first woman had been pushed under a train. She hadn't been seen underground since then. "She's with him," Coin said. "They're inseparable."

"No," I said, shaking my head, as if that might buttress my denial. But I was arguing against ineluctable evidence. Nuala had expressed her intentions to be with H. What was more shocking was the thought that she must have known about me. If she was protecting him, then maybe her move into the flat above mine was more of a conspiracy than I wanted to believe. She had been keeping her eye on me all the time.

"It doesn't make any difference," I said, flatly. "I have to find them." A pool of sickness was spreading in my gut. I knew, but I didn't want to accept it.

I stood up. "Will you wait here, a little while? I need to have a look at what happened back there."

I didn't wait for her reply. Instead, I swiveled and stalked away in the direction of the tunnel from which she had rescued me. Away from her, I was suddenly aware of the tightness of my chest.

Nuala. How she had cried against my chest after showing me the video. The tenderness she displayed towards me. The outright affection. Was it all a sham?

I padded back towards the necropolis of trains, sucking in air that now smelled of fried dust and burnt synthetics. The clamor from above could only be Camden Lock. Every so often, through the iron grilles in the ceiling, I caught a glimpse of feet as they marched along the road above me, or a whiff of noodles, or pizza. It was the only light that came in: rays hit the walls like chalk marks ticking off a stay in prison.

I passed through other chambers, the tunnels used as stables for the horses and pit ponies that used to pull the old train wagons; the canal basin, close to the Lock itself.

At last I entered the chamber containing the broken Tube stock. The trains had been blackened by the fire, their windows shattered by the heat. Some pockets still smoldered, and the heat was noticeably greater in the cave than in the tunnels that fed it. Through the open frames I could no longer pick out the seats; they had become a single molten mass. Up ahead, where I had seen the figure consumed by fire, was a sickening pile of ashes and blackened bones. I approached carefully, picked off a length of metal that was hanging from an engine and, steeling myself, began raking through the cinders, looking for a clue to the victim's identity. I hoped I'd find the chain that H used as a weapon, or an arm that had escaped the flames, complete with his tribal tattoo.

Instead, I found a shark's tooth.

"Nuala," I gasped, and slumped to the ground, all the strength in my legs vanished. I rubbed away the ash on the curve of enamel, until I could make out the serrations. I remembered the shock I had felt when I first saw it dangling from her sex, simultaneously the most uninviting and enticing object I had ever seen. I pressed the tooth against my mouth and prayed that Coin was right. If Blore and Mistral—H and Nuala—were inseparable, then he must be dead too.

COIN PUSHED HERSELF TO HER FEET AND SHUFFLED OVER TO a large tea chest, from which she pulled a plastic jug. She motioned to me—*want some*? I nodded, despite my impatience. She poured grayish water into two beakers and brought them over. High above us, the hiss of hidden streams and pipes filled the caves with reptile music. It was strangely comforting, but I was still glad Coin was with me. Alone, these caves would have scared me half to death, even though I seemed to have spent quite a portion of my life around here. That so much of my time was unconscious to me was a chilling, depressing truth. How much else of my span was unknown to me? How many other people and places was I a part of?

"The charts you saw at the sentinel's bivouac in Hyde Park depict what we at first believed was a mythical place, a subterranean city that our forebears had pursued for centuries, a place many of us thought never existed. The charts changed all that. They described a route to this city, and the area in which we might be able to find it. The Face was at the end of a long tunnel towards what we hoped would be the doorway. It really exists. And we are there now."

"What? Here?" I looked around.

"No. There is only one entrance to the Face. The way in. All of us, except for me, are through. I'm going too, soon, when I've taken you back to the surface."

She gave me a look, from deep beneath her dirty fringe. "Odessa wanted me to thank you, for your help."

I snorted at that. Some thanks.

"She asked me to offer you an invitation to join us, if you felt that your life as a Topsider was too painful now. If you are ready to return to us, rid yourself of this surface mentality."

"I don't believe you," I said.

"Are you ready to go? Do you feel strong enough?"

I nodded. "Thank you," I said to her, covering her tiny hand with mine. Such a young girl. Such a wise person. "You saved me."

"I didn't save you enough if you want to go back there," she scolded, jerking her head towards the ceiling.

It took the best part of an hour to get back to street level. On the way, we bypassed the cave where I had first seen Odessa. Coin ushered me in, keen to prove that Odessa's offer was genuine and that it wasn't just a titbit thrown to me to make me feel a part of things.

The cave was empty but for her chair and the small screen on the floor. It flickered, blue seeds of interference shifting across the washed-out image of that ancient woman. I could just about make her out in the tide of white noise, the filth coating the screen. The message was on a constant loop. The sound wasn't great but it was good enough. She said:

"If you see this, Monck, then it would appear you survived your bouts with Blore. We are grateful. Had you died, your sacrifice would not have gone unnoticed. We salute you. And I extend an invitation to join us, should you feel that your life as a Topsider is over. If you wish to return to the fold, you will know where to search for us. But be warned. We will not hesitate to act if you expose us to the surface. I wish you well, Monck... Underman.

"If you see this, Monck, then it would appear..."

"Satisfied?" Coin asked.

An hour later, I was standing in deep night near a fissure outside the Langham Hotel. Across the road, BBC Broadcasting house was a shell, gutted by an old fire that had long since burnt itself out. I walked parallel to Oxford Street, picking my way through the dunes of demolished buildings on Foley Street and Howland Street back towards H's flat. Although the shark's tooth burned against my skin, I had to hope that Laura was all right, that she would be there at the flat, alive.

I noticed, as I neared Charlotte Street, that steps had already been made to right the trashed city. Giant cranes clustered like yellow spiders around the worst implosions; makeshift roads had been carved through the rubble to allow dumper trucks to remove all that weight of failed concrete and steel. Rescue teams worked ceaselessly, sifting through the wreckage for bodies. Spastic blue light washed the city. The chatter of static and voices burst like sporadic gunfire through the silence. Nets of dust hung in the streets. I couldn't help thinking about Meddie, Iain and Yoyo. Here was some pocket for them. Here was some fucking pocket.

By the time I reached the flat, I must have looked like a ghost, coated as I was in gray powder. I thrashed at my clothes for a while before pushing my way through the main door, swallowing hard as the familiarity of the stairwell and what had happened here last time I made an unheralded visit hit home. Up the stairs, I crouched by H's front door, listening for movement from within. When I was convinced it was empty, I barged my way inside. I could smell Troake, his stale cigarettes; his wet, yellow bandage, but he was no longer around.

If I was expecting H's flat to be some kind of shrine to depravity, I was disappointed. It was as plain as a bowl of porridge. There were no ornaments or knick-knacks. No clutter. The surfaces were clean. An aspidistra flourished in a large terracotta pot—the bastard—but that was about it in terms of decoration. A futon was freshly made. At the far end of the flat was a second room, its door closed, a decal of a sunflower stuck to its center.

Clearly H had not been here for some time. In a desk drawer I found the only clue that this was his flat; cuttings, from various tabloids and broadsheets and free weeklies, reporting his crimes. Wherever he had been referred to as The Pusher, he had savaged the text with a ballpoint pen. In the margins he had scrawled *NO* and *IDIOTS* and *FUCKERS.* That he was prone to such bouts of vanity cheered me no end.

I went to the other room and strode in before I could conjure any foul images of what might be waiting on the other side of the door. Soft music, very quiet, spilled from an old ghetto blaster. I recognized the song. It had been playing on my first visit to Nuala's flat. Paperback novels spilled out of an overcrowded bookcase. A bed covered with understated linen, soft throws and cushions. I sat on the bed and listened to the song until it finished. And then it started up again.

It was important not to make any rash movements, even though she knew me inside out. Shock had turned her as white as salt. Very carefully I reached out and teased away the masking tape that was covering her mouth.

I moved slightly, and leaned against her. Her weight settled against mine as easily and as comfortably as it always had. Equilibrium didn't have to be reached; it was always there. Even when we were apart.

I said, "Laura? Are you okay?" She didn't appear to be injured in any way, despite the great amount of dried blood on her skin.

Her scalp was pale and shiny beneath the close-cropped hair, like ice just beginning to melt.

She nodded. I untied the knots that bound her hands and feet, watching her reaction, watching to make sure she didn't turn hysterical and start lashing out.

The music kept playing. Like Odessa's message to me, it was on a repeat loop. I tried to imagine Nuala sitting here, listening to it, perhaps thinking of me, before H barged in and showed her what his version of commitment meant.

The song ended again and started again. Smoothing Laura's hair against her forehead, and making sure she was warm and comfortable, I pushed myself off the bed and picked up the jewel case by the stereo. A Cocteau Twins album: *Four Calendar Café.* Track one, her favorite.

The spit in my mouth vanished.

I led Laura to the front door and told her to wait for me while I set fire to H's cuttings and let the flames spread to the furniture, before their color and heat upset me and I had to run outside. Grief enveloped me halfway down the stairs and by the time I stepped into the street, I couldn't see for the blur, and I fell over and grazed my knees.

*Know Who You Are At Every Age.*

The song's title was the same as the message jammed into Greg's throat. The tears were coming so hard and painfully that I couldn't work out what was fuelling them: Grief? Anger? Madness? I was crying so hard that I couldn't see the figure reaching out for me. I said, "Mum?"

At the last moment, before she reached down for me, I recognized her and recoiled. It seemed too much like one of my dreams. I couldn't bear the rejection that would settle on me when I wakened. But then soft, real hands gripped me and hauled me out of the gutter.

It seemed those hands had never done anything but.

# CHAPTER TWENTY
## MONUMENT

We spent long evenings talking. He'd bring me a beer and we'd sit in the garden, smelling the wood smoke as the sun tumbled and next door's cat chased moths across the lawn. I got to know him well in those weeks, and we achieved a rapport that was better than usual for a British lad and his British dad. But somehow, no matter how great my love for him, or the level of respect, there appeared to be a strange law somewhere that banned any emotive trading between Dad and me. He'd shake my hand on my birthday, nudge his shoulder against mine on the day of my departure after a weekend visit. There was distance at the same time as there was none.

But here we were. Now.

After Laura had coaxed me back to life, she called my dad and he drove down the M1, as far as he was able. We met him at Toddington service station, coming the other way, having cadged lifts from strangers leaving the city. There were lots of people leaving the city. We spent a few hours in the back of a VW Campervan with six cats and a sweaty child who was being copiously sick into a bucket. The mother kept patting his back and offering him tea from a flask. "You have to top up your fluids after you've been sick," she said. The boy would take a sip and then hoick his guts up again. Laura sat him on her knee and read him stories from a book about a patchwork elephant. He hiccupped a few times, but the vomiting stopped. *That's what you do to people,* I thought. *You calm them down. You bring them out of the moment.* I could do with some of that.

Dad drove us back to the northwest, and I slept all the way. When I woke up, Laura was gone. Dad was sitting in the driving seat, watching me in the rear-view mirror.

"She's having a bath. And then she's going straight to bed," he said. "And you. What about you? Where are you going?"

All I could do was meet his gaze. And then I said, "Thanks, Dad."

WE DISCUSSED SUBJECTS THAT HAD NEVER BEEN BROACHED before. Mum, his childhood, his father and grandfather. His time in the Army, stationed in South Korea just after the end of the war in 1953.

Laura. Nuala. Greg. London. Narcolepsy.

Sitting on the benches in his back garden, Dad's voice coming slow and easy, it was hard to believe that this hadn't happened before. He was articulate and funny. His tone seemed to convey the message: *You only ever had to ask.* Laura kept out of the way, spending her time resting, reading, walking in the garden. I wanted to speak to her, but I didn't know what to say. The silences were perfectly comfortable. Sometimes we smiled at each other. I could deal with that.

Dad didn't probe me about what had happened in London; I suppose he could see what I had been through. Raking over those coals might only make me clam up, or withdraw into myself, to a place even deeper than the one Odessa, Coin and the others had found.

That's the only thing we didn't discuss. I was concerned that he might think I had lost it completely if I told him about my other life, my secret history. A part of me wondered about him—how many masks did he own? How many different roles did he play?—but I quickly realized I didn't want to know. I liked Dad Mark I. That was good enough for me.

As I surfaced from all this mess, I started getting curious about London again; gradually, the metropolis was sucking me back in. Dad and I scrutinized the newspapers and watched the news for bulletins about reparations to the capital. The death toll was many, many thousands. There were warnings that some people might never be found, that their bodies had been obliterated by the trauma. London was their graveyard. Only London knew where they were.

On the television we saw pictures taken by satellites trained upon the south-east of England. From above, the fracture resembled a pencil score that measured its own damage. The bisected city would have to be rebuilt, knitted together. The initial panic that this had been part of a terrorist plot were quashed when no evidence of bombs were found. The Underground had been damaged beyond repair. It was decided that it should be completely sealed off and tenders sought for a new overland transportation system.

Well then, I thought.

I DREAMT A LOT, DURING THOSE WEEKS AT HOME. AT FIRST, I thought the restfulness of my surroundings might bring me soothing images. Close my eyes and I would be confronted with great swathes of green, in more shades than could surely be possible. Thrusting blooms, bursting with color, broke the foliage. Acid yellow bracts like sodium lights in rain. Every leaf I touched, every stem I breathed upon, responded as though I had been gifted with some Midas-like ability. But then I saw that these lush surroundings were nothing more than screens thrown up by my brain, an attempt to conceal what lay beyond. My dreamscapes became infected with the terrible, patchwork faces of Blore's victims. The ruined flesh was knitted together crudely; rough seams that promised to spill their features if they or I moved. They swam out at me from tunnels, peeling away from the dark like ghoulish stickers on a schoolboy's exercise book. Through this terrain, Blore pursued me. He was a hulking, blackened cinder, his eyes shining out through a crisped mask. Despite this disability, he moved swiftly, heralding his arrival in my dreams with the sound of scorched limbs creaking and crackling. He shed carbonized fragments of himself as he swung his chain at me. Fat spooled through the red raw splits in his body like hot mozzarella....

Still, as the days passed, I rallied. I had healed well and now my mind was purging itself of all those shocks and anxieties. I began to relax. I began to grow bored.

Like I said, I was hungering for the city again.

Dad, to his credit, didn't try to put me off. He simply asked me if I was ready. It had been three months since he picked me up off the street, a wreck in every possible way.

"Where will you stay?" he asked. I hadn't thought about it but I told him that my boss, Cherry, had a spare room I could use until I settled in. I didn't know if this was true, but I didn't want to give him cause to worry. I didn't know if the flower stall was still standing and, if it was, whether I wanted to work there anymore. Maybe I could hire Marlon and set up a protection racket.

London had quickly been stitched together. A string of benefit concerts for the relatives of the dead had been planned across the planet. The quake was a blessing in disguise. The designs that had already begun to be considered for the center would see the streets completely pedestrianized, with plenty of green spaces instead of roads choked by taxis and buses. Shuttles that clung to tracks on terraced buildings would provide transport around the heart of the capital. The government pushed for people to get their bikes out. Adverts for cheap microlite aircraft began cropping up. The city was being given a facelift and people were buying into it.

And then, the night before I left, I was sitting in the dark. Dad had gone to bed and I was alone with Laura. The TV was off. Headlights on cars coming down Troutbeck Avenue took our shadows for a ride around the room.

I said, "Can you tell me what happened?"

"I'd rather not. I don't know if I'm ready."

I said, "His face... did he make you—"

"Yes."

I said, "I wish I could have been there to help you."

"You couldn't have been there. There was no reason for you to be there."

I said, "I'm different, Laura. I've changed."

She came out of the dark and pressed a finger to my lips. She held me. She said: "So have I."

I CAUGHT THE FIRST TRAIN DOWN FROM BANK QUAY ON A misty winter morning. Dad dropped me off at the station and we hugged each other hard. Tears sprang to my eyes. He was looking at me strangely.

"Goodbye," he said. That was all. Laura was standing away from the train, her back against the wall. She was going to stay on a little while longer, until she had worked out what she wanted to do. She thought she might go north, at first. Spend some time in the Highlands. As high above ground level as she could get.

She waved as the train departed. I watched her until she became a speck, and was lost as the train canted to the right, as it curved out of Warrington and headed south.

There was nobody else in my carriage. England streamed past the windows, and it was easy to believe that beyond the confines of those gray, feathery borders nothing existed. But London was at the end of the line, and every time I thought that, my heart took on the rhythm of the train on its tracks. A couple of hours and the sun made a push to be recognized, a slow wound seeping though gauze. We stopped, I got off.

I walked for miles. Thinking of you.

HOW IT ENDED.

I remember your profile edged with troubled light falling from the tower of neon angles at the Hayward. This was our first night together since you told me you didn't want to see me anymore. One of those bad nights that people arrange to make it official. To cap it all off. Where you struggle through the conversations that involve the words "still friends."

I remember it being bitter beyond the confines of your car. Flapping like anxious pigeons, we hurry across the road, skirting the brutal, colorless aggregate of the complex till we find the glass doors. The weather scowling behind us, we duck into a civil expanse of espresso and bow ties. You buy drinks at the bar, but before we have chance to finish them the gong is ushering us to our seats. In the concert hall, you smile at me; it's enough to charge me with hope.

Occasionally, I sense a yield in your voice, a softening in your eyes that suggests all might not be lost.

The first time, I remember the first time: April dying beyond your window, on the heels of a dovetail kiss, you moved over and sank upon me till I had no measure of where I ended and you began. The curtain of your hair moving pendulum slow above my face; the sound of the fountain outside the only thing pinning me to reality.

Onto the stage, to understated applause, comes a kind-looking man with a trained side parting and a wolfish woman in a red dress. She sits at a grand piano. He takes an age over the position of his cello before smoothing his hair and taking in the audience while exhaling levelly. Then, with a disconcerting flurry of movement, the instruments find their voice, driven by manic stabs and jerks of arms and hands. I can't equate the disarray of their movement with the beautiful sound of their strings.

The music creeps around the auditorium, stealthy as oil, settling against the skin during low chords, spirited away like a rising helix of bubbles during the high. In this moment, there is only you and the music; a silent proximity exerted by the loose arrangement of your clothes, the way your leg climbs over its partner, your left hand gently grips the right. I can smell your perfume (and if I turn my head a little, I see the wet flash of your eyes and the threaded chunk of metal infected by your pulse in the gully between your breasts).

You called me from Heathrow (on your way to a conference in Naples) to leave a message on the answerphone. You thanked me for taking you to the airport, explained that you were about to board the flight and then, whispering: "I... I love you, chicken. Very embarrassing to say that with all these people around." We talked twice while you were there. When I came to pick you up, you were tired but you looked well, had picked up a little sun. Back home, you went straight to bed and we made love when I joined you, your face as you came taking on the expression of a person frantic to swallow breath after a long time underwater. A week later, you said we were finished.

After Barber, after Bach, the musicians play Debussy's Sonata and you shift slightly, the hard edge of your forearm meeting mine on the armrest. The playing of music evolves on the stage in several leaves, like cels in an animation: the man turning pages of music, the pianist, the cellist. The cello. I see details that might have eluded me at other times, but with this heightening of sensation, it does not appear strange that I notice the cellist's hand: a white spider skittering up and down the cello's neck. Or the polished part of his knee where the bow brushes it at the limit of its stroke; filaments of horsehair; the slender, toned muscles in the pianist's arms.

In your letters to me, you outlined your apprehension about relationships, how you'd been stung by the end of a long-term commitment but not so disenchanted that you didn't want to risk another affair of the heart. You'd told me how you would fight this time. You wanted this to work. And yet here we are, just shy of a year together, and your voice is full of regret.

I can't concentrate on the encore. Outside, you make small talk with an old friend you didn't know was sitting a few rows back from us. You hold my hand till she goes, then slip from my fingers with cruel professionalism. Why, I don't know, but driving back we talk about the first time we met, at a birthday party in a loud, sweating basement club. It had been too loud to talk. Your eyes were wide and full of me. I wanted to kiss you so desperately that when, later, you leaned across your kitchen table, as the dawn chorus began in the copper beech in your street, I had to break away, gasping with relief.

You carried me. I was weak. As a puppy. As a chick.

At your house, you set about making tea. I riffle through your CD collection until I find Borodin's String Quartet No 2 in D Major. The first night I spent here, you and I looked at each other from opposite sides of the room for an age before you came to sit by my feet and hold my hand. This is what you do now, after placing the tray with the teapot and mugs on the table. I slip down onto the floor and you move between my legs, lying back so that your head finds the dip of my right shoulder. We don't say anything. There is a beautiful, haunting phrase that Borodin uses over and over during the *Notturno*. The cello's voice is plaintive and hopeful, rolling around the other three string instruments like an invocation. Although you don't move against me, I feel a settling of your weight, as if your muscles and bones have slipped beyond the threshold at which they find their usual repose. I become aware of your heartbeat and the measured journey of your breath. Everything is right in a way it hasn't been for weeks. Slowly, with as much tenderness as I can muster, I place my hands on your shoulders and squeeze, allowing my fingers to work your arms and the flat gloss at the top of your chest. Your clavicle, the small cob of bone at the back of your neck, the flat planes of your shoulder blades—I touch it all, trying to pass on something of my need for you: all my warmth and good feeling for you. Nothing is so important. Can you feel this? Eyes closed, I move my hands to the swell of the music, following the ebb and flow of the cello's ache. In my touch is all the tenderness we've shared before. The raw center of you is where I'm trying to reach, softly plucking and drawing upon the area that remembers the good times and wishes for them to return. I know this can work. Can you feel? I know this can work. Along with the charity of my hands, I send a message, forcing it through my fingertips and into the knot of pain and confusion we all carry at our center. Please let me try. Don't throw me away just yet: wait and see. I won't let you down.

You stay my hands. Bring one to your mouth and kiss the palm. *I'll think about it,* you said. *I promise.* But just like the cello, all your promises were hollow.

The door, when it closes on you for the last time, always sounds different.

ALL OF THE ANIMALS HAD BEEN ROUNDED UP. LONDON ZOO had been overhauled and now sat beneath a pale blue umbrella cage that completely ensnared the complex.

I wandered around Regent's Park for a while, wondering what I should do. I couldn't afford to stay at a hotel and I had no friends left who might have been able to help me. I thought of Cherry then, and thought *why not?*, although I wasn't expecting her to be at the flower stall. Nobody was buying flowers, and the demand for other kinds of labor was rocketing.

But she was there, in her jumper, jeans and Doc Martens, arranging stems and leaves, expertly wrapping bunches of flowers in cream sheets of paper. I could have cried.

"Cherry!"

She looked up and smiled as if I had never been away.

"Been on holiday?" she asked. I laughed out loud. It felt pretty good.

"You could say that," I replied. "Business booming?"

"It's gone off in the last few weeks," she said, and then: "What?" when she saw that I'd creased up again.

"Cherry, you're an absolute stick. Unflappable. Where were you when the world ended?"

"I was at home with my gran in Lewisham," she said. "We watched it all on TV." Like it was some kind of fly-on-the-wall documentary.

"I hope you locked up here beforehand," I said, and I was off again.

"You want *another* holiday," she said, looking a bit nervous now. "Get away from it all... oh, by the way," she handed me a shrub in a pot. "I wanted to give you this," she said. "It's a—"

"*Euphorbia griffithii,*" I interrupted. "Fireglow. Thanks. It's beautiful."

It was. A bushy little shrub with mid-green lanceolate leaves bearing pale red midribs, professionally speaking. When it flowered, it would appear orange-red.

"Use gloves if you ever think of cutting it," she warned. "The sap burns.

I think it's poisonous."

"Hey," I said, "me and it both."

A LOST CITY.

An ancient, underground civilization. I sat in the corner of the demolition site in Stag Place and picked through the fragments still stuck to the wall in the bivouac where I had met Reef and the suffering Sloe. At the time, they had been so many squiggles and hieroglyphs, as indecipherable as a GP's scrawl. But into the imbroglio I could now force new knowledge, and a shape emerged. *Beneothan,* they had called this forgotten country of theirs. If the faded map of London and its outskirts was to be believed, the blue pencil shading that engulfed it was the area beneath London that Beneothan occupied. The blue made an oval that my eye lingered over, as though it was a smooth, dusky jewel I was viewing. I ran my fingers across the paper and the soft whisper that returned was as deep and as sweet as any of the echoes that had winged through the dark of the underground.

*And I extend an invitation to join us, should you feel that your life as a Topsider is over.*

I thought of Dad at the station, looking at me in that odd way, as though he were drinking in my details for the last time. The way he said goodbye.

I had had a bad moment, as I reached the north side of the pontoon bridge at Victoria Embankment. I had heard the scrape and rattle of chains and swore I heard my name called, flayed almost beyond recognition by strangled vocal cords. But when I swung round to see, the chains belonged to a tug that was anchored to the jetty and the voices were those of two drunks murmuring thickly in their alien language.

Blore had surely died in the fire. It didn't seem conceivable that he could have escaped. He had drenched himself in petrol, after all. The exit I had taken was the only one. Yet still it nagged at me that I had found the remnants of only one body in the ashes.

I moved through the center of London cautiously, not wanting to get lost. I saw a sign that pleased me because it had been something, along with quacking ducks and side partings, that made both Laura and me laugh. HEAVY PLANT CROSSING, it read. And here was something. Thinking of Laura, for the first time, didn't trigger a pang. Especially now I knew she was all right. We were both different. Both new. Both alive. That was what mattered.

Diggers, cranes, piledrivers and Portakabins dominated the city. People moved through it all like nocturnal creatures venturing into the sun. We blinked and stared, trying to come to terms with the change. Trying to spot something recognizable that might make our repossession of the city a little bit easier.

Where the English National Opera had once stood, I caught sight of a figure as it rushed down one of the alleyways that linked St. Martins Lane with Charing Cross Road. I recognized his movement before I had chance to see his face and I had taken after him before I realized that it was Lucas.

I caught up with him as he entered Leicester Square, its cinemas crippled, splintered monster billboards advertising broken mosaic names: LEONARDO CLOG... WINON WITHERS... BRAT PISS....

"Raglan!" I yelled and he wheeled in mid-stride as though shot. We stood and looked at each other for a long time. "I didn't know," he said finally, spreading his hands. "I'd never hurt anybody. Do you know that?"

"I understand," I said. "I know what it's like."

"I haven't been underground for weeks. Months, even. It was fucking up my head. I've been running for days. I can't get a grip." He looked much thinner than the cocky chancer selling copies of the *Big Issue* by the flower stall. He looked hunted. But didn't we all? Panic came off him in lazy great waves.

"There's a way back," I said, not believing I had said it. I hadn't considered the option myself. Not much. "If you want it, there's a way back."

He inched towards me, licking his lips, his eyes ranging madly around the empty square. Our voices caromed off the shattered façades. On the wall behind him, in white chalk, that infuriating logo again. Like a bottle, lying on its side.

"What?" he said. "How?"

"They've found a new home. You... we can be a part of it, if we want it. I think I know the way, but I don't know if they'll keep the access open much longer. Maybe they've sealed it already."

"I need it," he said. "There's nothing here for me. What's the point of selling a magazine to help the homeless if the people buying it are homeless too?" He laughed an ugly little desperate laugh and licked his lips again. "I want it. How do I get in?"

Bottles stacked up in my thoughts. Bottles everywhere. All my narcoleptic episodes had been infected with the teasing shape. They were more real than the friends, the imagined friends, that had held them. I gave him an address and told him to meet me there in the evening, at eight o'clock. I was relieved. I was grateful to Lucas for forcing my hand. Although I hadn't really needed my arm twisting too much. It seemed right. It felt spot on.

"Lucas," I said, as he was turning to go.

"Yeah?"

"Blore. Have you seen him?"

A beat.

"I haven't seen him for fucking ages."

I watched Lucas twitchily leg it towards Piccadilly. I didn't know what he was going to do for the next few hours until we met up again, but I didn't care either. I needed this time alone. I had things to do.

"Blore is dead," I said to myself. "He's toast."

Lucas, ducking right, disappeared around the corner. I thought I saw his shadow but the sky was too overcast to create any.

Bottles. A bottle, on its side.

I took out my mobile and tried Yoyo's number, but there was no reply. I dialed Meddie, but before I punched in the last digit, the battery died. I walked, knowing how far it was but needing to find someone I cared for in all the chaos. A face I knew would be just the tonic I needed. One foot after the other, counting them off, all the steps north. Just shy of Fortess Road the land leveled off and normality seemed within grasp, if you ignored the silence, the absence of traffic, if you didn't look over your shoulder. I found an abandoned bicycle and pedaled to Meddie and Iain's place; all the way there I didn't see another soul.

The door to their flat was open when I arrived. I dumped the bike and stood in the hallway. I could smell fried onions. The sound of water tumbling into a full bath came from deeper within the flat. Half a dozen of Yoyo's novels were scattered on the stairs leading to the upstairs flats. I picked one up. It was called *The Blue Tiger*. I leafed through the pages; all of them were blank. Okay, I thought. Okay, it's a notebook, that's all. I saw one that she had been reading recently, *The Vanishing Road*. Empty. They were all blank.

I threw them on the floor, angry that Yoyo had duped me with such a cheap little trick, although she hadn't really gone out of her way to deceive me, and it wasn't hurting anybody. Still, I felt misled; I thought Yoyo trusted me.

"Hello?" I called, a little snappily. I heard footsteps all around me, but none of them were approaching. I headed for Meddie's bedroom, but she wasn't there. I thought I heard movement in Iain's room, but when I put my head around the door, it was empty.

I padded to the kitchen with my head tickling with something that seemed urgent. It was like half-seeing the picture that emerges from the stereogram, only to lose it before being able to recognize what it is. Half-finished mugs of tea sat on the table, along with the remains of minute-steak sandwiches. Iain's chemistry set was out. He liked to make toast with his paraffin-fueled Bunsen burner and drink his vodka from test tubes. Peanuts were arranged in an agar dish. A pipette contained salad dressing.

From the hallway, I heard Meddie call out: "Oh hi, Ads." Exasperated, I hurried back to the front door but there was nobody there. Just the sense of a space recently vacated.

"We're going to watch a film," Yoyo said, and I turned to see the wedge of a shoe slip from view over the last riser on the stairwell. I raced up after her and stood on the landing staring up at the unoccupied stretch to the first floor.

"Yoyo? Meddie?"

"Down here," Iain called.

I retraced my steps, trying to keep my shaky legs from spilling me. Back in the living room, the blinds had been drawn and Iain's projector was neatly set up on the table, the soft white gloves he used to handle the machinery and the reels folded neatly next to it. Whenever he wore them, he looked as if he should be creeping around a snooker table. Light was coming from a candle on the table in the kitchen. The dishes had been cleared away. I exhaled very slowly and went searching for a drink. In the fridge was a bottle of Stella Artois. I cracked it open and took a long, long swig.

I sat down on the sofa and waited for them to join me. Hoping that they would join me. Someone blew out the candle. The projector stuttered into life. Someone sat down next to me; I felt myself tip incrementally as the sofa's cushions were realigned.

From somewhere to my left I heard the legs of a wooden chair scrape against the floorboards. I smelled Meddie's perfume, maddening as ever, but this time for different reasons. None of the shapes in the dark would resolve themselves into anything I could identify. I inched my hand to my right, expecting to feel Yoyo's duffel coat, but there was nobody sitting next to me. My heart leapt. It suddenly sounded very loud, so loud that I almost didn't hear what Iain had begun to say to me.

"All my life needed was a sense of some place to go," he quoted. "I don't believe that one should devote his life to morbid self-attention. I believe that someone should become a person like other people."

"You talking to me?" I asked, and tried to force some laughter. The white space on the wall suddenly jumped with colors and shapes. Me in the cellar of The Pit Stop, my trousers around my ankles, fucking an empty space. I felt the area inside my head bend and thought, *I'm gone, I'm out of it,* but then the light roared back into the room and I was suddenly *recovering* from a narcoleptic attack. Nobody else but me in the room. No sound except the *flap-flap-flap* of film at the end of a reel.

BEFORE I LEFT, I WENT BACK FOR ONE MORE LOOK IN IAIN'S room. What I thought was Iain's room. Whoever the fuck's room it was.

I studied the film posters. Dozens of them. *Alien, The Deer Hunter, Chinatown, Heat, Barry Lyndon, Don't Look Now.* And there I stalled. Julie Christie and Donald Sutherland peering out from a photograph frame that was seeping blood onto a table. Above them, the tag line: *Pass the Warning.*

"Yoyo," I said. I dropped the bottle from my hand. It smashed. And I remembered.

A hot, panicky journey on the Underground many years ago with Mum and Dad, on a visit to London, a hasty, stress-inducing daytrip. I remember Dad pointing out the shape of the Circle Line on the Tube map, trying to distract me from the crowds, my nausea. "Look Adam," he had said, "it's not really a circle, it's bottle-shaped. We're riding a bottle." I'd laughed a lot when he said that, the pattern of the line rising out of the tangle of colored lines like something always known.

That logo I was seeing everywhere. It wasn't a logo after all. It was a map.

I found an A-Z eventually, a whole host of them, sticking out of the dirt at a petrol station. On the back, where the Tube map was printed, I traced a line with my finger, diametrically, from one corner of the base of the Circle Line's "bottle" to the mouth. And again from the other side. The lines intersected at St. Paul's. Bang on the money. I set off on the bike immediately, clasping the Fireglow plant to my chest like a beloved toy.

Who was the cartographer? Who had been scratching and painting and chalking these clues to Blore's whereabouts around the city? Had it been Greg, who had tried to help by giving me the note that originally led me to Blore's doorstep? Was it Iain, Meddie and Yoyo—myself, ultimately—trying to nudge me towards understanding by projecting myself into imagined friends in my narcoleptic blackouts?

Was it H? Did he *want* to be stopped?

IT STANDS IN THE TUNNEL, ITS ARMS OUTSTRETCHED. THE tunnel is too wide for It to be able to touch the sides, but It can as good as feel the damp bricks, their rough texture under Its fingers, as well known to It as Its own skin. There is no graffiti down here. Nobody ever sees the walls, or it might just be that they are too moist to take the spray paint. Litter is wadded into the angles between wall and floor: a maroon crate, a blue Calor gas bottle, skins and wrappers, newspapers and cardboard tubes. A sock. A torn shirt. The arch above Its head is studded with cable routers. Dark shadows show where the cables once ran: all are naked now. Reinforced lights punch into the dark; perspective draws them closer together. At the end of the tunnel, lilac light spills across the walls like a painting accident. Its light. Its nest. Its focus. Here It can sit and feel London spin out around It and above It. The tunnels take all its weight; by extension, It takes it too, deep into It where it nourishes It, fills Its veins with heat. All the deadweight loads, vibration loads, soil and water pressure, the seismic activity. All the tons of gravel and aggregate and Portland stone, the oxblood tiles, the steel, the wire. Sumps, pumps, storm drains. Electrical distribution systems, switchyards, ventilation ducts, utility tunnels. It is it, and it is It. It is a machine. It is London.

It enters the broken room, with its switch-boxes, circuit breakers, cable chases and valves. A mercury arc rectifier sits on a table, its condensing chamber glowing like something from a science fiction novel. It sits and places Its hands on the glass. There are many fingerprints on the glass. Some red, some brown. Some still wet.

"I am London." It says the words and they sprint away from It down the tunnel, as if afraid of the creature that formed them. "I am London."

I HEARD THE WORDS. I HEARD THEM, BUT MY MIND TRIED ITS best to persuade me otherwise. It's the air in the tunnels. It's the ghosts of trains. It's the rats, the hiss of the rats. It's my brain, decaying on its stem. Refusing to open up and show me what was what.

Paternoster Square expanded around me, a bright, clean, traffic-less area filled with pristine buildings, shops and restaurants. Pedestrians strolled along the piazza, or the landscaped gardens in St. Paul's Cathedral churchyard. The lights were coming on as the sun set. Everything was scarlet and blue for a short time. Everyone was smiling, as if they were extras in an advert for toilet roll.

I was exhausted. My legs ached from so much exercise, and my back was filmed with sweat. The handlebars had re-inflamed my healing fingers.

I had to lean over and touch the ground, to check it was real. It shouldn't be like this. It hadn't been like this, the last time I was here. The place had been a shit heap. It was always a shit heap. The woman had come at me out of a wreck of condemned buildings. But no, the ground was solid enough. Maybe this was part of what recovery meant for me. Maybe I was doing my brain a disservice. Here was truth, at last. Hadn't I realized something was remiss on my last visit, when the boarded-up shops and office buildings contained no glass to trap my reflection, to show me the falseness of my surroundings? It must have been a narcoleptic landscape, something that had seeped through from my past, perhaps projected by the fear of my proximity to Blore's lair, a background for Yoyo, Meddie and Iain to play against. I was mapping my way out of the past, adding color to the uncharted white spaces in my head.

This place had been twenty years waiting for the wrecking ball, marooned by recession and its own poverty. My head or Paternoster Square? Take your pick.

I scooted into St. Paul's Tube and fought a path down to a platform partly blocked by the ceiling, which had collapsed onto the tracks. Water was spraying from a ruptured pipe. I dropped down between the rails and closed my eyes.

It didn't take long to find him. I imagined I could hear the vast echoes in the Cathedral permeating down through the soil, and hanging in the clammy air like nets of dust. Footsteps on the tiles, on the hundreds of steps up to the dome; European and Asiatic languages piling into each other on guided tours; coins being dropped into a charity box. I was so attuned that I thought I could hear the lovers in the Whispering Gallery, murmuring their seductions and betrothals. I thought I could hear the pigeons landing on the balustrade around the drum. Through it all, I heard him.

*I am London. I am London.*

I trudged towards his voice, knowing that he was waiting for me, that all this scorpion dancing had been leading up to a moment when our claws were about to close, our stingers ready to be deployed. I no longer feared him. What was at stake had nothing to do with Beneothan, or Nuala, or Laura. It was me and him. It was my past and my future. It was happiness or gloom. Everything had been simplified by the earthquake. It was life or death.

A tremor ran through the tunnel and I pressed myself to one side, thinking a train must be arriving. But there were no trains. There might never be another train. Not down here. Aftershock, then? Fragments of earth unpacked themselves from the ceiling and rained around me. Tiles smashed in the station behind me. The shuddering leveled off. I heard the depths sigh and groan as they realigned themselves against each other. I went on.

A tunnel threaded away to my left. Lilac light spat across the point where it curved out of sight. I followed it and found myself in a room that had been some sort of electrical center of operations. Weird-looking apparatus lay around—circuits and valves and coils—like something from a James Whale film set. And there were photographs on the wall. Pictures of hard-faced men in overalls, their eyes shock-large, very white, but only because their faces were heavily ingrained with grime. They stood together scowling at the camera, carrying that strained expression of people being photographed many, many years ago. One man in particular stood out, but only because of the bloody thumbprints that were smeared across his body, or arranged like a terrible halo around his head. His face was left untouched. That part of his image, in terms of the print at least, was spotless.

Around me lay the bodies of eviscerated mice and rats. A bucket of human excrement was tucked under the table. The sour smell of urine raged from the walls. I opened the cupboards and found only more switches and levers, warning lights and embossed plastic labels.

I was thinking of leaving—the smell was forcing me to leave—and wondering whether I had imagined his voice after all, when a shadow of a figure trembled across the far end of the tunnel, growing impossibly large. It seemed he might never appear within it, that the shadow would continue to spread until all of the available light was snuffed out. The knife in my pocket suddenly felt very warm, as if it recognized the flesh it was meant for.

"The cathedral above us took forty years to build," he said. "Did you know that? Not a long time, really, as cathedral-building goes, and this fucker's a biggie. But still, a lifetime for some, living in the 1600s."

There was nowhere for me to go. I was trapped. I looked around me for some sign of egress: a grille in the ceiling, a baffle leading to a ventilation shaft, a hidden door, but there was nothing. This was the end of the line.

"Imagine a life devoted to the cathedral. Your life would *be* the cathedral. Maybe you'd be working on the great Corinthian columns, or the west towers, or the dome itself. Maybe you were at the quarry, cutting Portland stone. You'd start out on it as a strapping teenager and before it was over, you'd be pensioned off, ready for the grave, if the work didn't kill you first."

"Get a job. You become the job," I said.

"That's right." His shadow paused on the wall, as if considering what I had said. "But what a job. That's what I call a job. Sacrifice. Dedication. People die for the cathedrals, for the bridges. For the tunnels."

I reached for the handle of the knife. Withdrew it. The sound of the blade whispering against the edge of my pocket empowered me. "And yes," I said, "you pushing people in front of trains has forced people to appreciate the finer points of life, yada-yada-yawnsville. Well, circumstances have meant we're all doing that now. You're out of a job."

"It isn't just about the routine," he spat. "The nine-to-five, the sheep, the kowtowing to suits who don't give a fuck about you or your contribution, as long as the coffers are being filled. It isn't just about all that shit."

The shadow came on. Measured tread. Something slithered from his grip and jangled by his side, catching and turning in the filth on the floor. Another distant aftershock sifted earth through the cracks in the ceiling; caused the mugs on the table to chatter. He appeared. He had shaved his head. Light glanced off the sweating curve of his scalp and caught in the ruined weave of his face, what had once been his face. Part of it had become infected; his left cheek had swelled to a grotesque size, as if he had tucked a tennis ball between his teeth and his cheek. The color of him was angry red, black, the puce of the membrane on squid.

"Those photographs," I said, beginning to understand. "The man in those photographs. Who is he?"

He stopped again. I couldn't tell whether I'd angered him with the question. I didn't care. He switched his weapon to his other hand, then back again. I did the same. Blore chuckled.

"He's my great-grandfather. Henry Glaber. They knew him as The Mole. He could tunnel like no other. Strong. Staying power. He worked like three men. Four."

"What happened, Blore?"

He swung the chain suddenly, striking the wall so violently that sparks flew. Scars remained in the brickwork, like claw marks. "He died, of course. Clever boy, you'll have picked up on that."

Every sibilant he uttered went through me like a knife through cooked fish. He was suffering with each breath he pulled past that lipless mouth, but the pain seemed to fuel him, as did the rage. Each step closer to me was another half-turn on the standpipe of his emotions.

"He died in 1887. There was an *accident*. He was working on what started out as the City of London and Southwark Subway. The City and South London line. The pins keeping a bunch of rails on a cart failed. Two iron rails fell forty feet into a shaft where he was working. His wife was sent a letter of condolence. I think she might have received some flowers too. But no blame was apportioned. No settlements were reached. She went into the poorhouse not long after that. And died within the year. The guy he was with saw it all. What he said has been passed down through the generations. He said one of the rails ripped his face clean off. He was eating a cob of bread at the time. Even after he was dead, he had hold of that cob, reflexes lifting it to a mouth that wasn't there for a bite."

"You could let go," I said. "I mean, it was a long time ago."

"Water under the bridge, hey?" he said. He was close enough now for me to smell the badness that was eating through his face. Lymph drenched one half of it like tears, turning him into a grotesque Pierrot. "Bygones. Sleeping dogs. Spilled milk."

"Something like that. It's over, Blore. H. It's over. There's nothing, nobody left to rage against."

"There's you," he said. He charged.

I stepped away and raised the knife, but I was too slow, too soft. Too many cans of lager in front of the TV. Too many curries and apple pies; late-nights and lie-ins. The chains flashed and a red mist filled the space where my hand had been. I heard the knife clatter away down the tunnel behind him. I backed off, what was left of my hand I rammed into my left armpit. I squeezed down hard against a pain that threatened to turn me inside out and fill all my spaces with darkness. I felt the heat and color drop out of my face. He was roaring now, despite the warp of his face, the pain that was arrowing through it. He was acclaiming the moment of my death. So where was it? Come on, I thought, get it over with.

He had stopped. He wasn't making any noise at all. Black lightning played across the ceiling. Black rain fell from the cracks. I heard the muffled thump of something hitting metal and then a gray shadow painted itself against the weakening walls. In the moment when I thought the brickwork was sweating, it parted, and a great torrent of water flashed into the room. The cupboard toppled forward and I twisted my body, trying to avoid its path. It caught my ear and heat flared across the side of my head. The cupboard smacked into Blore's thigh and I thought I heard, felt, a deep, snapping sound, as you do when you pull apart the joints in a chicken. He opened his mouth to scream at the same time that about a ton of soil fell through the ceiling, burying him. Through it I saw him struggling to stand up, blood filling the leg of his jeans, turning the denim from blue to black. He was choking on dirt, his eyes collecting red. The wall to my back buckled like wet cardboard, but I was moving fast before it could help me on my way. I clambered over the hill of earth rising in the center of the room, but Blore grabbed my foot and tipped me into it before I could hurl myself free. I felt him dragging himself clear of the earth, dragging himself onto my back, pressing my face into the mud. He wrapped the chain around my neck and lights began to pop out all around me. My useless right hand was trapped under my body. I tried levering myself up with the left, but I couldn't get it to support my weight: it just sank into the soil. Another shockwave rippled through the tunnels; the tightness around my throat slackened as the floor tipped and all the water slid away. I went with it, but Blore was still trapped by the heavy furniture. The tightness returned as he tugged on the chain. But now my arms were free. The Fireglow plant fell into my hand from the V of my jacket. It was flowering. In the dark, gorgeous red blooms spread, like spots of red ink on vellum. I mashed it hard into Blore's face and he yelled as the sap spurted into his exposed tissues. He let go of the chain and I flipped myself over as the floor of the room separated and he jerked violently into it. I saw him bite the tip of his tongue clean off as the back of his head struck the edge of the hole. Then he went slack and slithered into the dark, his eyes on me all the while. I didn't know if he was still conscious, or if he had simply resigned himself to death. As I turned and pelted along a tunnel that was trying to stop being a tunnel, I snatched up my knife, and in that instant heard music drifting into the chambers from the cathedral above, the impossible sound of a choir in full flow.

*Yea, like as a father pitieth his own children; even so is the Lord merciful unto them that fear him.*

*For he knoweth whereof we are made; he remembereth that we are but dust.*

And then Blore's voice behind me, chasing me along with the cracks and the water and the thunder.

*"You did not die in vain! Si monumentum requiris, circumspice! Si monumentum requiris, circumspice!"*

I STOOD OUTSIDE THE REMNANTS OF MY FLAT AND WAITED for Lucas. Cold air found the ruined meat of my hand and tore at it, like crows hungry for carrion. There were nasty lacerations in the fingers, and some of the nerves must have been damaged because there was a numbness, a deep feeling of cold. But the nurses would put everything straight, I hoped.

The sky was dirty ochre, its lowest edge stained deep blue. I got a lurch in my chest when it hit me that I might never see it again. The plant pot, empty now, and stuffed inside my zipped-up jacket, was uncomfortable, but I could live with that. I stroked it, glad of something to take with me. I was grateful to Cherry; she had saved my life. I was sure that she would do things with the flower stall that were up there with the best bouquet sellers in the land.

I got another little hitch in my chest when I thought of Dad, and it dawned on me that he had foreseen this moment. I could write to him. I was sure Coin could somehow smuggle letters to the Surface for me. And....

He wasn't coming.

I kicked at a piece of brick and watched it bounce into the road. I left it another five minutes and then tiptoed through the rubble of the house that had stood next door to the building that contained my flat. The trench had been filled by the collapse of the front, but it was still possible to forge a path to the front door.

Inside, the darkness fell about my shoulders like a cloak. I felt the pull of the Underground immediately, an insistent hand, the hand of a child, or a lover imploring me to come closer. I caught a whiff of something charred as I swung my foot into the shaft and onto the first rung of the ladder. Pay it no heed. Your mind spooking you.

I sank into the shaft but had to pause halfway down to reposition the plant pot within my jacket. It was awkward, negotiating the ladder with only one working hand. Hanging there, I thought I could hear footsteps above me, gritting through the plaster and cement of the front hall.

My jaw clenched involuntarily. A dark shape filled the shaft at the top of the ladder. I clearly heard the clank of metal as something clouted the rungs.

I got to the bottom and began walking, allowing the tunnels to inspire me and draw me in. Nourishing me. I felt lit from within, radiant, and enjoyed the sensation of myself budding, emerging, as I strode deeper into the earth, towards the Face, towards Beneothan. I was looking forward to exploring the new city, sharing the surprises of its sprawl with Coin, proving myself a worthy servant to Odessa.

At the alcove that gave on to the cavern where our workers had tapped and drilled and scraped for so long at the Face, I slowed. As far as I was concerned, what was Topside now—the rebuilding, the rehousing, the recovery—all of it was as real as anything my sleep-scarred mind had created. All that mattered, that was real, that had to be real, was here, now, in front of me.

I could hear voices up ahead, and smell good food. There would be friends willing to accept me here, where the city was as new as my expectations of it. Where I could develop as it developed. Where my future was bound up with the city's and I might have as much influence on it as it had on me.

I thrust my hand into my jacket as the reek of petrol snaked over my shoulder. The haft of the knife slipped into my fingers eagerly, as if moving to meet my hand. Closing on the gates to the new city, I heard him bearing down on me, his breath laboring wetly in his chest. The smoke wreathing him.

It ended here. I could never again risk exposing Odessa and her family, *our* family, to outsiders again. It felt good. It felt right. It felt as if I was returning home.